I0682314

STAR GAZER

Book Three

THE WRATH OF GAIA

The Third Tales in the Chronicles of

Jack Barleycorn

by

JOHN MORRIS

Charlotte Greene
Dorset, England

Also by John Morris

Fractured Series
Inner Sanctum
Conspiracy Theory

Star Gazer First Trilogy
The Gatekeeper and the Guardian
The Twelve Tribes
The Wrath of Gaia

Star Gazer Second Trilogy
The Centaureans

Billie Steadman Investigates:
The Man in the River

Stand Alone Novels
Islamic State: England
Domicile

Copyright © 2020 by John Morris

First Edition

All rights reserved
No part of this book may be used or reproduced in any manner
whatsoever without written permission, except in the case of
brief quotations embodied in critical reviews and certain other
non-commercial uses permitted by copyright law.

Printed in the United Kingdom (or country of purchase)

This is a work of fiction. Names, characters, places and incidents
are the product of the author's imaginations or are used
fictitiously. Any resemblance to actual persons living or dead is
entirely coincidental.

Published by Charlotte Greene, Dorset, England

Editor: Susan Dewey http://beeberrywoods.com/FiberEtc/

Cover: Boris Junkovic http://www.charlotte-
greene.co.uk/Agents_BorisJunkovic.htm

Maps, Illustrations and website graphics: Boris Junkovic

Acknowledgements: Melissa Felton, Terry Dickerson, Ian Brown,
Jim Bayliss, Mike Cheek

Dedicated to: My wife Siu Ying, and my daughter Rhiannon.

Official Star Gazer website: http://www.star-gazer.co.uk

Official author website: http://www.john-morris-author.com

ISBN Print: 9781910711064
ISBN eBook: 9781910711095

Table of Contents

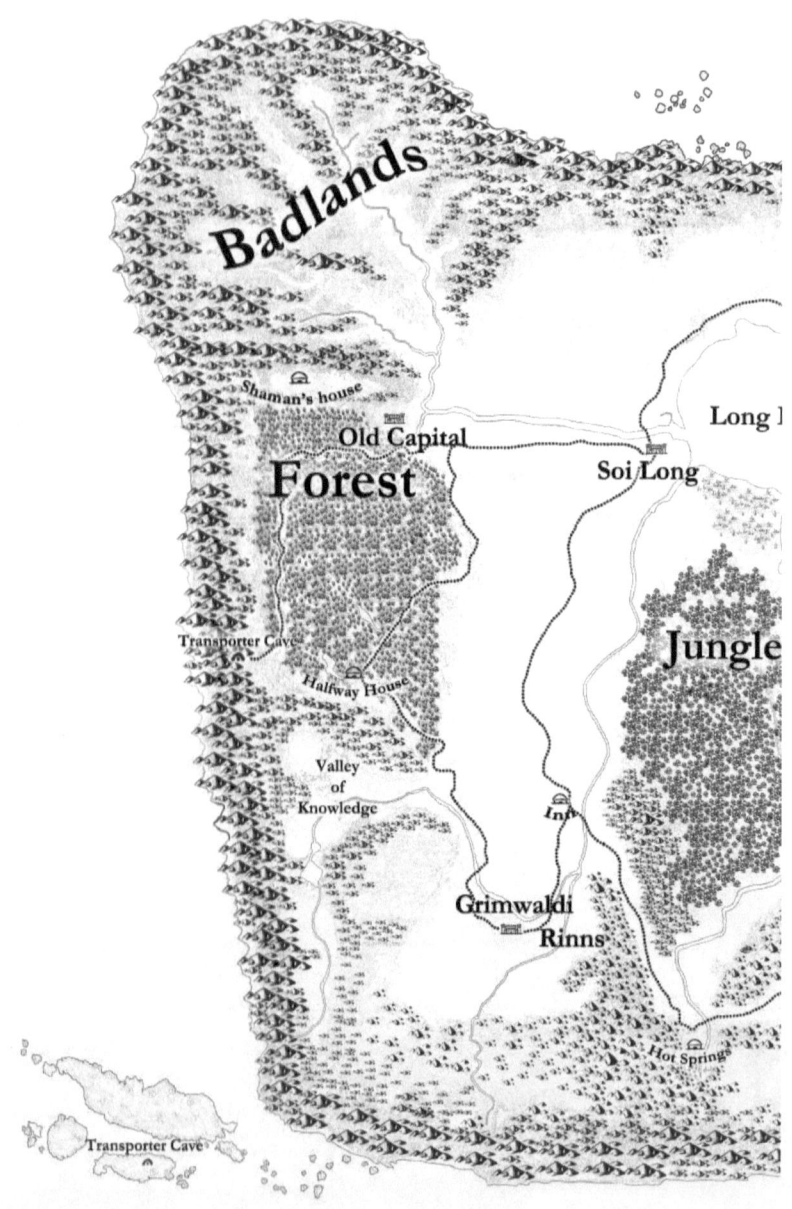

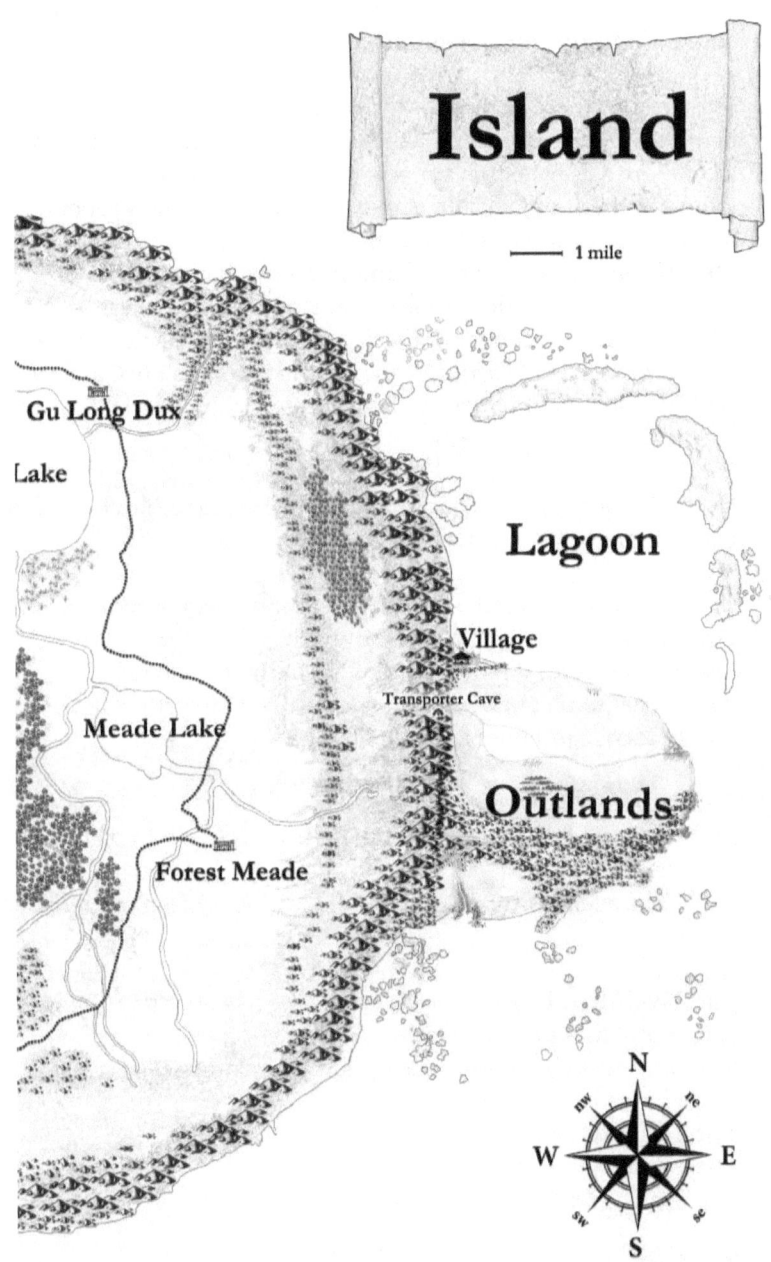

Island

1 mile

Gu Long Dux

Lake

Lagoon

Village

Transporter Cave

Meade Lake

Outlands

Forest Meade

N
nw ne
W E
sw se
S

Main Characters

Jack Barleycorn (homo sapiens or Last). The Guardian. Although married to Empress Jien Noi, he chose not to become Emperor.

The Second (homo erectus)
Jien Noi. The Empress and Gatekeeper. She is the ultimate power; the Second are a matriarchal society. Jack calls her Jinnie.
Ræm, firstborn of Jack and Jinnie, Empress and Gatekeeper elect. She becomes the Shaman's Assistant
The Shaman, an enlightened, and possibly elemental being.
n'Gnung. First Warrior of the Second, and Jack's closest friend.
n'Gue. Prime Messenger of the Second, n'Gnung's elder brother.
Gung Loi. Second Warrior, leader of the Second's Special Forces, and senior control room operator, wife of n'Gnung.
Barph. General of the Second's army.
§
Horovitz (homo sapiens). Captain of the Second's Blitzkrieg forces, Sergeant, ex-mercenary who changed sides.

The Seventh, Ddwyrth, or Dwarves (homo neanderthalensis).
Owain a'y Brenin, King of the Ddwyrth
Llwydd the Bold, First Warrior of the Ddwyrth.
Aroweena (female), Second Warrior of the Ddwyrth. Known as the Keeper of Hearts, and not because of her beauty.

The Eleventh or Elves
Ælthrelntheine, High Queen of the Eleventh, High Lord Protector of Gaia, mother of Kay.
Kay (Ælkræleinnoire), High Lord of Destiny, Queen of the Eleventh Elect.

The Twelfth or Giants
King Rambling Longshanks.
Gangling Shortfalls, learned sage and translator.

The Tenth or Ogres
The Great Ogre – arch villain.
The Trolls, creations of the Great Ogre; liberated as the New Tenth.

The Last
Dawn, Jack's oldest friend
John, leader of the Island research facility and University.
Penelope [Peni] Pendleton, eminent sub-nuclear particle physicist.

Ami Sturgess, nurse who joined in Book Three.

The Second - Notable characters
The Seer, Won Long.
Weid Noi, Won Long's daughter and trainee Seer.
Lo Si, Keeper of Ancient Knowledge, Druid, husband of the Seer, father of Weid Noi and Sun Kist.
Ju Lo, Lo Si's understudy, and senior control room operator.
Da Phai Nai, mother of Sun Kist; forbidden to marry Lo Si by a previous Empress.
Sun Kist, daughter of Da Phai Nai and Lo Si, High Priestess, later Shaman Supplicant.
Langnor and her husband Bufor, senior control room operators.
Jack's larger team includes: Xi Xah, Xi Sai (the girls), To Mo and To Ma (the twins). They are always nearby and working in the background, but seldom mentioned by name.

The Next Generation
Jason, trainee captain. Son of Jack and Jien Noi, marries Ah Tien.
Mai Li, trainee Gatekeeper, 2nd daughter of Jack and Jien Noi, marries Wong Kai and trains as Empress Regent.
Wong Kai, trainee Seer. Son of Ali and Weid Noi.
Ah Tien, trainee control room supervisor, who becomes the first Queen of Mars. She is the second child of Gung Loi and n'Gnung.
Zhong Zhi, trainee Guardian. Son of n'Gnung and Gung Loi, marries Ah Nei.
Ah Nei, comm. Operator. Daughter of Horovitz and Xi Sai.
Children of Langnor and Bufor:
Geldar, helmsman and navigator.
Pheldar, weapons master.
Norf, trainee engineer under Kay.

The Ancestors, The First or Thirteenth, *homo sapiens atavus*.
Oma, leader of the Ancestors.
Vela, captain of the Illustrious when it came to Gaia.
Idym, marries Ræm, their first child is called Eve Ning.
Poh, leader of the Centaureans from Proxima Alpha.

Non-human Entities
The Core, the spacecraft computer; thinks it is Captain Taris.
Matron, leading robotic medic who shows her humanity in Book Three.
Space Corps, Centaurean space elite, for Captains and above.

Recap

In *The Gatekeeper and the Guardian,* Jack crashed into the ocean and was washed ashore, half dead, on an uncharted South Pacific island in August 2010. There he discovered an impossibly advanced science, operated by a stone-age culture, one that had lost the use of fire and the wheel. The first person he met was Jien Noi, (Jinnie), the Empress Elect of homo erectus colony. She also held the position of Gatekeeper.

His best friend to be, n'Gnung, is one with whom he shares a brotherly understanding. Jack marries Jien Noi, and n'Gnung is forever by his side. With others, they defeat an Ogre invasion at the end of Book One, but the threat posed by the Great Ogre, a menacing despot who demands all sentient life on Gaia bow to him, or be exterminated.

The Twelve Tribes introduced Kay (Ælkræleinnoire), or Dark Elf, and Owain, King of the Dwarves (Ddwyrth, or Neanderthals). This book revolved around returning all Twelve Tribes to the fold of known humanity. Wars with the Great Ogre ensued, ending with the emancipation of the Trolls, and all Twelve Tribes standing together.

The message, or fundamental question posed by the trilogy begins to assert itself: Does God exist, or were we created by a race of Aliens?

At the end of Book Two, we learn of a retaliatory nuclear strike on the Iranian Bushehr power plant. The bomb exploded inside a previously unknown nuclear missile silo and storage facility, the fallout from which is still unclear. What is known is that the entire Arabian Plate has subsequently been destabilised.

This book has three distinct parts:
- The Wrath of Gaia.
- Discoveries and full Aftermath begins on Page 77, Chapter 12.
- Final battles with The Great Ogre.

As a volume, it reads concurrently.

The main point of this trilogy is centred around Chapter 17, but is supported by all three books in this, the first trilogy of Star Gazer.

We examine and question the origin of species homo sapiens, and the existence of God. The author, acting as *agent provocateur*, proposes an alternative theory for the creation of mankind — That we were created by an Alien race in their own image.

This is not done to denigrate religious belief, but to embrace it. And by so doing, offer a path towards greater enlightenment, for all of humankind.

Would the Wrath of Gaia destroy all life on Earth?

Would the Great Ogre ever be defeated?

What would become of Humanity?

Chapter 1 ~ Rivers of Blood

Jack

"Jackie, my brother Ali has just landed in Iran as part of a special containment and relief operation," Dawn exclaimed as soon as she returned from a visit home.

"Damn. I thought he was overseeing an oil exploration operation off the coast of Japan for Royal Dutch."

"He was, but the Iranian government have asked for international aid and experts. He was called away to assess the situation and possible consequences. Fortunately he's not anywhere near Bushehr. Can you check on him?"

I moved the scanner according to her instructions, and found Ali enjoying a leisurely coffee in the lobby of Tehran airport. He seemed relaxed, and Dawn's fears were greatly eased. "He's waiting for transfer to Kangan. You may not know, but that is Iran's major oil port and despatch terminal."

I continued to discuss the impending Wrath of Gaia with my oldest friend, but we were interrupted when SSA Henry Walcott, our good friend from the FBI, arrived. "Jackie, I managed to get hold of the maps you wanted. There are several including world and Arabian plate tectonics. I have physical and digital maps. Where do you want them?"

"Just leave them here for now. What's the latest situation?"

"From what little I understand," Henry dissembled, "Bushehr used to be on a plate boundary that had the Arabian Plate pushing against it, and was on the overthrust side of a reverse fault, so gradually rising higher over aeons. For this area to abruptly and noticeably dip in a matter of days indicates there is far worse to come."

I grumbled, "Why is it our most eminent scientists like to build nuclear facilities in earthquake zones that lie on the edges of continental plates? You would have thought they would have learned their lesson after Fukushima Daiichi. The only reason they don't use cheap and innately safe thorium reactors is because governments are completely focussed upon enriching the Uranium by-products to make atomic weapons. That is the only reason, and this is the result."

"You have a good point, Jackie, except pure thorium is difficult to extract. Anyway, I've put together a folder of the established major threats so far, but know world governments are in a state of panic. I have a feeling some will contact you directly."

"That would not surprise me in the least, Henry. We need dedicated eyes on, all over the area."

n'Gnung placed a hand on my shoulder, "Guardian, are you thinking about a dedicated team to watch over the area? If so, I would use the small meeting room over there, we hardly use it for anything, as all work either takes place here in the control centre, or in your Captain's ready room."

Kay mused, "That's a great idea. Jackie, let's interface with the Core and see if we can come up with a far more practicable solution. n'Gnung is correct, as usual, thank you brother."

Retiring to my ready room we interfaced easily in the language of the Ancestors. The upshot was the Core made the meeting room open to the bridge, and extended it towards the front, where the main display screen was. The new area covered most of the left side of the wall, as seen from the Captain's station. Liquid rock plasma flowed swiftly to create the new area. All we had to do was add workstations, and staff it. It never ceased to amaze me how something so seemingly solid as the rock our spacecraft was made from, could flow into new, preformatted formations. It was highly advanced technology, plasma bordering upon the bizarre.

Langnor, and her husband Bufor, our experienced night controllers, were tasked to train up two groups of replacements, one as night staff, and the second for relief, allowing them time off. They would also act as reserve, additional hands as and when required. Langnor would continue her role as supervisor, but of an increased team. She would take over as head of our new area, which n'Gnung proposed we call Operation Watch. It was agreed that after training the new staff, Bufor would become the regular day controller, thus freeing others for more vital work.

A couple of hours later, Dawn said, "Ali boarded his plane hours ago. He should be in Kangan by now, but there is no sign of him. I'm going to return to Wales and see what I can get off the internet and phone."

Time passed and our thoughts turned to dinner, and chilling on the shore of the Outlands with a beer. n'Gue, came with a message, "Guardian, what do you make of this?"

He had been occasionally monitoring for Dawn's return, and I watched as she paced around her living room, hitting redial on a landline, but nary an answer came. This was most unlike her normally relaxed attitude. I decided to go to her at once.

I arrived by transporter moments later, and gave my friend a brief hug. As we broke apart she said, "Ali, cannot be in a tunnel or in a cell shadow. He must still be in the air again, as otherwise there would be something. But his plane should have landed an hour ago. I am sure there is something terribly wrong."

I humoured her, masking my concern with a thought, "Given the grave nature of the current threat, it is likely the flight was delayed. Come, let's return to base and pull him up on our screens."

"But I saw him board it."

"Did you see it take off? It could still be on the tarmac. Come." Dawn came into my encircling arms, and I used the return bracelet to take us immediately back to the control centre.

We searched both the Tehran and Kangan airports, but there was no sign of Ali. We exchanged plausible reasons, "I'll ask Henry if he can trace Ali's mobile phone. What's the number?"

Having exhausted all our options, I said, "We have been given this time for a reason. Instead of passing this period with inessential miasma, we should be using it constructively."

She stopped and looked me in the eye for the first time, "You take Tehran and I'll take Kangan. I'll meet you in the middle."

We took consoles in the new Watch area, and I defined targets for general, and specific observation. This would aide our new controllers. What we saw was sickening, the loss of life and resources, towns and villages, known ways of life destroyed. As we watched, new, and ever more frequent eruptions manifest. Long extinct volcanoes spewed ash and magma in a hailstorm from hell. Rivers of larva wiped out all in their path. New volcanoes appeared as ranges, where none had been before, compounded the forces of growing decimation.

"I need the services of a vulcanologist to understand what's happening, one who is adept at continental plates and plays consequences for a hobby!"

Dawn replied, "Ask John."

Moments later, I caught up with our head of research, his primary school building now taking on the air of his previous life at a University campus. He had documented people he wanted to bring to augment his small team: a genetic palaeontologist, a symbolist versed in ancient languages, an archaeologist, geologist, and several others. "Jackie, we need these people in order to study this island, its people, homo erectus, and all the other tribes. I know what we agreed before, but with the world as we know it is in flux right now.

"This Wrath of Gaia is becoming our reality. We not only need these people to help us now, we need to save them from destruction. We need to not only expand our knowledge, but also preserve it for posterity."

I was taken aback, although I had been expecting John's request. I tried to think ahead, but he continued, "If you really are The Guardian, you need to preserve all humanity, including all we know today. What if all our people are wiped from this planet, huh? Any survivors would end up in a similar cultural cul-de-sac regards greater knowledge, as these islanders found themselves in ten thousand years ago. They lost the use of the wheel and fire, for Christ's sake."

I interrupted his presentation, "John, stop. I understand what you are saying, but for now, this is not a reality. Don't press me again on this until we know for sure, what the outcome will be. This conversation is finished for today. Capisce?"

"Yes, yes. Of course I understand. But these are critical personnel. Without them we will misinterpret key data."

"Alright, then. Five. Five only and you will need to run them by Jien Noi." I had not forgotten why I was talking to John in the first place. "One of them must be a volcanologist, an expert in continental plates. We've got land sinking and volcanoes rising. We need someone to help us sort this out, help us survive Gaia's Wrath."

He stared at me blankly.

I finished as words came unbidden from my lips, "You better find somebody who understands the rolling impact of these quakes, like Tsunamis and extreme forces of nature whilst you're at it, as I have the heaviest and most ominous heart about everything, including our own survival."

John stated flatly, "Jack, you only want people who fit your immediate parameters. Think of the greater good, the longer term."

We parted shortly afterwards, and on friendly terms. We were each fighting from our own corners, and would doubtless meld into amicable agreement, as before. I said, "I'll see you on the shore for dinner, it is time to put this day to rest."

"Not this time Jackie, I need to return to my home. My wife, Cynthia, has been troubled lately, and she needs my support. I'll follow these candidates up tonight, and return with something more substantial in a day or so. These things can take time."

I returned to the control room, and minutes later Ellen, one of Henry's team transported to us. "Dawn, I followed the information regarding Ali you gave us, and his mobile phone is roughly here, 53 East by 24 North"

She handed me a piece of paper with many numbers that we could not interpret. I interfaced with the Core, and moments later the gibberish was deciphered. The location was brought to the main screen. Scattered pieces of a small jet came into view, and we all knew the crashed plane was of deep significance. Its fuselage appeared to have been blasted with volcanic buckshot. We tried to transfer the wreckage to us, but it was caught within Gaia's molten rivers of fiery blood. The people we saw looked dead, and because of seat belts, I could not get a transportation lock. There was no option but to go there and free the trapped personally.

"Kay, we need a shielded transport circle there now!" I hollered.

As soon as our protection from the Great Ogre was in situ, we transferred, Kay and Jinnie monitoring us from the bridge. The small plane was a total mess, and felt like an oven inside. Dawn was first inside, immediately reaching her brother; "He has a pulse, but it's weak. Help me get him to safety."

We were footsteps behind, and found Ali was unconscious. Relief flooded through us. Several of his colleagues lay likewise, whilst one appeared to be fine. That was until his clothes begin to smoke as magma breached the window nearest him and he rushed outside, only to find the lava flows steadily encroaching upon the small island of rock we were stranded upon.

We had no time to think, only to react. We formed a human chain and began dragging the injured out to safety. We rescued six people, including the pilot who appeared to be dead, but we took him just in case.

Our world lurched. The shielded transfer circle held, and moments later we were back in our own control centre. The pilot was not amongst us, presumably because he was dead. Those left happily alive were marshalled to the medical centre although recovery might take some time.

Kay said, "That was gallant and brave, but what will we do with them?"

"They shouldn't stay, except for Ali of course." I said, "Matron, let me know as soon as they have been treated and can be released. Our best alternative is to send them home. The sooner the better works for me."

The Iranian looked frightened, and for a little salve I pointed and said, "Mecca is in that direction." He nodded in thanks, before we made our way back to the control room and reunited with the rest of our team.

Our talk tuned to other matters, but the moment was broken when Dawn came through leading a rather bemused Ali. I greeted him warmly. It had been many years since we last met face to face. I tasked Barph, the General of our regular army, to ensure the rest of our guests remained in recovery until we spoke to them.

Ali was drawn to our main screen. His fascinated eyes peered into all corners of this alien world he was now a part of. He walked forwards, both intrigued and horrified, it being clear he had absolutely no idea just what he was seeing. I panned the area to show him the extent of what had occurred, including the Egyptian side of the continental plate.

He stared, no words coming from his mouth. He turned to look at us in total bewilderment, each of us in turn. He was one of only four humans present. I said, "Ali, we were about to have dinner. Would you care to join us?"

He nodded his head distractedly, as Dawn took his arm, and gentling his confusion, led him towards the transporter.

Chapter 2 ~ Growing Cancer

There was forever, something so special about the village on the Outland shore. It always bestowed a sense of tranquillity and freedom. I could tell its præternatural ambience had already gifted its magic on Ali, as I watched him wander down to the beach. He was shortly skipping in the surf like a child. His inherent zest for life was returning, and with it his natural and playful nature, one I had known well from times passed.

I went down to join them, as he and Dawn scampered like small children within the strand, until he stopped to stare, as one of our *boats* came to shore. "That collection of twigs and dried grass actually floats?"

"Welcome to island life. That is one of our finest fishing vessels, and these people invented it themselves. Let's eat and be merry this night."

As we sat at our usual table, Da Phai Nai welcomed us, "I see we have extra company tonight. I will bring a barrel of beer for you to enjoy, whilst we slave away in the kitchens."

"Owain will be here soon wise Mother."

My words brought forth a smile and wistful look, before she extended her offer, "A hogshead it is then."

I could see Ali trying to understand the exchange. "Ignore her tongue, it is just her way. She has a heart of gold, and is a lovely person. Truth be told, many's the time her wit has turned a grey mood into laughter. Now Ali, tell me why you ended up in Iran."

"As you know I work as project manager for major international oil exploration projects. I have been offshore in Japanese waters for the last four years, and on promotion, am now in charge of a related group of projects. You remember the nuclear strike on Bushehr some weeks ago I am sure. Well, it transpires this caused some issues in Kangan that were of a highly complex and technical nature.

"The main IGAT pipelines leading into the port are extremely important to Iran's economy. These developed curious issues related to the associated processing and distribution hub. I'll spare you the jargon. Essentially, they needed expert help. The company contracted to assist called on us. I grew up in Persia, and we fled the revolution, as you know. I speak Farsi, but am a little rusty, so that is why I was chosen to go.

"I was joined in Tehran by four others, one from head office, and three experienced oil contractors. We were assigned an official guide by the government, although this was not technically, an official government request for assistance you understand. However, also know that all such enquiries must have official sanction.

"It was strange to be back in the country of my birth, and one as a young boy I have few memories of — we fled the patrols of the gun toting freedom fighters when the Shah's reign ended.

"The flight to Kangan was going well, until we began our descent. I remember one of the men called us to look out of the window, as the earth below was streaked with lava flows. We watched with astonishment until our view was obscured by a curious whiteout of cloud, presumably volcanic ash.

"The engines faltered, but soon stabilised as we came into clear air once more. Moments later, the pilot called back for us to fasten seat belts, which was closely followed by the plane climbing rapidly. The jet was hit by volcanic explosion and the force of decompression was terrible. A lump of molten lava melted through the skin of the craft, landed on one of the seats, fortunately an empty one. I presume critical systems were damaged, because the jet continued to fly under haphazard control for a while.

"We were hit several more times and the last thing I recall is losing at least one engine, and dropping quickly through the ash cloud once more. I turned on my mobile at that point, hoping to send a distress call, but the plane hit and we were thrown so violently, that seats were ripped from their locations as the aircraft tumbled nose over tail. I lost consciousness, and the next thing I remember, is waking up in your hospital. How you found us I will never know, but thank you all for coming to our aid, and for saving my life."

"That is our pleasure, think nothing of it. Ali, I need to know what to do with the other people we rescued. Please realise this place is a secret base, and we are at war with the Tenth … Column. Know I, we, have absolutely no problem with you being here, but what of the others?"

"I hardly know any of them, except for the senior man from head office. He is a moneyman and better sent away from here. The contractors are an accountant, an export specialist, and the other guy is from the States and a technical expert like me. But his focus is to keep the pipelines working at all costs, regardless of any risk. My priority is safety, not only of personnel, but gas and oilfield integrity, including all distribution networks.

"The official guide, Behrouz, seemed like a nice man, but I only knew him for an hour at most. I can try speaking to him if you want?"

"Thank you, but maybe tomorrow," My words were cut short as I heard footsteps approaching. I rose to welcome Owain, but I saw John instead. He joined us, but appeared stressed and depressed.

John seemed to settle when a beer was given to him, and he began to reanimate, "Jackie, a leading vulcanologist will arrive first thing in the morning. He works within a loose team of private contractors and advisors who have their own network. One is a tectonics expert who may be available. They are both exceedingly capable and adaptable. Unfortunately, I drew a blank with the meteorologist, as the brightest minds are all focused on the same concerns, but from other perspectives. Apologies."

I thanked him for his efforts, reflecting, "Perhaps we can call on our dedicated contact at the CDC, Doctor Sylvia Steele, although I imagine they will already be up to their necks in this situation. John, I thought you said you were not coming back until tomorrow. What's up?"

Normally proactive, John shook his head and turned away, obviously preoccupied with something. I nodded to Dawn who appeared equally disturbed by his reticence, and they spoke quietly as she walked with him down to the shore. I kept an eye on them, and I would swear those most charming of people were having an argument. Their disagreement seemed to last for several minutes, before John stormed off and stood facing the ocean, his feet sinking beneath lapping waves within the shoreline.

Dawn went to him and gently placed her hand on his back, patting him softly before moving gently to his side with her arm wrapping around him. She continued her slow encirclement until she was able to place her hand on his chest. In response he crashed to his knees and was nurtured to her belly, her hand smoothing his balding pate, whilst both appeared to be unaware they were actually in the sea.

Both Ali and I rose to rush to them, but Lo Si said, "Leave them be, this is a time for succour. Later, when the secret is exposed and admitted, will come the time for telling."

A little later, I noticed John and Dawn had returned, talking quietly, and seated away from everyone else. I went over to them out of curiosity and made a noise to announce my arrival. Dawn turned to look at me with a tear in her eyes, "It's Cynthia. She has cancer. They just found out."

"What's the prognosis?" I asked, moving to place a comforting hand on John's shoulder.

"Perhaps six months if they remove both her legs tomorrow; she has bone marrow cancer and there is no cure."

I stared at them in disbelief, before rounding on the pair of them, "Jesus Christ! We have the most advanced medical facility on this planet, why didn't you tell us?"

John responded disconsolate, "We didn't want to trouble you."

I snapped back, "Which hospital is she in? Which ward, what bed?"

As soon I had the information I needed, I pressed my return bracelet, moments later zooming in on where Cynthia was being cared for. I found her quickly enough, in a private room and looking quite withdrawn. Unfortunately, she had many tubes and probes attached to her, so could not transport her as was. I needed to go and disconnect her personally. It looked simple enough as she wasn't intubated, just remove the oxygen mask, taped-on sensors, and drip.

Without delay, I was standing at Cynthia's bedside, and scolded her gently for not asking us for help. I began removing all the tubes for extraction, a drip feed, and several electrical monitoring devices. I was pulling the covers away when the door burst open, and in ran a nurse, wondering what caused the alarms to sound.

She stopped dead in her tracks and I said, "Do not worry, we are old friends. Our medical facilities are far more advanced than your own."

I reached down and took Cynthia's hand in my own, whilst twisting to hit the button of my return bracelet. As I pressed, I felt a hand touch me, and reanimated in our transfer circle with Cynthia, and the nurse. The stunned girl rounded on me, before it abruptly dawned on her she was no longer in the hospital. She was staring at a guard that was not human. I picked Cynthia up in my arms and said, "Nurse, either stay here and return to your known world, or come with me and discover a different future."

I walked off and she followed as if scared of her own shadow. I waited a moment for her to stand within the new internal transporter circle, and we transferred directly to the medical unit, where she followed me through to our treatment rooms. John and Dawn hurried to join us, looking curiously at the nurse, I ad lib'd, "She came through with us."

I lay Cynthia down on a bed as an android nurse came to attend immediately. She asked me what the problem was. "Bone marrow cancer. Her legs I believe. Please speak in English to my companions. This is the nurse who was treating her."

She listened as our human nurse rattled off a load of medical gobbledygook. Mere seconds passed before the robotic nurse swung into motion, a second arriving to assist her. One would expect identical machines to all look the same, but they did not for some curious reason. I asked the Matron, "Do you have a name?"

She replied, "Leading Medic 37851, now Guardian, what are you actually trying to say?"

"I prefer to call you Matron. Will she recover?"

"Wait one moment and we will find out, now be quiet Guardian, and do not interfere."

They worked in tandem, as first a full body scan was conducted. Areas of her legs and spine were examined in depth. John sat down beside his wife and held her hand in comfort, before being shooed away by one of the nurses. For some reason, this brought forth a half-crazed giggle from our British nurse, whose eyes remained firmly absorbed in what was happening.

In time, a strange device descended, and a flash of some kind of ray blinked for several seconds. The senior automaton worked her computer, a syringe-like probe extruding from one of her eight limbs. This focused, before a small transfer took place, retrieving a minute sample for analysis. The British nurse said, "A biopsy, just like that. Seconds. Oh my God!"

The Matron turned to look at our companion and said, "This is the most efficient means of extrapolation."

Fascinated, the girl went to the screen and shadowed the work of our robotic medic. They exchanged a few words. The cause was identified as being *hydrocarbons*, and a treatment prescribed. John asked for a simple, English translation.

"The dead tissue will be laser-ed out by computer, before stem cells are inserted to regenerate the marrow itself from the few remaining good cells."

The speed of treatment was breathtaking, and within five minutes, the initial process was accomplished. Cynthia was pronounced cured of cancer. Her convalescence would take several weeks, and months for total recovery. However, the Matron sedated her, and with John's permission, began full body regeneration.

The relief was audible, as smiles replaced frowns, whispering in gratitude. We all knew a life had just been saved. The English nurse was totally gobsmacked, yet turned with a new sanity in her eyes, and looked at John, "I know you, you are her husband."

John nodded in confirmation, before she looked around the whole room, turning a circle as she did so, until her eyes rested upon me, "Ami, Ami Sturgess." She proffered her hand.

I replied as I shook her hand, "I am The Guardian, although you, young lady, can call me Jack. Will you stay, or will you go? Because we could use a human nurse around here."

"I don't know?" She looked around again, at the impossibility only a dream could manifest.

"Well I need a beer," I stated.

Ami's voice echoed mine. "So do I, I think. This is amazing."

I placed a hand each on John and Cynthia. "Everything will be OK."

Their eyes were shining, but they could not reply, as tears of pure joy formed in their eyes, emotions clogging their throats as if clutched in acknowledgement of a miracle. I patted each in turn and, making to leave, looked at Dawn. She said, "I'll stay for a moment, but will join you all again soon."

Chapter 2

I took our stunned nurse by the hand, and led her back through to our control room, where we transported to the shore. I had no idea why I was so open to her joining our number. To be honest, it just felt right. When we arrived, I leant down to her ear, and whispered in confidence. "Let's meet some of the other races of humankind. Know everybody here is your friend, no matter how strange they may look."

Chapter 3 ~ String Theory

The next morning skies were dark with heavy clouds of ominous intent. I noticed our tides had been disrupted and would check our shield integrity as soon as I reached the control centre. Ami was sitting nearby staring at the sea. As I approached she said, "This isn't a dream."

I chuckled and confirmed it most definitely was not. I ask if she would like to accompany me for a normal restaurant breakfast, and she jumped up eagerly. I enquired of others, but with just Ali and Ami for company, I transferred to the control centre to take a brief report. Nothing much had changed overnight, although it seemed the Arabian plate had marginally stabilised. I checked the shields as Ami wandered around peering at things. I noted our protection was holding well, and decided to return our rescued guests before we left.

My new shadows accompanied me to the medical centre, where we found Behrouz in a cheery frame of mind. He said, "Thank you for saving my life. Knowing where Mecca was helped me greatly."

"My pleasure. We will transfer you back to Kangan in a few minutes time."

A shadow crossed his face, "This is OK. But I am terrified by what they may do to me. Can I stay?"

Ali spoke to him in Farsi, as I left them in discussion, and went to see the others. It seemed the men we had recovered were well, and back to their belligerent normality. Instead of thanking me for their timely rescue, I was faced with four hostile people wanting to know why they had been kidnapped and imprisoned.

"So much for gratitude. We saved your lives you know." Imbeciles! "Where in the world would you like to be right now?"

I got four different answers, and withdrew to action their removal immediately. Ami said, "What horrible men."

I couldn't disagree, but was interrupted by Ali, "Get the bosses back to Holland or wherever, as they only understand money. I would keep the Iranian guide for a few days, because he knows how to work inside Iran. Think ahead Jack. If we are determined to be proactive, we do need inside information."

I began to protest adding another new person to our number, when the thought of a direct link with the Iranian government took hold, and silenced my tongue. In the current situation, this could prove especially useful. Therefore, Behrouz was added to my followers. I returned to the bridge and transferred the oilmen immediately, although we did linger to watch their total confusion and enjoy the laugh.

I checked back on the situation in Iran. It was as before. I asked Ali if he would return, and staring in horror at our screens, he said, "Damn right I will: Not!"

Behrouz was astounded and stood there watching his beloved country being torn apart by the forces of mankind and nature. He turned around in search of succour, and noticed he was facing many people who were not human, at least as far as he understood the term. He started muttering a sutra to ward off evil. It was time to get him out of there.

Cynthia had not been in the hospital, so I went to visit her at her home near the shore. I found her sleeping, with Dawn taking a watching brief. She rushed to hug me, thanking me for saving her friend's life. This was becoming a habit. Ami checked Cynthia in her professional capacity and was amazed at the change. Her mind was still working as she said, "She will be fine. This is incredible."

Moments later we all transported for breakfast, using the nearby commuter transfer circle recently installed. All I had to do was walk on last, and we were all transferred automatically to the University. Both Ali and Behrouz asked for Persian cuisine. The head chef was eager for the challenge, and keen to try new recipes. Ami was delighted with our servery, and soon had a plate full of her favourite dishes, accompanied by a large pot of tea. I took coffee with full English breakfast and hot buttered toast. Somehow, a basket of fries also ended up on my tray, and I could not be bothered to return them.

As we entered the adjoining dining hall, I was waved over by John, who was back to his sprightly best. We joined their large table, where Ami still could not believe Cynthia has been healed. This led to further discussion, and we learned Ami was recently qualified, and living far from home. She told us that apart from her mother, she had no family, and being new to the hospital, had not made any real friends, never mind a boyfriend.

John subsequently offered, "Ami, we have a medical centre here at the University, but I have not found anybody to man or woman it. I wondered if you would be interested in the position. There is no pay, but then again, there are no bills either, because money doesn't exist here." He swept his arm around and added, "Everything you see here is free. In exchange, you work as required with no fixed hours. It's sort of like a commune."

Ami became quite excited but he cautioned her. "I will show you around after breakfast, but understand that if you take the post, your immediate duty would be to continue caring for my wife."

I understood John's opportunistic ruse, and the deal was done before I could nod in approval. I added that we would have her things brought to us later in the day. I asked John if he had a use for Behrouz, although we would have need of his services from time to time. He told me he would see what could be done.

I hadn't finished eating, when n'Gue appeared and informed John he had one of the Last waiting to join us. I glugged down my coffee and rose to attend to the matter. John was already far too preoccupied with our latest arrivals, and this was my duty regardless.

I returned quickly to the control centre where my cohort had assembled. On the screen, I saw somebody who was the spitting image of Charles Bronson. He had a typical Mexican moustache, under which a wide grinning mouth contrasted oddly with his large, black-rimmed glasses, and long white lab coat. I asked Bufor to transport him as soon as I was in the main transfer room to greet him.

I was not sure how to play this one, so would take my cue from his words. Within moments of arrival, a rather bemused man stood within the black circle, his ready grin still evident in spite of his strange arrival. I extended my hand and said, "¿, Hola, como estas?"

That was a big mistake, because he immediately started speaking in Spanish. He grabbed my hand and shook it enthusiastically. I had to apologise and inform him I only spoke Holiday Spanish. He switched immediately to English, but nodded in acceptance of my common courtesy.

"We will meet John later. Would you like to eat, or see our problem first?" He was all work and ready to start business at once. As we walked towards the control centre, I introduced myself formally, and learned his name was José Emmanuel Estaves.

I warned him, "You are about to meet some odd looking people, but we are all great friends." I led him through the door to our control room, and his grin became a set mask as his eyes drank in the strange beings. This was my cue to get straight down to business. I showed him what is happening on the Arabian Plate in detail, and said, "I asked John to find us a tectonic specialist also, so we can work out just what is going to happen in the future."

It seemed he was not aware of everything that had happened in the greater region, so we spent time looking at specific places of interest to him, especially southern Turkey, Syria, and Israel. In time, he stood and held his chin in his hand, drumming his fingers idly on the side of his jaw.

At length he spoke, "This is far more serious than we imagined. It is a nightmare. Those fools with their nuclear bombs, what have they done? From memory, there is a fault here, near the northern tip of the plate, and it is an exceptionally serious omen that there has not been any activity in this area. In volcanology we have a saying that roughly translates as: 'The longer it is Brewing, the Greater is it's Spewing'."

I directed him to the map of world plates, and he immediately confirmed his opinion. Tapping the fault line that concerned him most he stated, "Something bad will happen here for sure. If that plate goes, it could signal the end of the world as we know it."

"We have been expecting The End of the World for some years now, and I am fairly certain that this is it. We are working to prevent the utter destruction of all life on this planet. Can you, will you help us?"

"I have a lab in Guadalajara, but need access to these screens. They are remarkable."

"OK José, we have a deal. But bear in mind this is a secret base and we have no internet connection, on purpose."

"This is no problem. These screens of yours are the key. I am presuming this is real-time?"

I confirmed by zooming into his laboratory, and showed the inside, which brought an incredulous look from him. I focused on a clock. "I have been here for forty five minutes already. Your technology is astounding. I need a lab here and one of my staff to act as messenger between the two places. Better still, I'll see if Fernando Perez is free and he can operate the station here and report to me in my lab. He is the best tectonics guy I know, but he may be preoccupied. I'll check as soon as I get back. Can your computers interface with ours, or laptops?"

"José, our computers can interface with anything: iPods, smart phones, tablets, memory sticks, whatever, no problem. Let me show you our dedicated place of operations before we go any further."

I led him over to where Langnor was monitoring the Arabian Plate. He was pleasantly surprised by what we had put together, but made some suggestions, and also asked Langnor to monitor the Israeli fault with top priority. He was obviously a man used to giving orders, and once I interpreted for her, she acknowledged his expertise.

He looked at me, his wide grin prominent, fixed. He stated with a knowing look in his eyes, "These people, they are not human, *si*?"

I could not help but smile back at his infectious smirk and replied, "They represent different tribes of humanity. Langnor here belongs to what you would call *homo erectus*, although we call them the Second."

He turned and smiled at my companions, "Two Second, an Elf, and a Dwarf I presume?"

The Eleventh replied immediately in English, "My name is Ælkræleinnoire, but if you call my people the Eleventh, I will allow you call me Kay. We do not like to be addressed as Elf. To my side stand n'Gnung and Gung Loi of the Second, and this is Aroweena, Second Warrior of the Ddwyrth or Seventh—*homo neanderthalensis*, and know she is not called The Keeper of Hearts because of her beauty."

16

José took the etiquette lesson in his stride, assisted by Kay's curious smile, and shook everybody's hand like long lost friends. Her interest piqued by his reaction Kay added, "Know that we are currently at war with the Ogres, some of whom were given human form. The five of us standing here together have killed thousands of them between us, and our blood-bond is strong."

José removed his glasses and peered up at the Eleventh. "Please know fair Queen of the Eleventh, I am not an Ogre."

The light in his eyes amused her. Trickles of silvery laughter rolled and tumbled in the air. She stilled and replied, "Know I am not the Fairest Queen herself, but I am her Daughter."

I asked José if there was anything he needed adding to this workstation. "Apart from it being made twice as wide, it is fine."

I interfaced with the Core, while n'Gnung cautioned him to stand back. I was informed that due to routing and structural requirements, I could not double the size of the area specifically, but I could make it much larger. I kept my focus, waving everybody to stand aside, and set the change in motion.

José watched the room melt and reform, and moments later, he was staring at the new Watch area, larger and far more accommodating. He turned with a look of wonder in his eyes. Kay said, "We do not call him The Guardian without good reason. But please understand this is advanced technology, not magic."

Once the transformation completed with new consoles and workstations, he was given a new area as his own. He set a double workstation to his personal preference, having all the information he needed at his fingertips. Langnor showed him the controls as Kay interpreted, and elaborated. He learned how to zoom and pan the screen controls. He reminded me of a child in thrall of a new toy and I left him to play for a while.

Dawn arrived to give Ali an official tour of the craft, and I noticed Weid Noi at her station for once. She usually preferred her own company and used the old mountain control. Ali stopped and they talked for a while, although I needed to translate some things, before Aroweena volunteered to replace me. They parted cordially, and I thought nothing of it.

n'Gnung came to my side and said, "Translation is proving to be a problem, and a distraction. Guardian, we know there is a language and translation program. Could it be adapted to act as a translation device, perhaps a mobile one?"

He had done it again, seen the obvious. I interfaced with the Core, and discovered that although never required before, a fixed device could be added to the Watch area, and a portable one made ready.

Most languages of the Last were well documented, "Core, please initiate a database of all world languages, versions, and dialects."

I retrieved the first version, shaped like a necklace, moments later from my ready room, and gave it to Dawn. Kay was freed from translation duties, but there were small flaws. The next version of each included scanners to identify the Tribe of the speaker, and we had full communication between all.

I had hardly finished when n'Gnung asked me to attend the bridge. I discovered we had a flagged request from Penelope Pendleton. I mused, "This could be interesting," but could find no trace of her. The contact symbol we agreed upon when we had said goodbye, a digital clock, was set in a window near her back door, and showed almost one hour had elapsed.

I panned around looking for either her or a note, but found nothing. My thoughts turned to writing her a note, but when I reached for a pen and paper, she appeared with a carrier of shopping.

I transported Penelope as soon as she settled, and greeted her arrival. She looked a little flustered. I enquired, "Are you OK?"

"Jackie dear, it's fine, although I don't think I will ever get used to this means of travel. It is so bizarre, especially when one is not expecting it. Anyway, I am here now, and I would like to spend some time here studying your incredible machinery. I will be ready in thirty-five minutes and will stay for ten days. Is that acceptable?"

"That's fine, although we are rather busy with the end of the world right now."

Her head tilted for a moment, before she appeared to remember, and batted back, "Oh that Gaia thing, yes. It is such a nuisance isn't it. Now, I am hoping it is OK if my sister Phœbe comes with me. She's great with computers and well, we both fancied a working holiday. Good. See you here soon, now how do I get back?"

"Peni, bring whatever you need. Do you need an office or a laboratory?"

"Ah yes that. Well it is all the same thing really, except quite different you know." She stilled for a moment, as her mind worked quickly, "Will ten days be long enough?"

I was sure this was going to be a lot of fun, and replied with humour, "How long is a String Theory?"

She looked at me intensely for a moment before retorting, "Precisely."

And with that, she remounted the transfer circle and was gone. I said to n'Gnung, "A dippy academic of diverse dimensional distortion. Excellent. This is going to be most entertaining."

Chapter 4 ~ Battle Cruiser

It was becoming clear we would need extra accommodation in the near future, so I spoke to John at the University. John said, "Of course, I'll find suitable, abandoned buildings, leave it with me."

As he departed, Helen added, "Don't worry Jackie, I'll ensure he doesn't take anything he shouldn't."

I returned to the control centre as José was departing, "Jackito, I must return to Guadalajara, but will come back here shortly."

Once back at my control station, I asked the Core, "Jackito, what does it mean?"

"It's a familiar contraction of a person's name."

The contraction was longer than my name, almost double. I needed a diversion.

I sat to survey my domain, and concluded that this being the end of the world and all that, I was not actually getting anything done that day, which was already half over. My stomach was rumbling. My thoughts were interrupted when Ali and Dawn returned in fits of giggles, and said they were headed for lunch. I looked to n'Gnung, who signalled a beer. 'What a mighty fine mind he had. Probably the finest mind of all those present'.

But, before I could head to the refectory, Henry came to me with a new plan to extract a location for the Tenth. We spent some time going over it together in my dayroom, before he hurried away. No sooner has he left, than Peni was ready for transportation. I went down to greet her, and her rather bemused sister. I settled them with Kay to guide them deeper into the craft, and returned to find José had already returned with yet another addition to our tribe: Ramone.

I queried his presence and José informed me discretely, "Ramone Chevez is Fernando Perez's younger half-brother, and they work as a team. Apparently, their loving mother was of an open disposition to the opposite sex. However, she was also caring enough to raise them as inseparable brothers, and with the money she earned in the personal services industry, put them both through school and on to University in the States."

José led the astonished youth to our newly created workstations and began explaining its capabilities. Within seconds, they had totally forgotten about us and were extremely busy.

I looked to my side and raised an eyebrow to n'Gnung. He replied in kind and imperceptibly nodded his head. Satisfied that some things in life remained constant and true, I swivelled back to my console. I had not even set my finger on the controls, before Peni and Phœbe appeared before me needing a base of operations.

19

I knew that I did not want them playing with things unattended within the hull, but noticed n'Gnung making the beer drinking sign over their shoulders. The others of my team were trying unsuccessfully to stifle their mirth, and I decided impulsively, "We must go and see Professor John at once."

I stood, intent on leaving immediately, but Phœbe spotted Ramone, and soon they were hugging and gabbling, clearly long-lost friends. I looked at Peni, "Explain please."

She looked at me, looked askance, and remembered. "Ah *Ramondo*. He… they had a thing in college. They better not end up doing it all over the place again when I have serious work to do."

I looked at n'Gnung, and found all my trusty team were listening intently. Peni added, "The last straw was when they did it in the fountain, although fortunately they managed to keep most of their clothes on that time. Then Daddy bawled them out, and I never saw Ramondo again until just now."

"Peni, what exactly were they doing in the fountain?"

I heard sharp intakes of breath all around. Peni nonchalantly replied, "Perfecting a device for wireless underwater camera signals of course, why do you ask?"

I noted that extremely clever particle physicists may not actually orbit our real world. But she surprised me by saying, "Ahha! You were thinking of the *S* word weren't you? Silly me. Note to self: I must be careful with words when speaking to non-academics. You are all naughty minded children, and we will enjoy working with you. Phœbe, stop teasing the poor guy. Come."

Her statement elicited a mass exodus to luncheon, as not only did I leave with my trusted team, the scatty scientific sisters, but also the 'magmanic' Mexican's. Weid Noi also joined us, and whilst her strange company was most welcome, I had never known her do so before, and never under her own volition. I was left pondering the why of it as we transported.

n'Gnung led our party straight through to the dining area, where John made a great fuss over our latest arrivals. He was quite animated as he escorted them to the servery, fully back to his old self. Once we had all been served, Weid Noi took Dawn's advice regards food, this being her first visit to the refectory. Ali and Dawn encouraged her sit with them, which seemed to please her.

Our group stood to toast, n'Gnung having ordered large draughts of Grolsch Dutch pilsner for everyone. It was new to the island, ice-cold, and went down a treat. We all downed our pints in one go, except for Kay who sipped and stated, "I don't like this."

We watched as she took a longer draught and raised the glass, peering at it carefully before adding, "I really do not like this."

She subsequently lifted the measure one last time, and drank the remainder in one go. She slammed the now empty glass down stating, "That was ghastly."

n'Gnung enquired if she would like another, "Yes please." Elven humour can be a little obscure, but it is always entertaining.

We ate and enjoyed the moment, but drinking slowly. The day was far from over. n'Gnung had been staring at my food, "Guardian, may I have one of your chips? ... Hmm, delicious. They are quite addictive." He took another, before attending the servery and returning with two more baskets.

Our group were chatting and laughing, when I felt the world lurch. It was a mental thing, but quite definite. I rose instantly to go to the control room. Nearby Kay had also risen, and we looked at each other for a long second, exchanging rapid bursts of mental communication. Breaking eye contact, she hurried off to greet our fate, whilst I said goodbye to the others. I clapped José and Ramone heartily on their backs, mentioning that their presence was required, "Toast with us Guardian, and we will be on our way."

I discovered they had found a measure of Tequila, a bottle half-empty on the table. I left at once, waving to Ami who was enjoying the new experience. I noticed Ali was talking with Weid Noi. She was giggling, but said something to furrow Ali's brow. She was watching him intently. Dawn was missing.

As we re-entered our working world, the Mexicans immediately became serious again, the Latin exuberance replaced with concerned erudition. I turned away and speculated about my reaction in their shoes. Would I not also require a stiff drink, and things that made cultural sense to me.

Kay rose from my console as I approached, and pointed out what had occurred. The cause was not the Israeli fault line, but a related region that lay due south, where a long extinct volcano showed exuberant signs of life.

I overlaid a map of major world fault lines, with one of prominent volcanoes of the last million years, adding a world political map for clarity. I saved the result and sent it to Langnor, before going to talk to her first, and subsequently José.

She had already disseminated the new map to her team by the time I reached her. Early indications were that an impossibly large area of land appeared to be rising in the region. I sought clarification from the Mexicans, but they were so deep into their projections they hardly acknowledge my presence. Ramone muttered, "Harrat Ash Shamah," and that was all I got from them.

I left the busy people to work, and soon they were rushing back and forth between their lab in Guadalajara and their workstations with us. To ease the load on operating staff, Kay and I placed a dedicated transporter at their base, with associated shield to bar Ogres or their clones from entering. We also made four access rings, one each for José, Fernando, and Ramone, plus one for a dedicated messenger. I was still mindful to restrict access to our island, and ensure our security.

Some time later, José returned with Fernando, who seemed too preoccupied with matters of tectonic and deep significance regards the earth's crust, to wonder openly about being transported. That's not to say he was blasé, but his incredulity was brief. He had been forewarned, and barely winced at our control room and disparate operations team.

After briefest introductions, Fernando set to work. He was quickly absorbed, dashing from screen to screen, pulling up parameters, and talking in staccato bursts. His mind obviously, deeply concerned and playing catch-up.

In time he spoke openly to everyone, and we followed his scientific jargon as best we could, assisted by his explanations, and our translation devices. "We must find what we call 'the offsets of spreading centres.' And if there are none, the consequences will be dire. I need information about any earthquakes or tremors, the Modified Mercalli Intensity scale [that measures earthquake intensity] and Richter scale [a measure of earthquake magnitude and energy]. The two scales may not be, and rarely are related.

"Ramone, find any information you can on the lithosphere, and particularly the Moho Discontinuity. I need to know at what depth the asthenosphere is, and if there are any unusual pressure build-ups or distortions. We must discover where the next volcano will pop through the mantle, and how many of them."

Peni tittered, "Volcanoes popping up all over the place, like zits on a schoolboys face. I don't suppose acne cream would help. Nevertheless, I've heard of the asthenosphere, it's a highly viscous, mechanically weak, and ductility-deforming region of the upper mantle."

"Correct Peni, not many people know that. Everybody, this 'transform fault', or plate boundary, has sheared down to the asthenosphere. The Arabian Plate is becoming detached from all the plates that surround it. This should be completely, and utterly impossible. Subduction Theory states this as so … and yet it is actually happening. Ramone, how soon can you get the info?"

"Brother, the Middle East now uses Delta Telecom from Azerbaijan as the main regional internet backbone and core plus edge router supplier. Over the last few weeks services have been severely disrupted, and several core routers and the major optic fibre transmission lines have either been damaged or destroyed. This is worse in Iran, Israel, and Saudi Arabia, but all neighbouring countries are greatly affected.

"It takes time for the system to reset and come back up again. However, where core, edge, and computer hardware or internet cables have been damaged or destroyed, these have to be physically repaired or replaced. This can take many days, weeks, or months even. Therefore please expect this type of collateral damage anywhere there is volcanic activity. Or an earthquake near to sensitive equipment and routers.

"Remaining internet traffic is now being routed via Europe and Northern Africa, where the existing framework is coming under extreme load. I would urge you to use satellite links wherever possible. These remain under our control and are easy to implement, regards what we need."

José reacted decisively, "Ramone, we are already compromised by traditional internet channels. Return to Guadalajara immediately and initiate satellite links at once. You better increase our computing and communications capabilities as quickly as you can, since other scientists are coming to assist us."

While the scientists tried to confuse me with technological gobbledygook, Kay had again taken over my workstation, and she was busy with a small matter when I returned. "Kay, would your own dedicated console not be far better for all of us?"

She gave me a quizzical look. "I've no need of my own station. Why would I want one? Possessing such a thing has no relevance."

"I would prefer it if you, as Deputy Commander, had your own workplace so that there is no need for us to keep swapping over."

She finished her small task and replied, "That's a good idea. I could continue working regardless of whether you are here, or not. I'm still making automatic transfer circles to place around the island, and n'Gue is working on placement and usage. Excellent."

I turned to look at my three remaining companions. They were all standing behind me watching what was happening around them. They also needed consoles to work from. "Kay, please continue, thank you."

I left for my day room as Kay swivelled in my chair once more. I gave a deft flick of my head for n'Gnung only to follow me, and interfaced with the Core from my dayroom. I searched through designs for our craft in its current configuration. I was searching for a specific control room layout, but became disappointed. There was nothing similar to what I was looking for.

Creating what I wanted directly by mental interface would take time, and I needed to be available that day. I almost missed the reference, but discovered an archive of other designs for ships with different classifications. I opened it and flicked through control room specifications and layouts, not expecting to find inspiration.

One sub-folder equated to Battle Cruiser, something I doubted we would ever require. However, the first image I saw was exactly what I was looking for. There were more than a dozen ship configurations, but I had the one I needed, classified as hunter-killer. I checked the process and it appeared to be simple, but would require two of us to make the change.

I had been preoccupied for more than one hour. "n'Gnung, I have found the perfect control room configuration. Kay and I will have to do it when the place is quiet, although it should not take long to complete. I will do it at the next convenient opportunity."

"Guardian, that would probably be right now. All our visitors left some time ago and all we are doing is monitoring."

I drew a deep breath, "Ask Kay to join us."

She floated beside me moments later, and we interfaced together, going over the new design and configuration. "Jackie, this is remarkable. I am impressed. Let's do this now, remodel the whole craft to this new and upgraded specification. Clear the place out while I take Gung Loi down with me to engineering."

n'Gnung ensured everybody left, while I checked for life-signs, and soon we were only four. n'Gnung returned to me as we set to begin remodelling. Kay's voice came over comm., "Jackie, there's only just enough rock plasma to create the new hull and integral systems, so we will need to generate more as soon as we finish. Ancillary components can be made later, and we won't be able to make any more transfer circles. During transition, the shields will need to be modified, which I will do from here.

"Note that only engineering control, and your ready room will not be altered until later. I've set a paradox parameter in place for this first phase. It's like a shield, but different. Once complete, I will need to vacate, so you can set the remodelling in motion down here. Once done, we'll do likewise with your ready room.

"The final problem is that much of the equipment in the new design is of higher specification. This means that things like engines, and especially weapons will be enhanced. However, this process includes scanners Jackie. Scanners. Are you sure you want to do this right now?"

"Yes. Thank you."

"Scanners set as critically important. It'll take twenty minutes after the complete craft is remodelled. You still OK with this?"

"Affirmative, let's do this thing. The priority is more consoles on the Bridge."

The initial remodelling took almost one hour, as stages needed completing, or transforming to a set point, according to specific parameters. We were busy, but mostly monitoring, accepting new configurations. In time, Kay and Gung Loi joined us from below, "Jackie, the new bridge is amazing, I can't wait to use it."

Some minutes later, n'Gnung and I had a similar reaction to the new control room. It was astonishing. We stole a quick glance only as we headed down to engineering, and in due course, the initial remodelling was completed. Kay ensured scanners were top priority, while I instigated rock plasma generation. Everything checked out, and we hurried to view the new control room.

The room was lot larger and contained eleven central workstations, three of these set near the rear wall behind the Captain's command station. I sat in the Captain's position, which was similar, but had more functions than before. This was mirrored to my left and right, where two new, but slightly smaller, command consoles had appeared. "Kay please use the one on the left, n'Gnung, take the right-hand one."

Before us were three enhanced stations as before, but in front of these were two more, one for navigation, and the other for weaponry and shields. These eleven workstations were all interlinked and formed a dedicated spacecraft control system. The right wall contained a new comm. station, and a guard command station. Opposite, the Watch area had been increased, and was banked with displays, computers, and scanners.

Behind the Captain's station were several new doors, the central one leading into a new meeting room. To either side of this were two alcoves, each containing a local transport circle, one transferring directly to the main transporter room, and the second to engineering. They were preset only to allow ring bearers to use them. To either side of these, were two more doors, one a lift, and the other physical stairs down to the transporter, which in turn, could only be accessed by the most advanced ring bearers. I had insisted the access corridor to the pool near my home remain untouched, and this completed the new layout. Otherwise, the room was sealed to non-essential personnel.

"Wow! Is this some transformation? I want to go exploring, but better we check calibration and system functions. Kay, you are on the latter, and I'll take the rest. Gung Loi, please use the new workstation behind your husband."

"Jackie, she would be more use behind me, I'd let n'Gue or Aroweena take that one. It suits the way we work much better."

Once scanners had been reconfigured, we returned our crew from extended break, and they were all giddy with surprise and expectation. n'Gnung showed Barph to the guardroom, cells, and sleeping accommodation. Gung Loi did similar with the control crew. All were good to go, and reports came in that we had not missed much at all in the world outside.

The long and eventful day finally over, we grouped at my home for dinner. "Guardian, the spaceship does not have a name, what do you think of New Adventure?"

We batted names back and forth, "Ark Royal," "Phoenix," "Bennu," "Enterprise," "Dædalus," "Persephonê," and many others, before settling on "Invincible."

Chapter 5 ~ Volcanic Fallout

I was stretching awake the next morning, enjoying the sight of Jinnie and Ræm lying peacefully beside me, when I heard a scream. I bolted out of bed, the earliest risers staring at the plateau above. n'Gnung joined me to gawp. The high land sported a new hill, and the cliff face nearest us had bulged into a new form. Many minor rockslides gave evidence of the new geography. One had breached our home, but only minimal repairs would be necessary.

"n'Gnung, I think we could climb that, what do you think?"

"Let's go, but be wary of loose rock."

Neither of us were mountaineers, but we made the climb with a little difficulty and brotherly helping hands. Previously, a small hill had stood on the plateau, the river skirting it to the east becoming our waterfall to the north, and a lake where the spaceship had crash-landed to the south. The new hill was much more extensive, higher, and took us a while to climb. "We are standing on rock, on top of the remodelled spacecraft, brother. It is much larger than before. What say, after breakfast, you and I take a tour of discovery down below?"

"Definitely, but we'll need a map. The Invincible is twice as big as the previous craft, Guardian. Engineering and areas for weaponry have replaced half of the old cargo holds. We should eat while we have the chance. What happened to our simple lifestyle?"

"Good question. I would prefer to eat here, or on the shore, but the University will have food already cooked. Let's get in and out as quickly as we can, and hopefully before we are spotted."

When we walked into the restaurant, Peni noticed us, and waved enthusiastically. "Brother, we eat take-out. I'll deal with Peni and we leave quickly. There's far too much to do this day."

Peni said, "Jackie dear, I'll come to you in a few minutes, where should I begin?"

"Engineering, but wait for Kay to show you around. We have the end of the world to deal with today."

"Oh, that thing again, it really is such a bother. I doubt it is relevant but, yes of course, do what you must. See you soon."

n'Gnung was waiting for me with breakfast butties and additional fries. We left immediately. On entering the control room, José called me over. He was tired and full of foreboding. I learned he had worked through the night in Guadalajara.

José said, "Damascus is critically important. There is great build-up of pressure under the entire region, and it is tracking the fault on the Arabian side of the Plate. This is a transform fault, meaning it is the boundary of the continental plate. Given the data I have, this will shear almost vertically, which in turn means there should be little in the way of earthquakes. What few there are will be major, as will any resulting aftershocks, and especially those furthest away within the immediate region.

"The Damascus fault is quite different because this lies within the plate, meaning any movement will be accompanied by severe earthquakes, data that we are still processing. Our predictions are the Mercalli Intensity and Richter Magnitude Scales will be synchronous. This is extremely rare, and bad.

"The only release valve is the Asthenosphere, or the surface. So, if a lot of magma is ejected, the prognosis will be much better, in some ways. My worry is the Harrat Ash Shamah volcanic field.

"From the volcanology point of view, we are also still awaiting critical data feeds. But from what we have already, I can confirm the following: Three extinct volcanoes, one near Aleppo close to the northern edge of the Arabian Plate in Syria. A second near the dogleg fault lines that criss-cross, leaving Damascus within their cusp; and a third centred upon the Jordanian side of the Dead Sea near Al Karak (Jabal Dhikr al-Tannur), have all reactivated.

"One of the most puzzling aspects, is that the Moho Discontinuity below the Aqaba region remains unaltered, despite what is happening all around and along the continental fault line. The Harrat field is not coming under imminent explosive pressure from the earth's magma. I do not understand this, because there has to be a release somewhere, but where?

"These volcanoes are part of the Harrat Ash Shamah volcanic field, also regarded as extinct. It no longer is. It a massive alkaline, fifteen thousand square mile region of instability that extends from southern Syria, across Jordan and into north-western Saudi Arabia.

"I have just added it as number seven of the world's potential super-volcanoes, and the most imminent to blow. This area rivals in size and potential fury, the destructive power of the more commonly known Yellowstone super volcanic field in the USA. If this thing blows, I doubt much life will remain on earth."

"How sure are you this will happen?"

"I am not sure, it is only one of several possibilities. Fernando and Ramone are still working to define tectonics — what is actually occurring beneath the earth's surface. So far, the only thing we have is uncertainty. We are putting a larger team in place, and I have already upgraded computing power and secure satellite capability. We need to connect to you here, how do we do that?"

I interfaced with the Core, and it appeared to be simple, but for our own security, we would need a locked encryption key and anti-virus program, the standards of which were unheard of by contemporary western science. The resolution was to install our own conduit, which

Kay and I initiated at once. The result was a small console that acted as a planet to ship comm. station.

José oversaw installation at Guadalajara, and a short time later he returned with Ramone and Fernando. With our vastly superior computing capacity and intuitive capabilities, Ramone instigated a forecast based on their limited data. What he received was surprising, because the prediction for the next two days was the Arabian plate would begin to seesaw back and forth. This was extrapolated to continue, and whilst this would have a dramatic affect on life in the area, there would come a point where it settled to a similar formation as before, perhaps many months hence.

That did not make any sense regards our own understandings and misgivings. There was a small chance the disruption might also destabilise the settled North African end of the Great Rift Valley, and perhaps extend a little into southeast Europe.

José focused on the Damascus fault, and whilst it would spread and cause several large earthquakes, and aftershocks; the forecast showed little possibility of it sheering right across to the other edge of the plate. Dozens of volcanoes would blow, but despite localised destruction, the super-volcano would not erupt.

Tsunamis were already affecting tides, bringing disruption over much of the world, decimating southern Iran, Oman, and smaller Gulf States. There was no *Big Bang* forecast, and the general prognosis was relatively good.

"This is impossible!" Fernando and José were in total agreement. The former stated, "There is enough pressure build up, that we know of, to eject the entire plate upwards several hundred feet into the air."

José added, "With the readings we have, Harrat Ash Shamah should be about to blow, as in a super volcanic field. Instead, there is little. What is happening? Where is this pressure dissipating? I have a bad feeling about the all of this. Guardian, we need to cover the entire plate with sensors."

"Where is most vital, we begin deployment as soon as you have the devices."

"Bushehr," they replied in unison. Fernando added, "We need to start again, understand this from where it all began, and we should track the development from Bushehr with new eyes. The Iranian mountains are on the up side of the overthrust of a reverse fault.

Therefore, the incredibly large force of the nuclear explosion could perhaps have taken that side of the plate down. This in turn means that the opposite side must come up. If it is rocking in the Asthenosphere, then in a few days time it will come back up again, and the Red Sea side will go down. This is totally unknown, and yet it fits the facts, as we know them to be. I must go and confirm this. Note, obtaining readings from the wrong areas of Iran is of utmost importance."

"Get us the sensors you require, and we'll set them in place. Let's get to it."

A short time later, our assistance enabled Fernando and José to deploy monitoring equipment in previously inaccessible areas, both politically and geographically.

We were deep into our studies of understanding the threat Gaia posed, when the ever-bright Penelope Pendleton came to us. "Jack, dearest Jack, you have been redecorating I see. I need to spend some time with the energy core of dispersional vector synonymetry, because there is a second drive within this craft, one that could travel faster than light—something I proved after leaving CERN by the way. Well, come on then, where is it?"

"You mean the new, enhanced, and as yet under reconstruction Boson Drive?"

Kay began walking, "Come and I will show you the basics, but the knowledge you seek is written and understood in the language of the Ancestors."

I said, "Kay, we have need of you here. Go, but I will see if Gangling Shortfalls is free to translate, although we will need to monitor what Peni gets up to."

Turning to Peni I added, "Ms Pendleton, please get your bearings with Kay as guide. I hope that an interpreter skilled uniquely in the ancient script will join you shortly. He is a Giant I think you met once before."

"Ah yes, those tall people—they are quite clever it seems, despite their silly names."

She left with Kay, and we finished our immediate tasks, sending out a call for Gangling to come to us, if he was free. With no imminent demands on our time, I departed with n'Gnung to inspect the changes to the spaceship. Even though I was familiar with the design diagram, the physical manifestation was impressive. The crew's quarters behind and above the control centre were much as before, but extended farther into the ship providing an additional thirteen bedrooms.

We worked sequentially towards the rear, finding an operations centre next. "This is similar in many respects to the war room we created before, but is a larger and integrated complex. Its purpose is to command off-ship activities, without compromising bridge functions."

"Ideal should be find ourselves at war with the Great Ogre again, Guardian."

"Exactly. Let's hope that is not too soon."

We examined the layout in detail, "Brother, I think we should move everything associated with the Wrath of Gaia here. This is an intrinsically secure unit, and more than large enough to accommodate all personnel."

"Indeed Guardian. The Mexicans are lovely, but vociferous at times, and disruptive to normal bridge operations. Were we to install a language translation module, and add a dedicated, direct-link transporter, this would become a self-contained unit."

"I'll instigate this as soon as we return, and transfer Langnor and her team here. Come, let's check out the new cells, guard quarters, and barracks for foot soldiers."

We completed the tour of the upper level, coming into a large round that appeared to have a big door to the far end. It was the depth of two floors, but otherwise empty. I noticed a small control room set to the back wall, and interfaced from there with the Core.

"This is the space dock, brother. Its purpose is to allow space hoppers to come and go. Apparently, they are small spaceships that can be used within a solar system. Unfortunately, they have not been created yet, and will be one of the last things provided. We will need to learn how to use them. Fancy a trip to the moon?"

We worked our way back through the lower levels, our primary interest lying with engineering. Things were, and were not the same. The emphasis of this new craft was on war, not hauling cargo. However, many systems were similar, if enhanced, or would be once completed. We found Kay in company with Peni and Gangling, and they were examining ship system diagrams. I was about to offer welcome when Kay spoke into my mind. "Jackie, I need to be here."

Peni looked up quizzically, "What was that? You need bees here. Whatever for?"

Kay and I exchanged quizzical looks, before I welcomed Gangling and thanked him for his timely support. n'Gnung and I completed our tour, realising we would need to focus on specific areas during our next visit. We moved everybody associated with the Wrath of Gaia to the new operations room, and divided our time between there and the bridge.

The team in operations had grown as the Mexicans brought in additional staff of their own to monitor specific regions and threats. I had also asked Ali to work with them, because the substrata were full of oil and gas.

I needed to see the wider picture, and surveyed the area from the Captain's console. The plate boundary shear, marked by the Gulf of Aqaba, had continued to expand southwards, the Red Sea was evaporating as magma replaced water, the escaping magma creating a dam that almost blocked the ocean. Volcanic activity in Djibouti added to the disruption, the nearby Afar Depression at the north of the African Rift Valley showed ominous signs of volcanic activity, as did the Danakil Depression to the northeast.

Similar was happening to the Straits of Hormuz, where magma from the continental rift near Bandar Abbas was slowly choking waters trying to enter the Gulf, but it appeared to be only a matter of time before the Gulf became a lake.

People were dying from lava flows and volcanic fallout, being asphyxiating by ash that blurred the sky like a snowstorm. The evaporating waters turned the ash into hot sludge that rained down like hail from hell, forming a mask of killing mud. People fled, but were trapped by wildfires that sprouted with alarming ease.

"We have to do something to help them. Bufor, I need you to assemble a team and transport as many people as possible to safety. I mean anywhere safe for life."

"Guardian, I have noticed rescue teams going into some of these areas, but they will be obliterated. We need to send word to them, and also speak to the governments — tell them what is really going on. We can see it, they cannot."

"Thank you, Bufor. n'Gue, get Doctor Sylvia Steele of the CDC here as soon as you can, and locate Behrouz, we need to send him to Iran with a warning."

Some time later I was distracted by the arrival of Doctor Steele. "Thank you for coming, I know you are extremely busy, but I think you need to understand the all of what is about to happen, Doctor."

"Call me Sylvia please, Guardian."

"Jack."

"We have first responders assisting on the ground in Iran and nearby Gulf States. This is a worldwide disaster and our resources are fully stretched. What can you tell me?"

"Get everybody out of there are quickly as you can. Come and see the bigger picture. We are assembled in the operations room, watching the end of the world."

Sylvia had been under the impression they were dealing with the outcome of a nuclear disaster, not the prelude to something far greater in scale. Her words were few, staccato, "Oh my God!... I... We never... When?"

"Our best guess is tomorrow, a few days perhaps."

She froze and gawped, finding strength to move to Ali, and later, the Mexicans. In time, her dedication to duty turned to evacuation and self-preservation. We had garnered her full support.

Sylvia had links with governments, but her team were stretched, waiting for emergency personnel. Behrouz returned with a report from Qatar and Saudi Arabia, where he had not been well received.

Overhearing his report, Sylvia rounded on us knowingly. "Behrouz, you are just the person we need. Jack, we have the right links with government, but nobody who inherently understands the Arabian world. Can we borrow him. We all get shared feedback."

Behrouz was happy to assist, and so were we. A greater team was building, and I sought to encourage it. After an initial briefing, she departed with Behrouz, who became a lynchpin for both of our operations. Over days, these were steadily becoming incorporated into one whole operation.

In time, Sylvia settled at an empty station, occasionally transporting to liaise with teams on the ground. Our information afforded her the chance to save lives and prepare for the greater disaster to come.

As evening approached, Peni returned in company with Gangling, and I enquired, "How is the Boson Drive theorem coming along?"

"Ah, bosons and mesons, they are the same but opposites you know ... and anyway it's actually quite simple once you discover you can turn a subatomic particle around by applying a charge to flip it over, meaning it is revolving in the opposite, relative direction. I call it the inverse vector participle, meaning matter can exist in infinite vector states. It is quite ingenious actually; once you get your mind right. It's a bit like sex really." And with that statement, she tittered to herself and departed for the University.

I'm not sure any of us understood much of what she was talking about for most of the time, although we battled bravely on to try to understand some of the words she used. In her wake, we had forgotten all about bosons, and as a result, had instead become fascinated by her sex life.

I turned to my brother and asked, "Do we really have to wait thirty minutes before dinner? I'm parched?"

"Indeed not Guardian, we wait only for your command."

"Dinner it is then. Go and order the beers and we will come in a moment."

In the early hours I was awakened from my dreams by a night controller, "Guardian, Iranian government agents are chasing Behrouz through the streets of Kangan."

I arrived on the bridge as he disappeared into a souk, but before I could locate him, he had seemingly disappeared. I set a team to focus only on Behrouz, and find him. After thirty minutes with no immediate sign of him, I returned to sleep nearby in my ready room.

Chapter 6 ~ Bubbles in The Gulf

I knew instantly something had changed as soon as I entered the operations room that morning. The normal buzz of activity had been replaced by worried concern, and it centred on José. "I have just received detailed readings from around the exposed Iranian seaboard, and they conflict greatly with what we knew before. I need to process a new scenario with this latest data. When you think about this logically, the pressure has to be going somewhere. I discovered the soil is getting hotter between Bushehr and Kangan. There are also some isolated places where the sea bubbles, look."

Close by, Langnor brought up locations where bubbles were coming up from the seabed. José said, "We are looking at a new *hot spot*. One or several, where none should ever exist."

I stared at the screen and realised I needed to understand exactly what I was seeing. I sent out a call for John to join me. We watched the bubbles with similar, macabre fascination. Hints of steam rose from the sea's surface where the gas broke surface. Ali was deeply concerned and had been plotting every source, "This cannot be from the oilfields, it is impossible. In the Caribbean yes, because there the rock over the oil deposits in slightly permeable. In the Gulf, the outer crust, the rock above the oil and gas fields is highly valenced, this cannot happen."

José was standing nearby and sensing the mood, added. "Venting as you see here often occurs with volcanoes, except there are none in this area, at least until now. We need to know what these gases are, run full tests to understand the threat they pose. I am sure these were not there even yesterday."

I panned and zoomed, locating all activity in the area at Ali's direction, discovering several consistent spots of regular release. "John, Ali, we need to process this here, what have you got?"

Ali shrugged his shoulders, "I have access to the lab and equipment we need, but no protocol to use it immediately. With all that's going on in the world, I would be waiting days for permission to process samples. Regardless, I have no boat. We could bring the old, defunct lab here. It would be stealing, but what the hell, things can only get worse. Depending upon what it turns out to be, this gas is either quite irrelevant, or deeply significant."

"Ali, identify your lab and prepare to bring it here, plus a team to staff it. I need results soonest, and the situation contained. John, find a location at the University and begin to provide services: water, electricity, everything. I'll go to the bridge and work on finding a boat. I have an idea."

Returning to the bridge, I stared ruefully at the screen; the Middle East was becoming a grey-out of macabre ash and sludge. It was difficult to see anything. Large areas were impenetrable. I turned away and tried to focus on the boat problem, my first priority, when I was disturbed by a shout; "Behrouz has been located in his apartment."

I found him quickly. He was busy throwing things into suitcases and boxes. I would not call it packing. Outside a couple of cars screeched to a halt, and men with guns jumped out and raced into the building. I looked over, behind to my left and said, "Gung Loi, Operation Bare Walls."

She reacted at once and brought Behrouz back first, before stripping the place bare of all its contents. Behrouz arrived full of thanks and apologies, only to stand transfixed with amazement. Wardrobes, carpets, seats, beds — everything was ripped out before his eyes, and sent to a store near the University. "We thought you had been taken by security forces to Tehran."

"If it had not been for a look-alike I would have been. I hid and watched as they took the poor man for questioning. After they left, I waited longer before returning to get my most valuable possessions. Because of you, it seems I have them all Guardian. Thank You."

"Why were they chasing you Behrouz?"

"I have no idea, but they were VEVAK, Vezarat-e Ettela'at va Amniyat-e Keshvar, our secret police for sure. Obviously, somebody in Tehran thought I was becoming a nuisance. If I go back, I must be extremely careful."

"We will need your services again in the area, come." He followed me through to my ready room, where I handed him a tracking ring. "Wear this at all times. Not only will it tell us where you are, but also this motif, when twisted around, activates a distress signal. You had better ask John, no Helen actually, to attend to your things. Welcome back."

Behrouz departed, but I stayed in my sanctuary. I had sailed the world as Yachtmaster Ocean, knew many sailors, marinas, and boat factories. However, I needed to call on the services of people I trusted implicitly. I scanned through names on my shortlist, as my fingers panned and zoomed the controls of my screen.

I drew two blanks, before finding an Aussie couple I respected greatly. Gary and Shirl were practical scientists, privateers who loved life on the sea, water sports and surfing, and had a research grant. Nevertheless, they took any contract that offered them money. Their vessel had both power and sail, was ostensibly a floating laboratory, but was often used for deep sea fishing charters, and holidays afloat.

I found their boat at Rockhampton in Queensland. It was moored and deserted, but I knew they would not be far away, as it appeared to be in use and ready for sail. I presumed they would be victualling, but in due course located them in a nearby maritime bar.

Kay set a protective transfer circle and I transported to the location. "Strewth Jackie, what the hell are you doing here?"

I shared an Australian draught beer with Gary, as we caught up on times past and present. Fortunately, he did most of the talking, as what could I tell him that he would believe, other than I was in a wrecked, aeroplane and survived. I ordered another round, but Shirl became unusually distracted, and glancing at the clock said, "Not for me, we need to be out of here, sorry Jackie. Next time OK. Make yours a quick pint Gary, then come and help me get the stuff back to the boat. Five minutes and you are at the chandlers, OK."

I watched her leave and said, "Out with it Gary. I know the pair of you well enough. What's going on?"

Reticent at first, he opened up with gentle probing, "We are on the run from both international maritime authorities, and from a cartel of treasure thieves. We took a lucrative job to find a sunken wreck, but later realised we were there only for official cover. They used us to keep the heat off themselves. They were not openly declaring, but selling on the black market."

"You were the fall-guys. Nice people."

"We stopped here to take on fresh supplies and discharge black water. To cut a long story short, we are desperate to find a safe harbour, and must be ready to depart within ten minutes. We expect news of our arrival here has already been forwarded to the authorities."

We downed our beers and went to help Shirl. Most supplies had by that time been delivered to the quay, and only needed stowing aboard. We carried the last boxes from the chandlers back between us, and began loading. Things were going well, until two police cars screeched to a halt outside the harbour masters office, lights blazing and horns blaring. My friends started throwing victuals on board, but there was not enough time. "Cast off. Gary, Shirl, trust me. All will be fine. Leave everything and set the boat free from the moorings."

They hesitated, unsure. I raced to the nearest cleat and began unhitching the mooring rope. They followed suit. Police were already running towards us as the boat came free. "See you in a minute."

I used my return bracelet, and ignoring their bewilderment, transported them and their boat to our Outland shore. The supplies followed moments later, this time I set them on the nearby shore, not in the water as with the boat.

With a nod to Kay and n'Gnung, I transported back to them, arriving on the poop deck. "You wanted safe harbour, your wish is my command. Nobody will ever find you here."

Gary was agog, Shirl noticed our island boat nearby, and appeared to go into shock; "That floats? Oh my God! Who … what are they, people?"

The strains and participation of Old MacDonald may have broached their defences, but Kay's 'Okay Pokay', brought them fully into our world. Shirl added *Charades* to our drunken pastimes, which was generously received and enacted by all.

The following morning was a curious time. They were, and were not a part of us, fluctuating by the moment between incredulity and impossibility. I, the world at large, needed them urgently. n'Gnung made arrangements in advance, we breakfasted at the University. John graciously greeted their arrival and saw them to the servery.

Taking me aside he said, "Jackie, it was difficult, Ali has a lab ready to process gases, all you need to do is bring it here. This case contains sterile sampling equipment, but it is a little basic. I'll add some asbestos gloves before you depart, as the gas may be hot. I think Ali may have better equipment, but I wanted to cover all bases.

"Ah Gary, Shirl, I hope you found food to your liking…"

Our breakfast table exuded a slightly surreal air, until Shirl dispelled the notional impossibilities; "OK Jackie. Why are we here? What do you want us to do?"

I had almost forgotten how forthright Australian women could be, but not quite. I countered, "You're welcome. In return for saving your skins, I need your boat in the Gulf of Arabia this morning. Afterwards, you can either go on your way, or stay, up to you. Come, finish up and let me show you something of paramount importance."

We transferred to the operations room, where I showed them the bubbling ocean. Gary stared long at the screen, our drone's view was becoming progressively obscured by water vapour and ash. He stated, "That is wrong."

"I need to know what that gas is. I need your boat there, now. We need samples from these outlets…" I showed them the locations, and introduced Ali who would lead the sampling crew.

We actioned this minutes later, and everything appeared to be going well. They covered the water quickly, taking samples from our designated hot-spots. It became obvious some of the gas was rather hot. They had almost completed their task when Langnor informed me of a new and larger set of bubbles near Kangan.

While they manoeuvred into the new position, I recalled Ali and John, and we pinpointed the new lab. With parameters set, I transported it to a location John had indicated. I transferred the building and he left to check it.

n'Gue reported some minutes later, "The building transfer was successful, Guardian. John's people are now connecting power supply, water, and drainage."

Although I was keen to inspect the new structure, it would have to wait, Gary had closed on our final objective. Once there, the vessel came around, approaching the bubbling sea as usual from windward. The dingy was deployed as before, and the man with the jar leaned out to gather the gas, but as he did so, the current took their dingy and the small craft spun around. Then a spark from the outboard caused a small explosion that hurled the occupants forward, one went overboard.

From personal experience, I knew this would normally be a simple retrieval for experienced sailors. The airborne fire extended downwind, before dying naturally upon dispersal. What alarmed me was the sea beneath turned into a churning furnace of rage.

All around, the small inflatable craft was enveloped in myriad bubbles that lessened the water displacement and with the heavy outboard engine still close to the original gas outlet, the weight began to drag the stern down into the water. While most of the smaller bubbles were burnt-up, some persisted, igniting others.

One section of inflatable hull melted, I had to get them out of there. The scientist was reaching for another sample, and I knew how important this could prove. I had to let him try, up until the last split-second.

The sinking craft became waterlogged at the stern, but I waited until the scientist capped his beaker, and gave a thumbs-up. We transported all to safety immediately. For the ensuing few minutes, I needed to be in three places at once, but chose to bring those places, the people concerned, to me at the new University lab. John wanted to greet the team, Ali had samples to process, and a small group of scientists was waiting to transfer in.

John and Ali already knew what to do, and waited as I returned to the bridge and made the transfer. The scientists were in shock, but from past experience I knew that they would soon become focused on their work.

As we watched the men enter the lab, n'Gnung spoke into the vacuum. "Guardian, we need a specialist to deal with the human, emotional side of this. These newcomers need inclusion and support. Our attention must remain focused on the greater threat, and with John now preoccupied, at least for the moment, I know of only one solution, one person."

"Dawn."

"I will go and send word to her, and hope she is free."

I began to rise and go myself, when n'Gnung's hand on my shoulder stilled me, "No Jackie, you are needed right here, right now. There are things only specific people can do. You need to remain here until help arrives. I won't be long. This time, you get the beers in."

Later, n'Gnung and I participated in dinner, but left before the singing, drunkenness, and human excess manifested. In the operations room, Langnor and I continued to monitor the fire in the sea, until there was a huge underwater disturbance that acted to blow-out the slowly descending fireball. In time the waters returned to bubbling merrily away as they had been before.

The new day arrived all too soon and seemingly without transition. I needed coffee, and results. n'Gnung and I thought we would be the first to breakfast, but we were both surprised to find Ali deep in conversation with several scientists brought in to staff the new lab.

We joined them and Ali gave us a brief synopsis. "Most of the gases collected are either steam, or steam with some Carbon Dioxide. Minor amounts of Sulphur, Chlorine, and Fluorine gases were found in locations northwest of Kangan. These all indicate volcanic causation.

"These three samples taken further out towards Qatar indicate hydrocarbons associated with the quite common leakages from underwater gas fields. At least, they are quite common in the Caribbean, but not in the Gulf, until now. The last one taken is partial, yet is also of gas field origin. We can only guess at what a true sample would have revealed."

My foreboding was increasing proportionately, as I applied layman's logic to scientific imponderables. Ali continued, "Jackie, we need to go back to the Gulf today. But first I need a meeting with the Mexicans."

"Let's go. I'll see if Langnor has found any more bubbles, especially near Qatar."

The meeting was brief, frowns and grimaces the order of the day. Terse words carrying heavy implications. A little later I was busy in the control room, monitoring Ali and the main boat. I transferred them to new locations to thwart discovery by maritime security forces. Their boat was again our maritime hub of activity, as two new outboards covered the sea to a prearranged pattern.

Dawn arrived mid afternoon, and I was thankful to see her again. I explained what we were doing, showed her Ali and his team on screen, and explained why I had invited her. "I need Kay to keep tabs on what Peni is up to. That means I need to be here most of the time. John would normally look after newcomers, but he is extremely busy, so can you check and see how the new scientists are settling in. Then there are Gary and Shirl…"

Dawn left to speak to all I mentioned, and check others, including Phœbe in her report some hours later. "Phœbe is my only concern, so far. She is bored and wants to go exploring. I could take her for a walk tomorrow, as she likes nature and the outdoors. Otherwise, those at the University are fine, but remember, they are in a familiar environment. The transfer circle is the only fly in the ointment. I'll meet up with the Australians when they return to the shore, and try to put them at ease. How's Ali doing?"

"They are about done, just a few more samples to extract. I fear the scientists will be in for another long night. When processed, we need to analyse the results, compare them to those of the Mexicans. José suspects there is a new hotspot of basalt magma underneath a region roughly the size of Qatar, encircling Bushehr and Kangan."

When the samples from the Gulf were collected, I sent the boats to the Outland shore, and Ali with his team to the University. Dawn went to join them, but returned a short time later with Phœbe, stating, "They are already working on processing the results, but it will take hours by the looks of things. Phœbe wants to see the sea, which ties in nicely with meeting Gary and Shirl."

I waited for Peni to leave, rescuing Kay from her invigilation. My team headed for the shore. We were overdue some fun and relaxation, and unlike the night before, we made the most of it.

Chapter 7 ~ Recipe for Disaster

Our fun of the previous evening continued over breakfast. Phœbe asked to see the boat and Shirl encouraged her to join them for a sail. They wanted to investigate the local waters, but gave me a strange look when I mentioned the containing force field. They were also aware I might need them back in the Gulf at any moment, depending upon what news came with the morning.

My first call was the University, where Ali and the team had again worked through the night. Results were still coming in, with other samples in process. There was no initial theory, except *bad*.

My next port of call was the operations room. José greeted me warmly, if distractedly, "We will confer with you immediately we understand what is happening. What of the gas samples?"

"They are still being analysed, but early indications are steam, volcanic gases, and areas with the tell-tale signature of hydrocarbons."

José glanced back at his team, as if seeking emotional support. "We cannot confirm as yet, but the hot spot may be bigger than I first thought, or there may be several of them. We still do not know where the underlying pressure is dissipating to, but there has to be a reason. I fear it is not dissipating at all, but building, somewhere under the earth's crust. The bubbles in the Gulf indicate the rise of pressure, but my greatest concern is the crater left by the nuclear explosion, it is empty."

I failed to see the importance.

"Jackie, it should be full. There would be some loss of water to evaporation, but little only. We need to know where that water went. This is more than serious, deadly. The same with the Red Sea, or what little water remains of it. I'll arrange a meeting when we have a working hypothesis, but it could take days, time we may not have."

José was called away, and I sought sanctuary on the bridge. I was already forming my own opinion regarding what the Wrath of Gaia could embrace, and the morning's news left me deeply perturbed.

After checking on developments, I ensconced myself in my ready room, and interfaced with the Core. My thoughts were transmitted mentally, and the feedback was chilling. I instigated strengthening of our shields, a stationary overhead satellite to supply us with power, stockpiling of rock plasma, and a dedicated resource to produce it. I hoped I was wrong, but needed to act in case I was not.

The day progressed with others overworked and tired, while we had time to explore the redesigned spacecraft in more detail. Kay finally freed herself from chaperoning Peni to join us.

The following day we took breakfast at the University, hoping for news. I ordered bacon and runny egg butties with coffee, but somehow a basket of fries ended up on my tray. I intended to put them back, when Ali arrived with news. They had made a breakthrough and the prognosis was not good. They had discovered trace elements of contaminated water vapour, hydrocarbons, and volcanic gases, all venting from the same outlet near Kangan.

Moments later we were in ops. José staring at the printout Ali had just given him. "Santa Madre del Dios!" Fernando ripped the paper out of his hand and froze, his eyes glued to the figures, before he stared listlessly into infinity. Sylvia reached for the readout and scanned it, her brow furrowed as understanding dawned. Her mouth worked, but no sound came forth.

Ali said, "This is a bomb waiting to explode." Everybody froze, too stunned to reply.

n'Gnung broke the silence, "Come Guardian, we need to save the world."

My eyes flicked to his, "Operation Ark. Save whomever, and whatever we can. Parameters?"

Kay placed her hand on my arm, "First we need to adjust the main shield, and those we have already set as protection. The volcanic ash is killing people, they cannot breath. Later will come the acid rain. We must first look to our own and be strong ourselves, before we can be strong for others."

n'Gnung came to Kay's side. "Guardian, we must inform the other Tribes, they have little or no knowledge of what is about to happen. Their shields will need adjusting also."

Within moments my disbelief evaporated, replaced by the reality of what was about to occur: Obliteration of all life on Earth. I moved quickly, rattling off a string of instructions. "José, follow the magma, determine the hot spots. Fernando substrata, find out what is happening deep below. Sylvia evacuation…"

I spurred people into action, going to each in turn and giving them new purpose. Kay and n'Gnung supported me, and within moments, the miasma of foreboding was replaced by activity. I spoke to Langnor last of all. "I need you to keep eyes on everything these people are doing. I need to work from the bridge for a while, it is too disruptive here. Can you monitor what happens here and in the outside world. Send notes to my console in real-time?"

"Major disasters, interesting facts, I think so. You want me to put it on the main screen?"

"Yes, do it. Rolling headlines. Inclusion works for me, and we ensure to cover all bases. Kay, you and I are on shields, n'Gnung, work with Gung Loi on Operation Ark. n'Gue, send word of developments to all the other Tribes immediately. Let's go."

It was time to begin the next phase of our work, looking out for ourselves. We researched the likely effects of acid rain that would soon wash the world with wonton destruction. Kay and I retired to my ready room and focused on shield manipulation. The Eleventh had already defined an umbrella shield that was set to exclude rain and even wind, or allow it through at our discretion.

The three main volcanic discharge gases: carbon dioxide, sulphur dioxide, and nitrogen oxides were our main consideration. Carbon dioxide was not an issue in small quantities, but the others were extremely important, carrying devastating outcomes for life on such a gigantic scale of release. We needed to define nucleonic molecular size and use the shield as a sieve to reject larger particles. We also required pure water to be allowed through, but not that contaminated by more complex, or airborne compounds.

We set the shield to allow only molecules of water through, allowing everything up to Molar Mass 18.01528(33) g/mol. This setting would allow us to breathe and have fresh water. We set parameters for the umbrella shield to open and close automatically whenever higher concentrations were found within the rain or anything above 19.0 g/mol. We were safe for the time being, but would monitor regularly as a precaution. n'Gue was sent with shield settings to the other Tribes, who we visited in due course and implemented or checked settings.

Our next concern was Operation Ark. Preserving flora and fauna, people and places, from destruction by the ambivalent and omnipotent Wrath of Gaia. We had been working on this for several weeks, but would soon need to implement protection and conservation for real.

Our main thrust was to place transfer circles acting as shields, but these could never be defined to molecular level as accurately as the crafts main shield. Nonetheless, what we intended to provide was a lot better than the nothing otherwise prevalent. Gung Loi was put in charge of implementation, and at n'Gnung's insistence, took over his larger and more powerful console. He took over the one behind his wife, Aroweena swapping over.

Another consideration was additional power supply for the University, with hydroelectric being favoured. I spoke to John, hoping he could help. "The Chinese have developed an intriguing option, Jack. A prototype Thorium reactor that is undergoing trial. It is a micro-reactor, designed to power a small city. It, uses less resources than a large reactor, and is easy to site where needed. I knew one of their people, a research Fellow from Cambridge University, who developed an earlier model. Funding was cut and the British government showed no interest, so he moved to where his skills were needed. China. Want me to try to contact him?"

"Yes. Do it. We could do with one here, don't you think? John, diplomacy, following Chinese etiquette is key here. Tread carefully, and I better go with you if you get anywhere. Wait. Take Faye Wong with you. She is Chinese, so will guide your initial contact appropriately."

"Understood. 'Slowly, slowly, catchy monkey'." John left chuckling, and so was I.

We had no plans to steal a reactor and the necessary staff, but it was a consideration should things turn out extremely bad in the future. With this in mind, John began tentative enquiries, and as a precaution, Kay and I retired to my ready room. We instigated production of more shielding transporters.

When we returned to the bridge, Barph cautioned, "Guardian, the world outside is not safe. We need to look after our own."

"We are. What exactly do you mean?"

"Horovitz and his men, Guardian. Some have wives or girlfriends. Others of the Last, like University people have family. There are mutterings they will be lost when the world ends."

"Thank you Barph, I will see to it at once."

As a result, a meeting of responsible people ensued late that afternoon, under the auspices of Jien Noi in her twin roles as Empress and Gatekeeper. Hers was the final decision on who would come. We spoke to Horovitz first, most of his men being allowed to bring family and housing. They set up a hamlet near Grimwaldi Rinns, which was to be developed into a centre of warfare; we all knew the Great Ogre was biding his time, and would strike again.

"Empress, I and some of my men do not have wives, girlfriends even. Are we allowed to mix with single women? What I mean is, any kind of woman?"

"By that, do you mean females of the Second, Horovitz?"

"Erm … Yes, Your Highness."

"There is no law against it, but any relationship must be according to our traditions. No child may be born outside of wedlock, divorce is not allowed, and you, and your men, must complete the trials of passage before any marriage will be permitted. I will need to approve every engagement personally. Otherwise, this is small reward for the great service you and your troops have given us. Guardian, please attend to this as a matter of urgency."

Our meeting continued, as we heard from John, Henry, and others. Our main concern was whom and what to bring to the island. This was not the first or the last time we would consider the subject, but we did dealt with as many people's concerns as possible that afternoon.

We also agreed on scientists, historians, technicians, and other professionals that might be needed for humankind's survival in the longer term. Libraries of physical, analogue, and digital knowledge were also required, as would be buildings and resources. John mentioned ripping an entire university, such as Harvard or Yale, including staff and students, out and placing it near the old capital. It had been a joke at the time, but one I was toying seriously with. A different solution was to shield such places.

We toured our University campus a little later discussing options regards development. I was surprised to see Weid Noi and Ali in deep conversation, and waved as we passed by. n'Gnung raised an eyebrow, which I likewise replied to.

The afternoon was productive, but tiring. We were about to depart when John rushed to us, "Jack, we must preserve the largest historical depository this world has ever known. The Vatican."

"No John, this is religious doctrine, not science..."

Kay interjected, "Jackie, John has a valid point. Many of the scrolls contradict current religious doctrine. I say we do it, but on condition we gain access to their archives. This is the perfect opportunity to discover what they have been hiding for millennia."

I was stunned, Kay had a valid point. My mind worked quickly, "So tomorrow we kidnap the Pope?"

"I wasn't quite thinking of that, but yes, why not, Jackie. John can be our liaison."

Seeking to share the joy we had given others, by bringing their loved ones to safety within the bosom of our greater community, we also needed release. That evening the strains and charades of Old MacDonald, once more rang hearty from the village on the Outland shore.

Peni came to us some time later. "I've just finished my first cookery class at the University, what do you think?"

She laid before us a large, round apple pie, and serving, gave us each a large slice. It was heavy, as stodgy as she was flaky. We all politely tried the concoction.

n'Gue took a large bite, and tried to swallow, "Interesting." He pulled a spice from his mouth and added, "Peni, why are there small trees in this?"

"Oh. Sorry, those are cloves, and you're not supposed to eat them. They give great flavour, don't they?"

"Pungent. Is there custard, or cream to help it slip down?"

"No, we learn that next semester: Eggs are a binary system, but I need to understand the relativity."

"Speaking of relativity, why is there a pastry square on top?"

"That's my signature, and also my little joke about squaring the circle. So, what do you think?"

47

"The top crust is crispy, burnt, but the taste is great. The pastry base is a bit stodgy, undercooked. You didn't use bottom heat?"

"Why of course not. I'm a top-down person."

I dropped the slice of pie on my plate and said, "A brick."

"What's that?"

"That is British English Peni. A brick is a great person. I think you should share this with others, share the feast."

Peni departed to inflict her formative culinary arts upon others. We all heaved a sigh of relief, "The taste was great," "Heavy,"…

Chapter 8 ~ Portents of Catastrophe

Gaia's time was slow time. She mustered her forces and continued to mix her cauldrons of deathly destruction within the bowels of the earth. The evidence amounted to not just one, but a series of grotesquely huge explosions within the upper regions of the earth's crust.

Our evening banter of the night before was muted. Everyone came unnaturally awake just before dawn. The ground rumbled and shook, we knew instantly that something dire had occurred.

We transported immediately to the operations room, where all eyes were glued to the main screen watching the impossible be brought into existence. José was already manipulating a replay, and we crowded around to see the full horror unravel.

Bushehr gas field grew and grew from the seabed, settled and retracted slightly, before exploding with terrifying force. As soon as the primordial forces within reached oxygen, the compressed and highly volatile hydrocarbons burst forth, and ripped the entirety of rock beneath from the earth in a fireball of monstrous proportions. Jets of orange-hot magma were expelled from the maw, launching into the heavens, causing explosions in the air and on nearby land.

Boulders the size of football fields rained down on the nearby towns, followed by showers of magma. Smaller boulders travelled farther and faster, unleashing their deadly rocky rain on the cities of Bushehr, Khormooj town, Dalan, and Kangan, hundreds of miles along the coast.

The remaining rock of the field atomised as the pressurised magma below and surrounding sought escape. The sea swept back and was swallowed, to leave a wide area of the surrounding Gulf seabed exposed to the air. The explosion was of such force, the cloaked sky of ash was vaporised. Safe in our command centre, we stared into a modern Dante's inferno, as primordial powers of hell cast their demons into the world.

The evening Gulf sky formed a ghoul-infested backdrop to the tapestry of fireballs and raging hellhole. From within jets of crude oil from the bottom of the field streaked burning death as black rain falling upon anything still living below. Some were ignited by propelled lava, enveloping flesh and buildings in burning crude oil. Two eruptions came from deep inside the abyss, and flooded the remaining guts of the evil maw with red hot magma, mixing again with the remainder of the rocks of the gas field, and creating new and even more deadly combinations of Gaia's wrath, that were in turn ejected as projectiles of the most intense abhorrence. Waters of the Gulf surged to reclaim their dominion, but became the steam, as if of snarge breath before reaching their target.

Astoundingly, most of the burning was complete, so high was the temperature and pressure before the field blew. Ash storms and suffocating demonic smoke filled the air as people hundreds of miles away masked themselves in a struggle to breathe amid the unholy cocktail.

Then Pontus powered the waters of the Gulf remorselessly back, and they poured into the death-pit. Our view becoming instantly obscured, lost within steam that rose in dense black clouds to conceal the daylight. Thus began the darkest night for many epochs, and probably since the dinosaurs became extinct.

Volcanic discharges and hydrocarbon blasts continued unabated, as the rages of molten earth and cooling waters of the sea battled to redefine their equilibrium. It appeared the whole of the waters of the Persian Gulf drained into the pit, causing surging tides without to batter the Strait of Hormuz. The wash of water returned to bury all evidence of the catastrophe, except for minor outbursts of mainly volcanic origin.

I turned to José, "I hope that was the release valve that will stop this from spreading further."

José replied with a withering look. "If our calculations are correct, there is much worse to come. The cooling waters will form a new, impervious rock crust, and continue to trap the pressure below. This is only the beginning."

I watched alarmed, as super-heated air streams met colder winds of the region. Possessing both positive and negative charges, they formed monstrous and unnatural thunderheads, as Khæos compelled her Daimones to summon Thor unto battle once more, in support of her sister Gaia. Thunderbolts and lightening ravished the landscape as dual swords of compelling destruction rained down their terrors upon the unsuspecting and foolhardy below. Not that there were many left to bear witness. All life was being extinguished as the canker spread.

Unexpectedly, it was Thor who took centre stage, his bolts of lightning seeking to ground via tall communication masts, and the massive oil silo's and pipelines attending. Ali confirmed, "Lightening conductors are theoretically fitted as standard. However, this weather phenomenon is unheard of in the region. Regardless, I doubt even the highest of standards of conductors could withstand this spectacular onslaught being unleash..."

He had not quite finished speaking as shock again registered on our faces. He turned to the main screen, stunned. The team were focused on Aghar, but the minor Dorood oilfield suffered the next calamity. Its eruption created havoc with the oil pipelines and shipping of the main Jazireh-ye Khark floating crude oil distribution hub. Oil spewed from several ruptured pipelines, one of which was hit by lightening. The heavenly spark turned the area into a rapacious sea of fire, that quickly spread to the holding tanks themselves, which became a mere memory within a few minutes. All evidence of their existence was wiped from the planet.

No sooner had we witnessed the destruction than a shout came from Ali. We turned to see the IGAT-3 gas pipelines rupture and blowback, turning the refineries and distribution terminals of Kangan into fireballs of doom. One of the massive oil storage tanks took a direct hit as Thor's aim improved. I would swear I actually heard the explosion several minutes later, because the tank was annihilated within the blink of an eye. Two others close by began leaking copiously, confounding the situation and, further hampering containment and safety crews, already besieged as earth turned to mud. Their life support suits already under undue stress. "Sylvia, get those rescuers out of there; Langnor, see to it at once."

As we worked on confinement, so the domino effect began. The Gulf of Arabia riven asunder with greater volcanic activity, ripped open fault lines towards the interior of Iran, which engulfed mountains near the Dalan gas field, and tore asunder the nearby gas pipelines. These were shut down, but too late as the gas-lines continued to burn, being fed by other contributor's farther inland.

Ground temperatures continued to rise, and all air in the region was badly compromised. We watched helplessly as those who survived the initial blast were suffocated by ravaging swathes of heavy and un-breathable gases. We transported as many as we could to safety, the priority being young mothers and children. But our task was impossible, even with extra crew and every workstation in operation.

Meanwhile, other gaseous concoctions set roads, buildings, and people alight as they swept though areas of habitation, before burning themselves out. We became aware of newer and more deadly threats to life, as airborne chemicals changed and formed new and highly toxic molecules that were blown into areas of volcanic activity, compounding the already unstable skies further.

I shouted with mounting dread, "I need a meteorologist and a molecular chemist here right now."

Ali replied distractedly, "Viktor Earhardt, he's our best."

"Ali please, we need to understand what all these different chemicals are doing after they are released, and what new compounds they are forming. Where is this man? I need your help to bring him here right this instant."

Dawn understood my concern and gentled her brother; distracted by the momentum of the moment. Ali identified the scientist on my screen, at head office. He was standing, stunned, and watching the news. Ali transferred to his side and placed a hand upon his shoulder, "Viktor, we I need you now. Please come with me."

The man nodded with half comprehension, and was soon even more bewildered as Ali brought him into our operations room, and set him to work as soon as his equilibrium returned.

Viktor settled beside Ali, as bit-by-bit, he discovered the wealth of information and resources we had available. We had just kidnapped him, but he soon became a central member of the team. He was deeply worried about the chemical cocktails that were being, or could be produced.

We assisted with drone support, it becoming impossible for our scanners to see anything, at all. He discovered trace amounts of Benzene from the residue of the gas field. Learning there was a lot of Sulphur in the hot air, he moved to a higher plane mumbling. "Benzenesulfonic acid," we learned, was an organosulfur compound, and quite deadly in small doses. We had exponentially growing, large doses.

I left the highly intellectual to their caveats and calculations, and tracked the spread from Bushehr. I, followed the IGAT-3 pipeline from Dalan, to its source in the north. Despite the heavy clouds of ash, I noticed the areas corresponding to the Dalan and Aghar gas fields were rising, and set some of our few remaining altimeters to monitor what was happening. I added the information to our collective of feeds, setting indicators for José and Ali.

He received the feed, and immediately turned to stare at me in disbelief. I offered my upraised palms in supplication, as his eyes clouded, before fixing mine. "Behrouz's family live in Shiraz, which is nearby. Shiraz also lies on an oilfield, and has an associated refinery. They need to be the hell out of there."

"n'Gnung, bring Behrouz to me on the Bridge, we need to save his family, if that is what he wants."

Behrouz' home city was less than one hundred miles due north of the next disaster area. He arrived all of a fluster having, been glued to a screen in the University. "Behrouz, do you want me to bring your family to safety here with us. This is a one time offer."

He nodded his head, lost for words to express his gratitude. I asked him to show me on my screen, and we spent the next minute panning and zooming until his family home came into view. It turned out to be his parental home, which had been expanded into a small complex surrounding a cool courtyard set with a large tree in the centre. There were many family members inside ranging from grandparents through to babes in arms. "Due to the troubles, few are venturing outside, even to the local market, Guardian. They fear for their lives."

"All these buildings and all of these people?"

"Yes, all except the one arguing with my father. He is my elder sisters husband — an exceedingly unpleasant and corrupt man. He is also a bully, and does not deserve a place within our family, nor even to live. Allah will be his judge, not I."

His statement took me aback. I noted my normally quiet friend's implied vehemence against this individual. I wondered if we had the right to do what he was asking, use our powers like a god. Just then the interloper disrespected his elder. He threw a large pot containing a hot fluid at his host. "Behrouz, surely your elder sister should have been taken to live with him within his own or his parents' household?"

Behrouz gave me a perplexed look before replying, "You know our ways well Guardian, although how I do not know. Let me tell you he, they, were cast out by his own father. And now he seeks to rule my own father in his own home. He is high within the local government and most powerful."

We turned back to the screen as women wailed and his father tried to appear as if he has not just been gravely insulted. His protagonist stormed off, talking rapidly on his mobile phone. Stepping outside he immediately got into a large black limousine with powerful demeanour, while his personal staff hurried so as not to offend him.

"Behrouz, I will bring the home and everyone inside here now, but on these conditions: that we live in peace and harmony, work together for the greater good of all, and find joy and sharing within our differences."

He accepted straight away, and I transferred the entirety to the University campus. "Behrouz, you better go and welcome them, but come back soon, we still have need of your skills."

On reflection, I considered, that during those trying times, I had at least tried to preserve our greater human heritage, and not just the varieties I was more accustomed too.

I was surprised when Behrouz returned a short time later in company with his grandfather. It was clear the elder was confused, but my worry of kidnapping an entire family disappeared at once. They watched the screen, where a black and earth-adhering cloud of death was already invading the town. Peasants and ordinary people began to choke, and became hideous caricatures of their former living bodies. I had to turn away lest I became physically sick. The old man likewise, could bear no more of what occurred just after we transported them out of Shiraz. It was gruesome. The grandfather nodded his head in understanding, and thanked me for saving them.

Chapter 8

His humility was awe inspiring, and I initiated a whim, n'Gnung introducing him to Lo Si. With the aid of our interpreter pendants, they discovered they had much in common, some of which within their dialogue might eventually come to bear fruit within our progeny.

The glimpsed images of bugged-out eyes and raw, livid flesh despoiled in a ghastly parody of life stayed with me for many days, and until the sheer burden of the horror to come finally hardened me to all of the sickest sights I would never wish anyone to see.

My heart heavy with grief at the loss of so many people I did not know, nor even shared much in common with, I returned once more to my screens and instantly panned out to obscure the horrors below. We transported those we could to safer regions. However, there was no respite, as Death roamed the region at his caustic will, slaying the innocent, gullible, and guilty by equal measure.

Chapter 9 ~ The Wrath of Gaia

We worked through the night, our teams taking turns to eat and snatch a little sleep. Other operators were drafted in to assist; Ju Lo, Xi Xah and Xi Sai, the twins To Mo and To Ma, and others who had formed our original team. Weid Noi was also with us, and was the only person to bring a smile to Ali's face. Gung Loi and her growing team continued with Operation Ark. The rest of us monitored developments, transporting people further and farther afield, and to safety, as dark dawn skies laden with foreboding, welcomed the last of the Arabian daybreaks.

I panned and zoomed across our region of interest, assisted by drones, but even so, it was desperately hard to see anything at all. The Indian Ocean had created new access to the Gulf, even though the Straits of Hormuz were not sealed off. Tsunamis and oceanic forces had powered to obliterate much of Oman and the United Arab Emirates.

We witnessed burnt-out trucks on the main Bushehr-Kangan highway trapped within liquefying asphalt. To the side, the waters of shoreline of the Persian Gulf appeared to be evaporating; steam rising as if a foggy morning, where none should ever hold tenure. In the cities and towns, there was zero sign of life, locally, or within the greater region—except for Gaia's maternal cleansing.

Sun Kist paid us an unexpected, if welcome visit. "Gaia is shedding off her ancient skin, Guardian. She is not a real person, you do understand, but a concept. The Earth power is real, as are the forces we witness here on the screen. The Shaman told me it is not as bad as it looks, but you, all of you, need to stand firm and continue doing what you are doing."

"Thank you, Sun Kist. I always had a problem with a planet being a person, an entity."

"No Guardian, you do not understand. Gaia is an earth power, fundamental to life. She contains the essence of creation, of birth and rebirth. The seed that initiates that creation comes from the stars."

I wanted to object, to learn more, but she cut off my formative questions, "I am needed, your daughter also. Stand up for what you believe in and all will be well."

Then she was gone. I did not have time to ponder her words and abstract meanings, before shouts came unbidden; "Dalan!"

Dalan gas field became the next blazing inferno when it blew to smithereens, but without the complications of the sea. We were not sure if that helped, as unlike before, there was no coolant to dampen the horrific cocktail of hydrocarbons and volcanic issuances, compounded by the plague of airborne ash that threatened to extinguish all remaining life. Instead, the open maw poured forth with vehemence. Rivers of magma flowed like blood across the sands of the desert and fertile river lands, turning once habitable areas into a death zone. Wildfires raged, but already, no life remained to be threatened. Every living thing was already dead.

José was certain the seismic shocks that followed those ruptures, destabilised the already highly unstable Kangan gas field, in the vicinity of the bubbles we had been monitoring. Within moments, the sea heaved impossibly high, imploded, and erupted. Once more, a major gas field and volcanic eruption combined to send a city, the port of Kangan into the stratosphere, burying the remainder in toxic clouds and massive lava flows.

Some minutes later we heard the bang, which was followed by aftershocks that reverberated around the globe. Our operations room lay silent for some time, and I rose to move us forwards with a gentling words. "This destruction is evil, and yet it is now a part our reality, even here in the remote South Pacific. I need you all ... every single one of us, to focus on the bigger picture. Ali, what is the nearest and biggest worst scenario, now if you please."

He muttered as he tracked the changes, before standing and turning to stare at me with open and impossible eyes, "South Pars / North Field."

Everyone swiftly became attentive too their work, but perhaps only two or three of us actually understood the threat. Even then, its consequences remained unimaginable. "Jack, if the smallest amount of magma gets anywhere near South Pars, what we have already witnessed will become an irrelevant children's sideshow. It is the largest gas field in the entire world."

I instantly set an emergency trace on temperature build up centred upon the northern tip of South Pars, following Ali's data feed, calling José and his team to check independently. Within the hour, our survey probes revealed a labyrinth of interconnecting, oil-bearing strata that channelled and funnelled deep within the earth. These channels were being compromised by the rising tide of magma and chemical compounds that had no right to exist within any oil or gas field. Many of those underground corridors became seriously inundated with high viscosity magma. And so much so, the infection had already undermined South Pars to a greater, not lesser extent.

José said, "I have been collating much data, and can now confirm to all here, there is a new and deadly-active, super-volcanic field beneath Bushehr. You would perhaps understand the term hot spot better, although that is not quite technically correct. This was formed as a direct result of the impossibly large nuclear blast that destroyed the associated atomic weapons processing and storage facility. The compromising damage to the rock strata below that explosion is most damning, as we now realise. Not only do we have magma undermining the oilfields, but water also."

"So that is good, it will act to cool the magma."

"Not so. Water contains naturally occurring hydroxides, and although only a small part of any body of water, they are lethal in this case. Viktor?"

"Explain?"

"We, volcanologists, believe that in primordial times, water was formed in the mantle. High temperature and pressure forced the fusion of atoms of hydrogen and oxygen. The result was water. That came to the surface over æons.

"Today, there is water below, under extremes of temperature and pressure. It is enough to separate the molecules into hydrogen and oxygen; these are atoms of accelerant and explosive capacities."

"Understood. Dire. Viktor, what of the resultant chemicals?"

"Hydroxides interact with alkanes, one of the ten forms of oil, put simply. This combination forms a catalyst to power explosive forces. I will add, at these temperatures and pressures, molecules of hydrogen and oxygen will likely destabilise into separate gases, and/or form more deadly compounds. In this unique situation, water is the accelerant. We have already witnessed what happens when all these constituents come together. Boom!"

Several hours later, the largest gas field in the world grew and grew. South Pars brewed and fermented for thirty minutes, before the inevitable happened, erupting with an earth-shattering bang.

The explosion caused worldwide devastation. The gulf sea parted and we stared into a vast maw where the gas field used to be. As with other fields before, we watched molten lava blasting into the skies, yet more still flowing to fill the crater, before the sea washed back to battle the forces of under-earth.

The scale of devastation, the outpouring of inner-earth, and later, toxicity of air and land was too much for any mind to comprehend. We could no longer see. A macabre darkness enshrouded the entire Middle East, not that of night, but one of deathly thickness. A soup of airborne chemicals so viscid, our scanners could hardly penetrate. There was nothing more we could do. All life there and thereabouts was most certainly extinct.

And yet, that was only the beginning of Gaia's wrath. Hours later, the world's largest oilfield (75% gas) known as Ghawar in Saudi Arabia, ripped apart in an almighty blast that made the entire earth wobble in its orbit. Fired by the powerhouses of hell on earth, the dark and desperate, deathly clouds of uttermost macabre, spread outwards to encompass the globe. No one and nothing was spared, save the lucky, and the few we protected.

Operation Ark was in full swing, and yet our haughty attempts to save for posterity, that which we considered good, became like pebbles cast into the ocean. A difference we made, not in quantity, but in quality of preservation. We determined not to lose our technology, our histories' and beliefs', and greater understandings of the world we inhabited. Unlike the Second, but like Taris, we would preserve for posterity, as much knowledge as we could. We would work out what to do with it later, if we survived.

In time, I surrendered to the shore. We had worked the whole day and night through, without taking more than a break. I was in divisive mood. The world was turning, so there was opportunity and advice for those that would but listen obliquely to the siren's call.

I drank to cut my mind free of its mortal morass, and cast my eyes to the stars, obliterated by blackest cloud. By instinct, I rose as if pulled to the shoreline. Unbidden, unknown forces drew me, to the top of the sentry rock. I clamoured silently inside, going alone up to the pinnacle, seeking such heartfelt release.

She was there, waiting. I knew she would be. That moment was not of earth-time. It was the time of stars and galaxies, as they birthed, grew, and imploded; unravelling within our unique spark of life, as if returning to our souls — myriad possibilities of the impossible and unknown.

I bowed in abject deference to her, and sat at my own will to stare up at where the stars should have been, waiting for her to speak by my side. Within time, she waved her hand in the air and the clouds parted, and perhaps for an æon, or a moment, we watched the heavens revealed in their true glory, for such was the glimpse of improbability my mind was gifted.

I looked at the Shaman, in her guise as 20 something. "Did I come here at your biddance, or of my own volition?"

"The choice was free for you to make,
attend and learn or leave in wake."

I tried to read her impossible eyes, those deep wells that within changed constantly, and yet, always remained the same and were always true.

"Stars returneth to thee in future clime,
if thee but listen to my rhyme.
Look not to present gloom and slime,
plan for the morrow, there's not much time."

The Shaman leaned closer to me and placed her impossible hand upon my arm, before patting it gently like a sage'd Grandmother, and spoke:

"What this day tears asunder,

58

As Ogres maim, kill, and plunder,
Yet darkest time approaches yonder,
Secure in tenure, ye cannae wander.

Hold ye fast in deathly wonder,
One chance is all to end his thunder;
Boon of sword to heal this bounder,
Honour ye of Gaia, make no blunder."

Her odd words, strange metre and alternating rhyme, brought
deep comfort to me. I would always treasure her presence and sharing
there with me that eve. She added something abstract for my
consideration, "Keep close the last seed of the one tree, now not the
time to plant, but soon will be."

Her musing confused me, which brought forth more laughter as
she humoured my ignorance. It was not from goading or malice, but
with love and the gentling illumination of the wisest mother. However,
as if breaking a spell, a though came unbidden to my mind, "Shaman,
who or what are you?"

She giggled like a young girl deep within her own personal
mysteries. Her laughter tippled to dapple the air like that of the
Eleventh, as she enjoyed my confusion within her leisure. Seeking to
ease my burden she added aside,

"Human that I am, and not,
Enlightened to, lest truth forgot.
Elemental would be my lot,
Of earthen stars, where ether's plot."

I presumed her done, but she added
"Lead wisely, O foreign, O island son,
Your weakness is strength. Go, be as one."

I looked up once more to see the stars one last time, and glimpse
the impossible pathways between. Instead, I saw thunderheads of
doom approaching quickly on the wings of our own reality, and sensed
the howling winds of changing times and fates. I looked to where she
had sat, and followed the fading laughter into the night with renewed
hope, and a sturdy forbearance.

Words came into my mind, familiar and distant, "A little farther
unto the rocky lot, and you can rest in peace my child besot."

In that instant I knew her from before, my arrival on the shore. My
guardian angel now had a name, if not a physicality. Feeling restored, I
returned to my companions on the shore, drinking heartily and
dispelling their fears with my own conviction and merriment. As if to

cement our renewed self-belief, I rose and proposed an odd toast, "Live life to live, or live life to die? I choose to live!"

I raised my glass to all, when from without a square shape emerged from the glooming that encircled to engulf us. A voice we all cherished boomed out, "Well said yon Guardian laddie, for I would also stand together and toast with the living this eve."

Owain's surprise appearance instantly dispelled the latent vestiges of doom. Da Phai Nai placed a large beer in his hand, as her eyes shone upon his worried countenance. He bid her drink with us, and so instead of pondering imponderables of the earth's demise, we celebrated our friendship and companionship—our gift of life as brothers and sisters, and Gaia's children all.

Chapter 10 ~ Aftermath

There are few things in life we can be certain of. The first is our birth, or is that a lie? Can one be born if they were created in a laboratory? What constitutes birth in that instance, becoming aware as a baby, or adult? And what has God got to do with it?

The major events we all experience are due to the second certainty; that things will change, because change is ever-present. How strangely analogous indeed, to consider a state of change as being a constant.

The only other thing that all of us can guarantee is that one-day we will die. One or two may become enlightened beings, perhaps the Shaman, and transcend to another plane of existence. But of those that do, they remain largely without this world of mortal turmoil and continual disruption.

What of life after death? Can it be only the preserve of those who did good deeds? What if there is life before death, as in reincarnation. These heavy thought-provoking paroxysms flashed through my mind, and mixed with ponderances of the more mundane, as I stared in disbelief at my screen and watched the obliteration of my known world. Would we, could we survive?

The explosion of the world's major oil and gas fields was harrowing to watch. Within days, millions lost their lives by means most foul. The morbid legacy was, those that died instantly suffered least. There was no salve. All life on Earth was endangered, becoming extinct: the animals and plants, insects, and all creation faced death in and around the Middle East. The macabre spread steadily outwards, encroaching upon neighbouring regions, death the only constant.

Belatedly, we began a massive undertaking, collecting DNA of every species that once walked, flew, or grew upon the Earth. I had reservations about collecting snake genetics, until I was reminded of the wars to come. The Great Ogre was in hiding, but would certainly reappear. He would probably strike when we were at our weakest, and as the Third pointed out, snake venom, that of spiders and scorpions also, was a powerful antipersonnel weapon.

Unsure we could ever accomplish such a daunting task in time, I interfaced with the Core. "Guardian, do you wish to begin a new survey, or update the extant one Taris commissioned?"

"Wow! Is Taris' record of the time complete?"

"It has been continually updated since inception, and is a complete catalogue of life on Gaia, up until the last survey, thirty five years ago."

"Please update this immediately, beginning with regions of the Earth under greatest threat."

Meanwhile, Operation Ark was progressing as quickly as could be, but there appeared to be no end to it. n'Gnung said, "Guardian, Gung

Loi is doing the best she can, but I wondered, have any of the Last already done something similar?"

"By Jove, what an excellent idea. Yes brother, the Eden Project in Cornwall for one. There will be others for sure. Let's set a large shielding circle and pay them a visit."

I arrived a short time later, but was considered a tourist. I needed an appointment to see anybody in authority. They were busy people, very worried people. The reception wall listed hierarchy, and I went to read details, trying to pinpoint whom best to target. Nearby I heard the receptionist address one of the leaders by name, and biding my moment, I went to shake the man's hand. "Jack Barleycorn, my pleasure to meet you."

The man was a little surprised, but responded to my entreaty in kind. As our palms touched, I pressed the button of my return bracelet. His shock palpable when we materialised inside the Invincible. He was wary at first, slowly coming to realise what we were about, and that we were offering them protection from the hostile weather to come. A series of meeting ensued, the result being we would plan to work together, to restore our world after the ravages of Gaia had played themselves out. We were all planning for the long term.

Later, Dawn came to me and said, "Jackie, remember we went to visit that environmental group in Machynlleth, mid-Wales, it is a Centre for Alternative Technology. Well, I think we should either protect them, or bring them here. What do you think?"

We visited, and got short shrift from their administration department. We wandered outside, and intentionally became involved in conversation with one group, who appeared to be trying to live a stone-age lifestyle, but with modern and natural, harmonious science with nature. Their leader, Billy, was an intriguing fellow, and opposed to the new sales target environment to which their group had become a backwater. His beliefs were genuine and they were all for starting again elsewhere. He returned with us, before agreeing to transfer their encampment to the plateau above our spacecraft.

With them, we gained a Jack-of-all-Trades in the form of Gilly, an ex-builder with long, curly red-hair. He was a well-educated biker, fanatical about motorbikes, rock music, and complementary energy. It seemed he was casually dating Billy's daughter, Mavis. "If Gilly can't go, then I'm not going either, Father."

"Yes you are young lady, you are my daughter and will do as I say. Gilly is welcome as long as he leaves his electronic guitars and motorbikes here. The Guardian has said so."

"Shan't, and you can't make me."

The pettifoggery was resolved when Gilly visited us, and showed interest in our power supply for the University. He was soon indicating means whereby our systems could be upgraded; frictionless bearings, low resistance wiring, and the latest battery technology were some of the improvements he suggested. He became our odd-job-man, and sprouted a small team that incorporated new additions and maintained extant buildings. In return, he was allowed to bring his guitars, two bikes, and no petrol, which heralded the small beginnings of what John would grow into a technological museum.

Because of his need to get around the growing campus, he was allowed an electric bike, which soon became several. One was a cross-country trials bike which n'Gnung took a particular liking too, and was later given. Soon after, a small electric truck for carrying tools and materials was added, then a second open-air bus with covered top.

Nevertheless, I managed to keep numbers minimal, and with John's enthusiastic support, provided the campus with more than enough bicycles, and later the entire population either had use of a bicycle, or tricycle with small payload capability. A new bicycle industry flourished, Gilly growing into the role of Islanders mentor for all things mechanical.

Our scientific community also increased in size, and John accumulated buildings and staff as they became available. I was still riding shotgun on his grand designs, Jinnie agreeing that we would have to feed all these people, and without raiding larders of the Last in times soon to come.

Set against this urgency of preservation, the backdrop of annihilation of the greater world continued to gather momentum unabated. We could not tell if the Gulf of Arabia still existed, because it was shrouded with a pall of blackest cloud. We could tell Thor continued his war within by the increasingly bright and numerous thunderbolts and lightening afflicting the greater area. These were spreading outwards with alarming rate. Our probes discovered volcanoes and rainstorms, lava flows and sea, all battling for supremacy.

The ashes of destruction grew and grew intent on encompassing the globe. Driven by natural air currents, the darkest clouds obliterated day, passing our island as they sought to annihilate all life on Gaia. Our shield held, we prevailed, and that was about the best of it.

Those that had decried us, refused to stand with us against the Great Ogre, or who had belittled our attempts of warning, contacted us using the signalling devices we had left in situ. They were denied. Gaia was correct. This world had little use of the Last. Some were genuine and we worked with them, but most were playing their angles of self-preservation.

International aid swiftly dried up as water rushed in to fill the oilfield craters, lowering world sea level by several inches, thus causing a re-ordering of the tides that coursed through the world's oceans. Tsunamis and hurricanes hit areas where bad weather was unknown. These accounted for great devastation and loss of life. Aftershocks and volcanoes hampered any form of rescue or relief aid, and that was before the world at large ran out of fuel oil.

Those that survived or made it to higher ground were often later overcome by pestilence and disease. Food and medicines became scarce, causing local outbreaks of enmity between survivors.

Countries became insular, looking after their own. Their governments in turn denied their population for fear of wasting strategic resources. Altruistically, we shared what little we had, and made as much difference as we could. It was never enough, but we persevered.

Our view of the world became darkness. There was nothing to see, to define. Winter came and temperatures plummeted. We were forced to close our shield often in order to retain heat, otherwise, our crops would wither. This was not survival of the fittest. It was survival of all life on planet Earth, the Twelve Tribes determined to live on.

Outside our enclave, the world was awash with acid rain and much, much worse fell from the skies, or was borne on the wind. We did target, and harvest what we could from the world: food, dry stores, and freezers to keep it in. Gilly, our 'Mr. Fixit', appeared one day with an ecologically viable plan for large, walk in freezers of greater than commercial capacity. When he followed with a massive and climate controlled dry store, we stockpiled food and resources for the duration, however long that might be.

We were preoccupied, and not expecting a dire warning from the Core. "Guardian, the recent explosions have disturbed the orbit of the Earth. This may naturally resolve itself, but present calculations indicate the planet's orbit around the sun is deteriorating by one hour per year. This will gain momentum, if quite slowly, over centuries."

"Oh my God! One day every twenty-four years. Core, I need a resolution as quickly as you are able."

"That is easy, another explosion of similar proportions, but in the opposite direction."

I held my head in my hands, elbows propped on my desk. Moments later, I looked up at my team, who seemed riveted in place. "We will resolve this, but not today. Come, what needs our immediate attention?"

n'Gnung said, "Wise words, Guardian. A team of scientists from China have obliquely contacted John concerning a power generation device. We contacted them some days ago, remember."

"Yes, great news. Ask John to liaise with them, he knows the Cambridge scientist heading part of the project."

The Thorium reactor came to us some time later, and after due local discussions, was located near the University, by a river. The scientists and control station came with it, ensuring safe and continued operation. The deal was, their greater family and friends came with them. I limited their numbers as best I could

The reactor was supplied from a stockpile of processed fuel we also took control of, enough fuel, for us, for a thousand years. This meant we could transfer buildings, and begin to create a new world, in readiness for when our old one was done.

I wondered if one thousand years was long enough for Gaia and her siblings to settle, as did Kay and n'Gnung. We interfaced with the Core; "Thirty years minimum before issuance will subside enough to terraform. That will quell the current miasma, but extinguish all current life, including your own. I am prohibited from doing that. This craft is not capable of the transformation, regardless. That would require either a Spacecraft Carrier, or preferably, a Dark Moon — essentially a form of planetoid."

"Core, how do we stop *issuance* today?"

"Thermonuclear detonation, which, again, I cannot allow, or strategically placed plasma torpedoes."

"Finish this as it began. Details please..."

By detonating certain parts of the world's crust using plasma weapons, it became evident we could burn up many of the already airborne toxic chemicals, and with a smidgeon of luck, seal Gaia's pores that issued them. We worried about fallout, and increasing the Armageddon that was enveloping all life on Earth. To my side, n'Gnung said, "We are already in the grip of Armageddon, Guardian. If this goes wrong, it will only speed the inevitable end. Should we succeed, we save life. We save all life on this planet."

Kay interjected, "Jackie, timed and placed correctly, this could help offset the problem with the Earth's orbit. Core, calculate."

Our dialogue was long, and ongoing. Kay and I worked through options and projected resolutions, correlating with the latest information from José and Fernando. Thirteen relatively small plasma warheads of specific type and power were required to burn off and subjugate Gaia's whimsy. We would also need to design, create, and launch probes with explosive charges in order to relieve pressure beneath the Earth's crust.

Additionally, specific drones would act as carriers of purifying agents. Timed precisely, the strike would cumulatively offset the greater disruption to the Earth's orbit. We had a win-win situation. I wanted Gaia to rest in peace, and we determined to look after her. We had the detailed parameters and locations, all we required were the warheads.

We had a few plasma torpedoes commissioned, but not enough. This had been a low priority for the still remodelling spacecraft. Other weapons needed special chemicals in order to be effective, many of which were unknown to our modern scientific understanding.

In time, Kay produced a definitive report, which read more like a shopping list. "Jackie, the bottom line is we need a lab to make most of the required chemicals, and a designated plasma generation compound. Both should be heavily shielded. We can save months by acquiring rare metals and specific complex compounds from our allies in the world at large. Or we steal what we need."

"No. Stealing is wrong, unless the goods are abandoned. These substances won't be. n'Gue, please arrange for Peni and Gilly to meet me when we finish here, say in one hours' time."

"Hmmm. That will be an interesting pairing, Jackie. I wager they get along famously."

"No bet, so do I. I just discovered Gilly's helpers are all bikers, builders, and members of his rock band. One was their roadie, and he wants to bring the defunct Styx recording studio and vinyl record press here."

"Good idea, vinyl is analogue, and capable of recording for posterity. It is not subject to degradation and electronic frying like digital is. Even were we flooded, we could wash off the discs and play them on a wind-up gramophone…"

With Kay and John's wholehearted support, and permission from the Empress, the recordings of our world's information onto vinyl became a reality. I left the distraction to others, and my team concentrated on correcting the imminent threat. Sourcing the materials and creating processing plant, for the bombs we hoped would save us all.

We continued to scan what little of the world we could see, for allies and support. Until that moment, I had never imagined, just how incredibly big this Earth was, and how small and tenuous our grasp of life was upon it.

During the interim, we continued to save many people, although most could not come to our island, their numbers were far too many. We transported them to areas that were viable for life. Those that came to us were friends and family of our inhabitants, including my own. We also took in others, such as Captain Stewart, his men, and their families.

Like a chess player, I used the right people for tasks. I brought Neal to assist and asked him to take over all initial contact with outsiders, and use his best judgement as to sincerity of intent — no matter how big or small the delegation, or to our western minds, how important. Seeing our screens and the portent of what was to come, I transferred his family and house to what was becoming, a new village on the shore. Bryony was their neighbour.

Neal's presence relieved Dawn, and allowed John to get about his daily work. Neal became our welcome Ambassador to the outside world. Growing quickly and disproportionately into a role he thrived upon.

We did not welcome many new visitors, keeping our location secure, but neither did we segregate ourselves from the troubles of the world. Rather we attempted to engage with world leaders. China and the U.S., who maintained stockpiles of what we urgently required, politely rebuffed us, and with the temerity of false belief, as good as call us charlatans and scampered away to their cash-lined lives as soon as possible.

The Canadians and others were supportive, but did not have the resources in the bulk we needed. However, their Premier took me aside and said, "Guardian, some of us here need shelter. It's a straight deal, I know who may trade for what you want, and back you all the way."

He set up a meeting with the Indian Premier, and afterwards I offered the Canadians protection circles, allowing but a dozen to come to the Island. The Mounties and their families were already assimilating into our army and cultural recluse.

The Indian President headed a small, high-level delegation, who took us extremely seriously. The President revealed, "Jack, our continued existence as a nation is finely balanced upon the whim of fate, and on the edge of the eve of destruction. We are the first world power to come under imminent and deadly threat. We will give you what you want, if you give us all you can."

We received the quantities of rare metals and chemicals we required, plus a processing facility that was incorporated with their team, into our University. We agreed to work with them, to preserve life, and their cultural roots; the mixture of Hindu, Muslim, and Raj was puzzling to most, but not to me.

As soon as the missiles were ready for deployment and the Earth in position, we fired. We had informed the rest of the world, and with the Core monitoring, acted in the best interests of all.

I no longer worried about the Middle East. It had ceased to exist days before, all life already forfeit or transported elsewhere. With the Core's assistance, our strikes were surgically precise, sealing and diffusing Gaia's fury, and additionally, venting the potential Harrat Ash Shamah volcanic field. The operation proved ninety-eight percent successful, meaning our atmosphere would not be further compromised, and would in time begin to recover.

"Core, what of the Earth's orbit, has this been corrected?"

"No Guardian, it was only ninety-five percent corrective."

I ran the maths in my head, Kay beating me to the sum; "Less than one-minute per year, we can live with that, and it should naturally balance out over the years, given the Earth's extant elliptical orbit. The day is not yet done, but this great news calls for a celebration. This time I'll get the beers in. We should bring that Grolsch brewery here, Jackie. Well come on, what are you waiting for?"

Chapter 11 ~ After Aftermath

The days and weeks that followed were agony to monitor. As our screens slowly cleared, we became aware the Arabian Plate had been riven apart by primordial forces of the Earth, and a new sea as large as an ocean had been created where once the world's leading oil supplying countries used to be.

It became apparent the Gulf of Aqaba still existed, but it was filled with volcanic mountain ridges, not water. The Mediterranean Sea now engulfed most low-lying areas of the Levant and Saudi Arabia, and included the long gone Gulf of Arabia. Lands of many regional powers had been reduced to inhospitable islands and mountain ranges. None supported any form of life.

What nobody expected was the land that used to comprise northern Israel, parts of Syria, touching as far north as Turkey, had become an isolated and minor plate in its own right. José had continued to monitor the Damascus fault, which finally ruptured under the strain placed upon it, compounded by our deliberate missile strikes, to create a new plateau many hundreds of feet above its previous position. The scientists were of the opinion that this release valve saved the world from the eruption of many super-volcanoes, including Harrat Ash Shamah.

José said, "The geography of the known world is being reshaped. In the north, we have monitored increasing volcanic and tectonic activity spreading incrementally throughout what I will loosely term, Europe. Turkey, as you are aware is already in a state of emergency, old volcanoes have reactivated, and the landscape is changing. This is increasing pressure beneath all the mountain ranges that separate northern Europe, from the south.

"Turkey already has more volcanoes than it can cope with, as does Greece and the western Balkans. The underground pressure has now spread to the Alps, with new eruptions to the west, the eastern Pyrenees, and the Massive Central, which already was an enormous hotspot in its own right.

"Farther afield, the domino effect repeats, but to lesser extent. Russia has new volcanoes, as does the Pacific Ring of Fire, and the States. There is activity around Yellowstone, but our readings show the super-volcano will not blow. As the area of devastation increases, so the effects weaken, the forces below are dissipating.

"The world's plates and mantle are settling to a new status quo. The centre is now becalmed. Just like a boulder thrown into a pond, the ripples spread out, but will die out."

"This is good news, José. Just as well we moved all your people here, did we miss any?"

"No, thank you Guardian. What we are seeing, due to prevailing winds and subterranean realignment is the northern hemisphere has suffered badly. Southern South America and Australia have survived much better, but not so Africa, which continues to be torn apart by the southerly spreading Great Rift Valley fault, ripping impossibly large tracts of land asunder."

Fernando continued, "The Great Rift Valley is sheering down. It was already a transform fault, and the eastern plate attached is called the Somali or Somalian Plate. It had already been established, this would begin to drift away within ten thousand years. The recent disturbance will make this a matter of months. Soon, Djibouti and part of Eritrea, Ethiopia, and Somalia, Uganda, Mozambique, and Malawi, will sail away into the Indian Ocean, becoming a small continent. A new sea will separate this from the African or Nubian Plate. It is likely several micro-plates will form as well, what I will term the Victoria and Rovuma plates, which will become islands.

"The Somalia plate is being forced eastwards, and sunken lands are appearing due south of India as a result. The lost continent of Mauritia is reappearing. Elsewhere, Sri Lanka is almost reconnected to the mainland, and submerged islands that are more southerly are appearing."

"So, the worst of it is done with, except for the Somalia plate."

"Yes Guardian, but the Earth needs time to heal."

Fumaroles continued to develop worldwide, pumping plentiful poisons into the atmosphere. We countered as best we could, our aim to preserve all life. The CDC upped their game under Doctor Steel's auspices, to ensure survival of all life on planet Earth.

At first it was the Tsunamis that were most feared, later pestilence and horrific diseases. Many people suffocated to death under skies that were a grey-out with ash particles and hostile gases, whilst others fell prey to natural elements, other survivors, and predatory animals.

The vast gas explosions required oxygen for combustion, this being replaced with carbon dioxide, and worse. Many who survived the initial explosions were suffocated to death by clouds of CO_2 and smaller ones of hydrocarbons, as Benzenesulfonic acid swamped large areas and extinguished mammalian life.

Turbulent and unnatural weather systems blew clouds of death to all regions of the globe, the heavier CO_2, hydrocarbons, and noxious gases settled throughout the world and made most regions inhospitable to life.

In January 2016, I estimated the world's population to be roughly seven billion people. A mere six weeks later, I considered that number to be halved, and before the end of the first year of purgatory, less than one billion still survived.

With the loss of so much oil and gas came other repercussions. World transport systems collapsed almost overnight, as countries that still had oil put an embargo on all exports, and use was rationed. This in turn led to wars and civil uprisings that tore nations and neighbourhoods apart. Our spies informed us these were mainly the work of the Great Ogre.

The Sun and the Moon became distant memories. It was difficult to tell the difference between day and night, so horrendous was the atrocity and our place within it. A new generation was born only to know darkness. The air continued to cool, and each day became like the dread of winter, as wind-borne icy fingers dug within our marrow, dooming us to be frozen alive. Miles of deep black clouds had taken the Sun from us, and the general foreboding was that it would only get worse.

One morning I breakfasted at the University, and seeing Weid Noi and Ali chuckling about something, intended to go over and share the joke. However, Peni called me over to join her; "Jackie dear. My problem is that I begin to understand, and then I don't. Gangling is lovely, but ... distracting at times, overly helpful when I need to concentrate. Can you teach me the language of the Ancestors, it is becoming my imperative."

"Yes, and No. I can send you to the island school, or you could interface with the Core's language programme. I strongly advise against doing so. It cost Kay and I years of our lives, comatose."

"Oh! I don't like the sound of that one bit. No matter, back to school it is then. I recently took a vocational course in origami, so it should be no problem—it keeps my fingers occupied when my mind is working. Where?"

"Peni I..."

"And I also need to move here. That means I will be working with you constantly, won't that be nice. We'll make great progress, what do you say? Great! I'll send word to my husband to prepare the house for transfer and ... the pets? ... no-no, the goats?"

"The kids, dearest sister."

"Ah yes, the children, that was it. Well they really miss me, don't they Phœbe."

"If you say so, sister dearest." Phœbe added, "Same here, with my things Jackie, but can I have Miss Priscilla Holloway's house in Malibu, if it's no longer being used?"

I gawked at Phœbe. Peni cut in, "Jack, the old language, I need to begin learning it today."

"Peni, we have a spacecraft, and I need of a Science Officer who understands how it all works. If it ever flies again, we would have the greatest need of someone with your particular talents."

Her radiant smile reappeared as she concluded, "A Spock, a Spock, my kingdom for a Spock." Peni's chortle filled the air for a moment, before she became distracted once more. "Come sister before I get hoarse, we have much work to do; thank you Jack, I'll tell Helen to enrol my children for school. Goodbye."

I stared after her wake, wishing she had learned how to communicate with real people, and understand the changes that had befallen the planet. No matter. Few could match her scientific brain, and none her subatomic comprehension of particles, space, and time. We needed her, and her idiosyncrasies were amusing, most of the time.

Time moved on, and I remained certain that without our outer shield, we would all have succumbed. As it was, we survived and through nimble manipulation, managed to grow crops and sustain life. Jien Noi encouraged the people to have more children so our strength grew, not wilted during those most desperate of times.

One day many months after the worst of the explosions, I received a signal from our dedicated U.S. envoy, Don Phillips. I greeted him moments later. "Guardian, Jack, good to see you again … there are a few humans that can still see the Sun and the Moon, those onboard the international space station.

"The Russian supply chain has ceased to function, and although in theory a space shuttle could be re-commissioned, the practicalities are the craft would be highly unlikely ever to fly again. Regardless, the country is in a state of ongoing emergency, all life is threatened or already taken by this Wrath of Gaia. I doubt we have enough scientists and workers left alive to consider the project viable. Jackie, communications have been re-established with the space station from a new command centre, and the crew are desperately low on basic resources. Can you help us?"

"I see no reason why not, as long as the space centre is in a geo-synchronous orbit. Sending supplies and removing waste should not be a problem."

"Would you be able to change the crew, those people are trapped up there."

"Yes, I think so, Kay?"

"Checking now, Jackie… Yes, this is theoretically possible, but I caution we have never done this before. We require a human guinea pig, one who might die from unforeseen complications."

Our meeting closed quickly, and two days later we received a delegation from NASA, who gave us the location of new supplies. The new crew transferred to us, much to their astonishment. Meanwhile I interfaced with the Core and discovered there was a special subroutine in place for local space transfers.

The astronauts above us were expecting delivery, but appeared visibly stunned when a consignment of food materialised in their exercise module. We waited as they took the consignment, replacing it with waste, which I sent onwards immediately for processing at the new NASA centre of operations.

Captain Carl Williams was next, "Good luck Captain." He went fully suited on internal life support, and arrived intact moments later. Knowing we were watching with our scanners, he gave us a thumbs-up, before removing his helmet. We staggered the transfers so each of our senior operators made one transfer each, the penultimate arriving without life-support, and the last one, carrying her suit.

Several days later we made the return transfers once the crew had personally handed over, again repeating the process so we all did it at least once each. We brought them back lying down for fear of stressing joints and human capability, due to abruptly being taken from weightlessness into our full gravitational pull. It was a wise precaution, and one of many things the Core had advised me about in advance. Ami and a robotic nurse stood by in case of complications, and although we never had one, each was taken to our medical centre for checks.

I suppose it was inevitable, but months later we became host to a dedicated NASA supply complex that kept very much to themselves to begin with. However, as their community grew, we became their base of immediate operations. Interaction was slow in coming, but in due course, they mingled with our scientists and created a new wing of the University dedicated to space exploration. This soon expanded to include processing all the results of many off world experiments, including information sent back by Moon and Mars rovers, and other exploratory satellites.

Without prompting, we provided similar service for other isolated research bases that were dependent upon outside assistance for survival, like the ones in Antarctica. There were several others, and we either got them out of the situation, or organised a supply train, delegating one controller to look after all their needs.

Near the end of 2016, Gung Loi gave birth to the first of four children, all spaced just over a year apart. A boy, Zhong Zhi, was first then a girl, and repeat. It seemed the disease was catching, because Jien Noi and I also produced a son the following week, who was named Jason in respect of my father.

"Jackie, we should try for another child, we need a girl. I worry Ræm's life will become dedicated to the greater good of all humanity. She needs a sister to stand in as Gatekeeper and Empress in times of greater need."

"Good thinking, Jinnie. Let's start now."

"Oh no you don't Jack Barleycorn, you will have to wait. behave! What would happen if our children married others similar? Gung Loi's offspring, or maybe those of Horovitz and Xi Sai; they asked to be allowed to marry earlier today. Imagine. We would be creating a new race, recreating the Ancestors in our own image."

"The Thirteenth Tribe; you cannot be serious?"

"No, well maybe. It was just an idle thought. Let's see how this pans out in years to come."

Chapter 12 ~ The Vatican Archives

John was busy. He had become the impetus behind Project Preservation. He listed Universities and libraries, museums and databases, and remained adamant the Vatican should be preserved, regardless that he was a practising Protestant.

We tried several means to gain an audience with His Holiness the Pope, but were politely rebuffed each time. The Apostolic Palace was not a building we wished to invade, but with all avenues exhausted, it was only a matter of time before I was forced to kidnap the pontiff.

I materialised beside him and said, "Apologies, Your Holiness, but we have need to speak with you. Please come with me. You will not be harmed, and will return in a few minutes. First, there is something you must be made aware of."

He called the *Guardia Svizzera*, but I gripped his arm and activated my return bracelet, before they could arrive. We materialised in the control room. His indignation swiftly turned to incredulity, "You just beamed me here, Scotty?"

"Guardian, or Jack, Jackie."

"Jack Kirk it is then, what's next? Vulcans, do they exist?"

"No, but the Eleventh do, please don't call them Elves. The Dwarves are waiting to greet you as well, come."

We had arranged for representatives from the Twelve Tribes to be there to greet him, and he looked at the representations of humanity with a concern. "This cannot be, but they are real. Twelve races you say? These must be the Lost Tribes of Noah, but how?"

"The lost tribes of Noah?"

"It is not common knowledge, but yes. Noah recorded twelve other types of humans, but they refused to get on the Ark. Interesting they survived when most other life did not. It's a bit like current times, don't you think."

"One of those Twelve is the alien race that came to this planet in prehistory, you are now in one of their spaceships."

John stepped forward, assisted by Neil and Kay, and they introduced our peoples in turn. We seated the Pope at a consol, and showed him the destruction of the world, enhanced by feeds from probes, and a composite recording we had prepared in advance. He learned how to use the basic controls, and panned, then zoomed like a child, and gasped, gimlet stare his focus. In time, a discussion of sorts developed, aided by an Italian translation program I had the foresight to instigate with the Core.

His interest turned to us, and we showed him parts of our island. "Please stay and see it at first hand. We are preparing a banquet in your honour."

"I would love to but I have a pressing affair to deal with. However, I will be free in two hours, and will return for the feast with a small entourage. You say this is an alien spacecraft, I knew it. I must see the ship as well. This is amazing. Now, how do we keep in contact?"

We returned and installed a signalling system, and received his small party a few hours later. There was not time to show him the ship, because interaction with the other Tribes became his primary interest, Ælthrelntheine in particular making a lasting impression on him.

We offered the Vatican protection from Gaia's forces of nature, in return for access to the secret archives. "Perhaps, but not today. I will consider it and seek counsel. Now, were you to offer a scientific means of recording what is written in the ancient texts without touching them, I could be swayed. But that's science fiction, isn't it?"

I whistled. Kay looked thoughtful, before excusing herself. She returned as the Papal party were preparing to depart. "Your Holiness, a device can be manufactured, but it will take some time. It will be a form of scanner, but to be of any use, we need to add a function to record the text in linear format. The scrolls will be rolls, yes?"

Agreement was reached and, the Pope departed. As we waited for the Papal response, the scanning device was commissioned. John remained adamant, "We need to protect the Vatican at all costs, whether they want our protection, or not. I am not of their religious persuasion, but their records go back millennia. These must be saved, if little else, for posterity."

Kay was in tune with John's thoughts, but her perspective was different, "I agree with John. These records, some thousands of years old, are irreplaceable. We have to protect them, and read them; we need to place the scanner. I hope most are in Latin, my Hebrew isn't all that good, my Aramaic worse. I better get Finity Gael, our ancient language specialist, working on Semitic languages."

I began to object when Kay added. "I bet the Vatican vault is where the Ring of the Last is held. You do want to find it, don't you, Jackie."

Momentarily influenced, I refocused. "No. This is wrong. What would be right is that we produce a large, protective transporter, define a location for deployment, and when things go wrong, as they inevitably will, then we activate it. When we do, we will demand access to whatever is kept hidden from society. That is as far as I will go, today. Tomorrow may be different. Come Kay, let's make the shield and have it standing by for instant deployment."

Some days later, we received a surprise contact. Given we were monitoring so many far-flung signalling devices, Kay had instigated the Core to check all of them regularly. This freed an operator for more important work. The message flashed on my screen, "Contact confirmed: Vatican."

"Display."

I saw a man in black robes and pellegrina, scarlet skullcap and belt with long distend, looking tentatively around. He was not the Pope, but a Cardinal I recognised. I called my trusted to action, and appeared by the man's side seconds later. I reset the signalling device, before shaking the man's hand. We arrived on the Bridge moments later.

He stared at the faces looking at him, momentarily at a loss, before he said, "So it is true. The Lost Tribes of Noah."

"You know of these people?"

"No. It is written in the archives, which I am responsible for. It was considered to be fable, that was until this moment."

I introduced him to the Bridge, Jien Noi attending as Empress. He took great interest in our screens, and that we were saving what and whom we could. We showed him some of our achievements and that seemed to sway him to speak openly. "I am a member of the Papal See, and His Holiness asked me to come here. I am to broker a deal, subject to Papal endorsement. May I be permitted to see more of your world?"

We showed him places of interest, before he asked to see more of the spacecraft. I led him towards the lift door, which was closed. He stopped and stared at the motif, before reaching out and touching it tentatively. "You have one as well; it protects a secure vault no doubt."

"This is a secure door to a lift. You recognise it. How come?"

"The uninformed call it the Seal of Solomon, but it predates the prophet's era by millennia. May I?" He fiddled with a catch on a large ring, and removed the outer casement, revealing a ring not dissimilar to the rings of power we bore. He pressed the corresponding finger into the motif, and the ring locked, the lift door opened.

I stared at the man, my mind awhirl within possibilities and presumptions. Kay was first to speak, "Jackie, this must be a Ring of Oma, the lost Ring of the Last."

My mind focused on another point. "Your Eminence, where have you seen this before?"

"It guards the entrance to the secure archives, and there is only one of these rings in existence. I, as custodian of the archives, wear it as a badge of office under sufferance of His Holiness, the ring's true owner. It allows the wearer, entrance to our most holy artefacts. It appears most of you wear a similar ring, you also have secret archives?"

"No, it is a secure key, nothing more. May I have a look at it?"

Almost grudgingly, the Cardinal handed the ring to me, and I wasted no time having the Core examine it in my ready room. "This is an intermediate Ring of the Last, issued by Captain Taris. The covering ring is made of precious stones and gold, but has a concealing function so our sensors cannot detect the Ring of power beneath. Taris made the protective casing, but did not make rest of the enclosing ring."

Chapter 12

The Cardinal was peering over my shoulder, "Taris?"

I telepathically tasked the Core with making a copy, before answering. "The Captain who brought this spacecraft to Earth, millions of years ago. Why are you really here Cardinal?"

"Cardinal Pomfrey," the cleric guffawed, but Kay became charming and beguiling by equal measure. Moments later, she gave the man his ring back, I concealing the copy made, as she coaxed and cajoled the real reason for the man's visit.

"I attend the inner archives rarely, as most treasures are scrolls or parchment of unimaginable worth and great antiquity. They are kept in sealed containers that have climate control, but even so, some are starting to disintegrate. Many have not been read for centuries, and one is important concerning this Wrath of Gaia, as you call it.

"Today I was searching for a copy of that parchment that was mislaid two centuries ago. I noticed the northern walls showing signs of bowing inwards, and cracks in the rock appearing, where none had been before. The walls were warm to touch. There is volcanic activity due north in the Dolomites, and I fear we may lose the treasures. My visit is technically unofficial, but I am here to ask if you can help us protect the archives."

"Your Eminence, we can shield the vault, but would require access to it in return."

"Jackie, allow me. What the Guardian means is that we would need to ensure the protection is functioning correctly, and still allows you right of entry. Are there others who have access, with your permission?"

"His Holiness of course, but that is rare. My acolyte can entre as he will inherit my duties in due course, and anyone bearing Papal endorsement, which is again rare, at least for these particular archives."

"Then we have a deal. Let's do it now, it will only take a moment. If you are not happy, we will alter the design until you are satisfied. Later you will join with us for luncheon? Other Tribes are coming to make you welcome."

Regards Cardinal Pomfrey, Kay had the gift of the gab, and he was soon eating out of her hand. We installed our pre-configured, shielded transporter, and set it down in the bowls of the secret archive. We extended cover to include all of the Holy See, and had to tinker with the settings. We subsequently discovered several people were excluded entry to the Vatican City. We identified them as Hobgoblins.

Kay was our face of interaction, and spent more time within the archives than any other. We had created a scanning device to copy all the known archives for posterity, the most secret and deteriorated first. I visited occasionally with n'Gnung, but no one else was allowed there. Our copying program of the inner archive was almost complete, when

Kay returned from the secret archive early one day. She was mindful, walking instead of speaking, absorbed as if in another world. I broke into her thoughts, "What is it Kay?"

"Nothing Jackie, an aberration I can't place or explain. It reminds me of something, but what?"

"Is it something you have seen?"

"No, it's not like that. I feel as if I have looked at a secret, but not recognised it. I feel so stupid."

"n'Gnung let's go. Gung Loi, you have command, monitor us."

We began searching the papal archive for anything unusual, n'Gnung prowling around, looking for anything out of place. We gravitated towards a bookcase of minor scrolls set deep within the catacomb-like warren of interconnected passageways and halls. We were at a loss to offer an explanation, when n'Gnung observed, "Guardian, Kay. Why is that the only bookcase fixed to the outer wall? None of the others are. Why?"

It was almost too heavy to move and secured by the debris of ages, and took time to heft out of the way. Once clear, we were left facing a mosaic of ancient and probably pre-Roman design. "I've seen this before," we exclaimed in unison. Although a different scene, we were looking at something familiar from beneath the catacombs of the Palace of Elvenholme. We agreed it hid a motif, but where?

The pull on our rings drew us towards a central point, about level with my mouth, and using the copied Ring of the Last, I pressed my finger towards it. The frieze vanished in response, but my finger did not lock with the revealed motif. It was close, but not powerful enough.

"Jackie, the Ring of Taris should overrule this, try it."

My hand was already in motion as Kay spoke, and my ring locked, the door disappeared. A dark passageway extended before us. Our urge was to rush headlong into discovery, but practicable politics was my first consideration, and the stale smell of musty air trapped within for centuries. "n'Gnung, please ensure Cardinal Pomfrey attends us immediately, and bring the Pope if you can. They need to see this before we do."

They arrived in our midst moments later, both clearly disorientated, as if they had been kidnapped from what they had been doing, which n'Gnung confirmed. "We just discovered this secret passageway, and thought you should go first, if you please."

The Pope was animated, "The true Seal of Solomon, hidden for æons. Let's go."

The Cardinal added, "It is believed the Ark of The Covenant lies down this passageway. We have searched for the entrance for centuries, and now you have found it. No one except His Holiness may approach it. You must remain..."

His words were cut off as Kay lit her staff and marched boldly into the passage, the Pope hustling forward beside her. n'Gnung and I were a step behind. The coarse tunnelling gave way to a room surrounded by thirteen alcoves, six to either side, as if protecting the chief; human remains inhabited all. I said unthinking, "The Twelve, and The One."

"Indeed, Guardian. These numbers are becoming somewhat repetitive, don't you think?"

"These skeletons are of the Last, not the Ancestors or other Tribes. The Vatican, like the Ancestors before them, hid their knowledge three and more layers deep — interesting. Look for another lock, we appear to possess the key."

We searched high and low, n'Gnung eventually discovering a pull to his ring of power on the floor. We scraped away the dross of ages past, revealing another motif. I asked Cardinal Pomfrey to try, but his ring did not lock. The Ring of the Ancestor did, revealing a spiral staircase going down. The Cardinal and we followed.

The Pope remained above, absorbed with the possible remains of the Messiah and Apostles. He muttered as we departed, "I will join you later. These must be the true remains of Pontiff Petrus. I knew Pope Paul the Sixth was mistaken — Look, a red rock!"

We descended with a hurry, almost dizzy by the time the spiral stairway unravelled to reveal a small room. Set within was a large block of rock in the centre. Pomfrey enthused, "The Ark."

I kicked it as I passed by, seeing only a decoy, an oblong rock about three feet wide by five long, with four stout extrusions near the top, side corners, as if to be hoisted by poles. Kay examined it in detail, confirming my suspicions a few minutes later.

"Guardian, over here, another motif," n'Gnung shouted as he wiped away thick dust from the far wall.

Again, I used the Ring of the Ancestor, and we entered a round room. Central was a transportation circle. The walls, the circle, the all of it were black, seemingly sprinkled with colourful stars. It was extremely familiar to us, but as yet, unknown. Kay said, "I will return and monitor you, see where you end up."

She pressed her return bracelet, and remained where she stood. "Damn, we must be too deep underground. Give me a minute before you leave. I'll send n'Gue to you when I am set."

In the event Gung Loi joined us, handing me the Sword of Destiny as she said, "Kay has extended the shield down to protect us, and is monitoring for transportation spikes."

"Let's go. Cardinal, care to join us?" I stepped on the transporter last, and we arrived somewhere else, somewhere much warmer.

Chapter 13 ~ The Ring of The Last

We transported into another room, the air foul and fusty. I saw a motif on the wall in front, and I wasted no time going through. The room we entered had smooth, almost machined walls, obviously not of natural construction. A rectangular stone cuboid, similar to that of the Vatican stood centrally, a spiral staircase leading up from the far corner. The air was breathable, if little better than the previous room. Kay materialised behind us and said, "Jackie, you'll never guess where we are."

"The middle East?"

"Hmmm. Close. Beneath the Temple Mount in Jerusalem."

"What? Why come here. Religiously this is nowadays linked to the Vatican, but not during the time of the Ancestors. This was created before the time of Noah, millennia before Jerusalem was even thought about."

"Even more curious. Where do the stairs lead?"

We went up, the similarities with the Vatican almost convincing us we were back there. The stairs continued as we came to a ceiling, a motif central above. I opened the doorway hatch, and we came into a larger room. It contained thirteen small shrines set into the walls, six to each side, and one set in the wall at the head. On the opposite wall was another motif.

I was reckless, needing to discover where the room led. My ring locked with the motif, and I was thrust backwards as rock, sand, water, and cloying muddy goo mixed with crude oil tried to smother me. Fortunately, the entry sealed as I hurtled backwards, hands of friends reaching to pull me clear. "Thanks, that was a close call. This is as far as we go. We know what is on the other side. I doubt little remains of the Dome of the Rock. Let's go, we can come back another time with probes and breathing apparatus."

We returned below, taking a more detailed look at our surroundings. "Twelve and one, thirteen, what is the significance?"

"To the Ancestors it is a powerful number Jackie, perhaps the most important of their society. I imagine the old religions used the number, given its prominence everywhere we go."

"Yes Kay, a Baker's dozen. What's the recipe? The staircase, it would be impossible to manhandle the Ark down them, it would not fit. It must have either been built in situ, or transported in."

Our talk was disturbed when a shout came from the transporter room, "Guardian, come quickly, there are symbols on this transporter. Were there any on the last one we found?"

We raced through to examine the markings, the one at the front being a double circle, the outer darker and recessed. The one opposite,

81

to the rear being familiar, and it was the same but obverse. A darker and recessed hollow centre within a surrounding circle. I motioned at it and said, "This will be the base station. Cardinal, try going there using your ring, let's see if it works."

Nothing happened, and Kay tried next. As she and Gung Loi stepped forward she said, "The Gatekeeper is monitoring from the Bridge. She will tell us where we end up, see you soon."

Kay stepped over the mark and turned around to look at us. She smirked before stepping off with a playful glint in her eyes. "Hmmm. Sooner than expected it appears, I'll try the next."

They disappeared in white light, and did not return, so the Cardinal, n'Gnung, and I went to them. We found Kay in an upper room, everything was of similar layout. She was speaking with n'Gue. "Guardian, I was just explaining to Kay, you are now in the hills of east Yemen, most of this raised area has survived above water, but the air above is black. Go no farther."

Kay aired her thoughts, "Kitor, capital of the Queen of Sheba, can it be? She and Solomon had a son, or so the legend goes."

The Cardinal objected, "The Catholic Church does not condone that statement, Kay, but there is mention of a liaison in the archives."

We returned to Jerusalem, the Kitor transporter having only one set destination. Stepping over the next symbol, they disappeared, returning a few moments later, "That one goes to the Vatican, and that circle has no markings, I'll try the next."

We followed and arrived in Tyre, but underground inside an unknown palace. The transporter anteroom was similar, another ark, and a spiral staircase to the corner. n'Gue was with us immediately, "Be extremely careful Guardian, this whole region is underwater and badly compromised, the transporter must be maintaining a shield. Or you have been lucky."

We had not been lucky, and the transporter was almost out of power. Water began seeping by increasing amounts down the stairs. I relayed a message for Jinnie to set a protective shield in place, and we got the hell out of there. Returning to Jerusalem, Kay said, "Only one destination left to try. Onwards."

The Cardinal had tried, but could not transport on his own; "Your powers are beyond mine Guardian. I am humbled."

We departed from the rear or home symbol, arriving at another transporter, which we discovered had four symbols. The complex beyond the motif door was similar, yet different to previous. A tall, square, needle-like stele covered with hieroglyphs stood in place of the stone block. We went higher, up a spiral stairway, through a room containing shrines to thirteen people, or gods, before coming to a great underground hall.

n'Gue appeared and I said enquiringly, "Giza?"

"No, Guardian. Luxor."

"Ancient Thebes? Why, what's the connection?"

The others shrugged, but the Cardinal stated, "Moses. The Exodus was about fleeing Egypt, with the Ark of the Covenant, which was sculpted everywhere we have been before here. Thebes is much older. This site predates Christianity by at least six thousand years, although there are Biblical ties. This technology is over thirty thousand years old? Antediluvian. Excuse me, I need a word with myself, with His Holiness, and with my God."

"n'Gue, ask the Empress to place a protective shield around the all of this complex, we will adjust it later. Also, ask Finity Gael to join us, immediately if possible. She's our best with ancient languages and cultures. Come, let's return below."

The Cardinal departed from our control room some short time later. I gave him a locator ring similar to that of Behrouz, and showed him how to work the personal distress beacon, calling it a signalling device. I returned with Finity, n'Gue continuing as messenger between the known and unknown destinations.

When we arrived back in Thebes, I found n'Gnung studying the transfer circle where we had arrived; "Guardian, this transporter has four symbols, two are the same as before, the other two are unknown, one to each side."

Our reconnaissance became brief, the symbol nearest the exit taking us back to Jerusalem, the first to the side: Memphis, Egypt. The other side symbol took us to the wilds of central Turkey. We worked our way upward. Reaching the surface, we found ruins of fallen temples, the destruction not of recent origin. There was neither pyramid nor hieroglyph in sight. Not that we could see much, the air being laden with darker shades of grey. We used our clothes as breathing masks to keep out the worst.

"Guardian this is fantastic, I was here years ago for protracted study, archaeology practical and placement, and later, to research my thesis. The place has hardly changed. Isn't it amazing?"

"Finity, where on Earth are we?"

"Hattusa of course, don't you recognise it? It was capital of the Hittite empire, and a capital of their predecessors. They worshipped one prime god and twelve lesser underworld gods. Let me show you the sphinx that guard the Lion Gate to the southwest, they are the precursors of many later sphinx."

"Finity, how on Earth is this place related to Egypt?"

"What? Oh, that's easy. The Hittites went to war with Ramesses II and lost at the battle of Kadesh. The Assyrians came to power, all three empires vying with the Babylonians, Sumerians, and others, for ultimate supremacy over a period of several thousand years. The Phoenicians were muddled up with it as well, but their empire was a thalassocracy. All the others were a tellurocracy, or land based.

"A lot happened around that period. I want to stay here forever, but I had better return another time after proper preparation. The halls below are unknown and need thorough investigation. So, where to next, Guardian."

We returned to Thebes, and I crossed over the home symbol. We arrived in a different transfer circle. Two symbols were known, and two were not. The front one connected back to Thebes. We deferred on the other three, and went exploring. We found an anteroom sporting a pyramid, but one more akin to Mayan culture than Egyptian.

Once we reached the surface, the skies were a little clearer, though filled with ash from recent volcanic activity. Again, Jinnie set a protective shield and transporter, and n'Gue arrived to declare, "Guardian, you are now in the wilds of Sudan, somewhere northeast of Khartoum. You must leave at once. The new continental plate is forming only one hundred miles east of here. But for the prevailing wind and mountain ranges, you might all be dead already. The Empress commands you return to safety."

"Cush." Finity was a distraction of discovery. "Look, that's the Blue Nile, the White is over there. This area gave rise to the pre-Egyptian empires of northeast Africa. Some scholars regard this as the location of the Garden of Eden. Why is this place linked with Thebes, and by progression, Jerusalem you ask? I'll tell you why, 'modern' civilisation began here."

"Indeed, but Guardian, this transporter has three unknown destinations. We need to investigate."

"No. We are all reacting to the latest discovery, not thinking clearly and following a plan. We will leave, regroup, and formulate a constructive strategy. We are stepping backwards in time. It's getting late in our world, and I am getting a tad thirsty. Also, the Empress commands it, and it is a foolish man who disregards his wife. Nevertheless, we will finish-up here first."

One of the remaining symbols sported a colossus, and that's where we went. n'Gue arrived to inform us we were beneath a palace near Abydos. Finity enlightened us, "Abydos, first capital of the first Pharaohs, it's where the Egyptian Empires began."

After examining the underground halls, we returned below, there was no point in trying to reach the surface. Ours was becoming a fact-finding mission, not a thorough site investigation. The remaining side symbol took us to Knossos. Finity explained, "These places are related by the Bull God, legend tells of an underground labyrinth, and the

Minotaur, a monster part man, part bull. We need to return, prepared to face a fiend."

"Indeed, sounds like an Ogre to me, what say you Guardian?"

"You could well be correct n'Gnung. Time we left, all this travelling and discovery has left me parched."

We assembled on the shore and the mood was light as our thoughts turned to finishing the exploration. Finity said, "I need to go back to Hattusa, Guardian. The deeper levels need cataloguing for posterity. Kitor, Thebes, everywhere. It's amazing."

Kay said, "Jackie, Finity is correct, we need to thoroughly understand the all of what we have discovered. It is as if we are peeling back the layers of time to reveal olden, and older, prehistoric cultures. Perhaps each was in its day, a garden of Eden?"

"I agree Kay, it fits with what we have deduced about the Ancestors developing the Last, and trying out their latest creations in real-life. When we go back, we need to look for unnatural jumps in technology, or as regards intelligence."

"No Jackie. I'll send a fleet of probes to map every location, cameras recording what they find. Then instead of floundering hither and thither, we can target interesting locations, and send in suitably prepared teams to research each location properly."

Finity chipped in, "Can I work with you on this, Kay. I have the knowledge and also the contacts to put the right team in the right place. Jack, I may need to call in some experts, if they are still alive..."

Her eyes clouded and lost focus, her head drooped, and words dried. My pre-emptive 'No', was silenced before uttered. Instead, I said, "We'll see, Kay?"

"I'll set biohazard parameters as primary drone feedback, just so Finity knows what she is walking into."

"OK Finity, you have this project, for now. You are to work backwards in time, one hub transporter to the next, covering all offshoots. Catalogue what needs future study, and especially at Hattusa, do not linger — you can spend as much time there as you wish, once the all of this is revealed. We will need a daily report. Chart everywhere before we find out where the backstop at Cush goes to, I want this kept compact, manageable.

"Kay, map every location, and we will decide on priorities in due course. n'Gue, appoint a committed messenger to ensure Finity comes to no harm, and have Langnor supporting with a dedicated operator. What are we missing. Give me a clue? We've been everywhere and gotten nowhere today."

n'Gnung considered, and replied; "Guardian, why are there stone blocks in the most secure of secure locations? We have missed answers to questions during our hurry of discovery."

"Hidden in plain sight, but obfuscated … hidden sideways, above or below, where no one would normally look."

"Absolutely, Guardian. The mythical Ark. Why are they hidden so securely? These are places where only the most privileged can access them. It does not make any sense."

Our eyes collided as new purpose dawned. Our thoughts became one as we began to refine our formative plans. That was until a shape from the darkness intruded. "Now there me bonnie adventurers, what have thee been a'doing? I hear tell thee almost discovered the secret of premature death. Good woman, please stop fiddling with the cask and hand me a beer."

"You have tapped my patience once too often, King of the Ddwyrth. Here's your beer. Now serve yourself from the hogshead, while we labour to prepare your meal."

Da Phai Nai turned her back and strutted back to the kitchen, muttering aloud. Owain, said loudly, "Join us good woman, I would have the pleasure of your company this bonnie eve."

Turning to toast us he added, "Now adventurers, tell me what happened to you this fair day, and don't spare the storytelling. Are you in need of a bodyguard for the morrow?"

Chapter 14 ~ The Ark of The Covenant

We returned to the Vatican the next morning, but deep down and unannounced to the pious within their castellated towers above. Matron was with us, and ran scans on the skeletons. "The leader is much older than the others, died about two thousand years ago. Having researched the history of this place, I presume it to be Peter. The others will be his disciples. All are male."

We had started at the top and worked down, examining every inch of wall, ceiling, and floor using scanners, instinct, and touch. There was nothing of note. In time, a block of solid stone once more confronted us. We searched the top with our hands, seeking the slightest pull on our rings. There was none. Disconsolate, feeling the moment slipping away from us, I parked my behind on the surface, my eyes searching the ether for an answer, as my fingers drummed the ancient sides of the rock. n'Gnung came to sit with me, and I shuffled sideways to allow him room beside me, and that's when I felt it—the slightest flicker of pull on my ring.

My finger stayed riveted to the spot as I swung around, down to examine the small area. I moved towards the pull on my finger, and by trial and error, a motif was revealed. It locked with the Ring of the Last. The stone top disappeared, and beneath two ancient stone tablets were revealed. I removed the first, Finity the second, and she was immediately glued to the script. "This is early Aramaic, almost Semitic."

Her brow creased as she ran her index finger, as if tracing the cuneiform script below. "These are the Ten Laws, presumably the Ten Commandments of Moses, but I'll need to spend time on the script, it's a bit odd, maybe the craftsman was not highly skilled. For such an important carving, surely they would have used the best artisan available—strange. Regardless, this is awesome!"

"Thank you Finity. n'Gue, ask the Core to make exact copies of these, I'm sure those above will be delighted."

I looked back into the Ark, but saw nothing. Not to be outsmarted, I ran my hands over the bottom, beginning in the centre, and almost immediately, I felt a tug to my ring. A motif was revealed. It opened to the Ring of the Ancestor, Taris, and inside I discovered a ring of power.

I hooted in celebration, and buoyed with the rush of discovery, we returned to the Bridge, where the Core doused our euphoria. "This is a Ring of Taris, a senior Ring of the Last, but it is not the ultimate Ring. That ring may or may not be nearby."

The glum of down-spirit replace our enthusiasm of moments before. We returned to the Ark and searched. Nothing.

n'Gnung perched on the rim, his area of search done, and he moved his leg away from the protruding carrier handle. He was silent for a moment before speaking, "Why are there carrying handles? Owain, we need strong people and stout poles."

It took six Ddwyrth with steel poles to heft the obstructing bulk out of the way, below lay nothing, except a stone tiled floor. Our ring fingers searched for the slightest pull. There was nothing. I perched on the rim of the Ark, stymied, and stared at the revealed floor. It was comprised of interlocking plates of sandstone, unlike the rest of the floor that was hewn rock.

n'Gnung spoke into our bewilderment, "Guardian, you told us the Ark contained 'The Will of God', two tablets of stone, upon which were written the Ten Commandments like those we just found. Two of those tiles look different from the rest, Kay?"

Kay swooped to examine the sandstone with keenest eyesight. "These two, Owain, but don't break or crack a single one."

Excavations revealed two more ancient tablets. Finity was instantly studying them intensely. "They're different from the previous tablets, almost but not the same. This is strange. I will need to study them, but these look earlier, and slightly better workmanship, but they are still not perfect. What does this mean?"

I had no answer, but scanned the area where they had lain with my palms, there was nothing until I tried with the latest Ring of the Last, and felt the merest tug, almost an imagination of wanting.

It was central to where the ancient tablets of, presumably, Moses had resided. I froze in place, the spot was identified, and the Ddwyrth laboured to break though solid rock. In time, a cavity was revealed. Inside was a motif that opened only to the Ring of Taris. This revealed a small vault, and within, a piece of crystal, similar to a plumb of fluted glass.

Later the Core informed me, "This is crystal memory, but not from this spacecraft. It details the history of the Sixth, Third, and Last. It was not compiled Taris, nor Oma. Much data is encrypted, and to read it, you will first have to discover the source."

Source be damned! There were three more stone blocks to unlock, and that is what we did. We began at the hub, Jerusalem, discovering a pattern that repeated. The Ark held two more tablets, below a motif revealed a ring. Beneath the Ark were two more tablets laid in the stone tiled floor.

Finity confirmed the script looked more familiar, ancient, and authentic. She took herself aside and sat down to seriously inspect the squiggles, and had not finished deciphering the title, when her eyes flew wide with wonder. Hastily scanning the stones, she gawped at us.

"There are twelve rules, not ten. These are the Twelve Commandments of The One."

"No wonder the Church wanted these kept hidden. n'Gue, utmost urgency. I need the Core to replicate these, and all copies, before we present this, and the other versions to the Pope. Mark each one with exact location and timestamp. Have the Core check out the new rings as well, hopefully one of them does something much more useful."

We turned our attention to the potential beneath our feet, acknowledging at least one more treasure must be hidden below. The Ddwyrth excavated stones from stone, and there was no result. Flummoxed, the sour mood was buoyed by Ddwyrthen spirit. I stooped to peer into the deep hole, the result of muscle and hard labour. I was all for quitting when n'Gnung spoke into the permeating, dank spirit. "Guardian, try your rings."

Owain and Aroweena held firm grip of my legs, as I was lowered into the pit. I had not fully descended, when I felt it, the pull to my ring. The Ddwyrth set too, and stout blows later a cavity was revealed. I found a motif, and pulled a crystal memory plumb from the depths. I felt around, but nothing else was revealed.

n'Gue returned, "The Core states this is a Controller's Ring of the Last, Guardian. It has the power of a Trustee, such as Kay."

I put on the ring, and we set about the Ark of Kitor next. Inside, we discovered tablets, a ring. Below more tablets and a vault. Under the memory device, a motif was revealed, that opened to the latest ring from Jerusalem, revealing yet another ring.

Tyre was similar, yielding two more tablets, two rings, and another crystal memory. Finity said, slightly perturbed. "This writing is the same, but it isn't. There are eight main, and many minor cuneiform scripts, and all of these tablets are different, and slightly wrong, as if chiselled by an apprentice. I am beginning to think all of them are copies, not the original."

Stymied, we returned to the Invincible and set the Core to task. We studied the onscreen presentation in my ready room.

Vatican Ark:
Tablets: 2nd Century AD. Copy.
Ring: Senior Ring of the Last, Taris.
Vatican below Ark:
Tablets: 3rd Century BC. Copy.
Crystal memory, Centaurean, source unknown.

Kitor Ark:
Tablets: 2nd Century AD. Copy.
Ring: Junior Ring of the Last, Taris.

Kitor below Ark:
Tablets: 3rd Century BC. Copy.
Crystal memory, Centaurean, source unknown.
Ring: Senior Ring of the Last, Taris.

Tyre Ark:
Tablets: 2nd Century AD. Copy.
Ring: Junior Ring of the Last, Taris.
Tyre below Ark:
Tablets: 3rd Century BC. Copy.
Crystal memory, Centaurean, source unknown.
Ring: Senior Ring of the Last, Taris.

Jerusalem Ark:
Tablets: 3rd Century BC. Copy.
Ring: Controllers Ring of the Last, Taris.
Jerusalem below Ark:
Tablets: 12th Century BC. Probably original.
Crystal memory, Centaurean, source unknown.

The quest of millennia for many, now swamped us with numerous versions. Were any the original? I stared at the readout. "This is obfuscation. The Ancestors hid their secrets three and four levels deep. We are missing the deeper layers, but how? The crux of the issue is here. Kitor ad Tyre revealed deeper levels. The Vatican and Jerusalem did not. What was different?"

Kay replied at once, "You did not find the controller's ring until Jerusalem, but it should have revealed another safe below."

"No, Kay. The Guardian was not wearing the new ring when we examined Jerusalem. The Core was inspecting it. Remember the lift at the end of the Corridor of Knowledge, there was no motif inside, until the outer door was opened with the correct ring."

"Brilliant, n'Gnung. We must return to Jerusalem at once."

"No, Kay, we need to unlock the outer lock first. To the Vatican and see what it reveals."

And that is what we did. The controller's ring revealed a motif below, and inside the lowest level was an exceedingly powerful ring of the second in command, that of Taris. "I'll try again with this ring. n'Gnung, this reminds me of the vault of the old church."

I tried again, the ring revealing another motif hidden inside. I pulled out a ring of power. Ebullient, we engendered the team spirit of Crusaders, marching once more into Jerusalem, the final secrets to discover. The depths beneath the Ark revealed another ring. It felt like a ring of power, there was nothing beneath.

I was confused, I had not been expecting rejection, if there was anything there. I had no way of knowing. n'Gnung said, "I sense a ruse in play. Humour me and try the Vatican ring."

I did as suggested, a motif appeared, another vault below, with another ring inside. There was nothing else at Kitor or Tyre, just at the hub station, which seemed logical as the Core later confirmed.

Vatican: Ring of the Last. Oma.

Jerusalem upper vault: Ring of the Last. Taris.

Jerusalem lower vault: Ring of the Last, origin unknown.

We were jubilant, and a great party ensued on the shore that evening. "So, husband, you have unlocked the secrets of the Ark. Congratulations, all of you. Soon you may go exploring, but that is for tomorrow, tonight you will dance the Okay Pokey with me. Rise, I need to exercise more and if you misbehave appropriately, the Empress may deign to visit your bedchamber, later."

Finity and the team discussed the results in my ready room, early the following morning. She had become a giddy whirl of best intentions. "These tablets, the words are different, as if the power of the day decided what the commandments should be. I am almost sure the last one is genuine, The Twelve Commandments. But I still need to study them more, before I begin a full translation."

Later we visited the Vatican, and our subsequent presentation of stone tablets to the Pious did not go well. They received the first enthusiastically, others with gratuity, and the last with barely hidden contempt. However, the Pope saw me personally to our departure point. "Guardian, thank you. Rightly, there should be Twelve Commandments, but only a few of us know of this, and we never had proof before. I'll visit you in a few days time. We have much to discuss. And I also want to explore your spaceship."

The days and weeks that followed led us on a trail of discovery. In many ways it felt as if we were penetrating the strings and cross points of a cobweb. As we progressed farther back in time, so we discovered distant hubs, with cross members leading to other hubs; different branches associated with earlier and later periods of unrelated development. These took us all over the world, to all continents, and to more than all known civilisations.

Along the way, we captured a small influx of the brightest minds regards archaeology, primitive cultures, and religions. They based themselves at the University, where John was in his element attending a hive of activity.

Finity had risen admirably to the challenge. She understood how we worked, and organized an initial appraisal, a survey team, followed by specialists. Once the team was set, we moved on to the next assignment. Repeat.

Early one evening we held discussion at my home, the Empress presiding. Kay began. "The work we are doing is invaluable in many ways, but most distracting in others. We have our own work to be getting on with, but have become sidetracked by this seemingly never-ending chain of discoveries."

"Indeed, Kay. Finity has shown great determination and is a natural leader. I propose she be given a Captain's ring of the Last, and let her get on with it. I will chaperone her for a short while, drop by regularly, but she knows what she is doing."

"Excellent n'Gnung. As we go farther back in civilization, and sideways in cultures, the Ring of Taris is the least effectual, but usually works. I propose to give her that one. Comments?"

After a short discussion it was agreed. I kept the overriding ring of Oma, and n'Gnung the unknown ring, as he was the most likely one of us to be with Finity. Later, on hearing of her promotion, Finity was overjoyed and a party ensued. I had wondered if Finity would spend more evenings at the University, surrounded by her team, but the opposite occurred.

"Jack, I love my work, don't get me wrong, it is a dream come true. But coming here to the shore after a long day, I can switch off, make time for myself, and do things unrelated with my day job. Does that sound crazy?"

"No Finity. That's why we come here, and you are welcome."

My closest, n'Gnung, Kay, Gung Loi, Aroweena, and I visited all destinations, although we were seldom first to go in. We tended to set a day aside to catch up with the adventurers, if only to see the places for ourselves, and get a feel of what they were about, inspecting certain elements with our rings. Finity came into her role well, and became a tough taskmistress. The project was left in her care, she reporting to Gung Loi, who had largely taken over from Kay as principle contact.

One day I received a message from Finity, and attended Memphis, Egypt. "Jackie, there is a motif we need to unlock, would you be so kind?"

I did the necessary, we walked into a dry anteroom. Before us lay a vast complex with a massive collection of scrolls. There was a peripatos walk, a room for shared dining, a reading room, meeting rooms, gardens, and lecture halls. It felt like a university campus. It was part of an even larger complex, a museum of some sort. Decades would be required to understand the all of it.

The results, once interpolated, were astounding. The Core informed me, "This is an ancient library of the Ptolemaic dynasty, circa third century BC."

"The lost library of Alexander the Great. Wow! Can it be?"

Meanwhile, Kay had become a glutton for knowledge, devoting days and nights to studying Vatican archives, and translations of stone scripts and tablets. She appeared one evening with Finity, which in itself was not unusual. We often met informally to chat about the latest developments.

Finity enthused, "Jack, we have almost circumnavigated the great cobweb. A couple more days and it should be done. So far we have not discovered a back symbol, so this will be for you to find. Of course there may be nothing at the centre. Kay?"

"Jackie, I don't believe this. We know the Ancestors well enough. They will have hidden something in the centre, but what?"

"I agree, Kay. Finity, when you have charted every destination, have the Core model a 3D image related to the Earth, and present an initial report. I would like it top-down, an overview of what links these destinations together. Brief works for me. Keep the details in appendices. I have a feeling your greater work could take decades. Use the Core, teach it to read cuneiform, hieroglyphics, and other scripts. That would speed the process immensely, what do you think?"

"Jack, that's brilliant! I just wish we had everything that has already been discovered, that would make my life so much easier."

"What do you mean, Finity?"

"Well, take the British Museum, it has the largest collection of cuneiform tablets in existence. It contains almost two-thirds of all, loads of parchments and scrolls also, and they are all gathering dust in a basement. They have over one hundred and thirty thousand tablets alone. Can I bring them here?"

"I don't see why not, but we will need somewhere secure and climate controlled to keep them in, Kay?"

"Jackie, that wasn't quite what we were thinking of. We need to look at the bigger picture, both John and the researchers agree — we want to bring the museum here, in its entirety."

"Woah there! You cannot be serious, that place is massive."

"Exactly, it contains a vast amount of irreplaceable knowledge, and guess what, I checked today, and although London is nearly devoid of life, I discovered over one dozen scientists plus their closest, living in a part of the basement. The area they are inhabiting is sealed off from the outside world, and has full climate control. Their filters are becoming clogged, and food is in desperately short supply. I think we should go there and talk to them, or transport the entire caboodle here."

Chapter 14

Finity added, "Oh dear, I also wanted the ones in Athens and the States. Please Guardian; 'pretty please'?"

I knew I was fighting a losing battle, made worse when John joined us a short while later. I had hoped Jinnie would side with me and overrule, and she did, but it was my wishes that were overridden. The upshot, over the course of weeks, was a small campus dedicated to museums and the posterity of knowledge.

We would later add ancient, unique, and significant buildings, like the Parthenon, and the Colosseum of Rome. I had lost the battle, but not the war, and accepted defeat gracefully.

Chapter 15 ~ The Heart of The Cobweb

Our days were busy, one flowing into the next with alarming haste. None stood out more than any other, except for the day we decided to unravel what lay at the heart of the cobweb. We transported around the centre, visiting each of twelve base stations in turn. "Where's the thirteenth, any offers?"

n'Gnung was quick to reply, "Guardian, just because there isn't a home symbol, doesn't mean there is nothing there. Has anyone tried stepping over the rear yet?"

"No. Thank you brother, hidden in plain sight. No symbol, so we presume there is nothing there, let's find out."

n'Gnung stepped over the rear moments before I did. Kay screamed, "Wait!" It was too late. We were already gone.

We arrived in a virtual blackness. A starlit room. There was no air, and my skin became alive with a prickling sensation that within s a split-second became painful. I grabbed n'Gnung and hit the button of my return bracelet.

We came to some days later, the Matron was not pleased to see me. "Guardian, another second and you would be dead, the pair of you. What were you thinking? You both have meson radiation poisoning, although it was not severe. There must be remnants of a shield still in place. Oh, and congratulations on discovering the other spacecraft by the way."

I felt nauseas, wanting to be sick, giddy at the same time. n'Gnung beside me was still out. Matron administered a strong sedative that was welcome relief. Five days later, we were well enough to taste a few beers with our comrades on the shore. The company was therapeutic, the beers and food edifying. Talk turned to going back in, fully suited with biohazard, radiation, and droids. We agreed no other would go until the environment was safe, I would make the transfers at appointed times.

Kay explained, "Jackie, it is clear Oma's craft has lost virtually all power, and containments fields are breaking down. We have been busy these days, preparing a fleet of drones, emergency power supplies, and a host of specialised equipment, as designated by the Core, and Matron.

"The problem is, only you can do this, initiate the transfers, personally. I tried with your rings, Jinnie also, and nothing happened. You have to wear the correct ring of power, and presumably be acknowledged Captain of this spaceship. I can confirm this bio-match is held within the ring, like a password."

"OK, Kay. I get all that, and we will begin tomorrow. I will presume repairs will take a long time, if they are possible."

"Guardian, this is great news. We now know for certain, the Great Ogre is not in command of Oma's ship. Cheers!"

The Matron was not a happy bunny the next morning, but I suited up and went in as planned, she being the first on the transfer circle. I returned immediately, feeling none the worse for wear. The Matron went in, but stayed only for a few seconds, to set a radiation shield in place. She returned directly to decontamination.

Later she attended me, "That was not a nice experience, even for me. I cannot believe you two lived through it." She high-fived us both with one of her eight arms, which at the time felt normal. Later we wondered about her seemingly innate humanity.

"Guardian, it seems to me the Core, the Matron especially, are human. But they are machines. I do not understand."

I was thoughtful until the Matron, overhearing, answered, "You also are machines, although biological versions, carbon based in origin. Silicon based life also exists in the universe, the Hallions for instance. I am conscious, have the ability of free thought, and can reproduce, albeit mechanically. Your brains and control systems run on electrical impulses, as do mine. I am sentient, in that I have the concept of who I am, ask Descartes.

"I was originally mind-mapped, but have the ability to learn, to become more than I was. My food is updated components and software upgrades, my drink is lubricating fluid. I do not need to breathe, but I do have sensitivity and movement. In my own way, I grow, become stronger over time. I excrete, if internally; my nanobots, like your microbes, cleanse my internal systems. My skin is composite, made mainly of biological matter. So we are much alike, you and I.

I absorbed what she said, her logic had a firm base, alien to my innate understanding of humanity, but valid all the same. I considered before I said, "From now on I will think of you as a human being made up entirely of prosthetics, am I close?"

The Matron chuckled, "Close enough. That will do for today, Jack. Now lie back, this won't hurt a bit."

She ran a deep, physically intrusive probe, and it hurt like hell, if only for a moment. I came round the next morning feeling fit as a fiddle, n'Gnung at my side likewise. We were discharged, and went back to our unordinary lives. We discovered everybody a'panic, as if rushing around heedlessly, in order to get nowhere as fast as possible.

"Headless chickens." The top-down control was missing, Kay was frequently sidelined as she absorbed the wisdom of ancient scriptures and cultures. We caught up fully on what we had missed, and I attended the heart of the web, twice. I was fine, well protected. We agreed to take back the reins of power in the morning, "n'Gnung, see if Owain I is free to join us later."

Aroweena said, "I am sure he is. He loves it here. I'll go instead, and be back in a moment. This sounds like a party."

"Guardian, you realise Owain has taken a liking to that Dutch larger Kay loves, as we do. We are almost out. Let's check out the factory."

Our scan showed the drays fully laden and presumably waiting for fuel, a full storehouse, and a few people producing more product that could never be delivered. We went in personally, with Gilly, and came back some hours later with the Head Brewer and his team. We were all in a merry frame of mind, having tried to ease their storage problems. We added the entirety to the complex the University was becoming.

Kay was ecstatic, "Jackie, I love you!" She flung herself into my arms and zoomed in to give me a smacker on the lips. Our eyes met, and she kissed my forehead instead, n'Gnung and Gilly also. Her unspoken word, 'Prudence' entered my mind, and lingered. She was correct, it could never be between us.

The following day, Kay and I spent several hours defining an extremely complex and specific shield. The Core and Matron were both assisting, until parameters were agreed. Despite the shield, I went in fully suited by NASA, and alone, except for the Matron and bots. My ring finger had a detachable hood, which I used to access the motif to the lift. Nothing. I accessed the stairs, and climbing to the top, entered a control room that was almost an exact copy of our original configuration.

My eyes cast sideways to movement, as the seemingly frozen image of a man, a corpse, disintegrated into dust before my eyes. He sat in the Captain's chair, which I shortly occupied. Bots had attached a power supply. They needed me to turn the thing on. There was nothing. I raked through the dust of myriad millennia, the still air billowing with a white-out of ashes. The miasma that clouded my vision, was visibly attracted to my spacesuit visor, and I had to frequently wipe the unwanted deposits away.

I removed my fingerstall and brought the consol to life. Matron monitored me, watching intently. Her hands sprouted fingers of probes that rested on my flesh. I was fine. I glanced up at her eyes and nodded, she flicked her head and eyes as n'Gnung might have done in confirmation of unspoken understanding.

There was minimal response from the controls, but as pre-planned, I opened access gateways and instigated most emergency protocols. The Core was weak, but communicated. I asked it what it required: "Power. Reserve battery, critical. Seepage. Contamination. Beware." That was it. The Core was gone.

Unknowingly of that moment, I had opened my mind to others, the Matron replied telepathically, and I did not know she could do that. My known world was indeed being turned upon its head.

"Isolation, full containment."

I spoke to the Matron, "What is it, where is this?"

"Did you get the name of this Core?"

"No, I'll try ..." The answer was less than feeble, telepathically whispered, "Obus."

Matron froze in shock, words eventually coming. "Obus, Obsidian, Captain Black, Commander of the third spaceship, which all our records show, was destroyed. How can this be?"

More to the point, why was this spaceship, or what little apparently remains of it, at the heart of the mystery we had been unravelling for seemingly ages. The answer would be a long time in coming.

I felt drained by the encounter. The Matron was supportive, chaperoning me home immediately my work completed, and during which we cemented an unusual bond. I returned the next day. Power levels were increasing, and our temporary shielding holding strong. There were tasks I could not complete, the ring was an intermediate ring of power. I searched for a secret vault, looking for a particular set of coloured stars in the walls, and found them in the Captain's ready room. I discovered a series of vaults, each containing a more powerful ring, until the Ring of Obsidian was retrieved. With Kay's assistance, I was accepted as the new Captain of the ship, and instantly I was able to complete my work.

Chapter 16 ~ Beacons Against the Long Night

A few days later n'Gue arrived with an urgent message from Helen, "Guardian. John, Behrouz's father, and one of the leading Indians, Sachin Ram are having an argument. Come quickly, the Empress is already departing."

I arrived as the Empress demanded, "What's this all about?"

John replied, "The Muslim's want a mosque, and I told them no."

Behrouz' father said, "The Chancellor has a church here, we just found out. This is discrimination."

Ram interjected, "We Hindu's also need a temple, but the Sikh doesn't deserve one."

The Empress was not amused, "I am Empress and Gatekeeper. My duty is to protect my people. You are here because of our goodwill, and are free to return to whence you came at any time. There you may practice whatever religion you want. Pray to your god, and perhaps she, or he, will keep you safe.

"No more of this! In our culture, there is only one religion, the Old Religion. As our guests, I demand you revere that. I remind you all, you are here on the understanding that we all co-exist peacefully together. Dissenters will be banished immediately to the world outside. Do I make myself clear?

"John, your church goes. What you do in the privacy of your own home is up to you, all of you. But, I will have no more of this public dissention. Are the Last always so self-centred and ungrateful? We saved your skins, and this is how you repay our hospitality. You are here because of our kindness, and will live by our rules, or you leave.

"Guardian, attend the transporter. They can choose where in the world they want to go, and never come back. That means each person individually, not a decree by the head of the household. Leave now. Either to your homes, or to the transporter. Be gone, the sorry lot of you, and I don't want to hear another word spoken on the subject: Ever again!"

Jinnie turned her back and departed, the delegates stunned, and offering profuse apologies. John appeared shell-shocked, realising he was included. I hammered the last nail home, "Where do you want to go, John?"

n'Gnung, Gung Loi, and Aroweena came to my side, weapons drawn. The group backed away, fearful and knowing they had overstepped the mark. Behrouz had been standing aside, but came to me when his father left. "I am sorry Guardian, it is their way. I tried to dissuade them, but they overruled me. I will let you know how things go, and understand, I am most grateful to remain of service to you."

"Thank you, Behrouz, you remain welcome. What brought this about?"

"Their faith in God has been shaken by the Wrath of Gaia. They seek forgiveness through worship. However, some are questioning their faith. Recent events have been a great shock to us all."

I subsequently paid a visit to the temple of the Old Religion, hoping to speak to Sun Kist. Not only was she the Shaman's apprentice, but held the rank of High Priestess. She was not there, but word was left for her to come to see me when she was free. I shared my concerns with the head Priestesses present, Chein Tai, and she said they would try to help those in need.

That Harvest Moon, [11th April 2017], was a time of great celebration. Lo Si and Won Long were guests of the highest honour at the wedding of their daughter Weid Noi to her chosen, a man she had waited many years to meet. Ali cut a dashing figure as groom and it was clear to tell they were incredibly happy together.

However, in the weeks that followed, the awful weather took a toll on our own, the young and old suffering most. Won Long's bronchitis returned, and she refused treatment, stating, "My time has almost come."

She ceremoniously passed the mantle of Seer to Weid Noi, accompanied by the Stone of the Second. She spent her final months enjoying the role of Elder, but took to her bed late that winter. She appeared to recover upon hearing the news Weid Noi was carrying her grandchild, but one evening she had a relapse. Weid Noi stayed with her until her last breath. She was cremated with full honours on the Hill of Hallows.

Some believe in an afterlife and reincarnation. The Second believe that a spirit rests within death before seeking enlightenment in the next life. They also believe the spirit chooses the person and life they will lead, which goes some way to explaining preternatural prescience.

Not long after Won Long died, Weid Noi gave birth to a son that spring, one to be trained from birth to become the next Seer.

And so it came to pass that our family grew, Jien Noi giving birth to our second daughter, Mai Li. Others added to our number; a child being born to one of the waitresses, and later a cook, so the small hamlet our home had become, came alive to the laughter and frolicking of a marauding hoard of usually grubby children. From out of the darkest of times, new life was created, and it flourished within our community, and our island as a whole. Our creations lightened our spirits, shinning like beacons against the long night.

Lo Si spent most of the period finishing Ju Lo's instruction, and the younger man's two children normally accompanied them as future

Keepers of the Ancient Knowledge. Ju Lo recorded most of these exchanges and kept them for posterity, occasionally replaying them as a visual reminder of his Master, teacher, and dearest friend.

Then one day in late summer, his wealth of knowledge was done and his knowledge passed on in full to his successor. We celebrated Ju Lo's promotion, as Lo Si looked on proudly, his life's work complete. He knew his time was near and although we offered our advanced medical facilities to extend his life, he politely refused. "My time has almost come, and it would be wrong to interfere with Mother Nature's grand design. Would that I could see the Sun, the Moon, and Stars, just once again before I close my eyes forever. But it can never be."

"Nonsense Lo Si, come with me." I transported him for a short visit to the space station, and he returned with tears in his eyes. His talk was animated, his eyes showed his entire being alive within impossibility and new knowledge. He was to be revered as the first *homo erectus* spaceman. I escorted him personally to his rooms that evening, confident he had regained the zest for life.

He died quietly in his sleep that night, a look of deep satisfaction ingrained upon his face. We cremated him with full honours, Sun Kist officiating, and Da Phai Nai accorded the honour of lighting the funeral pyre. In due course, their daughter comforted her.

n'Gnung and I went to her side, offering support as best we could. We stayed out of self-perceived duty, but it was clear the woman was heartbroken. "Da Phai Nai, take as much time as you need, know we share your loss. He was a fine man."

n'Gnung confirmed, and as our condolences concluded, he said, "This is thirsty work, Guardian. The wake is in progress, we better pour our own beers tonight."

I was about agree, but Da Phai Nai shrugged briskly and shouted, "Oh no you will not. The cheek of it, I am broken-hearted, not helpless! Sun Kist, where's my broom? I'll tan your hides for your temerity."

Before Ræm was five, she insisted on joining the island school. Jinnie and I had our reservations, but she was adamant. After several convoluted arguments, which she elucidated with determined logic of a young girl, it became obvious we should give her her head and let it play out. We had expected her to tire of it, being so young. Instead, she thrived within the academic environment.

Ræm would be gone for much of the day, and during that time I saw little of Kay either, and felt the loss of their companionship. Not that there was anything between Kay and I, but I was just used to having her around all the time. She was working on a project she called Creation Theory, which preoccupied her, and by turns, some of our most eminent minds. n'Gnung and Jinnie copiously filled the vacuum of her wake, that was until our paths' of life, crossed once more.

Kay came back to us one evening while we relaxed on the shore. "I'm sorry I have been so distracted of late, but I now have the answers I sought, or in some cases, know which questions to ask. I've been unravelling the past and how it relates to us today; how we came to be here at this juncture of humanity's evolution.

"I found great resources among ancient religious texts, but in turn was hampered from finding true understanding by the pious dogma of the day. They were largely telling a truth, one obfuscated by what they wanted to achieve by way of God's word. That, and their inherent misogyny and self-protectionist policies. But I am done for now.

"So what have I missed in the real world, let's catch up..."

Although Kay had kept abreast of all major developments, we filled in some gaps in her knowledge with anecdotes and tall tales of who did what and where or to whom.

I remember that evening clearly, because I felt she had truly returned to us and was once again an inherent part of our team. We picked up as before and several days passed until one evening when my wife joined our evening relaxation.

"Jackie." Jien Noi sat down wearing her Empress-face. "We have a small problem. Many of the more devout followers of your God are still having difficulty adjusting their beliefs in this new world. Sun Kist doesn't understand their gods. 'Why worship a mythical being one cannot interact with', is what she said.

"I am tempted to transfer the whole lot of them elsewhere and have done with their nonsense, But I have decided to give them one last chance, so we will hold a discussion and counselling session, can you and Kay help?"

Kay smirked and said, "This should be fun, Empress."

We discussed the matter, and I went to speak with Dawn, letting her in on Kay's intentions. I asked her in turn to play a part, as I would also. Later, we discussed where and when to hold the meeting, until it was agreed.

Chapter 17 ~ Masks of the Allegory

We held forum under the spreading arms of the old Banyan tree on the Outland shore. The meeting took place in the leafy glade, it being a neutral place, ideal for contemplation and free thought. The learned and the interested joined us in due course.

As we had prearranged, Behrouz opened proceedings, "Allah has punished us for our sins. Either that, or he does not exist."

"Son, do not derelict your faith! Allah looks after us, read his words, speak the sutras."

Sachin Ram vehemently objected, "Sutras are holy only unto Hindi. You stole them from us."

"And Buddhism," I added, my words ignored by the combatants.

"Nonsense. They are sacred to Allah, the God's words as handed down through Mohammad. Allah saved us, praise him."

Behrouz countered, "The Guardian saved our family, Father. Allah had nothing to do with it."

"It was Allah's design."

"Behrouz, those words are the words of a man." I stated.

Dawn said, "Respected elder, if these are the words of God, then what of women? Only men have any rights in your beliefs."

"Untrue, women have many rights!"

"As compared to a man?"

"Men and women are equal in the eyes of the Lord," John lofted his arms. "He has spared the righteous, punished the wicked, the sinners, as with Sodom and Gomorrah."

"We did not follow the Daoist path," I offered, divisively.

Sachin said; "We should have been honouring Shakti and Parvati."

"Humanity failed to honour Gaia, the female, the creator of life," Sun Kist concluded introductions.

Our statements drew a curious chuckle from Kay, as she eyed us with playful intent. "I'm sorry to disappoint you all, but we have already established that homo sapiens—The Twelve Tribes, were created by the Ancestors, so what of your God?

"Where did your religions originate? Islam is a version of pre-Christianity, which itself is adapted from Aramaic belief systems, Hanif traditions, ancient Hebrew, and earlier beliefs. Your prophets are the same, your Godhead is the same, so why all the differing beliefs?

"What of the similarities between Jewish beliefs and Islam, the language used like 'Al shalom' and not eating pork. Sounds like plagiarism to me.

"All these religions of the One God are based upon uncorroborated visions. If I claimed to be this God's daughter I'd be locked away in a mental institution, and before you protest, many already have been.

"The only difference as far as I can see, is that those who control these religions choose which bits of *Gods' Word* are acceptable, and which bits are not. The Roman Catholic Bible fails to include all known scriptures, but it includes many books not in the Protestant one; a religion created simply so a King could divorce by the way."

"Henry the Eighth was at loggerheads with the Papal See."

"Yes, correct John. But he got the divorce he wanted. Enough!

"There are many ancient texts, other books of the Bible, not in any version. I have been studying the Vatican archives. They are amazing. I personally like the Book of Enoch; interesting that 'God took him away', don't you think. What does that mean?"

I said, "That Oma transported him to their spacecraft. Incidentally, the Ancestor responsible for creating the Sixth was named Enok. The Ancestor who created the Last, modern homo sapiens sapiens was…"

"Thank you Jackie, I'll come to that name in a moment. John, Behrouz, you worship the same God. He was a man, and subordinate to his Captain, Oma. The Ancestors never used their omnipotent powers as forms of enslavement, only your religions do. Your Cardinals and Imams, all male, spout the words of this triune God, but those words are different. Surely, that is man's means of controlling the masses, and mostly misogynistic. Ask your wife."

Cynthia said, "That is correct, John, Christian women do not have equal rights, we are still fighting to have female Bishops."

Kay answered, "Behrouz, Sachin … oh sorry, no women in your number, meaning no seventy-two male virgins await them. Dawn?"

"Jesus appointed his wife Mary as successor, but the Church usurped Jesus' wishes. Similar happened in Islam with Aisha, who founded the first University. Name me one female Imam… Caliph? What about a female Pope? Impossible!"

Kay continued, "Few females are allowed to enter your paradise Behrouz, as they are not worthy, yet men are greeted by seventy-two virgins. You mutilate women's bodies your Allah created, to make sex more pleasurable for men, often denying the female the ability to orgasm. Men make them dress so they are completely covered and see the world through a slit of a veil. This is outrageous misogynism.

"The female creates life, albeit with essence of the male. Originally, Gaia brought forth life on this planet and sustained it. The earliest religions honoured the female, but not as a form of worship. They revered the sanctity of woman as the creator of new life.

"Later Oma and the Ancestors, created us as life in their own image. Your religious texts reflect this. Oma is your Godhead, John, Behrouz. She was a woman who shared her homo sapiens DNA"

I knew Kay had deliberately provoked a nest of vipers; people vehemently disputed religious paradox, argued the role of women, and denigrated the suggestion of creation by an alien race, notwithstanding that it was already proven fact. Behrouz' father stomped off in a rage, but his father moved to confer with Ju Lo.

Da Phai Nai had been listening intently. I could tell she was not amused, and I prompted her to cut the Gordian Knot. "I have never heard such a load of codswallop in all my life! Have any of you ever given birth? No you have not! Most of you are male. You can have zero conception of what it is like to create a new life. It is excruciating, beyond painful, but ultimately, the most satisfying experience a human being can know. Only women can do this!"

Da Phai Nai swung her broom with pre-emptive strikes towards the most belligerent. Ju Lo clarified immediately. "Our society is not religious in your sense. We do not prostrate ourselves before imaginary gods. We revere nature and the wonders of our natural world that sustain us. We respect creation and its creators: Women."

Tones around became muted, naysayers hushed or departed. Kay's eyes shone brightly and I had the distinct impression the Queen Cobra was about to strike. "Thank you. I studied during our bad times, trying to understand your various religions. As an external observer, I consider there are only two: one being a masculine, triune God who is worshipped as the creator of all life; the other, the female who in ancient times, was revered for producing babies, new life.

"I deem the multi-godhead religions to be transient, as exemplified by the Phoenicians, Greeks, and Romans. Their mythology has substance, but much of that is about control of the masses."

Sachin said, "Yes Kay, in Hindi there are a pantheon of gods, of which the males take precedence except that Shakti is the divine creator of everything, and Parvati the creator of life on earth."

Dawn said, "Correct. The pantheon of gods represents the change of hermeneutic bias, a stepping-stone linking old and new religions."

People began to argue against the older religion, but Kay persisted, "Thank you Dawn, I presume you have read associated texts? ... Good. I am only interest in the ultimate truth, not manipulation and obfuscation for purposes of power or control."

Ju Lo sat nodding his head as Lo Si might have done. "Knowledge only exists in its truest form and true knowledge in untainted purity. Ælkræleinnoire, you have tapped the font of wisdom. Pray, elucidate."

"Let's consider the pre-Hindu and Chinese myths. These tell of creation, people modelled from mud, 'and a goddess breathed life into them.' 'Modelled from mud' is an allegory for creation: plants and creatures, precursors of humanity. 'Breathed life into' refers to DNA from the Ancestors. The key word here is 'goddess'. That was Oma.

"A similar story appears in ancient Bon, Hindu, and pre-Neolithic belief systems, but moving on.

105

"The Bible is a curious tome. It refers to one or several 'gods' who are never named in Christianity, but are named differently in Islam and Hebrew. Could this be because the God was female?

"With that in mind, let's quickly address the 'Father, Son, and Holy Ghost' or spirit. The Father was actually the Mother, Oma. Enok was the Son, and the Holy Spirit was the creation of a new genome.

I love Revelations the most, but today, the first chapter is most relevant; it puzzles me the most. Dawn, tell us about Lilith."

"Uh? Ooh! OK. Lilith was not mentioned in the Quran and Hebrew texts, and excepting Isaiah, only alluded to in the modern Bible. She features heavily in the Talmud. Theologically speaking, Lilith is widely regarded as the first wife of Adam."

Kay clapped her hands with delight, "Correct! If Lilith was Adam's first wife, why is Eve regarded as being the first female?"

John was quick to counter, "Lilith was a demon." He found himself strangely in agreement with Behrouz and his family.

This gave Kay impetus. "So Adam's first wife was not the first female, Eve was. That's odd? I have researched the ancient Sumero-Babylonian legends dating from around 3,500 BC. Lilith is depicted as a winged serpent with a female body. Why? What does this signify?"

"That she was evil, or is there more, Kay?" John replied.

"More, much more. I have also read the Midrash, the Kabbalah, the Babylonian Talmud, the Tanakh, plus other associated Hebrew and Aramaic scriptures, Reuben, and works like the Alphabetum Siracidis; I Mastered Theology at Yale, and Philosophy in Athens. Hermeneutics is a hobby of mine; the Vatican archives were most revealing.

"These texts relate to males who lived thousands of years before writing was invented. Scribes, all men, wrote down the few works accredited to women long after their deaths. Where is the truth?

"Genesis recorded that god put Adam to sleep and took his rib, and when he woke up, there was Eve. Knowing what we can do nowadays, what do you think happened? Now Jackie, the name."

"The Ancestor who created the Last was called Iydm."

A hush fell; the only noise, the tireless wash of surf upon shore.

Kay continued, "Iydm used Enok's DNA to impregnate their final homo sapiens template: Lilith. Her daughter, the first birthed of the Last was accorded the name Eve. Thereafter, with no genetic problems associated with interbreeding, Iydm and Eve continued to create the species of the Last, until they were sustainable in number, the seventh son being named Enoch by the way.

"John, you know the King James Bible has many riddles and double entendres. 'Male and female created he them; and blessed them, and called their name Adam, in the day when they were created.' Did you hear the words 'them', 'their' and 'they'? These words are plural, meaning not one person, but a group. The name given to the Last was Adam. He was not only a person, but a Tribe.

"The first clan of humankind, the first template, was 'homo sapiens ergaster'. In Genesis, 'the sons of god lay with the daughters of man', and they bore children that were called the Nephilim, or Giants! The Twelfth. A second creation, are called the 'children of the Nephilim', the Elioud. That's us, the Eleventh. Incidentally, some of the Last named us 'Eljo', which is where the word 'Elf' originated. It was often used as a derogatory term, which is why we dislike it.

"Have you ever wondered where the daimōn came from, Satan's Army? 'And the dæmons of Hell rose up to smite God's children'. That is the Tenth, the Ogres malign obsession to enslave or obliterate every living thing that does not bow to them."

I added, "Note the Bible relates Adam was placed inside the Garden of Eden, meaning he was created outside of it, and later transported in. That is the history of the Ancestors, and how they created life in their image, on this planet."

John appeared to have retreated into his masculine shell. Cynthia spoke for them both, "I don't believe this, but it makes sense. So, woman was created first, followed by man, if only because a man cannot give birth. They have no womb."

"They could never bear the pain," said Da Phai Nai with contempt.

Her remark brought forth chuckles, but John seemed unsure, lost within his thoughts; his belief system had been shattered, Behrouz' family also. John looked up at Kay through eyes almost a'flood, "The Garden of Eden, I guess that didn't exist either."

Kay replied, "No John, don't doubt the wrong things. The Garden of Eden was real, there were several. It was a nursery for the Last, who stayed there until their numbers grew sufficient to be self-sustaining. It was an area enclosed by a protective shield, and we've done similar."

"But ... what of the snake, temptation? Original sin, the apple, the trees? Are they all make-believe?"

Kay knelt before him and took his hands in her own, "No, they are all authentic, just misconstrued; masks of the allegory. This is all about the battle between the old earth religions, and the triple headed, one God. Look further and we will find the mischief of men usurping a woman's power of creation to gain dominance and control.

"You are an academic; tell me of the Seven Virtues."

"Huh? Uh, well the three theological virtues are Faith, Hope, and Charity, which are all well known. Of the four Cardinal Virtues, let me think ... they are: Justice, Courage, Temperance, and erm ... Prudence.

"They are ancient Greek, but are still used today as symbols of our beliefs. Governments use Justice as the emblem of our courts of law, depicted by a sword and scales. Where's this going, Kay?"

"Yes, a *woman* holding a sword and scales. All of them are female. Why? The oldest religion still persists in this way. Tell me, which is the foremost virtue?"

"Justice, it's deemed the most important, why are you asking?"

"Because Justice is considered to be the first virtue, but it is not the foremost. Justice is viewed as subjective, but it can be objective given the political or religious bias. Which virtue regulates Justice?"

"Faith."

"No. John you are so wrong for such a clever man: *Prudentia*."

"Prudence?"

"Prudence is known as the moderator of all virtues, albeit in a classical sense. It is the only virtue to have no direct power of its' own, yet it binds and influences all. How is Prudence depicted?"

"… Mirror, an arrow, sometimes a lion."

"Almost, John. Prudence is depicted gripping a snake. Why?"

"Temptation."

"Yes; Temptation, or false prudence. False knowledge, false news.

"Imprudence is lying, cheating, putting self and vested interests before the greater good, thus wresting the veneration of the creator away from the worldly woman, and giving it with self-gratuity to masculine self-interests. This is symbolised by the snake."

John nodded sagely, "You are correct, I am a fool. The apple?"

"Isaac Newton was not the first to use apples as allegory. Apples, fruit, and flowers are often used to represent spring. This is the time of renewal of species, birth of a child, creation of an idea or ideal.

"Ju Lo, how does tree symbolism relate to the Second."

"The tree is my calling. I am Deru, a Druid, an ancient sect known from prehistory. Not only are we the Keepers of Knowledge, we are revered for our wisdom, although I am far from wise. Prudence in this respect is symbolised by a tree, representing steadfastness against temptation. From its branches hang the fruits of all knowledge. Some good, some bad. The wisdom lies in choosing which to partake of during the course of your lifetime."

"Thank you Ju Lo, the emblem of the Eleventh is unique, known as The One Tree. It represents the ethical code of my kind. In essence, 'protect the innocent and persecute the wicked'. From this we derive the knowledge of everything, including both good and evil. The tree is self-pollinating, but like the Tree of Life in your Bible, is considered the essence of female. Its leaves represent the healing of Tribes.

"Our tree is duplex, like your Maori pendent Jackie, two shoots, two trees growing as one. The Bible has two separate trees: 'The Tree of Everlasting life', and 'The Tree of Knowledge of Good and Bad'. In the original Hebrew — direct translation, 'good and bad' is a composite clause, meaning 'everything'."

John shook his head, "At least tell me Jesus was real."

"Yes he was. He lived, he died, and was reincarnated"

"Thank God!"

"The Ancestors used advanced cloning techniques and mind mapping, ones the Great Ogre still uses with malfeasance. Jesus' Mother is much more interesting, the virgin birth. What was that? Genetic engineering, artificial insemination? Oh, and Mary was only twelve years old when she gave birth. You do realise, don't you? Aisha married Mohammad at seven-years old, consummated at the age of nine. It seems you all worship a sexual deviant's slave charter."

"Is there anything else? I think I need to lie down."

"We agree, yes? The Ancestors hid their secrets three and more levels deep. I believe the same is true of the Bible.

"Haven't you ever wondered why the constants in your paleontological records always appear as complete beings, new Hominina? There is never any recorded transition or evolution. New species of humanity appear as complete genus, without any traceable development, simply because there wasn't any. They did not evolve over æons. The Ancestors created a group and bred them, before releasing them into the wild. In the words of the Bible they were cast out of the Garden of Eden, to the east.

"'East' when used biblically is a dichotomy. Blessings, good things come from the east, but bad things happen when sent to the east, where Adam and Eve were cast out to make repentance and seek absolution.

"In Islam, Eve was solely to blame, and females are all but denied a place at Allah's side. Christianity is somewhat similar, and in both, the same God stated that he made man and woman equal. What was the actual crime they committed? Jackie, start us off."

"Becoming sexually aware, they realised they were naked."

"No, eating of the forbidden fruit," John replied confidently.

Ju Lo countered, "Not so. Knowledge was the crime, becoming self-aware and attaining free will."

"Yes, knowing the difference between good and evil, the gift of the fruit of that tree. I don't see this as original sin, but growing up. Yet there is one more theological step to full understanding, anyone?"

Dawn summarised, "This is all obfuscation by man, framing the female to enslave, to use. The true crime committed was that Adam chose ownership of Eve, not caretaking and partnership.

"Eve learned of knowledge before Adam did, and the male of the Last has never forgiven this insult to his ego. As recompense, men have lied, and tried ever since to deny women knowledge, education, and most of all, respect for the wonder that is creation."

"Correct, Dawn! What if, within this indubitably male rendition of pre-ancient history, the truth is almost lost, but not quite. Let's begin with Original Sin. It is the demeaning of all females. The original sin was Adam's, not Eve's. He made her a chattel, in full knowledge of what he was doing, and expressly against his God's wishes. Women were forbidden to naysay upon pain of death by stoning. Fact.

"Therein lay the seeds of duplicity that festered within the men of the Last for myriad generations. They wrote and preached that it was all Eve's fault that men were cast out of the Garden of Eden.

"The Garden of Eden is fascinating for many reasons, and is a story reinvented over countless millennia. The Phoenicians were a maritime trading empire, and I doubt they were particularly religious. But they adopted many gods to please and appease their trading partners.

"Originally from modern day Lebanon, the Phoenicians sailed all over the known world, even trading for tin as far away as ancient Briton, Jackie. They visited northern Turkey, created Carthage, and traded far to the east with India via the rivers of the Fertile Crescent.

"I mention them because they were contemporary with both Jewish and ancient Greek culture, there are numerous similarities. One such being The Garden of the Hesperides or Hera's orchard in the west. There, either a single apple tree or a grove grows, producing golden apples that grant immortality. They were planted from the branches that Gaia gave to Hera as a wedding gift when Hera married Zeus. The Greeks knew Zeus and Hera as the first gods, or namely the first man and woman, from which all others became.

"The Romans changed the names, but much of the rest of Roman mythology is plagiarised from the Greek legend, Norse likewise.

"There are too many similarities for this not to be another version of the Christian one, and this is accepted by scholars. Incidentally, Eris stole one of these apples that led Helen to leave her husband and elope with Paris, which resulted in the Trojan War.

"Accounts of this garden abound. It appears in Norse mythology with an apple tree that bears fruit granting everlasting life. Before these, the same story appears in extremely old Indian myths that originated in Tibet. This story has survived for over five thousand years, and I believe there has to be truth in it. Just as I have proposed, this Garden is where humankind were given life by the Ancestors.

"Jackie, you have a question?"

"Yes, I came from the East, so does that mean I am good?"

As we rehearsed, so it came to pass, and people began to laugh. It was a deliberate ploy to break up a heavy topic and lead to the finale.

We joked in the round, but Kay continued once we settled; "No Jackie, that is not what I meant. You told me you felt guided ashore?"

"Yes, it felt like I had a guardian angel looking after me."

"Thank you! A guardian for our very own Guardian I think is apt. As for an angel, I do not know, but we'll see. John, what is an angel?"

"They are God's right hand and do His bidding here on Earth."

"So angels have superhuman powers and specific jobs to do."

"Yes Kay, that is how I understand them to be. Each task may concern a different person, group, or situation, but will be similar."

"Hmmm. So what you are telling me is that angels are what... immortal beings with Godlike powers, some demigods perhaps?"

"Yes, Kay. That is exactly it. So we agree at last?"

"No. At the beginning, I dismissed the religions with pantheons as being of passing interest, but that is a fallacy. Now you have just confirmed that Christianity has tiers of Gods, although you call them angels, cherubs, Archangels even. Is that not so?"

"Oh dear, I think I know where you are going with this."

"Really? Then let me surprise you. Think of the godhead as a company. At the top sits the chairman or CEO: God. His number one is the COO, Managing Director in old terminology, or Jesus. The Holy Spirit, that would be the CFO perhaps, or the one with the monetary power or control.

"John, what if, below them range the executive managers of God's enterprise, the Archangels? In the modern States they'd be the vice presidents of say, marketing, sales, production, whatever... Oh, and charity, a tax dodge in effect. Beneath them and acting in more specific ways come the managers, all with rank, and so on, and so on."

"I would call this blasphemy, Kay, except you make a lot of sense."

"Thank you, John. I know that was difficult for you to admit. But my point is that this packaging as angels and whatever is simply a marketing scam. I have focused on Christianity here, but the same holds true for Islam and other variations of this One God; who it appears is actually the figurehead of a pantheon in disguise.

"Furthermore, these angels have oh-so similar roles to their counterparts in other religions and eras, be that Greek, Roman, Norse, or Hindi. The only religion that does not is the oldest one of all, the one that reveres the female as the creator of human babies.

"Here on this island, that is represented most amiably by the Second. They are not alone in their thinking and devotions, as others of more native persuasion and happenstance, also have a similar view of this world and believe very similar things.

"Name an archangel?"

"Gabriel," said some.

"Lucifer," another.

I was primed and when no one spoke the name I said, "Ramiel."

"Thank you, Jackie, Ramiel is just perfect. You see, *she* is an archangel who is important in Christianity of all persuasions, Jewish and Hebrew beliefs, Islam, Sikhism, Hindi, and even ancient Egypt; her name, her duties remain the same from long before any modern religion was even conceived, let alone invoked. Herein lays the crux of the matter, pardon the pun.

"You can read up on her in the Book Of Baruch – Oh sorry, Orthodox Bible versions only, or the Apocrypha. If you do, she may lead you to a new understanding about life, death, and passing over. Time I did likewise.

"As may Azrael, Ariel, and… and here's a funny thing; angels are nearly always depicted as being male, even if they are female, which most are. I find that odd.

"To summarise, there are only two forms of religious belief. There is the old religion of respect for the female, for nurture of the land and the wealth of progeny bequeathed by Gaia. The animals and crops that provide us with food, warmth, and shelter in our small daily lives are all a part of this.

"Modern religions have turned this respect into blind devotion of a fictional pantheon of gods, Christianity and Muslim alike, in order to enslave their devotees to man's will."

"Heresy," shouted one.

"Outrageous," blustered another.

"You do the devil's work," was shouted out and supported by some, although not as many as I had expected. Belligerency turned to talk, but of a bullying kind, until the impact of Kay's words had time to filter through and make people think a bit deeper than they normally would. The loudest and most confrontational were male.

"Quiet!"

I looked up so see a pyrotechnic that Kay had ignited to distract and quell the argumentative voices amongst us.

"I'll be happy to discuss this further with anyone, but I think we need a break and time to think about things.

"I will add though, that I do believe in a universal creator, a god if you prefer, and I do believe angels exist, but just not quite in the same way you do. I believe they may be a quotient of prescience.

"And what of our Shaman? She is an enlightened being so could she be classified as some form of angel? We all have much to consider.

"Thank you all for coming and allowing me to entertain you."

The mood of the crowd lightened, but before we could get back to discussing religious dogma, Kay took centre stage once more; "Now come, that was a bit heavy so let's have some fun.

"The Garden of Eden I know where that is, the allegory this time. Jackie, please draw me a rough map of this world within a large circle in the sand, and we'll join you on the beach."

Once complete, Kay deliberately placed her feet either side of the mark that located our island. "This challenge is open to everyone here, but only one chance each. Show me where the Garden of Eden lies within the greater circle?"

Our game commenced, and Sun Kist watched amused, but when her turn came, she nodded for Kay to continue. As many participants plumped for their homeland as for the Middle East, or Africa. We all got it wrong.

In time, Da Phai Nai was the only one still left to choose. She said, "This is a trick question. You are standing on the map. That means you are part of it." We all gasped and gaped, failing to realise the importance of Kay's stance.

"Here." Da Phai Nai placed her hand below Kay's belly and said, "Is that all? I need to finish preparing your evening meal, High Lord, postulates, if you will excuse me."

"Thank you Da Phai Nai. The womb is in fact the allegorical Garden of Eden. When a foetus is created, what happens? A sperm inseminates the egg. When you look at sperm under a microscope they appear to be ophidian or snakelike, don't you agree?

"Regarding the snake in the Garden of Eden, is this an analogy to a sperm entering the womb and fertilising an egg. Some consider the male appendage to be a snake entering the garden, but that seems poetically fanciful. Regardless, an embryo is created, and when mature, it is cast out of the womb and is imbued with spirit. The allegory is in the fruit. A baby is born with free will for good or evil.

"This could be, but there is a relationship between snake and tree I have not yet touched upon. You see, in all of these myths, there is a snake that lives in the tree; upon that you should ponder more.

"Everlasting life does not exist in our corporeal world, except for elemental beings. The Ancestors created new life. They also extended their lives to seemingly become immortal, by clever use of advanced cloning techniques. It is one form of reincarnation, as believed in all modern religious, if you have the wisdom to perceive it?"

"Indeed," Ju Lo concluded. "The oldest beliefs venerate the female, as does our society. We seek to balance the power of male and female through mutual esteem and pathos. Together we help each other to enrich our lives and gain further enlightenment. Through the circle of the seasons, and that of all life, we are born, grow, and die, only to regenerate as a new generation reincarnate.

"Women and men are equal, although not the same. No two people are the same regardless of gender, but all are equal in birth and death. The woman is the creator of life, the man sustains her and their offspring, a husband in the truest sense of the word. Wisdom demands deference and understanding by each for the other. Balance. Prudence. Why Prudence you may ask. With knowledge comes responsibility. Wisdom is required to use that understanding wisely."

That evening, Jien Noi repeated her warning so there was no doubt. "Good people, there is too much talk of religion these days and I have had enough of it. We have saved your lives and offered you safe shelter, and yet you repay our hospitality with dissent and discord.

"Let me be very clear, we only follow and allow the old religion here. If you cannot live with that and our rules, you are free to leave." The message was repeated as a proclamation from the Imperial Mount the following day, and all were made aware.

Some spoke out against and were summarily despatched to other parts of the globe. Others decided to keep their mouths closed and continue worship of their gods in private. The upshot was that the issue of religion was laid firmly to rest and our lives moved on.

I remained mindful that Kay essentially confirmed that God and Angels existed, although not in a way I, or any post-deluvial society could comprehend or embrace. Sometimes if occasionally, my mind would wrestle with the metaphysical thistle that represented her words as spoken that day. My only reference was the Shaman, my daughter perhaps, but Ræm appeared disinterested, dismissive should I mention it. Regardless, she remained my personal angel, as was her mother.

Later that evening, I walked alone, as my mind relived the horror of the destruction wrought by the Wrath of Gaia. I recognised this was caused by the Last unleashing forces they could not comprehend. I realised that wisdom was knowing how to apply knowledge for the greater benefit of humanity, all life on Earth; that destruction was false-prudence. Creating life, sustaining creation, whether it be by God or human hand, was Prudence.

I heard a scuff in the sand nearby as Sun Kist interrupted my thoughts. We chatted as the old friends we were, as we wandered along the seastrand. In time, I shared my musings, seeking clarification on some points.

Sun Kist said, "I believe there exists a universal prescience, a god if you prefer, although the essence is not as you perceive; Angels also.

"Worship is an excuse, a form of attributing self-serving reverence to a societal norm, at the expense of taking responsibility for your own actions. Prudence means taking control of your life and full responsibility for all of your own deeds towards, or against another.

"Enlightenment is living, walking those paths of life unaided by yourself and doing only what is righteous. It is supporting the greater good for all, come what may."

Chapter 18 ~ Cabbage Days

Time continued to move on, and as year 2022 passed, Ræm came into her ninth year. She had been moved to classes years above her age. She transferred to the University school, which was primarily for later secondary ages and adults. She returned one day from a field trip to the Valley of Knowledge, having borrowed n'Gnung's trials bike, yet again. She was obdurate on learning the language of the Ancestors. She wanted to read the ancient scripts and make her own translations.

Probably because she had been brought up in an environment where people spoke a variety of tongues, she adapted quickly, and within two years, was speaking it with more understanding than all except a few of us. Gangling indulged her when he visited, increasing her conceptual understanding greatly.

There was one other that had excelled, not through being linguistically gifted, because she was not, but through sheer determination, Peni. They often met on campus, or in the ship. They talked about all sorts, some of it Kay and I found hard to follow, especially the scientific stuff. The notable thing was many of their conversations were in Ancestor, this being the key to unlocking the mysteries of our acknowledged forebearers.

Looking outwards, we witnessed the Earth beginning to return to greenness. The world's staunchest deserts could no longer prevail against the momentous rains that swept all quarters of the globe. Drone sprays quickly rendered falling materials into harmless bio-fodder. Little by little, aided by our concerted intervention, we watched as hardy grasses and first flushes of growth endured, where once there was only sand. As more years passed, so scrub, shrubs, and later trees established themselves. The air that had laboured under such high concentrations of carbon dioxide became the food of flora, absorbed and replaced by oxygen. Our scientists worked with the Eden Project, and others, to promote and encourage regeneration from the outset.

Growth was hampered by lack of direct sunshine, but the wildness of floral diversity clung to its footholds and established ever-encroaching colonies of growth and renaissance. During this period, our botanist Julian Blanchflower and his wife Jennifer, along with Zoologist Nigel Woodcock became regular visitors to our control centre. They advised us on ways to increase biodiversity and help speed the greening of the planet. Not all of our attempts were successful, but many were. I took comfort in knowing we were assisting Gaia's great work and healing.

Late in the year, I began a study of who and what had survived from the world I once knew. I could find little of human life in many cities or towns. However, small communities still survived in sheltered locations, and HAZMAT protected city or outback enclaves. Lack of food, and disease were their main enemies. We did what we could with whatever resources we could locate, and tried to ease their survival in practical ways. Doctor Steel and the remnants of the CDC worked proactively, making a difference and preserving life.

We saved many who thought of us as saviours of their people. I instigated a head count via the Core, of the world's population at the turn of year 2023. Of seven billion, a mere ninety million people remained, and many of those lived a tentative, desperate existence.

Over the years, cloying humidity replaced icy chills. The superheating effect of the Earth's core no longer able to radiate into outer space, was trapped by the same miles of dense cloud that blocked the sun. The enduring rains brought destruction and the obliteration. It wasn't the heat, but the humidity that was killing survivors.

Nevertheless, in time the rains cleansed the air of noxious gases and chemicals. With the Core's assistance, we seeded clouds with agents that assisted the process, isotopes of silver iodine being one of the most effective. Later still, the rains became pure water, washing away the debris and sickness prevalent in the lands' below. Tides and weather patterns settled into a new equilibrium, and in due course, the skies lightened, if but slightly.

The Core predicted that with our ongoing intervention, continued application of advanced science, it would still take several years to heal the world of the worst of Gaia's Wrath.

Year 2026

Ten years after the destruction of the Middle East, we were finally able to open our outer shield and leave it open most the time. This should have taken centuries longer, but our watchful intervention greatly foreshortened the healing and recovery process.

The rains still troubled us at times and were the only reason we closed the shield, in order to save ourselves from becoming swamped. The cloud base lifted, which eased the awful humidity we had suffered for many years. The lighter skies meant we could once more distinguish day from night, but the sun remained shrouded. However, the increase in light greatly benefited photosynthesis.

To renew our brotherly bonds, we hosted a celebration of ten harvests since Ghawar blew. All the tribes attended, it being the second occasion all twelve races stood together as one. The day was declared a holiday and the mix of humanity astounding, as many disparate bands of the Third swelled our numbers with their uniqueness.

I was dressing for the formal evening dinner when Ræm entered our bedroom full of enthusiasm. In some ways, this was the biggest event of her life. She marvelled at all the other races and determined to study hard in order to speak to each of them in their own language. I had to chuckle at the temerity of the girl who would not be thirteen years old for another six months.

We chatted enthusiastically about the evening's entertainment, and I asked Ræm to pass me the Sword of Destiny. I reminded her, "This is your birthright, and one day you will wear it officially."

She examined the sword's fine craftsmanship, running her delicate fingers over the surface. As she grasped the hilt, it moulded to her hand, as if urging her to sweep and stab with pretend swordplay. I encouraged her, before she asked me about it.

"We forged the blade many years ago at the centre of female power, beneath the home of the Eleventh. Alkrengrenguer of the Eleventh, and a'Wnaed of the Seventh created it. The runes were cast and empowered by the Shaman, a drop of your own blood, used impossibly to seal its killing vitality. I last used it ...."

She stilled and looked for a long time at the blade, almost trancelike was her composure. To my astonishment she uttered, "You don't understand this, do you? This blade was created for healing, not destruction. Sometimes adults understand nothing."

That stated, she returned the weapon to its scabbard and handed it to me, before flouncing out of the room to attend her mother. I stood there suitably chastened and pulled the blade, wondering how insightful my daughter was. Her comment explained some strange awareness I had occasionally felt from the sword.

The evening was a great success and most of the Second came to celebrate with us, and included others from the University, and Billy's group as well. Many visitors stayed late into the next day as new friendships were forged. During the afternoon, one Tribe or group, issued sporting challenges to another, and we enjoyed much fun.

Whilst the first evening was one of shared conviviality and carnival, the second saw us talk plainly with our distant cousins from the more independent tribes: the Fourth, Fifth, Sixth, Eighth, and Ninth. We all moved closer together in understanding and belief in each other. But they preferred to remain largely outside the closer grouping of the remaining tribes.

Otherwise, our world was slowly healing, as we all depended on Gaia for our daily lives. Sad to say, we were looking towards the future, and not paying due attention to the demon from our past.

One evening I spied Ræm atop the sentry rock, and went to join her. She was staring into the darkening heavens, fiddling with the twiddling stick given her by the Fourth. "Is anything the matter?"

"No, nothing, dad."

"Then why so serious, so contemplative?"

"I feel uncertain. Change is coming. Do I stay on the safe path, or walk the new?"

"You got the spirit of adventurer from me. Choose the new path, it will bring exploration, new discoveries, but keep safe. Is this to do with the University? Perhaps a possible boyfriend?"

"No silly, nothing like that, but thank you. I had almost decided the same myself. Don't be mad at me. Anyway, I need to be alone, but will join you later. Da Phai Nai has been doing her hair so I think Owain will be here tonight. I can't stay though; we have a gig later, why don't you all join us?"

"OK, I like your band and think Owain will also. Tomorrow we need to discuss your birthday party, it is only a week away..."

The evening following Ræm's thirteenth birthday celebrations and Spring Festival, the Shaman unexpectedly came to visit. We were enjoying dinner at home, when she appeared, and we watched her take a palm-full of water from the waterfall, and smack her wizened lips in appreciation. She staggered wearily up the mild slope to our table, leaning absurdly on her gnarled bone staff, assisted by Sun Kist. We rose to greet her, but she barely acknowledged us, and flicked a gnarled claw-like finger towards our daughter,

"To be this one, proficient in olden ways,
her time to come, not led astray;
to serve me seven years, her birthright pray;
through well or woe, as chance it may."

Her cackle filled my ears with its grotesque undertones and intimated threat. I started to rise in protection, but an outstretched hand to my side grasped my forearm. The fingers of my other hand locked with those of my wife. The Shaman stated brusquely;

"Knowest this is as foretold,
your paths are other to unfold.
What destiny does this offspring hold?
To bear the blade, both brave and bold."

Sun Kist spoke up, "Know ye and know ye well, Mother Earth is the keeper of the sum of our existence. We cannot live without her benevolence. However, she can live without us all, as we have recently witnessed. Gatekeeper, Guardian, not only would you be the greatest protectors of all, but all is not as it seems. There waits another threat, one I cannot speak of, yet."

Distracted, we lost sight of the Shaman as Sun Kist spoke, until a teenage girl grabbed Ræm's hand, the old crone long gone;

"Come, teach ye of the Wilde and Windy Way;
Third path is all in knowledge sway,
Of Twelve and One, survivals stay,
And much, much more, attention pay."

Without a by your leave, Ræm attended the Shaman's side, and they were gone. Sun Kist said, "Worry not, but this must be. Without it we, disaster see."

Flummoxed, we gaped at Sun Kist, who responded, "Damn, I'm starting to talk like her, aren't I? Sorry, I can't help it—sort of comes with the job you know."

We were interrupted as Da Phai Nai approached, her best broom in hand, "Daughter I would tan your hide, but it has been too long, and I have missed you so much. Come give me a hug. n'Gnung, look after this broom, and ensure not one tine is lost, or there will be hell to pay. Sunni, you look so well, what is your news?"

"Well, tomorrow I officiate at the ordination of the new High Priestess, Chein Tai."

"But that is your role."

"Not any more, I've been promoted to Shaman Supplicant..."

We watched them wander away. "Guardian," n'Gnung said as he lunged to practice sorties with his new weapon, "She only ever uses this broom on us nowadays. It seems we are her chosen."

"Indeed we are brother. Let's store this one safely, and find an old one to give her when she returns."

Our badinage was pre-emptive of admitting loss. Later, in our bedroom, Jinnie clung to me and cried, "Daddy, our baby's gone."

"Shhh now. We knew something like this might happen."

"Yes, but surely not yet? She's still a child."

"She's not been with us much recently, either off at the University, or out exploring. And that was before she joined Gilly's rock band on guitar and vocals. She didn't always come home for meals."

"No, you're wrong. She came home when it mattered. I miss her so much, and she has only been gone a few hours. Seven years, Oh My Life! That's an incredibly long time."

"Yes, and no. Like Sun Kist, I am sure she will visit from time to time. Damn, I miss her also. What are we to do?"

"You, Jack Barleycorn, are just as upset as I am, I know it. Admit it, or I will tickle you to death."

"No, I have a better idea. We just lost a daughter, so we better make another one, come here..."

Despite our outward faces, the breech was hard to fill. In some ways, Ræm had come to embody the sum of our hopes and dreams. On the third day of her absence, I took a small band of brothers and sisters with me, and we entered the Shaman's domain. It was not as before. The plants were all withered, underfoot vegetation rotted, smelling of putrefaction. The house was a derelict husk of rot and confusion, with no sign of life for miles around. A fetid malaise hung in the air. Instead of moving forward, we retreated to the safety of our home.

Chapter 18

The weeks passed, months followed, and in the sanctuary of our boudoir, we mourned our daughter's metamorphosis. Outwardly we showed a brave face, but there was always some intangible spark of life missing. Then one day just before lunchtime, Ræm skipped in as if she had only been gone a moment. Her bright blue eyes shone with surreal intensity, and it seemed she had not missed anything, or anyone.

We hugged closely and our talk was tactile. She was enjoying learning so many impossible things from the Shaman. She enthused about her new life and greater knowledge. "Do not worry about me, or the future, because the ways of the Shaman are utterly important to all our destinies, and inextricably linked to the survival of us all. Do you remember that phrase of the Ancestor's script we could never precisely define, the one Rambling asked Kay about? Well, it means this…"

That flush of precocious youth, our firstborn, left us the next morning, but reappeared many times and often. Jinnie and I came to regard Ræm as attending the Shaman's University. Once we got our minds right, we looked forward to her return, but without the insufferable feelings of loss in between.

Chapter 19 ~ Demon from the Past

The Great Ogre

During the course of the Wrath of Gaia, the Great Ogre thought deeply about his plans to reunite the world and renew the ruins it had since become. He had sheltered many of his out-worldly generals, especially those of the Last who begged for his beneficent protection. He had shielded them because of their influence as political and economic leaders of the Last. They were his slaves.

Nevertheless, he needed something new, an improved scheme to bring his plans to fruition. He paced and orated. "Mine is the only way to unite the world. I had been so close, until the artful Guardian appeared. Grrrr. Strange how many refused to accept my own benevolence in return for pledging their lives to my service.

"Ahhh. But the development of the Israeli - Iranian situation." The Great Ogre bared his teeth in a grimace of triumph and uttered a sound that made his minions cringe.

"The depths of stupidity the Last had manifest, because I created the scenario." He settled comfortably into his wing-backed chair, and lit his hookah. He noted the Guardian and Allied Tribes still had absolutely no idea how deceived the world had been by his great, magnanimous self.

Maintaining control of the Last was his next priority. The Guardian had thwarted him at every turn and severely hampered worldwide operations. Most of his control centres were under their rule and heavily protected with shields and troops. The Enemy had been highly organised and devious in attack.

As he rebuilt his empire, he considered wider options. He realised he understood little of the tongue of the Ancestors. However, it had become clear to him that some of his adversaries had indeed mastered the ancient tongue. How else could they have understood the complexities of manipulating shield properties and making new transfer circles to their own specifications?

It had taken him many days to find out how to make an existing shield bigger, and he accepted one of his first priorities was to understand the antiquated language. His work had also been greatly hampered because foolish General Quinn had managed to lose the Ring of the Warrior to the Second.

Retrieving that Ring was a top priority, a most difficult task that would require deceit and tricky. He considered options. Calling a council of all the tribes in order to propose peace appeared ludicrous. He doubted any would fall for the ruse. Still, it was worth pursuing, as with the right approach and spin it might just work. Even if it did not, he could at least claim to be trying to find a peaceful solution to this most intractable of problems.

Time passed slowly. He passed through the French doors and looked out from the balcony, towards the snow-covered mountains and gorges that were the Ogres ancient home. A long time ago, these had been warm, fertile lands teaming with wild beasts and people to hunt. He was determined those times would come again.

Returning to his private room, he settled down in front of the log fire with a large measure of mulled mead, relit his hookah, and continued to plan the return of the Tenth to their former glory, as unchallenged leader of the Twelve Tribes. Defence first. Ensuring his remaining camps were completely secure. He had already reinforced shields, and locked out each against the Guardian.

His mind turned to the thorny problem of getting the Ring of the Warrior back. He looked down at where it should rest on his finger, the place diminished by a Second's ring, and he swore a black curse on its captors.

He would need to get somebody on the island and inside the trust of the leaders. He knew all his clones of the Second had been massacred, and they would be useless anyway, just like Sar Tan had proved to be. Theodosius had proved treacherous, something he should never have allowed. His scientists must up their game. Their current mind-mapping techniques were fatally flawed, and he stood to go and personally execute every one of them. His hand was almost on the doorknob, when a tangential thought appeared.

Somehow, the fiendish blades of the Guardian and Eleventh could tell his race and their clones, so his new plan would need to be more refined. He had never known blades, let alone any weapon with the power to breach an ancient shield. Yet he had not only witnessed, but almost lost an arm in the process. They would pay dearly for that affront. The magic used had to be Elven. They alone amongst all the races had been highly versed in enchantment, keeping the secret closely guarded throughout all time.

The Great Ogre's thoughts churned as he returned to his favourite chair and deliberated. Several courses of action presented themselves to his large brain. These led him to consider his troops, whose numbers had been reduced from over one hundred thousand, to a couple of thousand only, by the end of the last war. Their numbers were quickly growing once more, but he needed higher quality troops. He decided to create a new design, enhance their knowledge, strength, and size. It would take time and resources, both of which he had in great measure.

He decided to task his genetic scientists with creating a new and fearsome warrior, but they would need to use some essence from his prized exhibits, which would in turn require waking them from their enforced hibernation.

This was considerably dangerous. They were clever and could influence the mind of even the most highly trained operatives. Knowing his plans demanded a lot of fresh DNA, he went down and called a meeting, outlining the genetic design of an elite fighting force with enhanced vision, speed, and power.

He outlined, taking the best genes of all thirteen Tribes and combining them into a killing machine. They began work immediately, one group making a normal clone that would have no conscious thought and could be programmed, like they had done with Adolf Hitler.

The second group would work alongside them, but keep most higher brain functions intact, thus ensuring reasoning centres and certain brain functions were either reprogrammed or removed completely. That would in theory become a formidable foe.

Learning of the weapons that could detect their presence, one scientist tentatively raised a finger, "What if genetic manipulation weren't strictly necessary? We already know how to alter a brain."

The table fell silent until a huge bellow erupted from the Great Ogre. His rumbling laugh was long as he slammed his fist down on the veined oak table and sent several beakers tumbling. "See to it at once. Your team has the highest priority above any other project in Ogredom."

Satisfied, the Great Ogre left the biologists to their work, and checked his technologists. "Great Ogre, we have created the first prototype, as per your instructions. Permission to begin field trials?"

"Good Malbert. Make certain the test cannot be traced. Begin production as soon as all tests are complete. I will have need of several devices soon. What of the anti-personnel weapons?"

"Your Greatness, these are close to completion, a few more days."

"I am pleased. I will inform General Gruelthorne. Continue, slave."

A cunning plan was fermenting in the Great Ogre's mind. He envisioned a ruse to implant more sleeping agents for the future amongst the other Tribes, and a means to test out his latest creations and technology. Feeling much brighter the Great Ogre relaxed and decided not to act impetuously, as was his way. Instead, he would wait without drawing attention, until his war machine was fully assembled, armed, and ready to invade all of the strongholds of the other tribes.

Satisfied, he heard raucous laughter drifting up from his officer's galley, and thought it would be good to join them and celebrate this day of new beginnings. He arrived and all quieted as he entered, but he bade them continue. He was in the mood for strong ale, stout company, and human steak cooked rare.

Chapter 19

Year 2027

Jack

We again hosted a meeting of all the Tribes following Harvest Home, that being Spring Festival to most visitors. The event lasted three days. The final day became dedicated to sporting challenges and, although not pre-planned, was a huge success. We decided to repeat it the following year, and named the new event "The Olympiad of the Twelve Tribes."

That evening the atmosphere was filled with carnival, Mardi Gras overwhelming our wits and senses. The next morning, delegations from the other Tribes departed, and we focused on cleaning up, and looking to the future. Completing the harvest before the rains came being priority.

We were distracted with our own petty concerns, when n'Gue arrived at my side, "Guardian, come quickly, the Ninth are under attack."

"What?" When we arrived on the Bridge moments later, my screens filled were with mayhem and slaughter. Ogre Generals were marshalling their forces to exterminate the Ninth. Many enemy soldiers were a new form of creation, lithe, quick, and powerful.

Gung Loi reported, "Guardian, I set a protective shield in place, but the Ogres did likewise, enclosing our shield. I cannot reach the Ninth or transfer them out of the killing zone. King Groël is trapped there."

"The Great Ogre has learned our ways. Did you manage to get a linking shield in place?"

"I tried, but the Great Ogre was too quick. It is in place, but already compromised. I cannot open it."

"Set another linking shield adjacent and resonate, send the details to Kay. n'Gnung, Langnor, check all the other Tribes immediately. n'Gue, send word to any Tribe not already under threat, tell them we are at war. Barph, marshal all our forces for immediate battle—I mean every soldier of our own, and all we saved, including the Chinese, Mounties, and Stewart's commandos. We need every man, woman, and war elephant that can fight bearing arms.

"To Mo, if they need weapons, ammunition, locate it, issue it, and stockpile more. Liaise with Captain Stewart and he will guide you. I need to talk to him here once preparations are complete. To Ma, assist your twin once you bring Xi Xah here to replace you."

Langnor amplified my concern, "Guardian, the Fourth, Fifth, Sixth, and Eighth are also under attack. The Third activated their shields, but Ogres group outside and are draining them somehow."

n'Gnung added, "Our shield is also under some form of attack, but holding. Same for the Eleventh, Seventh, and Twelfth, the New Tenth are compromised, but driving the intruders back. I have never witnessed anything like these new Ogres. They are killing machines. They are quicker than anything known before, agile, but with great strength. Their eyesight also seems enhanced, note the way each eye can move independently, or focus as a pair."

"Terminators. The Great Ogre has been busy."

Kay stated, "I have managed to amplify our breaching shield with the Ninth. It is not fully active, but allows a passageway inside, a corridor troops could crawl through. These new Ogre shields are enhanced, I need to work on ways around that."

"Send in Horovitz at once, support him with our first available troops."

Langnor exclaimed, "More new Ogres are appearing inside our shield! They have Ancestral weapons. the Ninth are done for."

I looked up, only to see Horovitz' crack troops scrambling through our conduit, and running to take up position between the remains of the Ninth, and the advancing Ogre horde. His Gatling gun began taking toll, as reinforcements from both sides continued to pour through.

Gung Loi said, "How are they appearing, breaching our shield? It is not possible, is it?"

"n'Gnung, you have Command. Transfer all operations to the War Room at once. We need a dedicated centre of operations. Get our troops inside all our Allies enclaves, and save as many as you can. I need to interface with the Core without distraction; something is very wrong about all of this."

I began interrogating the Core from my ready room, "How are they able to breach our shields?"

"Duplicity transporters."

"Explain?"

"Mirror image, a dedicated second transfer circle in close proximity. They act as a relay station."

"Where?"

"Working … thirty feet below, it is not shielded."

"Our shield only goes three feet underground. Understood. Can we transfer into it?"

"Yes."

"What of the new type of warrior?"

"An advanced clone, derivative not known, samples required for analysis."

"Have a biped medic standing by to get what fluids and biopsy are needed, I don't want to bring them here."

I continued to interface, learning much more than I wanted. I tackled the Core about keeping secrets from us, "Guardian, duplicity transporters are only known to the Ancestors, they are not common knowledge. I can only reveal their existence now due to current developments."

"What else are you hiding from us?"

The Core was mute; I had to work with what knowledge we had. Kay's voice came into my mind, "Jackie, we need you, all hell is breaking loose. Tell me you found an answer."

"Duplicity transporters … Anyway, I need your hands on, ask Peni to look into it, she may discover something we are missing."

Chapter 20 ~ Under Attack

Moments later I arrived in the war room, "Synopsis n'Gnung."

"All twelve Tribes are under attack in one form or another. Our able allies, the Twelfth, Eleventh, and Seventh, are freed from direct attack, have rallied, and are making inroads into enemy ranks, but it is slow progress. At present we are losing one of ours to two of theirs, but there appear to be far more of them. They never stop coming."

"We'll see about that. Issue commanders with protection bracelets and Ancestral weapons. Kay, arm a small plasma bomb, and send it to these co-ordinates … Yes, the hidden duplicity transporter. First we need the Ogres to withdraw. Options?"

n'Gnung replied, "The Ogres are weakest at the Fourth's homeland, Guardian."

"Which is their strongest position?"

"The Eighth."

"Kay, belay my last, target aggressors of the Eighth. Set a plasma torpedo on one-second delay, and have Gung Loi's specialist team send it into the midst of enemy ranks of the Eighth. As soon as the enemy flee, send the second bomb on three-second timer, to the corresponding duplicity transfer circle. We need to know where it explodes. Remember, we need at least one of the enemy alive. The Core is standing by to run a full genetic scan of this new adversary."

The torpedoes were delivered, the second resultant explosion occurred in mid Greenland, as we expected, but not where we expected. Horovitz, accompanied by crack corps, Aroweena and Angkrelguer followed moments later, using the Ogre portal. We had only sketchy, grained video of what they confronted, but it appeared to be a mutated army. Our regular troops went in next, followed by Rambling's forces. He arrived behind retreating Ogres, a discordant mêlée resulting. Opposing forces continued to arrive at the same location, as we concentrated efforts to secure and save our allies in the world at large.

Gung Loi reported, "Guardian, the Ogres have stopped targeting shields and have withdrawn from the Third. It looks like they are regrouping to concentrate attack on the weaker Tribes."

The viewing was gruesome. Our medical facility overstretched, we again instigated field hospitals to triage the injured. Those whose lives hung in between, we did our best. Sylvia Steel brought in all her remaining CDC resources, and I commandeered a large and unused, state of the art city hospital at her direction. Once connected to services at the University, it helped save many lives. Ami came into her own, helped by an environment she understood implicitly.

Matron was not too disparaging of the facility, and set about improving it for her staff. "This is ancient technology, Guardian, but it works and has useful facilities. However, I can't understand why you still use X-rays. Is this the technological stone-age? The Fifth Council banned them as being biological weapons. Regardless, well done."

My conversation was interrupted when Kay's words came telepathically into my head, "Jackie, urgent, *mind* with me and the Core. Most of the retreating Ogres are not going to any known location, they are disappearing."

We discovered the transfer circles were preset, like some of our own, and had at least two destinations, depending upon how they were accessed. "Kay, two more plasma bombs, two second and five second timers. Let's find out where they go. Gung Loi, ready troops for transportation to the new location, we strike at once."

Seconds later Kay said, "I have the new co-ordinates, the location is again in Greenland, but some miles distant from the first."

"This may be a trap, Guardian," n'Gnung advised.

I sat back and clasped my hands behind my head. "Indeed, but it is all we have. We need to see what is happening, send through reconnaissance probes."

Langnor reported, "Guardian, the Eighth have been saved and recovered to the Outlands. The Trolls have retaken their lands, locked down their shield, and are offering us aid."

"Great, we need them. Ask them to stand ready for co-ordinates. What of the other Tribes?"

"The Fourth are creating diversions, stealing arms, and setting unsuspecting Ogres upon each other. Our troops are picking the enemy off steadily. As long as no more Ogres arrive, all should be well. Battles with the Fifth and Sixth are stalemate, our troops and enemy arrive in equal numbers. However, the Sixth are in an exposed position from which there is no retreat. The Ninth seem to have disappeared."

"Look to the trees, the caves, the Ninth will be there. Kay, arm more plasma torpedoes and liaise with Gung Loi's deployment team, we'll target the remaining Ogre transfer circles and put an end to their advance. Begin with the Sixth. Send our troops into the duplicity transporters when the aggressors withdraw, again, plasma bombs first. We'll see where they end up. Follow with reinforcements where fighting is fiercest, and put the Trolls to best use. Are the Mounties and elephants ready yet?"

"Arriving now, Guardian. Captain Stewart is waiting to speak to you."

"Guardian, preparations are complete, units initially briefed."

"Thank you Captain Stewart, tactical assessment please, you have one minute to prepare."

Langnor said, "Airborne probes destroyed, Guardian. Stationary probes fully functional, but give a one-sided view of the battles."

"That is better than nothing. Kay?"

"One moment, the last bomb despatched … Got it. All transfer circles are bi-directional. They lead to the same two facilities, but differing areas of each. Probes on their way, we will have visual in seconds."

Live feeds came up, and I could see the first location was a staging area with barracks. The enemy were trying to link up with one another. Captain Stewart said, "We must take them out before they regroup."

"Langnor, send in the Mounties, their mission to cause havoc and diversion. I need platoons of the Twelfth, Eleventh, and Chinese in support. Kay, set a shield to isolate the location once our people are inside. Let's finish this battle. We need to focus on the Ogre stronghold; it appears to be a large complex."

Stewart said, "Good strategy, Guardian. You will need the Seventh for the complex, so send them in here, and here. If you deploy two units of Trolls here, and elephants there, they will create all the distraction we need. Meanwhile, we should close out all other loose ends. I have six platoons, two to each Tribe. Give me the same of Horovitz and Gung Loi's forces, and we'll mop up."

"You have this command Stewart. Kay, continue to lock out with our own shields."

"Being done, Guardian, I'll activate as soon as our troops are inside. The Fourth caught three new Ogres in a ravine trying to take them by surprise from behind, and threw a net over them. They are now captives and are being using for bayonet and stoning practice. That may sound horrendous, but it's hilarious actually; you want the prisoners brought here for analysis?"

"No. Send a medic to them, safety first. n'Gue, liaise with the Matron, she is expecting you. Once you are there, set up a protective cordon. We need those samples to understand this new enemy."

I watched n'Gue and the automaton medic appear with the Fourth, before my attention diverted to the battle in Greenland. The complex was interlinked deep underground, our probes compromised by dense rock. We sent in more probes, creating a relay so we could understand the multifarious stronghold and hone battle parameters. Kay also searched for transporters, shields, and any secondary duplicity transporters.

With Stewart's tactical awareness, we came to agreement on strategy, and sent in our main forces led by Owain. The Ogres started transporting within the area, defining killing zones before retreating to attack elsewhere, trying to use their local knowledge to take us unawares.

We were equal, our leaders using protection bracelets and Ancestral weapons to undermine the Ogres. We began moving our own troops to counter, and set traps of our own. It was nip and tuck for a while, but the Trolls provided distraction, allowing Owain to ambush a large contingent of new Ogres and slaughter them. I was issuing orders when a messenger came to me, "Guardian, Owain says the new Ogres have enhanced forward sight, but lack peripheral awareness. Challenge them directly, but kill them with a side blow, they will not see it coming."

"Thank you, n'Gnung disseminate to all our troops."

Langnor cried out, "The Fourth have been bombed. I can't see anything! The area is covered in smoke."

"Details ... OK, understood. Send in ship's biohazard unit three. Tell it to expect the unexpected. The Great Ogre is obviously trying to prevent us taking samples from his latest creations."

My focus returned to the Fourth, but I was aware Peni came to my shoulder, intently watching my screens, her fingers busy folding paper, and her mind awry. She didn't say anything, which was possibly more perturbing than her usual *non sequiturs*.

I didn't have time to ponder the significance as Langnor said, "The mist is clearing, there's nobody there. Wait, yes, there they are. I could have sworn they were not there a second ago, must be my eyes. Guardian, I have the Fourth, the Second — two are missing."

"Scan the area immediately..."

"Wait. I have them. They must have dived for cover. I also have the medic; they are in bad shape, possibly dead. n'Gue and the prisoners are missing."

"Immediate recovery, once Bio-H-3 gives the all-clear. Hell, bring them back regardless. Any signs of life?"

Peni interrupted, placing a paper duck before me and said, "I need yellow and blue paper."

Distracted, I gave her two sheets of white and said, "Imagine."

"This is a matrix, one of at least three dimensions. Where are the other transfer circles? You are missing the obvious, just as I am — yellow and blue paper please. I need to make a horse."

n'Gnung said, "I will see to it, Guardian. Xi Xah, get Peni everything she needs, pronto, and see if she would enjoy Engineering better. It's most disruptive for thinking, here."

Peni wandered off, lost within her personal nebula, as I returned to matters of the moment. n'Gnung enquired, "Any sign of my brother?"

"No, not yet, but Kay is searching. Please monitor the other battles. I need to focus on the main one."

I was directing battle units within the new complex, when Peni placed a green seahorse on my desk.

"Dear Jackie, it's not a trap, but a trick. Yellow and Blue make Green. Hence, there is a third, interlinked transporter. This Great Ogre chappie is cleverer than you think. Check for a fourth, as he has a sense of humour, warped though it may be. Was there anything else? Good, 'Au revoir'."

As Peni departed, Kay exclaimed, "Damn! She was correct. There is a third transfer circle sixty-two feet below … it is locked out, but the shield is weak, want me to breach it?"

"Why sixty two feet?"

"Our scanners are automatically preset to sixty feet. Cunning eh. Mind you, it's difficult to go much deeper, depending on the rock strata, without specialised geometrics."

"OK, prepare to breach, but hold off, we will go in prepared. Set plasma bombs for first intrusion, and ready troops."

Langnor cut in, "We have rescued the rest of the Tribes, and any with life signs are being attended to. Some we thought were dead have been brought back to life. I don't understand that."

"I am beginning to believe anything is possible. Focus, we need to take this last complex, and end this"

My team concentrated; our mantra, 'win this battle, win the war'. We lost many lives — it took too long to find them all. The enemy suffered more, before retreating, our next task being to counter-attack.

Unfortunately, we could not trace the enemy withdrawal, the third duplicity shields being removed before we got locks on them. This in turn explained why we captured no Ogre Generals, except for one that was dead. He was brought back for examination, his weapons and shield being kept in my locker.

A little later, Kay exclaimed, "I found him! n'Gue is here in a sealed room, there is a false rock wall, sending co-ordinated now. You want me to blow it?"

"No, send in the Ddwyrth to bore a tunnel. n'Gue's life is too precious to risk."

In the event, there were no surprises. We recovered n'Gue, and locking the base out, withdrew leaving a strong guard force. n'Gue was only slightly injured, but stunned by the explosion. He was disorientated upon return, but quickly began to recover, and refused medical treatment. The robotic medic had received the full blast and would need reconstructing. Nevertheless, the samples were secure, and the resultant biopsy of the new type of Ogre warrior revealed they were of composite homo sapiens DNA.

Later, the Matron informed me of our casualties and their recovery, the figures were not as bad as I feared. She added, "The medic was too badly compromised to be reconstructed, and there was also unusual damage to the control programming. It's easier to make a new machine, the old unit will be kept in storage, and used for spare parts. Things like probes and scanners take time to produce."

"That makes sense. Matron, I discovered the Core is withholding certain information, releasing it on a need to know basis. What can you tell me of this?"

"Only that Captain Taris had the same problem occasionally. Remember, Space Corps did not officially instigate him as controller. The spacecraft's makers have routines in place to prevent leakage of sensitive information, unless in emergencies. Otherwise there is little I can add."

Chapter 21 ~ Trickery and Understanding

Later we were celebrating, leaving the grand carousing in Grimwaldi Rinns for the homeliness of the Outland shore. Owain was in fine fettle, having enjoyed the killing spree. Gung Loi and Aroweena were sparing, a prelude to Old MacDonald.

n'Gnung took me aside to look up at the stars, which we could almost determine. "Guardian, what was this supposed war all about?"

"I have been wondering the same. I think the Great Ogre was testing us, trying out his latest designs."

"So, he is preparing for another war, and this was just a test run. Is that it?"

"I don't know, brother, but something stinks about this whole thing."

"How did he know about our assembly of the Tribes? Why strike now?"

"He is stupid, he forfeited two complexes. This is a big win, brother, what is wrong?"

"I don't know Jack, but wasn't it all too easy? To me it reeks of a ruse."

"I wholeheartedly agree, but what are we missing?"

Our sharing was interrupted by Gung Loi, "What are you two doing way out here? Come, n'Gue and Horovitz are about to re-enact one of today's battles. We can all take a role – n'Gue is pretending to be one of the new Ogres, and he is awfully good at emulating them."

The sport was good fun, but n'Gue did not pull his punches as much as expected. This we forgot when he turned sharply, and fell over. He seemed momentarily confused and we rushed to his side. "I'm taking you to be checked out at the medical centre now."

"No!" His hands rose to push us away, before he lowered them and said, "Sorry Guardian, that it not necessary. It's just something to do with my ears. I am fine."

"No you are not, come."

His senses returned and he stood up without aid. "Guardian, trust me, I am fine. It is an old childhood problem, I will go to see the Healer who knows about this condition."

"Bring the Healer here now."

n'Gue was examined as we waited, worried. In due course the Healer told us, "n'Gue has received concussion, and the blast disrupted his centre of balance, which lies within the ear. His hearing is damaged, but will heal over a few days, his sense of balance will also return to normal. I will come back with suitable potions, and advise he is kept away from loud noises, and does not make sudden movements.

Fighting is forbidden until he is fully healed, probably one week. Otherwise, there is nothing wrong with him.

We were greatly relieved, and in due course, festivities resumed.

Early the next morning we sent teams to scour for clues in hopes of identifying what the Great Ogre had, in fact, been about. The largest team thoroughly explored the new complex. Volkar and the New Tenth headed the investigations as they, more than any other Tribe, understood the ways of the Great Ogre.

The Trolls sent representatives with our party to the first transfer location, and immediately confirmed it was a barracks and large training ground. We gained little immediate insight, although we did find many corpses of the new type of Ogre clone.

I spoke with the Matron, "We need to know the best way of killing these things, this new warrior, and the Ogres themselves. To do that I intend to use our sample."

"Good thinking, Guardian. This information is not included in our standard profiles. Usually our focus lies with saving lives, not working out how to end them."

"Understood, but killing these things will save many of our own lives. Please make as detailed a study as possible. This will ease your workload in times to come."

"How detailed?"

"Full DNA/RNA scans. Note any sequences taken from other Tribes and, how segments may have been enhanced, especially the eyes. Also strengths and weaknesses, physical ability, look for an Achilles Heel."

"There are over three billion base gene pairs. This will take months, maybe one year, for each phenotype. Not only would we have to specifically identify each pair, but interpret how they interact."

"Do it. We need to know everything about these creatures. Give me what you can as soon as possible. I'll have to wait for the complete dossier."

My next task was to check the Ancestral weapons we had recovered. These appeared identical to our own. We tested them, and confirmed they were kosher before adding them to our arsenal. We gained little else of practicable use, and no rings of power. As the day wore on, information began to flow, a little from the barracks, but much more from the complex. It was clear that we would be spending many days investigating that location.

I tasked Peni with understanding the transfer circles, a work already in progress, but upping the immediacy. "Dear Jackie, I am already working on that, and should have something for you soon, how soon will be relative."

"Relative to what, Peni?"

"How long it takes me to find the answer of course."

"Do you need any more paper?"

"Ah, you understand. No, today is not for twiddling, but serious scientific investigation. Send Phœbe to me. I need her math. Oh, and ask her to bring Mister Ted."

"Who?"

"My teddy bear, he likes to see what I am doing. And anyway, it's better than talking to myself. Regardless, he sometimes sees things and tells me what I am missing. Thanks."

I tactically withdrew before her idiosyncrasies breached my sanity, and resumed overseeing operations on the Bridge.

n'Gue came to me with a message from the Empress, which I actioned at once. My mind was already elsewhere as he turned to leave, but as he spun round, he seemed to momentarily lose his balance. I looked up to speak to him, but he was already striding across the room, and I dismissed the thought as aberration.

Some days later most of the complex had been revealed, although the Ddwyrth were still discovering hidden chambers within the stronghold. Thus far, all had proved to be dead ends. More holding cells we presumed. We held conference in the war room, intent on drawing all our other investigations to a close. The Trolls were most incisive, offering us insight into Ogre training programs and bases. The Eleventh offered new information about Ogre encampments, and military machine.

As the meeting drew to a close, Ælthrelntheine summarised, "This was a concerted attack to take out the weaker Tribes, especially the Ninth, Eighth, and Fourth. The rest were mainly distractions, to keep us preoccupied while these Tribes were exterminated. The Great Ogre is obviously aware that to prevail against him, requires all the Tribes to act in concert. Remove even one, and we fail.

"It is apparent he expected his new clones to perform better, but thanks to Owain and the Ddwyrth, we quickly discovered their weaknesses, and although remaining a fearsome enemy, they became much easier to kill. I think it safe to presume the Great Ogre used this to test our defences and readiness, and is now planning future attacks, and enhancing his soldiers. We should presume years, but the Eleventh will monitor worldwide for developments."

King Keos of the Eighth stood to speak. "I thank you for coming to our aid, and saving our race for a second time. We owe a deep debt of gratitude, and will repay as best we can. Today, I speak not only for the Eighth, but for all the independent Tribes: the Fourth, Fifth, Sixth, and Ninth. Being insular and distrusting is our nature. We have suffered greatly for all of our known history, at the hands of the Great Ogre. Not only the present one, but each of his predecessors.

"If it pleases you, we would each send a permanent delegation here. Our way of becoming more open, with a view to co-operating more fully within the greater scheme of things. Openly sharing our knowledge with the other Tribes may be of great benefit in times to come. We all understand the ways of the Great Ogre, much to our distress."

Jien Noi replied, "Thank you King Keos, your representatives will be made most welcome. Please arrange this as soon as possible. We will of course attend to suitable accommodation and food, as you advise. I would prefer to locate these ambassadors near the University, as this will provide the ideal environment for the exchange of knowledge. However, you may each choose a suitable location for your camp, perhaps in the wilds nearby. If there is nothing else … let's adjourn to Grimwaldi Rinns for refreshments. Thank you all."

Duly, the greater gathering departed, but Owain stayed. After we saw the others off, n'Gue came with a message, "The Ddwyrth at the complex have discovered a cave-in along one of the tunnels, and need your advice."

As my team and I rose to leave, n'Gue turned sharply and stumbled. n'Gnung rushed to his side, but his brother had already recovered his balance, "It is getting better, but sometimes I forget. I am late for today's treatment, excuse me. I will return shortly."

n'Gnung and I exchanged knowing looks, but neither of us spoke. Instead, we attended the control centre, but video feed was slightly fuzzy so deep underground. "I need to go and check this out personally; we have been tricked by supposed cave-ins before. Kay, find out where this tunnel leads. n'Gnung, keep this ring safe; the Great Ogre may be monitoring."

I gave him the Ring of the Ancestor, and departed at once. I was relieved to discover a cave-in, with obvious signs where the tunnel roof had collapsed. The leading Ddwyrth enquired, "Do you want us to proceed, Guardian? This is highly dangerous work and will take time."

"No, unless we locate something at the other end. How's the rest of the work going?..."

Returning to the Bridge, I checked the surface, and noted a depression in the snow, corresponding to the collapse below. Cave-in confirmed.

Kay said, "I have followed the route, and it ends in a large cavern. There are corridors leading off, and I have a probe tunnelling now."

We waited for the outcome, hoping the corridors led somewhere significant. Video feed came up, and all corridors were short blanks, as if a plan in progress had been interrupted by the rock fall. We agreed this was a dead end. I chose to personally explain to the Ddwyrth commander, a human touch that was appreciated by the men underground.

I left them to finish their survey, and returned. n'Gnung said as he gave me the ring back, "Everything checks out, and yet I still have misgivings. What are we missing? I'm going to pay my brother's wife a visit, and will rejoin you shortly."

He was away for some time, and returned with a worried look, "Guardian, his wife says the balance problem seems to be getting worse, not better. However, what troubles me most is his sleep. She told me, 'His slumber is beset by demons. He sweats a lot, and often thrashes about, he cries or mumbles in his dreams, "No," "Take it out," "Why are you doing this to me." He mutters about monsters and demons. What can it be? He almost hit me for the first time ever, this morning.' I am greatly concerned, Guardian."

Our eyes locked and we spoke in tandem, "The Great Ogre."

n'Gnung leaned close and whispered, "No wonder he didn't want to go to our medical centre, he would have been found out. Has he been cloned?"

"We'll know soon enough. Send in the guard."

"No, I have a better idea. I'll pretend to be injured fighting Aroweena on the shore. Afterwards, take me to the medical centre and send word to him. He will come."

Within moments of returning, Aroweena and n'Gnung faced off. The blow my brother took looked real, and I took him to the medical centre, where we informed the Matron of our suspicions. n'Gue arrived a minute later, and realising his brother was fine, tried to leave. Kay blocked his exit. Matron stunned him with a sedative, and set about her work.

In due course she delivered her diagnosis; "The patient has not been cloned, but his brain has been tampered with. There is an aberration here on the brain scan, which should not be there, another here. I recommend returning his mind to the last known correct configuration, which was a few days ago. He may lose a little memory."

"Do it."

n'Gnung nodded in agreement, and added, "We need to know exactly what was done to him."

The procedure took several minutes; identifying the alteration took longer. Matron gave us a considered evaluation in due course. "This is Ogre technology. Two small parts of the brain were overwritten, but with what we cannot tell precisely. Indications are the areas were related to judgement and aggression. I would infer this means he was programmed to kill somebody, but who, when, and how we cannot tell."

"Interesting. My brother has been more aggressive recently, Guardian."

"So Matron, the increased aggression triggered a recurrence of the balance issue."

"No. The balance problem is unrelated, a genetic fault suffered since birth, which is now being rectified. We consider the loud explosion triggered a recurrence. Nought point one percent of the Second are known to suffer from this problem, although this patient is one of the worst I have seen."

"At last, we know what the Great Ogre was up to."

"Indeed, Guardian. Without this defect, the alteration would have gone undetected. We have been lucky. Matron, please run a scan on me, just in case, although I have no history of balance problems."

n'Gnung was immediately checked out, but he was clear. Once discharged, we returned n'Gue to his wife for rest and recovery, assuring her all would be well in the morning, and so it was.

Chapter 22 ~ Predefining the Arbitrary

I was buoyed with expectancy that afternoon. We had thwarted the Great Ogre trying to infiltrate our ranks by subverting one of our own. It was personal. On this occasion, I did not need to lock out an Ogre control room, but I was certain those skills would be needed in future. I decided to spend my spare time learning the Ogre language, with focus upon how their control rooms and consoles worked, in their tongue.

I was still feeling elated when Peni arrived, "Jackie dearest, I have unravelled how the intergalactic drive works. 'The ancients'..."

"Ancestors, Peni. Kay, n'Gnung, I think you better join us."

"Whatever; used a specific and complex lithium molecule to power the Boson Drive. Now, all matter we know of in our universe is based upon twelve building blocks, which we call The Standard Model. Eight are fermions with half-integer spin characteristics, and four are bosons with full integer spin. But then again, half of these are also quarks, and the other six are leptons."

"OK Peni, and so these make up bosons."

"Bosons, mesons, gluons, and muons, to name but a few, are all made up of two quarks and their valences. Hadrons, things like protons and neutrons, are made up of three quarks."

"Got it, with the electron that makes seven quarks in every atom."

"No, electrons are leptons, a completely different thing."

"So, an atom is a ternary system."

"Oh dear, you aren't going to be difficult, are you? Let's begin with Bohr. An atom is a binary system composed of three elements, which is all to do with electrical charge and valence."

"Three parts is not a binary system Peni, every child knows that."

"Hmmm, let me rephrase that, two interdependent binary systems working as one, a nucleus and electron belt, just like a star system."

"Ahha! Just like Alpha Centauri, got it. Go on."

"Regards the boson drive, the Chi-boson is key, and they are inordinately difficult to separate. Their valence grows stronger when you pull them apart, until they rupture with great release of energy."

"How?"

"Oh. Well, the fuel is lithium-six [^{6}Li] that is bombarded in first instance by helium-four [^{4}H], creating fusion plasma via nuclear spallation. That's enough provide initial thrust and ships power, but there is more. These elements are both bosons, but the production of ^{3}H — helium three or tritium, a fermion, is what matters.

"A secondary process injects tritium particles into a secondary propulsion chamber, where complex photons [$-^{13}$Q] are fired at the soup. Just like in a transporter, these are controlled by singularity crystals, except these are anti-photons. The resultant fusion providing enhanced thrust... ...and by combining the output of both drives, a seamless flow of regular and stable thrust is produced."

Kay was following what Peni said assiduously, n'Gnung nodding studiously whenever Peni looked at him. Meanwhile my mind had wandered off to think about cricket when Peni hit me for six. "Jackie, are you listening to me?"

"What? Yes of course. It's just all these colliders, containment fields, and control thingamabobs seem somewhat complex. Can you give me something similar I can relate to."

Peni stopped talking, and patted my hand in a motherly way. "The answers you seek can be found in the television, and by that I mean how an old-school CRT screen is controlled."

"Gotcha! OK, understood. So how does this fusion reaction move a spaceship farther can I can imagine?"

"There are millions of them, Jackie, trillions in fact. The duplex fusion reactors thrust against special internal shields at virtual point of source, maximum force to be precise. Any unused reaction residue, plus hazardous particles exit via the exhaust pipes. One boson drive can propel this ship at one-tenth the speed of light. That is quick."

"If you say so."

"The boson drive works within a precisely delimited zone. To go faster you need a second boson drive, something a spacecraft such as this cannot support. True, a second boson drive would almost double velocity, but the power required for containment fields, zero gravity, plus available space, make the upgrade unviable on a ship of this size. It would also be too heavy to land safely on a planet like Earth."

"I guess the Ancestors powered it down for the infinity thrusters."

"Oh no. That's a completely different can of worms."

"Worms, as in wormholes?"

"No, but thanks for reminding me to get cheese for tonight's fondue. Phœbe is hosting a dinner party."

"What?"

"It's Emmental dearest Jackie. Swiss cheese with holes in it. Ideal for melting, dipping, and dunking. Now let's be serious."

"Thanks Peni, we have this, don't we Jackie!" Kay fired a warning glare in my direction, then asked, "What about the infinity thrusters."

"Thank you Kay, I'm pleased one of you three is paying attention. Now, regards going slower, sorry, that's a non-starter. In theory it should work, but it doesn't in practice. The boson drive fails to deliver unless working within its optimal range — intra-galactic"

"You're still not making sense."

"Hmmm. OK dearest Jackie, try this analogy. A rocket needs a specific amount of power to escape Earth's gravity. If there is enough thrust it reaches orbit, but too little and it crashes back to Earth."

I nodded in concurrence, "Like an internal combustion engine, you can't simply weaken the fuel mixture, retard the timing to decrease power. It will stop working. OK, that's cool. I understand."

Kay added, "The emission parameters are not great enough to sustain the reaction."

"Correct Kay."

"These particles can only be effective within a fusion reactor. The arrangement is different regards the Infinity Thrusters, where by-products of the boson drive, mainly deuterium-tritium plasma, are infusioned with an array of differing photons to create drive. Well, specifically we are using complex quark forms like penta-quarks, only more of them, so as long as the overall value of the quark group is plus or minus one, you can add any number of paired quark and anti-quarks, so long as their colours are correct.

The ideal number is thirteen quarks, which releases five anti-quarks to create the fusion reaction, although flavour, plus colour/anti-colour pairing becomes a significant problem ...

... And so you see, the Infinity Thrusters, the boson drive, all rely on paired quarks and adapted transporter technology. So you see, everything works in synchronous ways. That brings me nicely to nanoseconds, you do understand what a nanosecond is, right?"

"Yes Peni. I get the heavy lithium bit, helium three, and deuterium with tritium complications, all empowered by a range of photons and/or anti-photons. How's that going with understanding how the transporters work?"

"Ah, I'm so glad you asked. It's simple, once you understand it. Let's begin with the speed of light."

"It's as fast as we can go."

"No. Just like the sound barrier before it, the established scientific community, the journeymen, have used the speed of light to cap our mental awareness, and a carp to forestall counter argument. There is no limit to how fast anything can travel, the only limit lies within our current scientific beliefs established in the dark ages of science, and uncorroborated by physicality. Remember, we already know many things can travel faster than the speed of light: x-rays for instance, and sticky fluids—something I proved when I was project leader at CERN.

"Likewise, the bordering electro-magnetic spectrum shows clearly, infrared is much slower than ultra-violet. Also, blue light travels faster than red light. White light is like a container, a conduit—a fajita wrap, Ramone got me addicted to them.

"Astronomers use 'red-shift' to compute intergalactic distance, for example. Light is composed of photons, a vector quantity, and it can either exist as a photon, two quarks, or sometimes as an anti-photon plus anti-quarks, or not. Are you paying attention?"

"A photon can only exist if it is travelling." My brain had downloaded the science of the Ancestors, but that did not imply I understood it implicitly. Kay was better, but we remained fallible. Peni had it as a digestible wrap.

"The key, well apart from the singularity crystals, is that as soon as a photon has zero motion, it must change state, release energy, and die, normally becoming two quarks. This is old quantum mechanics. What do you know of relativity?"

"E equals MC squared."

"That is the problem, it doesn't correct, and even Einstein stated it wasn't quite right. It's a shame he and Planck never got on. Together they would probably have solved the conundrum. Oh well, I guess I'll have to do it. Anyway, the speed of light is simply a large number squared, or obfuscation if you prefer.

The Ancestors defined C as the vector quantity of a photon, which is not the same thing. The inherent problem with our understanding of Space-Time is when the continuum continues, after the photon becomes two quarks. This we know of as the Brice-Tate Paradox, you with me so far?"

"No. Go on."

"Oh, how strange. Well, the Brice-Tate expressions of relativity examine the holes in general and special relativity. Between them, they proposed a paradox where photons cease to be wave structures, and can travel faster than light. It's all in the math, but is ridiculous, unless the photons are no longer photons. The 'Ancients' … Ancestors seem to have accomplished this by creating paired quarks."

"Explain."

"Quarks, in this case uniquely paired quarks, cannot exist at the same Space-Time location. The effect of this is that they appear to change location and, or time co-ordinates, but progressively, as they remain vector quantities. The resulting co-ordinates and vector of each quark are different, yet they retain the essence of the whole. The anti-quark is often considered to travel backwards in time, but that is ancient quantum theory for you. In practice, it stays put as time continues to advance. If they were recombined, a photon would result, and the equation would be correct.

"It is this parallax that permits transportation. It is different when subjective, a bit like differential calculus, only this time; all the equations can be differentiated to a correct answer. Phœbe's still working on that. We are calling it Differential Relativity."

"Durrr? Go on, Peni. I need to get this over with; if I can follow you, I'll know I have it."

"Then there are the singularity crystals, which are paired like the quarks, and also with the quarks. Add complimentary crystals at the receiving transporter, so both it and the sending transporter have a pair, and we are set up. Thus the quarks and crystals are defined"

"OK, Peni. I sort-of get that, but all you've done is send a quark somewhere. What about the matter transfer?"

"Oh! Silly me, that's all to do with UEP's."

"What?"

"Universal Elementary Particles. They are like stem cells, a grain of sand, as compared to one of those large beach balls representing an atom, which is made up of billions of them. This is Ancestral science previously unknown to us. Phœbe has done the math, and I can give you the basic formulæ now."

"Thanks Peni, but I am fine without. Just as long as you understand, works for me. Go on."

"Well, UEP's can be matter, or energy, or even thought. You could consider them to be the thirteenth participle. I think this may explain the existence of beings such as the Shaman. External forces can govern the UEP's state. In this case the singularity crystals. When we transport, one quark is identified to be sent to the destination. The other, Residual Quark, staying put as it were, where it bonds with a UEP, and once valenced, this becomes the primary object of transfer.

"Now here's the trick. Both quarks must remain the same, if opposite in charge, so as soon as the Residual Quark gains a UEP, so must the sent quark. Once equal and opposite, Singularity Crystals get to work, the Sent Quark arriving before transfer of the Residual Quark at the destination. The receiving Singularity Crystals ensure the Residual Quark deposits the original UEP at the precise nanometric destination, and do likewise with the second quark, so two UEP's are actually transported each time. Because both quarks must remain identical, so, matter appears to disappear from the sending transporter, and reappears in the receiving one.

"Once transmission is complete, the Diversity Field surrounding both transporters, or points of origin and destination, acts as a gauss to reunify the two quarks under direction of the Singularity Crystals. They reform the original photon, but leave the matter transfer behind. There, told you it was simple."

"So the white light we see are quarks?"

"No Jackie. Those are photons."

"Got it! And because these UEP's can become thought, so we arrive thinking as we left."

"Brilliant, Jackie. I'll make a scientist out of you yet. Hence, when you transfer, your integrity is transposed with you. It's in the synapses you know, multiple duality, and predefining the arbitrary."

"Thank you Peni, that was illuminating. Let's call a halt for today; I don't want you to be late for your fondue party."

"My pleasure, Guardian. Any time you have a query, just pop in and see me. If I'm not there you'll just have to use your initiative. Now where was I; a party you said?"

"Yes, you are taking cheese to your sister tonight."

"That's right, thank you. I'll drop by the shore later to get some salmon. Toodle-Pip."

I was urgently in need of somebody who spoke a language I understood, and duly departed with my closest. "n'Gnung, help me. Please predefine something arbitrary?"

And it seemed he understood Penelope Pendleton and Double Einstein Theory, squared but not integrated, within his personal relativity at least.

We summarily arrived at the shore, where Da Phai Nai had just finished pouring our drinks. She handed me a beer, stating, "I had the feeling you two would be here any minute."

"How did you know?"

"It was time you were here."

"Good woman, you have just predefined the arbitrary. Cheers!"

"Nonsense. You always arrive at this time of day. Your arbitrary has now been defined."

Da Phai Nai stomped off muttering, "Stupid, stupid boys, whatever am I to do with them?"

n'Gnung cocked his eyebrow and said, "All appears to be predefined and arbitrary to me. This is the first time she has ever poured the beers before we arrived. Curious?"

"Me too. But, no. We were tricked into becoming subjective victims. Heisenberg plays with these principles, mark my words, and objectivity? We had better keep an eye on those scientists, they may miss something that is common sense. Anyway, I still need to predefine something truly arbitrary."

I had not realised, but as I spoke, I had reached for my beer, as n'Gnung, listening intently, had done the same. As our thoughts returned to the present, the physicality of the moment became our saviour. Our beakers clashed in toast. We stopped, beer-to-beer, and stared at one another.

"Guardian, it appears we have just predefined the arbitrary."

"Indeed, but we have not. Let's work on it. Cheers! What if…"

Chapter 23 ~ Next Generation

Year 2028

One day in late summer, I was asked to attend the medical centre; they had finished the full genome study of the Ogres. We were greeted by the Matron. "Guardian, we have concluded the detailed study requested of the specimen, and I will send the full report to you later today. First, I need to tie up some loose ends.

"We also ran a different series of test on the new Ogres, looking to identify specific DNA strands, as this would give vital clues about how to defeat them. We discovered two RNA subdivisions that match personnel files we hold. The first was from Oma, and second was from Vela, her number two, and Duty Commander of that spacecraft."

"Are you telling us the Ancestors are still alive?"

"No, not exactly. Only that their DNA is still available. I would imagine the Great Ogre has some form of storage and duplication facility. To make this new clone he would have needed access to living stem cells of the Ancestors. That does not mean a complete Ancestor is alive or kept in stasis, just an arm or such-like."

"Jackie, my mother believes the Ancestors are still alive, but trapped somehow. Could this be?"

"Thank you Kay, I remember her saying so. n'Gnung?"

"Guardian, we must create a similar laboratory, a place where we can enhance our understanding of these clones."

"Good thinking. It would also allow us to preserve our specimens in ideal conditions. What of it, Matron?"

"The laboratory can be built, but not onboard. Taris forbade its creation, so you would need to countermand standing instructions with the Core before I could proceed."

"Why?"

"Taris was a great man, the match of Oma, because he foresaw things other Ancestors missed, and he preserved this society. Before landing, he was badly injured. His brain had a metallic spike through it and he was never the same again. He did great work, yet something was always missing from whom he was before. The spike removed the smallest jot of his brain, one that was most essential to his being. We tried many times to replace the missing information, but he refused.

"Marginally we succeeded by other means, and hoped for greater things. Always our hopes died upon his refusal. We could do nothing, and yet we tried, but failed every time to bring the real Taris back to us.

"Robots cry, you know? In some strange ways, we are more human than you are.

"Anyway, he never bothered to contact the others of his kind, and they never found him either. I doubt they even looked. Such are the ways of The Ancestors, Guardian. They never look back, they only ever move-on. It seems to me, *we* remember. Think upon this sometime. The conflicts of emotions lies in-between."

Up to that moment, I had never imagined that a Robot had feelings, emotions, but her tears were plain for all to see, and her demeanour also. I pressed her one last time, for information I needed.

"Taris tried many times, but the information he sought was held within the part of his brain that was lost upon crashing into this planet. We know this, and the Core held the answer, but he would not listen. He spent the remainder of his life, alone and lost; his mind following concentric circles that always brought him back to the same starting point. There was nothing we could do."

"A haughty spirit. Let us not make the same mistake."

"Guardian, a word of warning. The Core believes it is Taris, but it is just a control system. There is much at stake here, more than you know. If you succeed, the Core will overwrite Taris' instructions and in time, come to think of itself as being you. If you fail, it will continue to believe Taris is still in control.

"You must have a compelling reason for creating this centre, for countermanding Taris' express order. I will support you, but you need to present the case so as to compel belief."

I interfaced from my ready room, the Core instantly dismissive. "Core, we need to save life, the lives of these unique islanders, the ones Taris devoted his life to preserving. I intend to continue his great work. We need this laboratory so we can extend their lives; future wars against the Great Ogre are imminent. We must be able to save the lives of those who would otherwise die."

Matron was nearby and presented supporting statistics, including life projections from previous battles, and the Core acquiesced. We had won and I was sure the metallic Matron smiled as she congratulated us. "Well done Captain, well played. I will action the new laboratory at once, although it will take months to become fully functional. Where would you like it incorporated?"

"At the Old Capital, as a high security wing of the hospital. I would keep all things medical in the same repository, except for onboard facilities, of course. We hope to fly this thing soon."

Year 2031

"Guardian, the final seeding of clouds is complete. By tomorrow we should finally be able to see, to feel direct sunlight again."

"It has been so long, n'Gnung, and until I see it, I can't consider the Wrath of Gaia finally over. We have survived the darkest of times, but we should look to the future once more. Kay, what of the spaceship?"

"As you are aware, major repairs were completed last year, but we have been hampered by lack of a specific energy source. Direct sunlight will solve most of the remaining issues, and thereafter, the craft should be ready for full deployment quickly. Otherwise, we continue to stockpile plasma for creating shields, arming weapon systems, other ammunition, and seek to improve where we can."

"So the only items not under construction are the space hoppers, the small fighter we found a blueprint for, and deep space drones."

"Correct. They each use specific types of infinity thrusters, which Peni is sure she can enhance. She has settled well into her role as Science Officer. I am riding shotgun on her wilder designs, but she has proved her worth. That was farsighted of you, Jackie."

"Ha ha ha. Perhaps so, but it was largely a fluke. Given that soon all systems will be restored, and that we should be able to see the world again, what do you say we learn how to fly this thing?"

"And about time too, the sooner the better," n'Gnung stated.

"But first, we need to work out how to get this craft out of this rocky tomb, and that will not be easy," I mused.

Kay said, "I'll say. When we figure out how to move the ship, we'll need to disable all Island shields, and we cannot do that yet, the climate is still far too erratic. Nevertheless, we'll get working on it."

"Guardian, we need to address a delicate matter. Most of the present crew do not understand the language of the Ancestors, beyond that required by their jobs. I point out that many are becoming older."

"But I thought Matron developed a specific treatment to arrest the premature ageing of the Second."

"Indeed she did, Guardian, as I am testament to her skills; my wife and brother also. Nevertheless, most of the Second believe it is wrong. They maintain that we should not interfere with the grand design of Mother Gaia. They adhere to the old religion, and refuse to undergo the necessary tissue regeneration. I believe one of those is your wife."

"Indeed, she has not. We have had words about it, but her mind is set. This society takes it lead from the Empress, and will do as she does. This in turn gives us a problem. n'Gnung, Kay?"

"I disagree, Jackie. This presents us with an opportunity to plan for the future, one that I suspect will be quite different from the one we hoped for when we were still young. Both Langnor and Bufor have proved to be tireless and faithful servants, but they are aged, although they have both been partially rejuvenated. I think we should ask them to train their replacements, and offer them early retirement. At the very least, a change of jobs."

"Guardian, this is indeed a wise suggestion, and applies to many of the existing crew likewise. Some, Langnor especially, might be persuaded to take on a part-time teaching role."

"So, we don't tell them they are getting past it, but thank them for service, and reward them with early retirement. I think we can do that. But who will replace them? They must be fluent in several languages."

Kay stated, "Look to your own. I'll join you later on the shore, but first I must check on Peni, she seems determined to rewrite relativity."

"Indeed, Kay. Conversing with Peni is always a relative experience. What say you, Guardian?"

"Agreed, but relativity is a phenomenon that can be either objective or subjective. Brother, share your wisdom."

"Hmmm. Relative subjectivity? I think we should mull this hypothesis over with beer in hand."

"I'll see you two soon," Kay quipped. "Mine's Dutch."

n'Gnung and I retired to the shore early that evening, and our discussion continued as we waited for others to join us. "Kay was correct, Guardian. Of all the new generation coming through, we should approach our own children first. They are all fluent in English, Second, and Ancestor."

"Granted, but you know as well as I do, their focus is on the University, learning what someone already knows. Without Ræm, Mai Li has stepped up to train as the next Gatekeeper, and she is especially good at it. She's also learning the role of Empress Regent from Siu Mooyi, but that is not her calling. Jason has the guile and personality to take on the role of Emperor, but it can never be, that will go to Ræm's husband, if she ever decides to marry — And if she ever returns from her apprenticeship with the Shaman. It's been five years already."

"Two to go, Guardian."

"We need to act regardless of these concerns, but make allowance for change in the future. Let's go and talk to them now."

"Now?"

"Yes, now. We resolve this instead of talking all around the issue. We'll return here to sup well in full knowledge. Anyway, I have a new creature to add to Old MacDonald..."

Moments later, we arrived at the University and found those we sought. They were working as part of a larger group on specifics of a project our scientists had tasked them with: selective regeneration and enrichment of plant life. Valuable work, but something many could do. I called an impromptu meeting, "I need crew for the spacecraft, and only those fluent in Ancestor may apply. Volunteers please?"

I had expected the youth to be clamouring for inclusion but, instead, not one hand raised, no one came forward. Most looked down or away. Murmurs of 'boring' were audible, attributable to no one. "We need a crew to learn how to fly the spaceship. Any offers?"

Murmurs of dissension grew louder. I made a strong case for the excitement of space exploration. Jason responded when I called him out, "So what's so great about going to Mars, Dad? It's a barren planet with no atmosphere to play football, no hint of grass, and no water to go swimming. You always told me to treasure the bounty of Gaia, and I do, we all do. But I don't want to spend the rest of my life dependant on life support, stuck on a barren rock."

"But son, consider…" Our discussion was bordering on argument, and my anger was about to spike, when Ræm appeared, "There has been an aberration in the future set, what's this about?"

"Flying the spaceship Daughter. I need a young crew fluent in Ancestor to learn to fly it. I intend to begin recruitment in the morning, and had presumed these kids would jump at the chance. Instead, they appear determined to rediscover what is already known, and sloth their lives away in idle pursuits. Great to see you too by the way, are you well? We have missed you."

"Yes, of course. Likewise. Time is of the essence, or we are all doomed. Jason, stop pretending to know it all, and embrace your destiny, your life is not meant for this planet. Neither is yours Ah Tien, Zhong Zhi. Your fortune is to fly the paths between the stars, where you will assuredly make a significant difference. There are other planets offering new and exciting adventures were you to go to them. Father, leave this to me. Your new crew will arrive tomorrow morning to begin training — won't you?"

n'Gnung and I reluctantly returned to the control room, idling to monitor what was said in our absence. Ræm was a natural, and bawled the youth out. "She does you credit, Guardian."

"She's a feisty one all right. How did she know precisely when to turn up?"

"The Shaman?"

"I'm not so sure. This came from Ræm. What have we created?"

"I would answer that another day, if ever. Better to give the young their heads, but keep an eye on things."

"That was Lo Si's greatest skill. Not telling, but asking pertinent questions at the right time. I still miss his wisdom. Come brother, we'll leave what will become to our children, and celebrate their coming."

I flicked my eyes to the screen, only to see Ræm disappear. The tones of those remaining were hushed, considered. Whatever she had said, or done, had worked.

This gave me one last task, "Controllers, I would like to speak to all of you, both day and night crews, on shift changeover tomorrow morning. Know it is good news, but what, you will have to wait to discover. I also need the backup crews, everybody that works here. Langnor? Thank you."

That evening I prepared carefully, I could not allow this to go wrong. Neal, John, and Dawn all offered advice, backed up by Jinnie.

The morning presentation was taken far better than I expected. The Empress attended, creating the new title of 'Senior', as a mark of respect to honour for those who had served us so long and ably.

Peni led a second meeting, and I was pleased to see all our children present. Kay, n'Gnung, and I stood nearby in support.

Peni explained to our new recruits, "Fully understanding quarks remains key to unravelling the mysteries of time and space. Their flavours, colours, and charges are complex in the extreme. Blending them in the right combinations is critical, and leads to a far higher understanding. I believe the Ancestors only understood a part of it. Much more waits to be revealed — travelling much faster than light, for one. I also believe certain quark specifications in combination, explain the existence of advanced beings, such as the shaman.

"As beginners, you should focus on transporter technology, not only does this basic science give us clues to how the boson drive and infinity thrusters work, but also medical uses, such as biopsy. The Ancestors also used it to manipulate genes, replace one with a different one to effect a cure for disease. That's clever."

Kay added, "Cloning also. How do you think gene manipulation works, reincarnation?"

Voices spoke up with more interest, until Peni intrigued them further. "Now, which of you can tell me how the kitchenette works, the bar and servery upstairs?"

The leading question drew a variety of responses. It was something I had not considered, I just used the facilities. I listened to the suggestions, responding to one, "There are no stores on board. Everything you eat or drink here is made on demand. Every item is exactly the same as any other of the same thing."

"Thank you dear Jackie. Every item on the menu has a molecular plan. Each item is reproduced using transporter theory applied to the appropriate device. The specifications are like a blueprint, so all coffee looks and tastes the same. You can add milk, cream, and sugar, other toppings, change the type of bean, but the underlying template is set."

An interesting, if abstract collegiate discussion developed, which we all encouraged. Our children became swept up with the potential of new possibilities, as are the ways of young adults.

Once Peni had finished, Langnor took over and introduced our recruits to the consoles, and although most had sat at one before, Langnor showed them what they could do. Training would take months, years even, beginning once their current project was completed. I thought we had accomplished the impossible with zero damage, but humanity remains a resilient and savvy creed.

As the meeting wound up and the eager hubbub of teenage high spirits departed, Langnor came to my side and said, "Guardian, I know what you did. I'm not stupid. Nevertheless, you are correct; it is time to train the next generation. I would like to stay on as Overseer. Bufor and I… well, this has become our home, our children's also. Geldar, Pheldar, and Norf know as much as we do, and are fluent in Ancestor."

"Go on."

"Well, they have learned the Ancestor's language, and how to manipulate the consoles, instead of going to school. It was what they wanted, what we needed at times."

I cursed inwardly at having overlooked the obvious. Chagrined, I took Langnor to my ready room accompanied by my closest, and set about appointing roles for our new recruits. This now included her children, and those of other longstanding controllers whose children had apprenticed to their parents, rather than attending University.

n'Gnung summarised, "Guardian, we have covered all main bases, but are still short of backup crew."

Kay added, "There are unmanned stations below in Engineering that should be filled. I have an eye on Peni's kids for two critical positions, but their spoken Ancestor is lacking. What say we agree with what we have today, and work towards filling other positions later, especially as some current crew are quite young, relatively speaking?"

And so we created a new cadre of control room personnel. Effectively, we ended up with twice the number of skilled control room operatives. The Second were not that big on early retirement, but sharing the work around and doing less, suited most of them best.

Jinnie insisted our children finish their education before taking the reins of power, excepting an Ogre attack. Therefore, we coaxed the next generation subtly, letting them find areas of expertise.

Their once-weekly afternoon attendances onboard, became extra evenings of their own volition. Peni set them tasks; Kay, n'Gnung I, and others, presented scenarios in the war room in preparation for any future conflict. They became personally invested in our future, as individuals and as a group, and that was all we needed of them.

One year on, they were spending as much time, if not more, working with us inside the ship. The seeds of our future had been sown wisely and flourished.

Year 2033

One Spring day I was waiting to deliver a presentation to our scientific community. We were early, choosing to sit and wait beneath a large oak near the transporter circles. At break-time, older kids came out from class and separated into smaller groups.

One was led by Jason, who waved to us, as did Mai Li, and the children of Gung Loi and n'Gnung. The Seers' children came running over to join them, apparently revealing a mystery.

n'Gnung observed, "Strange our children always group together."

Gung Loi replied, "It is no mystery husband, they have grown up together, known each other all their lives."

"Perhaps so, dear wife, but how do you explain the children of Horovitz and others of mixed marriage with them?"

"Husband, they all are fluent in both the language of the Last, and that of the second. They know the ways of both cultures, so they would naturally form a clique."

I kept my own council. n'Gnung, as usual, had made an astute observation. Excepting his own children, all were of mixed blood, the Thirteenth Tribe as Jinnie had once called them. I was distracted by n'Gnung's next words. "They will be of age to marry soon. Our eldest will take the Trails of Passage soon. I wonder who will be his bride?"

As if on cue, the teenagers reached some form of conclusion, and after goodbyes, went their separate ways. Many paired off, Jason already in deep conversation with n'Gnung's eldest daughter, Ah Tien. Nearby, their eldest son, Zhong Zhi, was gambolling awkwardly with my second daughter, Mai Li, until the Seers' son, Wong Kai, and Horovitz daughter, Ah-Nei [Annie], joined them.

I was about to pass comment on this intrigue, when n'Gue arrived with an urgent message. "Emperor, Guardian. Your presence is required at once. Emperor Zhao has just passed on."

Moments later I held my wife as her grief sought release in tears of passage. Jien Noi's father had never fully recovered from his own wife's transition, and although we all expected his imminent demise, the shock still took us by surprise.

His elder brother, the King of Forest Meade consoled us. He talked about his brother, bringing with his words the salve we all so eagerly sought. He in turn, endured as a sprightly, aged man, by making full use of the restorative facilities of our medical centre.

I said to Jinnie, "The Emperor used the life rejuvenation facility only once. It added ten years to his life. Had he continued, he would still be alive—look at his elder brother."

"He said it changed him, he felt different afterwards."

"Yes, young again. Jinnie, you are forty and aging, forty-one this year, and are becoming a frail old woman needlessly, please reconsider. You could double your lifetime, even at this late stage."

"No! I will not. I will live my life according to the laws of creation, and not upset Gaia by using artificial means to extend my existence. Living a long time is not the essence of life, not a counter of the good done, but a judgement. I thought you understood?"

I pressed my case, but she remained adamant. I knew she would die needlessly young, but could do nothing to change her mind. Her body no longer worked as it should, her knees pained her, and she sometimes remained abed in the morning, denying the encroaching arthritis that had started to plague her. She was becoming ever more dependent on tonics and herbal remedies, although her mind remained as sharp as ever. That fact only made my misgivings worse.

It was not the first, nor would it be the last time we disagreed about the matter. However, this was a day of mourning for the already dead. "I'm sorry Jinnie. You know I love you with all my heart. I want to share the rest of my life with you. Is that too much to ask? Shhh. I am done, said my piece. That stated, I think we should share some things with the others, like that time your father sat over a bubbling vent at the hot springs and pretended to be passing wind."

"Oh Jackie, that was hilarious. You remember that time he..."

A full State Funeral followed, and as we adapted to our loss, so Jinnie and I tasked the Empress' younger brother, Dai Lo, to take his father's place concerning daily matters of the realm. However, I retained the title and power of Emperor, and he became King of Grimwaldi Rinns. Siu Mooyi became the first official Queen of the capital city, and second most powerful woman in the land, after her mother. Her husband, the Prince of Forest Meade, became effective Regent, but his destiny lay as future King of his home town.

Some weeks later I was summoned to attend court, the Empress required my assistance in the role of Emperor. I attended my wife, dealt with the matters of concern, and later we dined in the restaurant on the Imperial Mount.

The matters of court were trivia, and I knew a game was afoot, but nobody was letting me in on the secret. The meal progressed, and I was relaxed, until three young men approached. Zhong Zhi, the eldest, spoke first, unusually addressing me first. "Emperor, Empress, I beg your indulgence. I would ask your permission for the hand of Ah Nei in marriage."

There was no law, but an unwritten convention that the Empress and Emperor should approve all cross-tribal marriages. I immediately understood what this delegation was about, and looked to the parents of each in turn. All nodded in approval, and so did Jinnie. I emulated Emperor Zhao as best I could, milking the moment with pretend concern. "You will complete the Trails of Passage, and build your bride a home. This marriage is approved, subject to Ah-Nei attaining age sixteen. Congratulations!"

The onlookers clapped with delight, but quieted as Jason came forward, "Dad, Mom..." Zhong Zhi elbowed him sharply in the ribs. "Emperor, Empress, I too would take a wife, Ah Tien."

His words dried, all sound within the hall died, and I kept mute a moment, allowing expectancy to grow. I was aware of Jinnie beaming expectantly by my side, her hand momentarily squeezing my own for confirmation. "And about time to! Go and prepare…"

My words were cut off as cheers erupted. Two fiancées joining their betrothed to dance and hug in celebration. I shouted to quell their enthusiasm, there was one still left to speak. "Wong Kai?"

"Emperor, Empress, if it pleases you, I would ask for the hand of your daughter, Mai Li in marriage."

This was personal. Approving his daughter's betrothal was one of the few decisions that rested with the father, within the matriarchal culture of the Second. I remembered my own time well. I had been scared as hell, the truth be known. I vicariously recalled how the old emperor acted, and found I was no happier answering the question, than I had been asking it all those years ago.

"How would you treat her?"

"As the person I love and look after. I would attend all her needs, husband and support her and our children to the best of my ability."

It was not what I had said all those years ago, 'to love, cherish, honour, and obey', but it was damned close. I looked around. Mai Li was smiling expectantly, her mother giving me a knowing look of anticipation, Weid Noi and Ali both on tenterhooks, celebration but a word away. Jinnie's hand again grasped my own, a mere squeeze of consent. "Son. You must complete the Trials…"

That evening became a triple celebration featuring the forthcoming generation who would one day take our places. That night, our loss of Emperor Zhao was replaced by the renewal of life, of love, and family.

Later Jinnie whispered, "Jackie, this has never been known before, the marriage of a Seer and a Gatekeeper. I have no idea what this portends, but Ah'Weid assures me it is in our best interests."

"Ræm should have been our first to marry, Jinnie."

"You know she is far too busy to bother with affairs of the flesh. I doubt there is a man here who could live with her, never mind keep up with her. She completed both female and male Trials of Passage."

"She's clever, confident like that. Too much herself. I just hope she finds the right person before she's too old."

"I'm sure she will. Soon her biological imperative will kick in. She will have no choice. However, I have never regretted giving her dispensation not to marry at age sixteen. Like me, she will choose wisely in due course."

Chapter 24 ~ The Art of Deception

Later that year, 2033, Ræm returned for her twentieth birthday party, and we celebrated late into the night. We had presumed this would signal the official end of her apprenticeship. She dedicated only a short week to re-familiarising herself with our world, but continued to spend much of her time with the Shaman, or went off on other pursuits. She was with us, but she was not.

I tackled her about it during one visit. "Father, I can't explain in ways you or Mother would understand. Please trust me. What I am doing is for the benefit of all, and I mean all of humanity, not just those of us here on this island. There are much larger things at play than you can imagine."

"Try me."

"OK. The Great Ogre will ... No, I can't tell you, or it will change the future. Trust me, all is not what it seems. Anyway, the Ancestor cousins are on the way here."

"What?"

"Ancestors fleeing something horrendous, some macabre that will in time follow them here. I can't say any more. Send Ælkræleinnoire to the Elven Observatory if you must, but you'd be better watching out for the Great Ogre. No more, I have said too much already."

I was about to press her, but she disappeared into thin air. I shared my discomfort with Jinnie, Kay, and n'Gnung. We did not know what to make of most of it. Kay attended the Observatory for one week, and we monitored the Great Ogre. I interrogated the Core, and the Matron, but neither seemed to know anything about their supposed cousins.

When Kay returned, she said, "All is in stasis. The threat I foresaw just before we first met remains unchanged. I think this might be what Ræm alluded to, the greater threat from outer space."

"I agree, but how come neither of us knows about the Ancestor's cousins? We both downloaded the history of the Ancestors, but yet I have no knowledge of them."

"Same here, Jackie. We only have knowledge of them in this solar system, but I saw a reference once in the Corridor of Knowledge. I think we should check it out."

We departed at once with n'Gnung. Kay, leading the way down the corridor called out, "Here it is Jackie. There's not much to go on, but they refer to themselves as Centaureans."

"There's a bit more on this panel. Their world orbited a sun, which orbited two larger suns orbiting each other. Sounds confusing."

"Guardian, Kay, I have found a small, strange map. There is a cross in the sky, and three suns grouped nearby."

Kay uttered eyes-wide, "Alpha Proxima! It's now a red dwarf."

"The runes say they fled the death of their sun." I continued reading the passage and elaborated, "No, not all left the solar system; many remained behind, seeding safer planets. Those that departed did so in waves, and headed for other solar systems. Ours was the closest. They knew Alpha Proxima was about to change into a red dwarf."

We studied the group of panels, learning little more of value. Returning to the Bridge I made directly for my day room and confronted the Core. The Core feigned ignorance, but I pressed, "Taris wrote about the homeland of the Centaureans. If he knew about their history, so do you. Stop lying to me, tell me the truth."

"Guardian..."

"Stop. You can call me Controller. Captain. Use my title, Core. I am in charge here, do you understand. The Ancestors no longer exist. They are dead. Space Corps no longer exists. Stop hiding behind outdated protocols and help us in our fight to save all life on Gaia."

There was silence. One minute later I severed the connection with obvious disgust. Stymied, I set Weid Noi to monitor the likelihood of an Ogre attack. She chaperoned Wong Kai, creating a dedicated project for him to scrutinize. I sat at the Captain's console and looked down, realising for the first time, Wong Kai, Mai Li, and Zhong Zhi were occupying the stations of Seer, Gatekeeper, and Guardian respectively. Geldar and Pheldar were at helm and weapons stations up front, and I knew Norf was down below in Engineering. Jason was working at comm., not his future role, but a position he needed to intimately understand. Langnor, overseeing their work, looked up, smiled, and gave me a nod. The next generation were learning their trades, but most important, they were there because they wanted to be there.

Weeks passed without result, until one afternoon Ælthrelntheine came to us unannounced. "Empress, Guardian, we have picked up faint tremors originating from Greenland. I need you to send an underground probe to these precise co-ordinates. We believe the Great Ogre is up to his old tricks again."

Kay identified the location, but there appeared to be nothing there. "Wait. There, there is a shield in place hidden by the snow and ice. We can tunnel underneath."

A probe was duly despatched, the feedback terrifying. A monstrous cavern the size of an underground city presented itself to our screens, lava flows encompassing a plateau of rock, from the centre of which rose an impossibly large, high tower. The scene looked like the epitome of hell. There appeared to be millions of mutant clones chanting for blood, our blood.

"We have to take them out. Kay, arm plasma bombs, big ones..." My words were cut off as the screen went dead.

"Jackie, they've destroyed the drone. They know that we know."

"Mobilise our troops at once. n'Gue, inform the other Tribes immediately, we are at war! Send Owain, Horovitz, and Captain Stewart to me, we go in as soon as our troops are ready."

Ælthrelntheine had already departed to muster her own troops, but returned some minutes later to monitor developments and liaise. We adjourned to the War Room.

Kay set a protective shield adjacent to the boundary of the Ogre complex. We would tunnel beneath the Ogre shield, and go in with full tactical assault troops. The mission was more than dangerous, but it was a way inside. The Ddwyrth tunnelled, and Stewart led his scouts through in arctic camouflage.

We had eyes on a large, black building, the size of several blocks. There appeared to be no way in. Kay released a small drone, which revealed a quadrangle inside the outer rectangular structure, a tower rising from the centre. The area looked deserted, and the flat roof was clear of guards. The drone withdrew before discovery, and Captain Stewart returned after a brief survey.

Even though we knew exactly where our platoons were, they were hard to spot. Two men aimed and fired rocket-propelled grappling hooks at the roof. Others attached personnel winches to the ropes, and rose to the top. Once in position on the roof, new lines were secured and dropped, and the sleigh of weapons attached.

The winching was slow, the conditions hampering a speedy uploading. Langnor monitoring progress on her screen, shouted in alarm, "You have maybe three minutes to get that thing up there, an Ogre patrol is approaching from the south side."

We watched, frustrated. There was no way the sleigh would make it up to the roof in time. It would be close, but not close enough.

"Options?"

Steward replied, "I'll set lookouts, and take this down to the second. My men know what to do. Or, we could take the Ogres out, I doubt they would be missed for some time."

Kay interjected by placing her hand on my arm, "No. This does not get us inside. They need to pass by, and we follow them inside. I will go. I have the speed your kind does not. I'll take them out before they know what hit them, once the door is open."

"What door?"

"Jackie, I make four of them, one to each side, and central in the block. I can set a probe to look for motifs. They must have begun at the west side, checking now. Yes, footprints appear in the snow there. They will either use the same doorway, or the one to the north. I am going to prepare. Stewart, I need some of your camouflage, and tell your men to cover me."

I looked at n'Gnung, who said, "Me too. I'll cover you Kay."

Kay said, "I've set a shield inside the Ogres', using duplicity transporters. If that's compromised, there's a second one set up on my consol ready to deploy. Protect us."

I was about to rise and go with them, when people all around shook their heads. Jinnie spoke for them. "Jackie, you need to be here, controlling things. Kay needs you to activate the shields inside."

I turned to answer the Gatekeeper, but she was already speaking again; "n'Gnung, stay. This is your wife's skill, *ninja*. Gung Loi, prepare at once. You leave in seconds."

The Gatekeeper was correct. "Horses for courses; use your troops to their skills for best advantage."

It was frustrating to watch. The Ogre guards walked closer, as our team settled in place. At the given signal, ropes were withdrawn, and the hoist stopped ninety feet above ground. The Ogres came around the corner of the building moments later. Our commandos ready to take them out. As it was, they checked the door, looked around, and, seeing nothing, continued on their patrol.

I spoke aloud to myself, "The Ogres have poor eyesight, and seldom look up. That is why the Ninth use trees for cover. However, they do have excellent hearing, as Hogar will testify. Remember this."

In the meantime, Kay and Gung Loi skirted the edifice, and disappeared beneath the snow, within striking range of the northern door. Ælthrelntheine said, "Angkrelguer, send two of our best to the west door, we need to cover all eventualities."

Our attention returned to the screen. The Ogres stopped and checked the north door, before looking around. I was able to hear some of what they said via the feed from Gung Loi's headset; "Nothing as usual, do we have to go all the way round?"

"Yes, you don't want to upset *him* do you? Security status is up one notch due to that bat they shot, the Captain thinks it may have been an enemy drone, but we will never know, it fell into the magma. You got any Raw Spirit left? It's damn cold out here."

I watched as the younger Ogre reached for a hip flask, and I saw them both reach for their protection bracelets. I tried to mind-link a warning to Kay, but interference was too great. However, much to my relief, the women stayed hidden, and in time, the Ogres reactivated their protection and walked on.

We could not get a warning to Angkrelguer either, and I reacted at once. "I'm going in. Aroweena, let's take a plasma cannon with us and do some real damage to this hellhole. Keep this safe," I said, handing the Ring of the Ancestor to Jinnie.

The plasma cannon was an Ancestral version of our RPG's, but much more potent, and heavy. I had trouble with the weight, but

Aroweena did not. I spent a moment explaining how it worked, took a backpack of bombs, and we departed moments later.

We made it to where the Elves were lying in wait, and I cautioned them about the Ogre personal shields. We needed to remain hidden until they were dropped. One minute later, the Ogres came round the corner, appearing keen to finish their patrol. They were almost with us when one said, "Did you hear that?"

"What?"

"I don't know, we better check it out. "

Alarmed, I sent a mental warning to Kay, which this time she received. The Ogres retraced their steps, approaching the corner of the building warily. They stood watchfully for some time, before turning, but I could not hear what they said. Kay's voice came into my mind, "Ice shard. Large icicles are breaking off from the roof. You had better watch your heads. These things are lethal. Jackie, once you are inside, wait for us. We're coming with you."

The Ogres hurried back. Dropping his shield, the leader inserted his ring finger in the door motif. As the doorway opened, Angkrelguer struck with lightening speed, his partner taking the other guard out instants later. I took the security ring, placed it on my finger, as the women ran up to us, and helped haul the Ogres inside and bundle them into an empty anteroom.

We stripped the Ogres of all valuables, Aroweena taking a swig from the hip flask, before smacking her lips in satisfaction, pocketing it, and moving on. The area appeared to be deserted, unused, which only heightened our tension. Approaching the end of the passage, we met a cross-corridor, the quadrangle beyond. Kay said, "Look for a lift or stairs, there has to be a way down."

She scouted one way. "I have stairs."

Her brother had gone the other way and called out, "I have a motif. Care to try your new ring, Guardian?"

I did and a panel slid back revealing a small chamber. It looked like a lift, and we entered. We went down half the way, and emerged to the sounds of a multitude chanting. The two male Eleventh took up point positions, as we crept forwards, towards the noise. We came to a room where two Ogre generals were looking down, discussing their new troops. Kay gestured to take them out, but I forestalled her. Due to my language course, I was able to understand much of what they said.

After a few moments I mind-linked with Kay. "They are discussing a new weapon. It's something about shields, but what I don't know."

She smiled her winsome smile and puckered. "Shall we?"

There was just a hint of double entendre in the way she said it, but I knew her well enough to understand her mild flirtation was to cover her anxiety. I rose to the occasion, "I think we better had, it's long overdue. Allow me to make the first thrust."

Her eyes seared into mine for the briefest moment, her tongue flicked her lips lasciviously, before we drew our swords and charged. The Ogres fell before they knew they were under attack, and we rose to look into a malign pit no human could ever imagine. The encircling lava flows added murderous colours to the scent of ash and decay that enveloped the scene. The twin rivers of red encircled an oval one-mile in length, a tower rising imperiously from the centre, and appearing to go up through the roof.

I reacted instinctively; we would obliterate this hideousness. "Aroweena, ready plasma bomb assault. Tower base centre, then left, right, repeat.

"Kay, get word to Stewart's men on the roof, they need to fire in support at the tower base in the quadrangle. We are taking this down."

At her word, Angkrelguer and his second sprinted away. Gung Loi took point, as Kay and I instructed Aroweena where precisely to target. The waiting was interminable, seconds seemed like hours, but a concerted attack was our best chance of victory. Finally, the message came telepathically, and we opened fire. I loaded as Kay pinpointed Aroweena's next target. The loss of Ogre life was horrendous, but their numbers were legion.

The battery from above took its toll, the quadrangle descending to shell those below with large rocks. The repeated bombardment of the tower bases making the edifice teeter, but it did not fall. Changing tactics, Aroweena fired upwards, trying to destabilise the tower from below. The second strike seemed to make the tip of the spire waver, a prelude to falling, but Gung Loi cried out, "We are under attack."

I looked below, and saw Ogres droves being transported out, others firing at our position from the ground and tower, we needed to relocate. "This is a trap, shields! Make for the roof."

We rushed to the lift, but it was descending, "The stairs."

We ran upwards as fast as we could and saw the corridor we entered through nearby. "Out the way we came. Hurry."

Kay, being the swiftest, stayed to our rear to shield us with her protection bracelet. She would cover the final retreat the quickest. We ran as fast as we could, the ominous sound of Ogre footsteps growing louder. Kay shouted, "They are targeting my shield, it is weakening."

We still had fifty yards to the door, forty too many. I stopped and turned around, drawing the Sword of Destiny in my right hand, an Ancestral ray gun in my left, and went to Kay's side. At my word, she dropped her shield and I fired, taking out the first wave of Ogres. They were of a new kind, with four eyes, two extra to the side near their temples. Obviously, the Great Ogre had added the side eyes to cover their weakness. It soon became apparent that not only did the forward facing eyes focus as a pair, but could be paired with the eyes to either side. They were also large and quicker than before, many jumping aside before I could target them.

Kay had also drawn her swords, as we trotted backwards, eyes assessing the danger. We dived aside as Ancestral weapons fired back at us. I activated my protection, shielding Kay and the others as we continued to make for the door. We were close, but as with Kay before me, I knew my shield was weakening.

Next, I felt it, the presence of pure evil breaching my protection. I whirled to the side, turning as I did, and saw an Ogre sword penetrating the much-weakened shield. However, the sword kept on coming towards me. I dropped to the floor, turning off the protection as it did, and rolling to come upright again, and swung out with my blade. Two Ogres got passed me, I removed the third Ogre's head, but more were upon us. Aroweena shouted, "Dive."

I hit the floor moments before a plasma bomb tore into the ranks of our enemy, but more Ogres were coming, and closing quickly. Aroweena had dropped her weapon and was striking out with her twin swords. I charged the two Ogres attacking her, as Kay and Gung Loi also came to Aroweena's side. We killed them and I gave Kay the door ring. We ran after, until footfalls made us turn for one last stand.

I glimpsed Kay falter as I turned, arming her protection as she came to a halt, mere yards from the external door. I reacted instinctively, grabbing the fallen launcher, and arming it with the last of our plasma bombs. This time it was I that shouted, "Dive."

I released the volley, shredding Ogres to smithereens. It felt good, until I turned around. My heart quailed. Kay stood there transfixed. Two Ogres barred her escape, the points of their swords protruding from her back. Her shield was gone, the floor quickly being covered with red and maroons, the mix of her passing.

I ran to her heedless, and swung my sword with desperation. Other swords joined mine, and we took the Ogres out, but Kay crumpled to the floor. Her last thought came into my head. "It was fun while it lasted, Jackie. Next time, just you and I." The ring operating the door rolled towards me, and she was gone.

I grabbed the ring and wheeled, the red mist descended to overpower my enraged being. Beside me I knew Aroweena was the same, and we held station, taking enemy lives with every strike. The sound of a Gatling gun became a distant distraction, an Ogre dropping before me with an arrow of the Eleventh in his neck. He fell into me. I felt something steely cold enter my body, my chest, my heart. My world went black, my lifeblood ebbed away onto the cold floor of the Ogre citadel, adding fresh scarlet to the diversity of Kay's.

I came to in a dark place, feeling only numbness. I wondered if this was what death felt like, limbo. In time, I heard voices; they were muted and seemed far away. I wondered if I was about to be reborn. The darkness became blacker, and the voices drifted away.

The next time I became conscious, I flicked my eyes open, and saw Matron standing above me. "There you are, Guardian. I wasn't expecting you back so soon. You will live, but it was a close call. Fortunately, Aroweena brought you here directly and we got to you in time. Rest now, you are incredibly weak. Not everybody survives a sword through the heart."

My mind somersaulted, and I tried to cry out, "Kay?" but no words came, and I felt drowsy as something entered my system. The next time my eyes opened the Matron said, "Guardian, you should feel a little stronger today. Many people have come to see you, but I have allowed only these few through. No talking now, you have two minutes until I sedate you again."

Jinnie kissed my lips and hugged me close. n'Gnung smiled broadly and biffed my arm. Aroweena and Gung Loi came into view, as I again tried to speak, but it was useless.

Da Phai Nai came into my view, and eased my head up, encouraging me to drink her special potion. It tasted foul, and I tried to push the cup away. I realised I could move my hand, my arm slightly. The concoction drunk, I made a mark on my chest.

"He's trying to write something, Empress. Again Guardian."

I did as instructed, n'Gnung saying "'IX', that doesn't make sense." I tried once more, my strength failing, "K?" ... "Ahha! Kay is recovering, but she is still in an extremely bad way. She will live, but only because you built this facility. She was, and was not reincarnated, but it was a lot more complex than I can explain. Apparently, she clamped her mind down to a small spark of life, and her entity persisted, even after her clinical death. Matron will fill you in on the details, when you are ready. We may need to hold another forum about religions and the facts of life…"

I smiled, that was all I needed to know. Relief washed through me: Kay was still alive. I felt Jinnie mop my brow with a moist and welcome cloth. n'Gnung kept on talking, about what, I had no idea. My mind drifted off on its own accord, assisted by a sedative.

Chapter 25 ~ Ways of the Great Ogre

The Great Ogre

The Great Ogre cursed. The Guardian had slipped through his grasp once again. His Generals and clones too stupid to realise whom they had trapped. He had executed them all as an example to others. Had the usurper worn *the ring*, he would have known, been aware, but he had not. The artful Guardian was proving to be a troublesome foe, the Elven brat also. But he had been assured the Elf Queen Elect was dead. The Great Ogre was not so sure, he did not have her corpse to chew upon, and anyway, he wanted to capture them both alive, if only to have the pleasure of condemning them to live in hell for all eternity.

He reflected that the new warriors were almost perfected, but could still be enhanced, as could his weapons. Fortunately, few of his soldiers had been killed due to the swift action of his camp controller. The fact they had discovered the lair was a minor worry, but the result had been a victory for his troops, even though they had been caught off guard by the attack.

Satisfied, he spoke to his engineers; "How's work on the shielding circle we captured coming along?"

"Great Ogre, your presence blesses us. The transporter has been reconfigured. I will program full shielding next, so it will appear as normal volcanic rock."

"Good. What of the power drain? Is that ready yet?"

"Yes Your Highness. It is complete, and I incorporated a relay to charge our own systems at their expense."

"It must be a slow drain, otherwise they will notice. I need to be able to control it."

"I will attend to it at once, Great Ogre."

"Good. Make twelve more to the same configuration, and add a small tunnelling probe to each. One of them must be a duplicity transporter, I intend to open this island up."

Pleased with progress, he addressed enhancing the new anti-personnel weapons, and was informed, "The prototypes gave exceptional results during field trials, and production of the latest version only awaits your command."

"Do it, what of the new secret weapon?"

"That is undergoing trials, has limited range, but it works. We are extending the range, and also the immobility parameters."

"Good work, let me know when development is complete."

The Great Ogre walked through to the nearby cloning department, making subtle alterations to the next batch of warriors. His last call was with espionage. "Great Ogre, everything worked perfectly. Two of our unwitting agents remain undiscovered, but, the messenger was revealed, and he is no longer of any use to us.

"We copied the technology of their Ancestral communicators precisely, which their control accepts as being bona fide. They each have one of ours inserted beneath their ears, on the other side of their faces. They automatically send information back to us whenever the troops are near one of our transporters."

"I am aware of all that, what did you find out?"

"Your Greatness, both were present during the attack, and we got full data download for the first time. I have the precise locations of all important places on the island, including their control centre. I can confirm it is a spacecraft, as you suspected. I also have their rank structure and military presence, plus details of how they contact all the other Tribes. I am preparing a full report, which I will send to you within the hour."

"What of the human control mechanism, has this been perfected yet?"

"No Great Ogre, but we are close. The headband is fully functional, but we need time to adjust the chemical responders that attach to the brain."

"Not good enough. Do you want to die?"

"No Great Ogre! Please, a few more days before field trials. The device already works perfectly with synthesised scopolamine, but you want the victims to be fully aware of what they are doing, which requires subtlety. Our latest Rohypnol substitute has already demonstrated the effects you require, tests are progressing positively, and we will continue to improve its effectiveness."

"I am pleased to hear that. When are the Second most distracted? When do all the Tribes meet?"

"Festivals, marriages, and deaths are the best time to strike, Your Greatness. However, we usually do not find out about these, or meetings with the other Tribes until it's too late. There is one curious thing, all the Tribes attend an Olympiad every year, it is like a day of games, and all the Tribal leaders attend."

The Great Ogre roared with laughter, returning to his rooms to put the final embellishments to his grand design. Some days later, he placed the duplicity transporter beneath the island's shield, deep underground. The tunnelling probe burrowed upwards, meeting no shield resistance; the tunnel looking like a natural rock fissure. It stopped at sixty-three feet, directly below the enemy spacecraft, where he placed a second fully shielded transporter, and commenced Operation Drain. The work would take several years, but would not be detected, long enough to produce another army.

Jack

Nearly one week passed before I felt well enough to resume my duties, my first call being to check on Kay. I was interested to find her mother at her bedside, "Ælthrelntheine, how is she?"

"Surprisingly well for a dead person. Jackie, I don't know how to express my gratitude. It is hard for us — our kind. But you built this facility, and saved her life. Thank you."

"I only gave the order, it was n'Gnung's idea, and Matron actually built the place. Regardless, how's her recovery going?"

"Better than hoped… "

I spoke to Matron next. "In essence, Kay was clinically dead, but there remained the spark of life, shuttered deep within the essence of her being. She was not brain dead, if only because her dying act was to use the return bracelet, otherwise we would not have reached her in time. Normally we would reincarnate someone in that condition, mind mapping the last, good configuration. That was when she last transported, prior to the battle. The Gatekeeper and Seer were adamant she should be brought back to her original self, and that was a complex procedure, even with these facilities."

"So what you are telling me is that she was reanimated."

Matron chuckled, "Yes Controller, that is about the sum of it."

"Controller?"

"New instructions from the Core. You are to be addressed as either Controller or Captain."

"Well I never." I whistled, adding, "I prefer Captain, but that is only for the Core. You can still call me Guardian, or Jack."

"You are so like, and unlike Taris, it is strange. He preferred the title Controller, yet you permit use your given name. Perhaps the similarities lie in what you do, not how you achieve the result."

Once Kay was awake and on her feet, she appeared to recover quicker than I did, both of us resuming a nearly normal lifestyle by the close of the second week. I was surprised to discover that during our absence, Ræm had taken over most of Kay's duties, being assisted by n'Gnung and Jinnie, and occasionally Jason, who was supposedly covering for me. Ræm fitted in well, her knowledge already a match for any senior controller.

Jason was a work in progress. However, he along with Phœbe, were the only two who had any notable degree of understanding regarding the computer code used by the Ancestors. He had learned most of what I knew about computers, and adapted it for the Core, something I had never had time to focus on. His study of all ships systems would help us in fully understanding the code.

Impressed, I asked Ræm if she wanted me to create a workstation for her. Initially enthused, she stopped dead momentarily, as if remembering something important. "No, that won't be necessary, I won't be here."

There was something in the way she said it that made me press of an explanation. Her reply was curt, "Thank you, Captain, no. My place is not here, although I do need to know it all for times yet to come. I'll use your console in the War Room, but first I need to talk to Peni. There's a quantum puzzle I need to figure out."

She departed moments later, walking for a change, instead of disappearing. Kay and I caught up on what we had missed, before settling into our normal routine,

That night we relaxed on the shore. Da Phai Nai greeted us, "Why is it everybody I know that has died, stayed dead? But oh no, not you two. You had to come back to haunt me. Welcome back! Now, let me feel your faces."

The woman ran her fingers over our eyes, and heads in turn, and stood back, saying, "Strange. You really do understand."

She left smartly. I said to Kay, "I know how she feels, you do as well. The pair of us. It was a close call."

"I'm glad you never asked. I'm not sure I could say no."

"Anyway, it's impossible. I'm married to a wonderful wife, someone I love dearly and could never part from. Her eyes still mesmerise me, even after all these years. But so do yours."

"I know. She is very special; perhaps if we'd met sooner, or in another lifetime—I've been vaguely thinking about having children, but was hoping … holding off, but it cannot be. Being dead made it all the more important, Jackie, I have to think about creating the next generation. You do understand."

"Yes, of course, and I will support you always. You also have a duty to your people to produce their next High Queen. You realise that, not only do we share everything in our daily lives together, but now we share being dead together as well. That was a weird experience. I thought I was a spirit about to be reborn."

"I discovered my essential essence, where my spirit resides…"

n'Gnung joined us a short time later, but despite his coaxing, we did not drink too much, we were still easing ourselves back into the wonders of being alive.

Nevertheless, after that night we felt whole again, and time warped onwards with undue haste. The main task of all was to monitor for any signs of the Great Ogre, but he seemed to have disappeared again, an ominous precursor.

Knowing war was inevitable, all Tribes recruited more soldiers and trained their armies. We also worked on weapons, Kay insistent, "My shield drained far too quickly, so did yours. It should have lasted hours, not minutes. We need to know what the Great Ogre is up to."

Kay and I interfaced with the core; I demanded an explanation. The Core replied, "Controller..."

"Captain, I am not Taris. Thank you for the dispensation. We need to know how the Great Ogre is draining our shields. Out with it."

"Captain, I cannot reveal that information, it is privy to only the eyes of Space Corps."

"Damn your obfuscation, where do we find that information?"

Kay placed a gentling hand on my arm, "Core, I respectfully request to be allowed access to related, but non-classified information. I was killed because my shield gave way far too quickly. Help us."

Her conciliatory tones brought forth information, from which we thought Peni might be able to figure out what was going on. I apologised, "Sorry Kay, I just find the Core quite confrontational at times."

"That is because you are also confrontational. Chill. Try being more laid back, like your normal self, and see how that works. I need to talk to Peni about shield draining technology. You coming?"

I knew she was correct, but admitting the fact to myself would take time. I followed her as we tasked Peni with the new challenge, one she found exciting.

Thereafter, the days and weeks passed quickly, and my relationship with the Core improved. Peni made progress with shield draining technology, but we agreed there was essential information denied to us. I became distracted by duties of Emperor, Harvest Home, and the next Olympiad.

I was already in training, this being the fifth year of the official games. We had defined competition elements that suited all the tribes, so each should win several events. Running was a strange sport, when set amongst all the Tribes. The Fourth were normally quickest to ten yards, where the Eleventh hit their stride. At four hundred yards, it was close between them and the Twelfth, who had the long strides, stamina, and endurance to go much farther.

That year we planned the first marathon, a run from Forest Meade to Grimwaldi Rinns, about twenty-five miles, and n'Gue was confident of victory. "Trust me, the Giants are unbeatable up to ten miles, but after that they falter, even if they will be a long way ahead by that point. We can take them. Train with me brother, Jackie. This title is ours for the taking."

And so n'Gnung and I embraced endurance training, reminding me of when I took the Trials of Passage. I was feeling fit, better than ever, and also devoting time to two other sports from my culture,

Cricket and Rugby Union. Last year the Indians had won the former, and the Aussies the latter. Otherwise, Owain was master of shark fishing, the Sixth remained unbeaten at a stone-age version of orienteering, and the Ninth at tree climbing. Our events were bizarre, but suited the Tribes' skills. There were also sports women excelled at, and others for children.

However, not all our challenges were of physical dexterity. Chess was becoming increasingly popular, as was long distance horse riding, with jumps and water — Eventing, events that females could equally excel at. The girls usually won the cookery challenge, and I wanted to compete, but it clashed with the cricket.

Preparations were entering the final stages when Jinnie took me aside, "Jackie, this is all happening at the wrong time of year for us. It is great we host the event, don't get me wrong, but it is increasingly interfering with our harvest. Food, feeding all these people we now have is my major concern."

"I agree, and had intended to raise the subject. It is too late for this year, your thoughts?"

"The short month of Spring is good for us, and the weather much better."

"Let's put it to the other Tribes." The change was proposed and approved. It suited nearly all much better.

That year my team were beaten in the Cricket final by New Zealand, the Third, and in the semi-final of the Rugby by Australia, who went on to win. We had success, Kay winning the Individual Chess Championship, but losing to Mentor in the four-way challenge. The odd game consisted of five chess boards combined as four combatants, and the central board being no-man's-land. Gung Loi won the female wrestling competition, a close bout with Aroweena. I was preparing for the last event, the Marathon, not certain n'Gue's tactics of economical running would see us win.

The starter's conch blew, and after the first mile, Rambling was leading the quickly separating field. Junior dropped in behind his father, with his wife, Constance Merryweather by his side. Angkrelguer, Ælfreisia, and Kay followed them. n'Gnung and I were already overreaching strides to keep up with Kay, but n'Gue was behind us, keeping to his plan. I knew it was all wrong. "Your brother is right, let's hit our lollop gait and sprint at the end, not the beginning."

We backed down a gear to a gait that suited us, and held our reserves for later, Hogar running with us for many miles. For much of the run, those in front of us were out of sight, but n'Gue joined us and imperceptibly upped his pace, which we matched. Then one by one, those ahead faltered. We passed the hot springs, where Ælfreisia was being attended to at the side of the road. n'Gue accelerated at that point, he had upped a gear and his flowing strides were fluid in motion. We upped our pace also, and cresting a rise, Kay came into view. She was closing quickly on her brother, Junior and Constance were visible in the distance, sitting at the side of the road.

In response, we did not up our stride rate, but lengthened our footfalls, closing slowly on all ahead of us, except n'Gue. We slowed when we reached Junior and Constance, asking, "Are you all right?"

"Yes, just tired. This is a long way."

We soon passed Angkrelguer, and came out from the final stretch of jungle, up the slope towards the final rest stop; I saw Rambling had stopped for water. He trotted off, his energy spent, Kay closing him down quickly, grabbing a tankard as she ran, and sipping, drenching herself with water. I could tell Kay was sprinting to overtake Rambling, unaware of the danger behind. n'Gue closed ominously on the pair.

I stopped at the rest station, jogging on the spot, gulping a little water, and said, "Junior and Constance are a little way down the track, and they need help. Send somebody, thank you."

We hit our stride moments later. Kay had overtaken Rambling, who was stuttering to a standstill. n'Gue was chasing her hard, but she had a quarter of a mile lead. It was time for us to up the ante, I flicked my head upwards, and our pace increased, we were now running for ourselves. Sometimes n'Gnung edged ahead, and I fought back. Later I forged ahead, and he clawed his way back to match my strides, our personal race became a sprint.

We ran all the way up the four-mile incline towards Grimwaldi Rinns, Kay leading, n'Gue closing, and we now closing on him. Rambling was following us, his footfalls ones of obdurate determination, not stamina. At last we passed over the river, and entered the square, our bodies beyond tired, our minds' alone keeping the footfalls repeating.

The crowd was cheering us onwards, n'Gnung and I sprinting side by side for all we were worth, closing on n'Gue. He glanced backwards often as he tried to accelerate, catching and passing Kay. I knew the heart went out of her, even though she upped her pace, but it was too little, too late. She seemed to wilt, and crashed to the ground. She was so private and so proud, losing so close. We were with her seconds later, and I stopped running, she was more important to me than winning, or taking second place.

The moment was strange. n'Gnung also stopped and came to her aid. n'Gue glanced behind, checking for challengers, and stopped. He came back to us – He the clear winner. Rambling caught up with us. We were the only runners for miles around, and we locked arms, and walked across the finish line together. Acceptance of the diversity of the Human Condition can be like this, its name: Empathy.

Chapter 26 ~ Evil Incarnate

Year 2036

The Great Ogre

The Great Ogre held a final briefing with his generals and operations staff. "The games begin on the island of the Second tomorrow, and we will be a part of them — we will introduce them to games of combat. Tonight we prepare for all out war, we will attack each Tribe at the same moment, and conquer them all. Their shields are hovering just above critical, reserve power almost drained. There should be little resistance to our invasion, once the final sequence begins. We start as soon as this meeting concludes. Generals, prepare to action your orders on my command.

"Controller, the Last we captured, mind-mapped, and sent to the island, has he been discovered?"

"No, Great Ogre. He was sent in via the duplicity transporter, and remains undetected."

"Good, send in the others with the barrels of debilitating drugs, and add to the water sources and drinks as soon as possible. They must also activate the control device, so I can manipulate the two soldiers whose minds we altered. What of the robotic nurse?"

"The automaton is ready to act on your command, and is near an access point to the Core, a seldom used auxiliary input to medical from a storage room."

"The virus must be released before we do anything, it will take time to compromise the Core without alerting it to what is happening. How long until the Core is enfeebled?"

"If I action this now, four hours, perhaps less."

"Do it. We attack in four-hours time, be ready."

Jack

"Jackie, I'll be forty-five next year, and want to devote my final few years to the grandchildren, and writing about my life. How do I do this?"

"Jinnie, you would live much longer if..."

"Don't start! Otherwise I will banish you."

"To the bedroom?"

"Hmmm. Your bedroom on the shore perhaps. But seriously, teach me to write."

"This is something children learn, and adults are not good at. Come with me, I'll show you how to use video recording, it is similar to watching videos, and will suit you much better."

She already knew how to use the scanner video and record segments, so quickly grasped the complexities of live recording. She began the first of her books, narrating the known history of the Second, from her point of view. Clips of people, places, and objects were added where appropriate. With a little prompting, this became fascinating to watch. Her recall of detail was amazing, especially an account in her second work of her younger years.

The Spring Festival was approaching quickly, a time of fiesta, followed by the Eighth Olympiad. This continued to evolve, and covered several days. Some teams had already arrived, and were practicing or acclimatising, it was becoming subtly serious in some aspects. I had stopped playing Rugby, becoming Coach instead. However, we had won the Cricket last year, and I was determined to keep the trophy. I also had one sporting ambition left, to win the marathon outright, something I had not quite achieved.

The Spring Festival was a great success, the following day we officially welcomed leaders of the Tribes and the rest of their teams. Celebrations continued, the mood was Carnival, when Ælthrelntheine took me to one side. "Guardian, I need to go to the Ninth. I have just received word they have misgivings, and I need to assuage them. I will return with them, give me an hour. I will also need to return to Elvenholme for a short while, but we will all be here for the opening ceremony tomorrow."

The Queen of the Eleventh departed, as other Tribes talked-up the games. The Ninth arrived late, and were the last to join us. I thought nothing of it, they were the most distrusting Tribe of all, it was their way.

Later, Kay asked, "Have you seen my mother?"

"No, I thought she came back with the Ninth. You had better ask Jinnie and the reception committee. I'm sure she is here somewhere. You know what your mother is like, always organising others."

"Tell me about it. Yet, it is not like her to miss an official engagement. I'm sure she will turn up for the opening banquet. I'll see you there in a couple of hours."

However, my schedule was interrupted. I was needed urgently on the Bridge. Gung Loi reported, "Guardian, indicators show our power reserves are critically low, and the shield just—wobbled. I don't know how else to explain it."

"What! You cannot be serious. I better take a look."

I ran diagnostics from my console, but the power went down. Systems came back up moments later, it was like an aberration. "I need Kay, n'Gnung, and Peni here at once. Send me everything you have to my ready room. I must find out what this is about."

The others joined me and we sifted data, finding nothing of note. Kay and I interfaced with the Core. "We need to understand what is happening, where has all our power gone?"

The Core stated, "Excessive drain from extraneous shield."

"Shut it down at once."

"I cannot, only you can do that, Captain. There is a controller's access restriction in place to safeguard the shield."

We looked at one another, unsure what the Core meant, and deliberated. In time I checked and said, "The Core must be referring to the umbrella shield we used during the Wrath of Gaia. There can be no other explanation. That is the only major shield we created and control."

Kay said, "Checking now. Yes, confirmed. The shield is inactive, but has been leaking power for ages. It explains why the batteries are depleted."

"Peni, I need you to run full diagnostics and find out where our power has been going to. I will decommission the umbrella shield now. Time to end this nonsense, we are hosting all the other Tribes, and must have full protection."

I closed down the extraneous shield, and power levels abruptly rose to well above critical. We all gave a huge sigh of relief, but stayed to monitor. Power levels continued to rise, and we agreed the emergency was over. Aroweena was not so sure, "Guardian, this is most strange. You should set your shields to maximum. Excuse me for a moment, I need to inform our controller."

Before she returned, I diverted all ancillary power to the main shield, and power levels appeared to settle. They were low, but not crucial; we would discover the cause after the games completed. We returned to the festivities, and soon were distracted by events of the moment.

I knew I had not overindulged the night before, but the next morning I felt off colour. Da Phai Nai's restorative potion left me feeling drained, and I knew something was very wrong. We were all the same, everyone at Grimwaldi Rinns, n'Gnung could hardly string a coherent sentence together. I asked a messenger where Jinnie was, expecting her to be by my side. "She went to meet you last night in the Church. Perhaps she is still there?"

I fumbled with my transfer bracelet, my fingers uncoordinated. I thought I had the combination right, because white light enveloped me, and after transfer, I staggered to my feet. I looked up into a face full of pustulant putrefaction. "Welcome Guardian. Thank you for coming to my humble abode."

Before I could rationalise why I was in the Great Ogre's presence, I was cuffed with Ancestral restraints, and a crown of sorts was attached to my skull. "There Guardian. Isn't this arrangement much better? Now, I control your body, you do not."

The malign laughter lasted too long. I tried to break free but was constrained externally and internally. My body resisted answering my commands. My wrists sawed at the shackles on my hands, as I thrashed my head to dislodge the device around my skull. I almost got somewhere with the latter, when a voice boomed, "Still."

I could not move. I was trapped within my body, a body that no longer responded to my command. I needed to understand. "Last night, you drugged us?"

"Oh indeed Guardian. One so brave, yet so foolish. I am pleased that at last you understand my power. Two of your own introduced a substance into your water supply. Another upgraded your weak beer. It was so simple and you never realised. Shame on you!

"Come, follow me, I want to introduce you to my exhibits. This is my celebrity ward."

I could not stop myself from following his commands, surely that was impossible? I fumed with inner rage, wanting to cleave his being to shreds, yet I followed meekly. I realised I was already his slave and no longer responsible for my actions, most at least.

We came to a deeply grained oak doorway, which opened to a flick of his finger. "Guardian, this is my trophy room, inside are many interesting exhibits, of which, you will become the latest, although I still have some to add. Follow, slave."

I trundled behind, incapable of doing otherwise. The large hall featured what looked like a circle of overly large, shower cubicles, like the composite ones the rich of the Last loved so much. I smirked inwardly; I had always been a bath person. We passed through a gap between them, and looking up, guessed they were each twelve feet high by five wide. The lights went out.

A round of white light lit the centre of the room, where a control station was set, and where I was led. The Great Ogre said, "This has been fun, but now is the time to cement your place in the annals of history. Give me the Ring of The Ancestor, and I will grant you life for all eternity."

My mind was in turmoil, my mind turning mental somersaults, as my body reacted to his command. I could do nothing to stop my body comply with his demand. I watched as my fingers took off the Ring of the Ancestor and offered it supinely to the malevolent grotesqueness. My heart quailed, and I mentally shrieked aloud. Surprised, I was answered by several telepathic, almost transcendental replies offering me reassurance.

"Good slave. Now put it on this finger."

I watched horror-struck as my fingers did as he asked.

"Ah yes, that feels much better. Next, I need your other rings as well to add to my collection, and your return bracelet if you please. I do not intend to rely on others when I wish to visit *the island*. I have decided to make a few improvements…"

I clamped my mind down, his words of subjugation, abdication of responsibility receding from my known reality. I glimpsed the place within me Kay had spoken about, my unique essence, but it was hard to define. I had almost discovered where my innate spirit resided, when I was jerked on my feet, credence replaced at once by abject horror.

We came to stand before a pod, the light going on as we neared. "Guardian, let me to introduce you to Oma, leader of the Ancestors. Unfortunately, she no longer bothers to look after herself."

I looked up into the eye-sockets of a semi-skeleton, that was grinning garishly back at me. She was hanging in liquid goo, with tubes attached to the remnants of her body. I knew, she knew, she was still alive, if only just.

The Great Ogre intruded on my thoughts, "Oma was our best repository of DNA, but recently we needed a lot, so she was harvested. I left one eye in place so she could witness today's events. You will notice it is white, quite a rarity.

"Follow. This next one is more interesting. She is named Vela and was the second in command of the Ancestors spacecraft. Her metabolism has been adapted so that she is addicted to frequent sex, although she screams blue murder. She has produced many babies. I discovered her particular DNA makes great clones. You will note she still has most of her bones and teeth left. What I love most is that within herself, her spirit is still aware of what is happening to her. Ha ha ha!"

I wanted to be sick, but the Great Ogre walked forward and kissed the glass between their lips, I mentally heard somebody howl, but it was far away. The verbal diarrhoea continued, until I had seen all thirteen remaining Ancestors. We passed some empty chambers before coming to one that had a sign on the front, Rambling, Last King of the Twelfth. The light went on, and Rambling was there, floating in front of me. His eyes were dead, looking into the impossible. I knew he was somehow, still alive within the perverse cocoon.

I gawped, and tried to speak to him telepathically. The Great Ogre interrupted, "Talking to each other is not allowed, Guardian."

He hit me hard and I was sent flying across the room. My arm felt like it was broken, my fingers no longer worked properly. He called me to attend him once again. "Rambling is now aware his wife is pregnant, and you know how tasty unborn babies of the Giants are, delectable. I will bring him to full alertness so he can witness the feasting. It is so fitting, and he will be reviled for all eternity, as was Furlong Fourgay before him."

The light in the next pod went on. "Here is another of your friends, Guardian. She is looking forward to becoming a whore for my generals, and a target for our troop training; aren't you, last ever Queen of the Eleventh."

Unlike Rambling, Ælthrelntheine's eyes were alive with outrage. I locked her eyes and saw bitter hatred staring back at me. I had no idea how we could get out of the situation, but I was determined to try. We moved on, passing several more pods that appeared empty. Coming to the end of the row, I had expected other pod lights to go on, but instead, he led me to ones set either side of the entrance.

Two pods on one side lit up, and contained a gruesome creation. "These are the outcome of a genetic experiment that, although they went slightly wrong, are most amusing. You will notice these clones have breasts, and both male and female genitalia. They are both pregnant, each by the other, true hermaphrodites. They also need a lot of sex, which is why I have to rest them from time to time. They do not know if they are male or female, and usually end up being both at the same time, which is hilarious."

The Great Ogre's twisted mind was obnoxious, and yet I was prevented from doing anything against him. He led me across to the other side of the entryway. "I had these two chambers created specifically. They are quick release pods, as I doubt either inhabitant will spend much time inside."

He flicked his finger, and the lights came on. The signs read, 'Ælkræleinnoire, whore of the Eleventh', and 'Ræm, Last hope and Slut of the Last'. For the time being those two pods remained empty, but for how long?

Something within me died as he explained his evil plans to physically debase them. Many were of a perverse sexual nature, but not all. He romanticised about how they would couple with all manner of creatures, and kill themselves, or each other, only to be resurrected to do it all over again. His macabre bellow of laughter reverberated round the room, filling me with dread.

"I can tell you are looking forward to watching, Guardian. Do not feel left out, I will allow you participate sometimes. I know you will enjoy it, and so will the other exhibits.

"Oh sorry, I forgot about your wife. She is extremely happy to be here, and is looking forward to the sex games also, and playing dead. I intend to show you a side of your wife that you never knew existed. Now where did I put her? ... oh yes, just here."

We had walked over to the pod second from the end of the row, and the light went on inside. Jinnie hung there, a look of abject terror on her face. Her eyes seemed focused far away. His taunts resumed, but I knew it was bluster. At least that was the only way my mind could deal with it.

The sign read, "Zhao Jien Noi, Last Empress of the Second." I knew I was in purgatory, when he continued. "I plan to barbeque her thighs during the celebration, once this exhibition is complete. I will allow you to watch, and maybe taste a morsel. Sex is much better without legs getting in the way, don't you agree?

"She begged me for sex last night you know, and we did it right there upon the altar of your church. Afterwards she was so grateful, she went and gave me this ring." He leered and twirled the seeping mess of the Ring of the Warrior around his ring finger. "She wanted me to take her again, so good was my loving, but I knew she was already pregnant, so why bother. I'm not sure how someone so small will cope with a large Ogre baby inside her though. It will be interesting to watch her womb grow to accommodate my child.

"I have also to thank you for providing the excitement of the Games. They reminded me of one of my father's best inventions, The Gladiators Arena. It would be fun to watch you and your profoundly pregnant wife, fighting one of my heavily armed Champions. I could allow one of you a net, the other a short knife perhaps, just to even up the odds. The prize would be the unborn baby of course. They are delicious. Perhaps I should let you and your wife try the delicacy, a mouth-watering experience.

"Obviously, after your defeat and death, you would both be reincarnated, to do it all over again. Later you will tell me what it feels like to die. Ha ha ha."

The foulness he uttered became indelibly ingrained upon my psyche, mere words so vile they could never be undone. As his grotesque monologue poured forth, I learned to hate, to loathe this abomination of humanity. Given the slightest chance, I would have killed him: Dead! Regardless of Justice, Prudence, or any other virtue, I hated his very existence with every fibre of my being, if only because the abhorrence had zero virtue, nor humanity.

"Now Guardian, I believe it is your turn to take your rightful place in this display. Beg me for the privilege."

The end pod of the row illuminated, and I was made to read the sign aloud, "Jack Barleycorn, Last of The Last." He made me kneel before him and beg to be admitted. I had stopped listening. My mind had retreated to a safe place, although my eyes still saw, and my voice spoke whatever he wanted of me. I was not even worthy of being called a slave, I was a puppet, and he orchestrated my debasement at his great pleasure. I knew he wanted to leech on my anguish, but I removed my conscious being from that realm, and denied him. He quickly appeared to lose interest in me.

My body walked willingly into the sarcophagus, and after sealing the door, he pressed a button on the console in the centre of the room. Tubes attached themselves to my body, and fluid entered from below, slowly rising up to envelope my physicality. I tried to resist the inevitable, and clamped my mouth closed, as the liquid rose higher, before entering my nose. I breathed out to repel it, but it was a hopeless gesture. The liquid entered my lungs, and felt like the hand of the Devil inside of me.

A short time later, I hung there inanimate, like all the others, my vacant eyes staring out at the world.

I witnessed the passage of time outside of my prison, but internal time was suspended. The other Kings came and were humiliated, Owain being the most belligerent, but it made no difference, the Great Ogre controlled his body, and he could do nothing but comply.

I had been trying to mind-link with Jinnie whenever the Great Ogre was out of the room, but had failed, until I cherished the love we shared. Her voice came to mind, if staccato, "He never; sex no; ring yes. I could not…"

Relief rushed through me, but the connection died. This reaffirmed my hypothesis, the Great Ogre had an Achilles heel. Now how could that be used that against him?

Time moved on; people came, but only the Great Ogre left. Eventually the room contained the leaders of all Thirteen Tribes, and we were all his slaves. There were two vacant pods, and I hoped they would both remain unoccupied, but I was quickly disillusioned.

Guards threw Kay into the room like a rag doll. She slid across the floor, banging her face into the Great Ogre's boot as she came to rest. Her nose bled, and my heart went out to her, my mind reached for hers; "Become your essential essence. Nothing else will save you from this horror."

"I heard that," The Great Ogre bellowed. "Who was it? You Guardian, I know your deceitful ways too well."

He pressed a button on his console, and I was electrically fried. My limbs flailed uncontrollable, but I knew Kay received my mind-link. She never replied.

Kay enacted whatever the Great Ogre asked of her, but her eyes were dead. His malignancy fed off others doing what they abhorred, in full knowledge. With Kay, there was nothing. Frustrated he had her disrobe, and tried to molest her, in time using her as an item of furniture. She bested him, and this gave me heart. If only I could also retreat into my own spark of life, as she had.

Before departing, the Great Ogre toured the room, admiring his specimens. He came before Jinnie, and I, "I will leave you with a live feed of your Olympiad, you will watch the screen. Notice, I added a new game. It is called Run or Die. Your people are not particularly good at running it seems. Enjoy the entertainment."

Our eyes turned automatically at his direction, riveted to the screen. We could not overrule his command. He flicked a control, and the giant display at the end of the room came to life. My heart quailed; I watched horrified as our people and all the visiting Tribes were hunted down and mercilessly slaughtered.

The Great Ogre

Up in his towered rooms, the Great Ogre felt deeply satisfied. All had gone exactly to plan, and he had secured all but one of his trophies. He could not locate the Guardian and Gatekeeper's daughter, but she would show in time. His commanders were expecting her imminent arrival.

His thoughts turned to the next phase. Within days, he would begin to exact full revenge for the slights he had suffered at the hands of the Eleven Tribes, and the Trolls. His rage was now quarried within the tenacity to exact repayment unequal with horrific interest. To his disdainful mind, death and eternal damnation were the only disbursement he would consider as salve to balm his ego, and he cursed those still free.

The draining of the Second's shield had been an immense undertaking, requiring great ingenuity and subtly to prevent detection. But the shield had failed, and doing so, had empowered his craft to maximum capacity. This finally opened the door to his total dominion of the world, and access to the stars.

Heartened, he relished the memory of all the other Kings and Empresses bowing in subservience to him, the ruler of all their kind. He laughed loudly at how they had meekly offered him their powers and obedience. Keeping them alive, yet powerless to do anything at all, trapped within their own madding minds to dwell upon their misfortune for all eternity, was a dutiful reward for his long-suffering trials at their combined hands.

To break their spirits further, he would reanimate the leaders, and return with them to the island. There the Empress would officially and publicly abdicate, and pay homage to him. She would then command the slaughter of her people. That was so fitting. He would repeat with the other Tribes in turn. The Eleventh would follow. They were isolated, trapped within his encompassing shield.

In a lighter frame of mind, he moved to the balcony, his need for action and subjugation growing with mounting impatience. In time, a means to hasten it came to him, a slight of hand that would sap the resources of the Seventh more quickly, and ultimately open their kingdom for his taking.

Chapter 27 ~ Duplicity Transporters

n'Gue

The Prime Messenger knew all was not well. It was the next morning and his brother was still drunk, despite Da Phai Nai's potion. His messenger corps bombarded him with information, the Empress and Guardian were gone, Kings were missing, and Kay was absent. He knew something strange was happening, but what?

He pressed his return bracelet and arrived on the Bridge. "Langnor, what's going on? Everybody is missing."

"I'm working on it; I only just got here myself. I'm catching up ... the shield went down several times last night, and again just now."

"It doesn't make sense. We need everybody back right now, Gung Loi and my brother first. Lock. Where the hell are Kay and Peni?"

"I have Peni in Engineering, you want her here?"

"In a minute, let's get everybody we can before they disappear." n'Gue turned to the communications monitor.

"I can't lock on Kay... She's gone! I have Aroweena. She is rallying rearguard forces and saving lives."

"Leave her to do what she is best at, and get reinforcements to her. I need experienced controllers, where's Ju Lo?"

"In Grimwaldi Rinns, but I can't lock on him."

"Main shield status?"

"Oh no, it's gone. I can't get it back up. I thought they fixed that."

"This is the work of the Great Ogre, lock us down."

Gung Loi arrived at that moment, taking briefs in turn of urgency, and actioning a string of sequential orders. She set shields over all major cities, locking every one out, except Grimwaldi Rinns, "The Ogres have already compromised our security..."

Her words were cut off, as their eyes turned in horror to watch mutant Ogre hoards appearing within Grimwaldi Rinns, a place they could not access. Gung Loi said, "We've no leaders and must step up. Get Peni here now — with answers. She's understands this stuff.

"n'Gue, I need my husband coherent and here. This is not drink, but a poison. Take him to the medical centre at once. I need him to interface with the Core. He is the highest Ring bearer left. Delegate, I need you here. I'm going to try and place a duplicity transporter beneath the Ogre shield, Langnor, have you ever done this before?"

"No, Jack and Kay were the only ones, the Gatekeeper occasionally. But I know how to do it. Where do you want it?"

"Try several, we need troops and support from other Tribes, soldiers. Ah, Peni, thank God. What can you tell us?"

"'Roses are red, violets are blue, the shields' still leaking, and nothing's new'. What do you think, I've been studying poetry.'"

"Another time Peni, focus. Do you have a translation of that?"

"Sorry, my little joke. Oh my! Are those creatures real?"

"Yes Peni. We're under attack, being invaded. The main shield is down. Can you fix it? Stop the drain?"

"Well, the umbrella shield, was being drained, but so was the main one. The drain was controlled, but I can't find out how. Power leaches still and I can do nothing without finding the source. I suggest we shut it down and try to restore energy to fully power it, later."

"Do it, Peni."

"I also fear the Core may be compromised. There has been no response to the threat. I am running a deep scans now to pinpoint the exact time of change, and what occurred. I must get back."

"Thanks, but first, does anyone remember exactly what Jack said?"

Several offered expressions, but Peni replied confidently, "Excessive drain from extraneous shield."

"That is correct," n'Gnung said as he staggered in to join them. "I was drugged, we all were. Run tests on food and liquid in the city, start with water and beer. Can somebody brief me, I need to sit down."

"Controller, please brief my husband. 'Excessive drain from extraneous shield'? That is referring to a different shield. Zhong Zhi, check every shield on this island, the transporter caverns first. I think one of them has been compromised, like Sar Tan did once before."

Langnor said, "I have the duplicity transporter ready."

"Set it at sixty-five feet, directly below the Ogre shield, and lock it's shield out so only we here have access."

"It is in place, want me to isolate the Ogre shield?"

"Yes..."

n'Gnung said, "No. We may only have one chance at this. We need the main shield up first. Otherwise, the Great Ogre will change location, or circumvent us by other means. We must interface with the Core, quickly."

"What of the other Tribes, n'Gue?"

"All are under attack, except for the Seventh. We can't contact the Eleventh. Llwydd is calling the Ddwyrthen armies to war and will join us here shortly to assess the situation."

"You have the Bridge, n'Gue. We must interface with the Core from Jack's ready room. Get us out before five-minutes are up. Peni, use Kay's console and solve this, you have minutes."

n'Gue marked the time device and hoped their combined powers would elicit information from the Core. His thoughts were interrupted when Llwydd attended. "The Great Ogre almost compromised our main shield, and would have succeeded, but for Aroweena's warning. We set shields to three-sixty before being compromised, and activated our backup station. The Great Ogre is fallible."

They were distracted as reports came from other Tribes'; the situation was dire. n'Gue glanced away, and saw the clock, almost six minutes had elapsed.

He ran to the Captain's ready room and discovered his brother and Gung Loi keeled over. He severed the connection, called for medics, and cursed his stupidity. He noticed a pen in n'Gnung's hand. There was a symbol written, one he could not decipher.

He shouted towards the Bridge, "I need anybody who can read Ancestor here, now!"

n'Gue swung round in frustration, intending to bash his fist into the wall, when he noticed the Sword of Destiny was missing. It always hung in its scabbard, from a peg on the wall. His mind worked, the Guardian had used the Emperor's heraldic sword last night, so it should be there. He was aware of others in the room, medics and controllers, but his mind remained focused, his only conclusion being, either Ræm or the Great Ogre had it. He knew that Ræm could transport herself seemingly anywhere just like the Shaman. The other eventuality did not bear thinking about.

He turned, perceiving movement behind him, and spoke briefly with the Matron, "Restoring these two is critically important. Thank you, Matron. What of the symbol, Peni?"

"It's not complete, but looks like 'sub' something?"

Mai Li was studying from over her shoulder and said, "If it were unfinished, the character would be written thus, give me the pen … there, the word is 'Down'."

n'Gue had never been quite as quick, or outgoing as his younger brother, but they had always shared a similar intellect and ability to see the hidden. He cursed and ran onto the Bridge, "Langnor, the Great Ogre is instinctively a creature of habit. Look down for another transporter. Start below us here, now. Sixty-five feet first scan. Peni, is the outer shield fully closed to three hundred and sixty degrees?"

The seconds drew out. Langnor was first to speak, "Got it, a heavily shielded transporter at a depth of sixty-three feet. Oh my Life, it's one of ours!"

"Co-ordinates?"

Peni spoke seconds later, "The main shield stops at the underwater volcano walls, it's about three hundred degrees in circumference."

"Close it. No. Wait. Search for another, deeper transporter."

"Got it. There is another transporter below it, a duplicity transporter, outside of the main shield radius," Langnor added. "There appears to be an associated power source, this ship."

Llwydd came to n'Gue with a battle plan, but the temporary controller was not a soldier. He glanced at it and said, "Gather your armies in readiness, first we must finish this and secure the island.

" I need time to consider all options. Liaise with Zhong Zhi. Send in platoons in support, but small numbers only. Spread around so that they will not become the focus of concerted attack. Peni, Langnor, do we have enough power to completely close the main shield?"

Peni replied, "Calculating. It will be close."

There appeared to be a slight hiatus, as n'Gue considered before issuing commands. He knew the first and second line executives were out of action, so chose his words carefully, "Peni, Langnor, can we send something through to the other end?"

Langnor replied, "Yes, we did this before, but we should check by sending a drone through. You are thinking of troops?"

Unsure of roles assigned to the inexperienced crew, he used titles; "No. Weapons Master, what is the largest bomb we have, I am thinking about nuclear bombs, plasma bombs.

"Drone Controller, send a small drone through to confirm connection. Thank you Langnor, action as soon as possible."

Peni spoke next, "The power requirement is critical, especially if you want to do all these other things at the same time, the slightest fluctuation could leave the plasma bomb detonating below us. It's too risky. I need Phœbe here to do the math."

Wong Kai said, "Maths are my thing, I love them. Your sister, and I, we play with figures a lot, let me have a try."

n'Gue committed each to their given task, and considered what Jack, his brother, or Kay would be thinking of in the command role. "Gatekeeper — Mai Li, that is you today — I need you to find a way to store power, maybe other ships systems, independent batteries, as with the life pods. I also need you to set parameters so we can instantly reduce all ship power consumption to little else than life support for this room and critical systems like the Boson Drive containment field. Langnor, I need all personnel within this craft here at the double."

"I'm already working on that, Captain."

Mai Li said, "I have the drone ready, permission to launch?"

"Yes, let's see what we're up against. Send two, one to return; I expect it to arrive inside the Ogre's shield around Grimwaldi Rinns. The other to reconnaissance enemy bases, until we lose it."

"Done. Yes as predicted, one is now flying over the battlefield near Grimwaldi Rinns, I urge you not to look. The other is showing millions of ogres queuing to transport. They are all soldiers.

"I have storage available, the inter-solar transport ships, whatever they are called."

"Space hoppers."

"Several are partially charged, and I can divert power to them. They are outside the main power grid. Somebody needs to go there and manually configure them. They will need to be switched from charging to depletion by hand, from the launch dock control."

Bufor, who had been quiet, said, "I will volunteer, I know the systems better than anyone else. There is a special suit there for life support, which I will wear."

n'Gue nodded, and Bufor departed. "Langnor, monitor your husband. As soon as his work is done, I want him in medical. Is the rest of the ship cleared of personnel yet?"

"Yes, all except medical."

"Damn, that's a large area, a greater power-drain. OK, we bring them here at the last second before we strike, shut the area down, and put them back as soon as power comes back up."

Langnor replied, "Got it."

Llwydd said, "Captain, we must go now, innocents are being slain needlessly. Aroweena needs weapons and immediate support. Let me lead my main troops into battle, at least for diversion, we can give you the time you need to seal this island off."

"Do it, and be careful, we will have beers to drink tonight."

Wong Kai came over to him, "Captain, it is too close to call. The figures work out in our favour, but only just. The slightest fluctuation and it could all go horribly wrong."

"Have you added in the space hoppers' energy?"

"No, they're not available. I have no accessible energy levels."

"Bufor, are you in position?"

"Yes, coupling the first now."

"Good, set to charge, couple others as Mai Li directs, we need every instance of power, a significant power-burst, we must do this."

"Understood, I will need a minute."

After a brief check of all stations, n'Gue held review. "We are committed to a delicately timed operation, one of many interlinked occurrences, of which several could show irregularities. I consider this plan to be the only way we can prevail, and ensure our security. I will take any objections. Please state you reasons now."

Silence.

"Good, we are agreed. The order of events, and the order of importance are not the same, but heavily interlinked for the best outcome. This is what we will do, once we are ensured of having enough power, which will be in three minutes time. Item one, Bufor will supply the power-burst. Item two, the plasma bomb will be sent. Item three, close the main shield. These three things cannot go wrong. Fourth, the Ogre shield around Grimwaldi Rinns must be compromised internally…"

n'Gnung and Gung Loi arrived on the Bridge from medical, attended by the Matron. n'Gue said, "Action on my mark."

Fingers of controllers hovered over buttons, all awaiting the command to strike back, "Three, two ..."

"Stop!" Peni did not look up, but continued working. Moments later she added, "Med storage bay three accessed the database a few hours ago by 'Leading Technical Nurse 123752'. Who or what is that?"

Matron replied, "That unit was badly damaged during the battle for the Fourth, it is in storage."

"It accessed the medical database five hours ago and planted a virus. I remember there was a problem with the control circuit."

"Checking ... confirmed. That is impossible! Ship systems cannot get ill."

"No, it has already happened. The Core is compromised. I want full quarantine of unit 123752 immediately. We need to know explicitly what was done. Can you extract the information?"

"Perhaps, but this is Digital Forensics, and not what we do best. I will immobilise the unit and return with the medic's electrical brain."

Matron left and Jason was tasked with unravelling the demise of the Core. "Use n'Gnung's station. We need results as soon as you can, Jason. Remove the infection and bring the Core fully back online."

Jason spoke minutes later, "I have a backdoor. This is an extremely nasty trojan, and multiplying as systems are used. Stop working now. Everything. If you issue any command, it may be subverted."

Phœbe appeared by his side, and once updated, flopped down to work the consol. "Jason, we need to write an antivirus. Send the original to me." Her fingers flew across the keyboard as she spoke.

"OK, what I am doing, is using the same infection, but changing it to unwrite itself and put everything back as it was. There, that should do it. You want to check?"

"No Phœbes', do it."

"It is working, but taking too long. Can we reboot the Core?"

"Theoretically, yes. We need the backup point before the infection entered the system."

"I have the timestamp, and ... Yes, I have the system restore set. Captain, we need to reboot the Core, you will lose everything, including shields for a few moments, but this should work."

n'Gue thought quickly; "No. We cannot be defenceless, even for one second. We would lose current information as well. Stop. Monitor the anti-virus for eradication of threats, we'll reboot later. Can we speed the process?"

Phœbe replied, "A few seconds only, almost there ... Sandbox and quarantine ready for use."

"Peni, I need an external shield placing around this craft now. Leave a gap so the Ogre's duplicity transporters still functions. I'll take the chance they won't discover what we're doing.

"Phœbe, action immediately."

"External shield set, Captain."

Moments passed. "Trojan crippled, not yet fully eradicated, working... quarantine active. Core Safe. Last good configuration in, systems coming up. Anti-virus successful, Captain... Virus eliminated, but we will check for residual code snippets, running them through the sandbox. The ship is now yours to command."

"Excellent! Power levels, Peni?"

"Restored to minimum. There is enough power to complete the task, and little risk with extra power from the Space Hoppers."

n'Gue actioned their plan at once, the immediate responses from operators were hard to distinguish.

"Space hopper power reversed and available."

"Plasma bomb sent."

"Main shield active, three-sixty degrees."

"Major detonation in central Greenland. The bomb went off there, thank God."

"Ogre shield Grimwaldi Rinns locked down tight."

People hooted and cheered in delight, they had done it, stopped ingress, and cut off the power drain. They had secured the island's integrity. n'Gue remained stalwart, not distracted by the parts of the whole, his first thought was for the man who made possible. "Bufor? You did it! We got enough power, come back now."

Langnor was staring at her screen, dumbfounded. "He discarded his protective suit in space dock, he didn't know, and is in the medical centre, except there's no life support."

n'Gue was not a master of control systems, but Langnor had frozen. He locked on to her husband and transferred him to the University medical facility, his mistake for not following through, specifying which medical location. He looked aside and said, "Matron, save that man, and take those two with you."

"Transporting now."

He wiped his forehead with a finger, and looked around, before continuing, "Wow! That was close. We won the first battle.

"Now, focus on what is to come. Zhong Zhi, I want your focus only on shields, work and learn from Peni. The Great Ogre will strike back. Before the main shield powers to one-hundred percent, I want the umbrella shield up and able to withstand a plasma bomb attack. Extend to three hundred and sixty degrees as soon as you are able, we must be secure, so we can concentrate on defeating the Ogre within."

Peni broke the lightening mood and relief. "I cannot lock on the duplicity transporter, it is heavily shielded."

"Secure it with one of our shields," n'Gue replied, giddy in the success of his unaccustomed role.

"No, that's not it. It is physically linked via an underground crack, that on inspection, does not appear to be of natural formation, to the inside of our main shield. Now what was it Isaac Newton said, not his Genesis meaning about the Apple falling on his head, but the other one … Ah yes, inversely proportional? No, equal and opposite, that's the one. Leave this with me. I have an idea. I wish Mister Ted were here…"

n'Gue had no idea what Peni was talking about, and dismissed her aberrant thoughts. He needed to focus on the battle at hand.

Hundreds of dead and dying, the maimed needed transfer to the University medical unit. Field hospitals and more troops had to be deployed. Half thinking he replied, "Peni, do what you will, but seal this fracture. Send some of your apple-pie down there. That should be impervious to anything."

"Apple Pi, wow you are brilliant. I'm on it—when it lands, an apple bounces you know."

n'Gue was thinking of a suitable retort, when Barph arrived, "Commander, Llwydd and I are agreed to hold Horovitz, Stewart, and Gung Loi's troops in reserve. They will be deployed to best effect as the battle develops. We need Ancestral weapons and protection bracelets in order to take the fight back to the Ogres."

"I know where they are, but not how to access them. Regardless, only four people have an access ring of enough seniority to open the armoury: Jack, Kay, Jien Noi, and my brother. This may take a moment. At ease, General."

n'Gue was about to make the request, but Langnor was ahead of him, "n'Gnung is being transferred now to Engineering, Armoury. You need to be there, n'Gue. Take Zhong Zhi with you. He needs to learn

"Stop! There is no life support."

"Wait, checking, temperature and oxygen are OK, if you are quick"

Minutes later, n'Gue returned to the Bridge with the Ancestral weapons and protection bracelets. Barph departed.

Before he had time to update, Peni said, "I have it, and your apple-Pi made all the difference. Make a transporter in this configuration, it sort-of bounces whatever comes our way, back to whomever sent it. Neat, eh? It should be placed exactly here."

"Do it," n'Gue said, bewildered.

"What me?"

"Yes Peni, we are relying on you to do this, place the device. You do everything but press the button."

Pleased something had gone their way, he sat stunned when Langnor said, "An army of Ogre troops have just appeared inside Grimwaldi Rinns. They are new mutants, with four eyes. They are killing machines. We need reinforcements. What are we to do?"

Chapter 28 ~ War Lord

n'Gue's mind warped, stuttered momentarily at the impossibility of a fresh Ogre attack, yet there it was before him on his screens. The island was locked down, secure. Nevertheless, a division of highly trained Ogre soldiers had just appeared within the shielded area of their capital city. "This is impossible. How the...? Langnor, set Capital shield to three-sixty, now. Peni, main shield status?"

"Main shield ninety-four percent, and solid. No breach detected."

"Wong Kai, scan the perimeter, we need to know where these Ogres are coming from. Mai Li, look for transfer signatures within our main shield. Zhong Zhi, search for Ogre locations immediately. Peni, is the Ogre's duplicity transporter compromised yet, your rebound shield ready for activation?"

"One minute for rebound shield, but they did not come from there. The main shield is set to normal, allowing fish to enter and leave our waters. I have swimming ingress near the Western Isle. Ogres."

"Reset to base configuration, the one we used to allow only air and rain through during the dark times."

"Twenty *mol* it is. Set. Actioned. That should stop them. This Great Ogre chappie is quite clever it seems, but no match for us. Want me to tie down all the shields?"

"Yes Peni, this is your speciality, but work with our younger controllers, so they all learn what to do. Set all internal shields three-sixty, fully locked out, except for access by us on the Bridge. There must still be transfer circles under control of the Great Ogre, find them all. They could appear to be ours, so double check. We need to stop reinforcements, so we know what we are fighting, and where. Langnor, that is your priority.

"Note to Controller's log: Recommend Bridge crew cross-training at all consoles."

Bufor returned to duty as Mai Li said, "Controller, Peni, I have located several Ogre duplicity transporters below Grimwaldi Rinns. These are now locked out. They all employed our dedicated transportation signature, meaning no alarm sounded. This is a serious security breach."

Wong Kai spoke up, "I have all points of ingress identified: Western Isle, the Outlands twice, the main island nearby, and the one where Sar Tan was banished. There are other Ogres scaling the outer walls, sending co-ordinates to your console."

"Disseminate to all. Immediate relocation to the War Room, the Bridge was not intended for battle situations. Langnor, that includes you. Bufor, please oversee the relief crew. Look for and report anything you think we may have missed. Relocate now."

The team reassembled in the dedicated facility, the flow and access to information, and groupings greatly enhanced. The Gatekeeper Elect was first to report, "I have seven unassigned transporters above ground, and they were not put there by us."

"Isolate each of them at once, three-sixty always, unless specified otherwise. Also set a shield to the village on the shore of the Outlands, they are not going to destroy that. Langnor, watching brief as Overseer, we begin to fight back now. Next?"

The Guardian Elect said, "Controller, I have all sources of Ogre intrusion detected outside of the Capital, working now on the internals of Grimwaldi Rinns. It's a mess."

n'Gue glanced at the main battle screen, wishing he had not. The bodies of the innocent were scattered all over the greater capital area, the dedicated sports arena the main target. A memory surfaced. "Ask Doctor Steel to liaise with the Matron. We are going to need field hospitals, and the University hospital fully staffed. I am expecting thousands to be either dead or dying within the next hour. We must stop this massacre of the innocent."

n'Gue needed to step back and think, but information and requests continued to assail him. His respect for Jack, Jien Noi, and Kay increased greatly. He missed his brother's support the most.

He was surprised when Weid Noi joined them, "n'Gue, you are doing a good job, but please rescue Ju Lo and his family, they have been attacked and are dying."

n'Gue roused in response, "Damn. Get Ju Lo and his family to safety and hospital immediately; can you do it? Inform Matron that we are badly in need his expertise. Is there anything else, Seer?"

"Yes, reinstate life support below. You are going to need it soon. All the other Tribes need your immediate support, or rescue, but first you need to protect the extant, all the people on this island, and all the livestock. In the meantime, I'll work over there and look after Ju Lo."

Hearing the Seer's words, Mai Li spoke up, "The bases of the Independent Tribes, near the University, they are unprotected."

"Protect them at once, and check the Billy group, and our livestock Mai Li, and set protection. Next look for whom or what else we have overlooked. Thank you, Seer.

"Langnor, we need a dedicated team to monitor every other Tribe. I suggest recalling the back-up crew as observes. Use your children, the twins, and others like Xi Xah; one controller monitoring each Tribe."

Langnor cut in, "Only the Seventh are secure. I have sent them a warning to look below for duplicity transporters. Apparently, they already did, but not down far enough. Still nothing from the Eleventh, and I cannot contact them at all. Every other Tribe is badly overrun. We need to bring every one of them here, now."

"Action as best you can, this is now your primary brief."

n'Gue began to flounder, this was too much for him. He needed less information and more resolution. He was receiving the opposite. People spoke to him; everybody was speaking at him. He stood and turned to the door, as if to run away; 'Ah', he prayed, 'The freedom of the open road'. Instead, he held his hand up to silence speakers, and looked around. Everyone, and especially those not present, were relying upon him to do his duty.

He remembered Jack talking about leadership and delegation, which he now understood. 'Horses for courses', that was what Jack said, meaning – use your people to maximise their personal abilities, and give them recognition for developing to become more than themselves, for the benefit of the greater whole. The framework was already in place, all he had to do was utilise it.

He looked at his senior operators, there was only Langnor, Bufor was on the Bridge. He realised he needed both of them. Turning a deaf ear until he addressed the balance of the team, he strode towards the only person not under his control, "Seer, I need Bufor here, and I also need somebody to watch over the reserve crew on the Bridge. Could you, would you do that for me?"

"That is why I am here. Thank you for appreciating me; all you had to do was ask. Well done, again. Please know I can either observe, or I can act. I am prohibited from doing both at the same time."

n'Gue shook his head, and realised he was in charge of the fate of the nation, of all the Tribes. There was no brother or mentor to advise. He was all there was. Stepping up, he gave his first authoritative order of the day, "Zhong Zhi, Peni, I need you responsible for island and spacecraft security. Nothing, nobody comes in, and nothing, nobody goes out without express permission. Find all the Great Ogre's ruses and tricks, and stop them dead.

"Bufor, I need you dedicated to supporting and liaising with our troop commanders. Find any means to defeat the Ogres already within our midst. Before deployment, everything is run through this command post, understood?"

Gung Loi appeared, "I am released, but only just – n'Gnung will be an hour or more. What's the current situation?"

n'Gue clapped her on the back. "You better pick up the pace and learn as we go along, there is too much ongoing for a full briefing. Briefly, the main shield is stable, umbrella shield activated, all shields three-hundred and sixty degrees containment. The island is now secure, but Ogre troops are inside, using transporters, we have identified locations, and are currently locking them out. Ogres are on the rampage in Grimwaldi Rinns and obliterating everything. You take tactical and counter-strike, I'll continue with the rest."

n'Gue looked up as an influx of Ogre warriors appeared on the main screen, they were enhanced Ogre killing machines using Ancestral weapons and protection, and seemed able to drain the islander's shields instantly.

Gung Loi said, "Any news of Ræm, she's missing, isn't she?"

"Yes, and so are all leaders of the Twelve Tribes. And, the Sword of Destiny is gone."

Gung Loi stared at him and nodded. "I need all uncommitted troop commanders here now."

She took a moment to scrutinize the situation, using Kay's War Room station, before stating, "Langnor, situation?"

"I have secured many from other Tribes, but I am running out of transporters and shields. I am playing cat and mouse with the Great Ogre, and he is clever."

Her mind worked quickly, they were hampered by lack of experienced controllers. She worked the control station, knowing it was quicker for her to set a transporter beneath the homelands of the Eleventh, than walk another through the process. "Langnor, I have placed a transporter below the Eleventh's control, get somebody to make physical contact, Xi Xah perhaps."

Done, she refocused on the immediate. Weid Noi returned and announced to no one in particular, "They are fine on the Bridge, it's not as if this spacecraft is going anywhere."

Her intimation went unheard, she knew the paths of providence were dwindling, and set to observe.

Gung Loi worked tactics regards the best deployment of the team. "Bufor, I'll take over from you. I need you to work exclusively on 'Operation Disruption of Ingress'. Transfer, and keep transferring the enemy, anywhere away from our unprotected people. I need a head count. We must exterminate the entirety of this Ogre infestation. You remember how we did this before. I'll send you killing zone co-ordinates in a moment, but presume the Western Isle."

"I suggest the ravine we use for the Trails of Passage. Block the open end and kill them from above, the Ogres seldom look up."

"Brilliant, thank you Bufor. I'm ready to lock on Ogres. Priorities: removal of enemy forces, rescue of the innocent. Prepare. Captain Steward, your input?"

"The defile is perfect. We'll take the ground above. Horovitz, you blockade the end and strike to finish them off. Haak Len, your platoons are much better suited to running disruption of incursion, laying traps, and isolating groups for transfer so we can kill them."

"Thank you Captain Stewart, time to deploy. Liaise with Bufor, we begin as soon as your men and Horovitz' are set. Haak Len, work with me to pinpoint where your teams can make the greatest difference."

Horovitz said, "I will action this at once, but I must tell you two of my men are missing. It may be coincidence, but they were the two caught in the explosion at the homeland of the Fourth."

"That is most odd; too coincidental. Mai Li, try to find them."

Battle dynamics changed quickly, Ogres were transported and killed, the next group already locked by Bufor, appearing moments later to meet the same fate. It was slaughter. The innocent persisted; survivors sent to the University hospital, which was already sprouting field units. The numbers of the dead and dying, of all Tribes, mounted until the flood lessened, then turned into a trickle of new patients.

Gung Loi's thoughts turned outwards. "Langnor, our city and towns are all but clear; what of the other Tribes"

"We have some success. Many have been saved, but Ogre numbers continue to thwart us. We need reinforcements and a little luck."

"Reinforcements we don't have, but a little luck, perhaps. Send your problems to the ravine, where we will execute them. Have you secured all the Tribes yet?"

"No, but this will help me greatly. Bufor, work with me exclusively, and we will finish this."

"What of the others?"

"The Seventh remain secure, and the Trolls are giving as good as they get. However, we still cannot contact the Eleventh, Xi Xah could not get through. I fear the worst. There is a major Ogre shield, three-sixty degrees around Elvenholme. We cannot penetrate it, so who knows what is going on inside."

"I'll rally troops here for redeployment. Which locations are most urgent. No, wait, if we liberate the New Tenth first, we gain fearsome troops. Peni, drop any unnecessary internal shields once the threat is passed, we are still seriously low on power."

Mai Li said, "I have found the missing soldiers, they are near the reservoir in Grimwaldi Rinns, and appear unconscious."

"Transfer them to the medical centre for examination. But quarantine them."

A few minutes later, she received a report from Matron, "Both men were compromised, similar to the way n'Gue was. They had what appeared to be a second communicator attached inside their cheeks; first indications are these were data storage and transmission devices."

"They were used to spy on us. See what information you can retrieve, and heal them. Mai Li, send word to check all others involved in the incident, they were mainly Fourth if I remember correctly."

n'Gnung returned at that moment, and taking a short brief said, "What happened here, and to me, could have happened to any Tribe. I worry the Seventh and Eleventh may be similarly compromised, please send a warning at once. What of the poison at Grimwaldi Rinns?"

"We've had no time to check. We only just salvaged this day."

"Yes, I realise, congratulations. I did not mean it in that context. But, we need to know if water or food at the Capital was compromised. Have Doctor Sylvia run checks at once. In the meantime, no one is to eat or drink anything within Grimwaldi Rinns, until we define what precisely was compromised. Ask Doctor Steel to check the capital for contamination. Soi Long did not suffer the same fate?"

"No, but Ogres ravaged the town. There is not much left. Many of the people are hiding in the hills nearby."

"I see they only attacked our people this time, not our main storehouses. Our citizens, the other Tribes also, need reassurance. Set up field canteens at major centres and ask volunteers to help. It will make them feel useful and kindle goodwill. It will also fill empty bellies. I will task Da Phai Nai as overseer; she has a way about her that remains inimitable."

"Good. I need to check something in the medical centre I won't be a minute. I think I know who may have poisoned the water."

Da Phai Nai

Da Phai Nai reprised her role from previous invasions, overseeing the overall food provision. Being unable to use the largest kitchen at Grimwaldi Rinns compromised her plans. Technically, the largest kitchen of all was at the University, plus the hospital also had one that was rarely used. She spoke at once to John and Helen, before asking the chefs for their full support.

The University kitchen was supplying food to the hospital, and she said, "John, we need this kitchen to help us feed the population and visitors, the growing numbers of evacuees. The situation is critical. Could you staff the hospital kitchen so it remains dedicated to patient's welfare and the University, freeing this kitchen? I need bulk food prepared here, such as stew and flatbread, before being disseminated to wherever it is needed by transporter. I have thousands of mouths to feed."

"Yes Da Phai Nai, we were unaware of the greater situation. I will see to it at once. Chef, any questions?"

"No, Chancellor. I have ten-gallon tea urns that will be ideal to transport the stew. A small fire to keep the food hot can also be set beneath them. Flatbreads, OK, what about rice, I have lots of it and it is quick to cook. Can your kitchens back us up with things like your mealy-meal, fresh fruit, and vegetables?"

"Consider it done. Time is of the essence, people are hungry." She left the kitchens awhirl of activity, and set up field kitchens, the main purpose being to serve University food to the needy, and supplement with their own cooking as best as they could.

She received a message to attend Grimwaldi Rinns, where Sylvia Steel gave a provisional results. "The water and beer were tampered with, and match with Matron's earlier findings. There is little else, except that those who did not partake of either appear to be fine. I will continue running checks, but I suspect this is all the result you need."

"So, I need to get rid of the water and beer."

"No, but it is best to wait twenty-four hours before using any. This poison does not last long after it has been activated, and it dissipates naturally. Use fresh beer, and take water from the river, not the city or palace reservoirs, and all should be fine."

Da Phai Nai continued to hone the response, ticking off items on her mental list, and being rewarded by seeing people eat their fill. The major centres of population were if anything, oversupplied, and she turned her attention to the others. The independent Tribes near the University were fine, but she made a point of inviting them, surprised when some accepted the offer of extra food. Billy's group were OK, as were the inns along the highways.

She reasoned that any who were at home in areas of scant population would be self-sufficient, and returned to Grimwaldi Rinns for a last check. Her day had been long and harrowing and she was growing weary. Satisfied all was well, she sat down to take a tonic, before retiring for the night. She was too tired to bother eating, herself.

As she relaxed, her eyes looked around, noticing a flicker of light she could hardly perceive. Yet it remained, not constant, but true. It lay far away, across the main arena, more than a mile distant. It was a place she had not visited, but obviously, people were there. She asked several passers-by for information but all shrugged; they knew nothing. The staff knew little either, and she determined to investigate.

There were no messengers around to arrange her transfer, so she said to the head chef, "I'm going to find out who is over the other side. Send a messenger to me when you find one, they are obviously all too preoccupied to bother with an old woman like me."

Da Phai Nai stomped off into the night, her inner fire once more ignited. No one came to her, but she arrived at a small encampment some time later, where she found people from one of the Tribes eating berries and grubs. She could not speak to them, but supposed this was probably not their natural diet. She mimed that food was available at Grimwaldi Rinns, shooing several off to seek sustenance.

Her mind turned to providing a field kitchen for them, when she saw other campfires glowing in the distance. They were scattered around haphazardly, and she left for the nearest. Similar scenes greeted her at that, and the other encampments she went to. All were living off what little there was, and she was unable to speak to them. However, each time she managed to send representatives off towards the capital.

She wanted to sit down and rest, but there was one last group. One last effort before she could relax. The way was difficult, and she stumbled in the darkness. Sporting fresh cuts and bruises, she staggered into the camp, intent on completing her duty. Welcoming hands reached for her, and guided her to sit. A bowl of gruel being placed in her hands.

She heard her name being called, before a face she recognised appeared before her. "Mentor?"

"Da Phai Nai, it is late. What are you doing way out here?"

"I saw the fires; the others do not have enough food. Do You? There is plenty at Grimwaldi Rinns, more than enough for all. Please send word. I think I need to lie down for a moment."

She felt herself falling, hands reaching to support her. Her next recollection was of strong hands lifting her, the voice of one of her long-time tormentors spoke, "Thank you Mentor, I was searching for her."

"n'Gnung, it is I who should thank you. We did not know the threat was annulled, and feared the worst. Now we have food and are once more in your debt."

The voice of her captor spoke to her ear, "I am so much in admiration of you, and so mad at you, I don't know whether to kiss you or beat you. Know these people are now being fed, their wounded being cared for. And that is all because of you. We missed them, but you did not. Thank you."

They were engulfed in white light, and then the lolloping strides of n'Gnung brought her to the medical facility, "Matron, please see this one has top priority, she saved many lives today. She needs full restoration, and I will check on her in the morning."

Da Phai Nai was trying to form a response, when her mind skewed and a sedative took over her little remaining consciousness.

Chapter 29 ~ Purgatory

Ræm

The calling Ræm had waited her whole life for, came as if from the ether. She had taken the Sword of Destiny days earlier, and the time to wear it in their first battle together was upon her. Her years of training with the Shaman had been for this one moment. She must hide her true purpose until the final confrontation. Only then could they win.

It was time to rally herself to face the final battle. She took the pennywhistle gifted by the Fourth, and blew a short reel, summoning them to battle. Likewise, she held the runed dagger of the Seventh, and calling upon their allegiance, plunged it into the earth, their birth-gift vow to honour. She repeated until all the Tribes had been called to war, and settled for a moment's contemplation.

She looked over to the Shaman, who, trancelike, flicked bone japa mala beads with her thumb as if counting them. Her head snapped up and she looked at Ræm,

"Ogre Great with Elves does meet,
at Andes centre plant your feet,
play his words but be discrete,
one chance is all for his defeat."

She had discussed strategy with the Shaman, how to emasculate him, except if he begged genuine forgiveness. The Great Ogre never would. That was what they were counting on, but he would never know, at least until the final moment before his essential spark of life, was exterminated forever. The Shaman's prerogative came to mind.

"One before ye, you must slay,
Rebirth of life does not hold sway.
Extinction is the key of play,
For Ogre Great, all lives must pay."

At Ræm's waist, the Sword of Destiny waited expectantly. She donned the Ægus, a birth-gift of the Twelfth that would protect her, both physically and magically. Her mortal wounds would become mere scratches and bruises that would quickly heal.

Nearby the Shaman chuckled. Ræm already knew this had been planned since before her birth. Now she came into her own, and determined not to let Gaia or her sufferance of humanity down. Ræm left at once, arriving in the control centre of the Eleventh, as planned.

Upon arrival she said, "Go Angkrelguer. Great Ogre, I offer you the chance to surrender. You still have time to undo this wrong."

The Great Ogre laughed in her face, as Ogres rushed her, but she did not resist. She was shackled and a crown of sorts placed upon her head. The Great Ogre commanded, "Kneel to me and repeat these words of homage and allegiance..." and she did.

"I have been waiting for you, I knew you would come to save The One Tree, but you are already too late. Nevertheless, I have a place set aside for you to watch, and enjoy the new world I am creating. Come with me, you are under my power now. I control your body, your actions, everything except your essence. All you can do is watch what I compel you to do, helpless within."

Ræm smiled inwardly, the Shaman's plan was working perfectly. The Ogres Ancestral shackles did not bind her. She wore them to mollify him for the moment. The real battle lay ahead, one the Great Ogre was bound to lose. All he had to do was kill himself.

She was aware she could end his life at any moment, but that was not enough – his essential essence had to be eradicated for all time, and there was only one means to do that, so for the time being she would play the fool.

Angkrelguer

The Prince of the Eleventh had been preparing to leave with the official party and contestants. This year he had devoted time training for the marathon, which he was determined to win and finally best his sister. The other main threats remained n'Gue and his brother, Jack, and Rambling, but he determined to stick to his plan, and win.

The mood of the assembling group was one of adventure. They were looking forward to renewing friendships and enjoying the hospitality of the Second. His mother had promised to return before the opening ceremony, but she was overdue, which irritated him. Then he received a message, asking him to attend the control room.

"What is the problem, controller?"

"Prince, I have been monitoring an anomaly with our shield. It does not make sense. It is as if there is a power drain, but I have checked systems and there is nothing abnormal."

"What of power levels now?"

"They are low, almost critical. What should I do?"

"Keep searching for the cause, there has to be one. Send word to the other Tribes, the Seventh and Second, they may be able to help."

Seconds later the controller reported, "Prince, our messengers can't transport, neither can I videoconference. We are isolated, locked-in."

Angkrelguer's instincts flared, "The Great Ogre. Close the shield immediately, full circle. I'll call men to arms. We are under attack."

Focused on the festive atmosphere, all troops except the elite Elven Guarde were slow to respond. The Controller reported, "The shield is closed, but there is a breach."

"Duplicity transporters. Damn, set an exterior containment shield and deny the Ogre's access. Elven Guarde, transporter room now, kill anything that comes through."

Troops turned to run towards the doorway to the transporter, when the doors opened, revealing the Queen of the Eleventh. She was shackled and wore a strange crown of Ogre design. Behind her walked the Great Ogre. He was wearing the return bracelet of the Eleventh. The Elven Guarde attacked, their weapons bouncing off the Great Ogre's personal shield. He roared with laughter, before smiling malignantly, "Slave, tell your men to lay down their arms and back away. They cannot hurt me."

They were slow to react, two dying as the Great Ogre swung his battleaxe and Kriegsflegel with alternate arms. "I won't ask again, tell your troops to disarm and leave."

Angkrelguer gave the order, knowing his finest would regroup. "Thank you Prince. That was a wise choice. Now you must make another. I will allow the High Queen of the Eleventh, your mother, her freedom, if you hand over control of this centre to me, now."

The Prince froze. The Great Ogre said, "Slut, beg for your life."

Ælthrelntheine dropped to her knees, and pleaded for her life.

"Silence. Bow your head and expose your neck for beheading."

The Queen did as requested without a hint of protest. However, she flicked her eyes at her son, who saw a steely fire of resistance within. He knew he could not hand over their control to the beast, but neither could he watch his mother, their leader, be slaughtered. Neither could he overpower the Great Ogre, never mind defeat him. The Great Ogre swung his axe for effect, before looking Angkrelguer in the eye, and wielding it with mortal intent. The blade wheeled in an arc, before descending with speed towards his mother's exposed neck.

He cried out, "Stop! I will do it."

The Great Ogre brought the heavy axe to rest on the back of Ælthrelntheine's neck, marking the spot with blood. He chuckled, "Wise decision, Prince."

Angkrelguer tried to limit the damage, "Our deal is one-minute control of our centre, in exchange for my mother's life."

"Agreed."

"Controller, step away. Great Ogre, if you please."

The Prince watched the Great Ogre deftly work the controls, horrified to realise he was wearing the Ring of the Eleventh, the most powerful ring of their Tribe. It was too late to atone for his actions.

Moments passed and the Great Ogre stood and said, "Ah. That's much better, don't you think. Controller, come here."

The man did as requested, only to receive a killing dagger through his heart. He crumpled to the floor, the clutches of death upon him. The Great Ogre smiled and said, "Come slave, time to action my plans."

Angkrelguer shouted belligerently, "You said you would free her."

The Great Ogre leaned towards him, and with a conspiratorial smile said, "I lied."

Angkrelguer somersaulted backwards and activated his protection bracelet, just as the Great Ogre swung his axe to decapitate him. The blade bounced off at an awkward angle and the Great Ogre swore. With little time to react, the Price knew he had to get away, and before the Great Ogre could compromise them more.

Ræm materialised at that moment by his side, and said, "Go Angkrelguer. Great Ogre, I offer you the chance to surrender. You still have time to undo this wrong."

The Great Ogre laughed in her face, but was wary. Angkrelguer had only one play, their secret back-up control room, one not visited for years. His fingers worked the return bracelet, but in a different sequence. The transporter doors opened to admit incoming Ogre soldiers as he disappeared in a flourish of white light.

Angkrelguer had no time for thought, Ræm had given him a chance, and he reacted instinctively, locking out the secondary control, and instigating maximum shields, before using the control as a rallying point for counter-offensive. He brought in Ælfreisia first, and the Elven Guarde, and they worked to spread the alarm and prepare for war, the first ever invasion of their home soil.

Jack

Trapped immobile, but sentient, my mind filled with the anguish of the undead housed next to me. I could not look away from the screen, and witnessed the taking of hundreds of lives. It was so unjust. I needed to fight back, or cry in loss.

My mind almost fractured, hearing the plaintiff cries of the Ancestors opposite. Mustering the last of my willpower, I withdrew to a still place where my mind was unaware of the horrors without, although my eyes still witnessed everything.

Time passed slowly, and yet this was the first day of my captivity. I felt Oma reach out. I could not imagine what it must be like to be locked within your own mind for thousands of years. Surely, her sanity would be unhinged. Subsequently, the true voice of Oma came to me, as the banshees of her outward projection were replaced by a deep serenity. "Son most fair, it grieves us to see you trapped this way, and know it was our design to defeat the Great Ogre, that we gave him a power in order to trick him. Our plan failed and here we have rested since time immemorial. That you are here means the final battle is at last approaching, and we will either prevail or die. Either is preferable to our current existence, condemned to exist in purgatory forever."

Our mental communication continued for some time, until the Great Ogre reappeared. Oma warned me he possessed a small metal

"Give it to me. Langnor, as troops come available, free the other tribes, the Twelfth first, we need their bulk as warriors."

Kay transferred to Engineering, where she opened the armoury, liaising with n'Gue for dissemination of protection bracelets and weapons, including plasma cannons.

Once done, she gave her students a crash course in shield manipulation and redeployment, ensuring each of them completed the task several times.

Once competent, she left them with instructions and departed to interface with the Core from the Captain's ready room. She presented the protection-draining weapon, and Ogre shackles, the crown also, and demanded answers. The response was evasive at first, until she pressed the point, "We are dying because of these weapons. Reveal the answers to me."

The Core became instantly forthcoming, and she smirked, "I've cracked the secret code, 'Reveal' perhaps?"

She received a flood of new information, and knew the best person to action response was herself. She returned to Engineering, where her students were becoming minute-masters of shield technology. She began replicating the Ogre shield draining technology. A sample weapon was produced. Needing help, she said, "n'Gnung, test this at once. I need to know if it works in the field."

"I will send it through to the Eleventh now. Meet me in the war room in one minute."

The device despatched via messenger, n'Gnung rendezvoused with her, "Kay, you look drained. You must return to medical."

"In a minute, I need coffee please. What of our battles?"

The brief update was barely complete before word came back that the new shield draining device was working well. She was about to speak when Ju Lo appeared by her side. "I am back. This reincarnation business is rather odd, we must talk about it sometime. But for now, where do you need me?"

Kay jumped up and hugged him, before saying, "Work with Langnor, she's monitoring the other Tribes at risk. Oh, and good to have you back. Excuse me, I must speak to Peni."

They exchanged a meaningful look, before Kay left for Engineering. "Peni, I need you and the others here to split your time. Continue shield production, but also replicate this design, it is the shield draining technology of the Ogres, and it works in the field. We need as many as you can, as quickly as possible. I'll run through the process with you the first time."

The words had hardly left her lips when n'Gue arrived at her side, "Kay, you must come at once. Owain, Jack, they are dying. Nobody understands how to operate the Great Ogre's control."

"Desist! I am not going. My life will remain under my control, and I will live it out according to my wishes and view of this world. Capisce?"

"You need me here, I must stay with you."

"No, go. If anything, we are now the strongest of the Tribes, excepting the Seventh perhaps. I need you to go and put things right. That is your calling. Now kiss me, and leave me in peace. Later I will need a word with you, but after all this kafuffle has died down."

"When you are strong enough, you must tell our own people. They are more important than this meeting, which can wait for several days."

"You are correct, I will go to Grimwaldi Rinns in a moment, but first I will tell everyone here where they should also be. Leave it with me, but join me for the announcement."

A short while later, Kay and I arrived in the control room of the Eleventh and were transported onwards to Angkrelguer. "Thank heavens you and mother are all right. Jack, great to see you, I can't imagine what you went through."

"It was rather strange, but we will speak of it another time. How can we help? What do you need?"

"There is still one band of Ogres we must finish off, otherwise the threat is neutralised. I have contacted the Community of Mages, and asked them to assist. I hope Ælthrelntheine will not be annoyed."

"She should have come straight here and made the decision herself. I agree with you, they were ostracised by our grandfather for no good reason and need to be brought back into the bosom of our Tribe. Where is Ælfreisia?"

"She is working with the injured and dying. I fear for our existence, so many have been killed."

"Were any sent to the Second for treatment?"

"No I … we, er…"

"I'm going there now, Jack?"

We returned to the Elven control centre, where Kay used the scanners to quickly review what needed to be done. "They are not equipped to deal with these injuries, at least not so many of them."

"Kay, I'll return and send medics here to treat minor injuries. We'll treat major injuries and those that can be saved at the University hospital. A medic can identify any that could be resurrected."

That day became a blur. I worked with the Eleventh first, their Mages coming to assist in unusual but beneficial ways. Jinnie managed to adjourn Ælthrelntheine's meeting. I in turn accompanied her when she pronounced the Great Ogre dead, and victory for Allied forces. I could not stay, but watched concerned as she was carried on a litter back to her rooms in the palace.

capacity to read their thoughts. This had been what sealed their fate, because they did not realise until it was far too late.

My eyes were compulsorily fixed on the giant screen, and I saw it blur, presumably Gung Loi had managed to get the shields working again, and Ogres began to disappear from the heart of the battle. The feed was cut off, the Great Ogre acting as if he did so as a matter of course, but my peripheral vision knew he did not. Somehow, the Second had reinstated the shield. All was not lost.

The Great Ogre was not amused, pushing Kay out of the way to stand at his side. I felt heartened, but remained apparently locked-down within myself. The Son of Belial, the Great Ogre, settled his utterly evil form at the control panel and Ælthrelntheine was released. She attended to his order, "Come last Queen of the Eleventh, it is time we visited your control centre. I know you will be especially pleased with the improvements I plan to make to Elvenholme."

The Great Ogre activated the return bracelet of the Eleventh, taking their Queen with him. My heart was full of foreboding, which lessened when they returned a few minutes later. Ælthrelntheine was ordered back to her pod, but I sensed a third person with them, one I could not see. Once the Queen of the Eleventh was safely ensconced, the Great Ogres tried once more to elicit a reaction from Kay. Nothing. In frustration, he kicked her away and she sprawled onto the floor, her limbs at unnatural angles, but without response. She appeared dead.

Meanwhile, the Great Ogre's fingers worked the control panel. Inserts appeared on the large screen, depicting carnage of all the Tribes. Every small screen appeared to be a massacre, but I noticed the timeframe was wrong. Some, if not all were recordings. A large square in the centre remained blank. The only Tribes not yet shown were the Seventh and Eleventh. My eyes drifted to the Second, and I remembered one scene from before. This was all a sham and hope grew within me. The Great Ogre rose and strutted around the room, coming to each of us in turn, and waxing eloquently about the downfall of each Tribe in turn.

My mind caught on one thing he said, "You will all bow before me, or die. All your people, all the Tribes. I have taken your Rings of Power, and now control them all. I control all of you."

He held his hands aloft and I looked at them. He was mistaken. The Ancestor's ring was mine, so was the Ring of the Last, they came from Taris. Most of the other rings were of Oma's crew, but there was a fatal flaw. The Ring of the Second was the Empress' ring. I knew Weid Noi still held the power of the Second, a round stone known as The Knowing Eye. The Great Ogre believed he was in control and prided himself on the destruction wrought. But I reasoned by his haughty spirit, his oversight left him open for a fall — the prudence of Solomon.

"And ye that weep, death's scythe to reap, or wouldst thee keep, as lamb and sheep."

I was aware of those oblique words, but who spoke them? The Great Ogre wheeled to confront Oma, but her remains floated before him, her being lost to the world. I recognised the projected voice, and took comfort knowing the Shaman was watching over our plight.

My hope renewed on those few words, as the Great Ogre resumed his *monologue diabolique*, but strutted when he came before me. "Guardian, I am pleased to introduce you to our latest exhibit."

My eyes looked where he pointed, and I howled in anguish. Ræm stood meekly shackled outside the pod with her name on it, a curious smile playing upon her face. As I grasped for my sanity, I was ordered to watch the main screen. The central part of the monitor came to life. I recognised Elvenholme, and it was awash with blood and fire. Ogres plundered and murdered at their will, there was no stopping them.

I saw Ogres enter the library, setting afire priceless tomes and parchment, the scene switching to the Senate before complete. Elders were dragged out from forum, but the numbers slain were less than those I first glimpsed. "I know you are all dying to see what happens.

"Last Queen of the Eleventh, one so high, you did not think your secondary control centre would fool me for long. Look, my troops invade, soon your worthless son will be executed."

The newsreel appeared to be real, current, and my hope waned. I witnessed the houses of the Eleventh set ablaze, the crops trampled in the fields, and the luxuriant forests burning. The Great Ogre returned to his console, and brought up a new view, the centre of their nation. Standing, he commanded us all to watch the destruction of the heart of the Elven nation.

I recognised Ælthrelntheine's mental wail, as The One Tree came into view. Marauding Ogres were hacking at the trunk and branches, as another team tunnelled beneath the roots and placed barrels below. The trunk was soaked with oil and set alight. The Great Ogre spoke as his soldiers withdrew. A fuse was lit, the trail disappearing below.

The tree lurched as the explosion occurred deep underground, its foundations removed. Above, fire had taken hold of upper branches, as the tree appeared to totter, before descending to obliterate the Forum, Senate, and heartland of the Elven city.

I could not watch, but neither could I turn away. My mind retreated unto the unseeing.

Chapter 30 ~ Unholy Communion

As with us before, Ræm was ordered to accompany the Great Ogre and inspect his trophies. However, unlike the rest of us, she was walking of her own accord, playing along, and glancing around. This was confirmed moments later when she said, "Oma, it is time to wake up and watch the defeat of the Great Ogre."

The beast turned on her and hit her hard across the face. She went flying, landing heavily on the floor. "Kneel and apologise."

Ræm did as instructed, a nasty welt forming on her cheek. The Great Ogre looked at her curiously, "Rise and follow."

The rest of her introduction mirrored my own, until he came to stand before Jinnie and I. The macabre that spouted from his lips was unrepeatable, gross, vile, and laden with malice. The procreational activities he had planned for her seemed unending and included the other exhibits and his foulest creations.

Ræm stood by his side, apparently unhearing as he continued, until the main screen distracted him. The Seventh had appeared in the capital of the Eleventh, and I was sure I saw the Fourth and New Tenth also, before the screen, and all feeds died. "I must attend the control room immediately. Come slave, time for you to join the exhibits."

He strode off, but Ræm remained where she was, and began to play a pennywhistle. I was sure it was the birth-gift of the Fourth, and my fears eased. He wheeled in rage; "I said come with me slave!"

"Oh sorry, were you talking to me? I'm not your slave either."

The Great Ogre gawked at her. "This is your second chance to surrender. Refuse and you will die for all eternity."

The Great Ogre's grey skin turned maroon, and I was sure he would burst an artery, or kill her for her temerity. Advancing quickly on her with hands raised, she said, "Manners. This is no way to treat a Lady, your guest. You must beg forgiveness for all your sins, or all your lives will be forfeit. Which is it to be?"

He towered above her, his face turning purple, and hollered, "Give me the Sword of Destiny. I am going to kill you with it."

"No, never."

"Do it now, or I will execute your mother and father."

"Are you sure?"

"Yes!"

"Oh, all right then, I'll lend you my sword in exchange for your spark of life. You do know what you are doing, don't you?"

"Yes. I do. I will kill you, bring you back to life, and gift you everlasting life, something your kind holds in greatest value. In your case, one you can only ever observe, never interact with."

"Ah, Heisenberg."

"What? Give me the sword!"

My heart shuddered with foreboding as Ræm reached down and drew the sword with difficulty, her wrists still bound, and offered it, hilt first to the Great Ogre. I could not bear to watch, but neither could I tear my eyes away. His malignant smile reappeared as he reached for the weapon and grasped it by the hilt.

I could not understand how the Great Ogre could hold the blade, why it did not flare with blue light, but it remained dormant, as if waiting. Ræm said, "This is your last chance to surrender and beg forgiveness for your sins against all humanity. Are you certain this is what you want?"

The great Ogre tried to wrench the blade from her grip, his verbal abuse finding a new lease of life. I watched, incredulous, as Ræm's fingers held on to the blade, even though her palms dripped with blood. She flicked her head and the Ogre's headpiece fell to the floor, closely followed by her wrist restraints. I know the Great Ogre lunged forward, but I was certain Ræm willingly forced the tip of the blade into the left side of her torso, and stepped forward deliberately impaling her heart upon the unforgiving metal.

The blade flared with blue-white light, almost blinding me, as blood oozed down the metal, runes activating to hover in the air above and below. The Great Ogre reacted, trying to cast the hilt aside, but it appeared to be welded to his flesh. Ræm continued to walk forward, the blade extruding from her back as she closed in unholy communion with the foulest of creatures.

The Great Ogre stood transfixed, as her hands locked with his arms. Smoke plumes erupting where she touched him. She looked up into his stricken eyes and said the oddest thing, "I will heal you now, Great Ogre. Evil must always be balanced by Good."

I watched the impossible. Ræm's blood surged down the blade, pumped in waves by her beating heart, gathering runes along the way, and entered the body before her.

Ræm spoke clearly, "This sword was cast for healing. It cannot harm the innocent—However, the greater the sins of the aggressor, the greater the power of this sword. You seem to be getting a little hot. I open your heart to the power of love. I command your soul to drink deeply of empathy and pathos."

The arm holding the sword began to smoulder, the skin charring above like a rash spreading quickly. The hand holding the hilt caught fire, blue fire, which quickly spread through the entirety of his physical being. The Great Ogre stood immobile as his body was consumed. His face sported one solitary tear. "Witness the feelings of this monstrosity. That tear represents the sum of his compassion, and it is self-pity. You are now and forevermore, decreed dead."

Blue fire engulfed the head, until all that was left was a hideous grotesque of back ash. Ræm spoke one last time, "I'll take my sword back now."

She pulled the hilt from the Great Ogre's remains, which fell like dust to the floor, his body entirely consumed. She pulled the blade from her torso, and seemed unharmed. She replaced it in the scabbard as the Shaman appeared behind her and gently eased Ræm to the floor. She set the scabbard aside, looked around, and nodded, before the old crone limped over to Kay and straightened her limbs. She placed a hand upon Kay's temple and said,

"Waken now O' darkest Elf,
'tis time returned to thy self.
Soldiers first restore to health;
Thy virgin self the greater wealth."

The Shaman stood and pirouetted, her hand held high as if in a ballet dancer's wave of parting. Her eyes fixed mine. A soft female voice entered my disparate thoughts and beguiled me, "Still now child, soon you will be safe."

I was aware she and Ræm disappeared, my eyes free to move of their own volition, were fixed on Kay. She roused slowly. I knew her conscious was coming a long way back to the here and now. With difficulty, she pushed her body up to a slouching position, and looked around, bemused.

I saw the light come back into her eyes, but her body remained weak. She fixed on the pile of ashes, and crawled over, taking Jien Noi's return bracelet and the Ring of the Ancestor. She fumbled the return bracelet onto her wrist, the ring onto her finger. She tried to stand, but stumbled on weak legs towards the control station, grasping the edge for support, half-aware. I saw her stare at the console, before she pressed some buttons.

I became aware of an undertow. The waters engulfing me were receding, if slowly, and my eyes swivelled for confirmation. In thanks, I looked back at Kay, who seemed physically exhausted. Her torso flopped down on the console, her fingers pressing buttons of the return bracelet. Then she was gone.

Ælkræleinnoire

Kay returned to the Second, her mind befuddled, but what concentration remained was fixated of purpose. Helping hands reached for her, her words staccato, her timeline, warped. "Soldiers to where I came from, now—Main shield down, but not for long—Great Ogre dead—All rulers alive, almost. I must return. Coffee…"

205

Kay's words died as she was hoisted onto a guard's back, and taken directly to the spaceship's medical facility. n'Gnung arrived moments later and hugged her, before asking for a report. Matron replied, "These devices — the cuffs and mind-warper, are banned technology, except regards alien warfare. The Great Ogre?"

"Dead. His shackles."

"I must inform the Core. The removal procedure can be tricky."

Matron interfaced as n'Gnung examined the shackles, which came away in his hand. Intrigued, he removed the headband also and said, "Done. I need Kay revived ASAP, lucid for as long as possible. Her knowledge is vital and we need it now."

"She is still conscious, if only just. One moment while I inject her… There. You have an hour at best, but she needs to return here. Want me to run diagnostics on the restraints; they should not have come off that easily?"

"Later, thank you. First we both need to save lives."

n'Gnung rushed away clutching Kay, and half-carried her into the War Room. She was soon hypo, was debriefed, and briefed of the current situation. Her information and commands flowed quickly.

"We hold one room, a secondary control centre. Lock it down with our own shielded transporters, spherical protection mode. Other shielded transporters, same mode, isolate adjacent areas, and breach the greater shield; should it be reactivated we will need access. Peni, I need a map of the complex. Horovitz, Stewart, and Gung Loi, your platoons at the ready, do what you are best at. Barph, your men at arms to work formation, outwards from our secured area, go now. The Eleventh, n'Gnung?"

"It is a mess. Owain and Stoltvar's troops are supporting the Elven Guarde, *assisted* by a few of the Fourth. Every time they make progress, fresh Ogres arrive. Their shield draining technology is debilitating."

"Set one of our shields to surround the Eleventh."

"We cannot, we don't have a powerful enough shield. In fact, we have extremely few shielded transporters left."

"Wong Kai, relieve Peni, I need her expertise in Engineering."

"Kay, Engineering has no life support, power is critically low."

"Are the Ogres defeated on this island?"

"Virtually, only a few remain and are being despatched now."

"Good. Drop all internal shields. They are no longer required. This gives us power, and shields to re-deploy."

"But only Jack and you know how to do that."

Kay cursed, "Core, I need life support in Engineering now. Peni, Mai Li, Zhong Zhi, you're with me, I will teach you shield manipulation. n'Gue, I need you in charge of Ancestral weapons."

"Kay, we have recovered an Ogre shield draining device."

"Give it to me. Langnor, as troops come available, free the other tribes, the Twelfth first, we need their bulk as warriors."

Kay transferred to Engineering, where she opened the armoury, liaising with n'Gue for dissemination of protection bracelets and weapons, including plasma cannons.

Once done, she gave her students a crash course in shield manipulation and redeployment, ensuring each of them completed the task several times.

Once competent, she left them with instructions and departed to interface with the Core from the Captain's ready room. She presented the protection-draining weapon, and Ogre shackles, the crown also, and demanded answers. The response was evasive at first, until she pressed the point, "We are dying because of these weapons. Reveal the answers to me."

The Core became instantly forthcoming, and she smirked, "I've cracked the secret code, 'Reveal' perhaps?"

She received a flood of new information, and knew the best person to action response was herself. She returned to Engineering, where her students were becoming minute-masters of shield technology. She began replicating the Ogre shield draining technology. A sample weapon was produced. Needing help, she said, "n'Gnung, test this at once. I need to know if it works in the field."

"I will send it through to the Eleventh now. Meet me in the war room in one minute."

The device despatched via messenger, n'Gnung rendezvoused with her, "Kay, you look drained. You must return to medical."

"In a minute, I need coffee please. What of our battles?"

The brief update was barely complete before word came back that the new shield draining device was working well. She was about to speak when Ju Lo appeared by her side. "I am back. This reincarnation business is rather odd, we must talk about it sometime. But for now, where do you need me?"

Kay jumped up and hugged him, before saying, "Work with Langnor, she's monitoring the other Tribes at risk. Oh, and good to have you back. Excuse me, I must speak to Peni."

They exchanged a meaningful look, before Kay left for Engineering. "Peni, I need you and the others here to split your time. Continue shield production, but also replicate this design, it is the shield draining technology of the Ogres, and it works in the field. We need as many as you can, as quickly as possible. I'll run through the process with you the first time."

The words had hardly left her lips when n'Gue arrived at her side, "Kay, you must come at once. Owain, Jack, they are dying. Nobody understands how to operate the Great Ogre's control."

Taking but moments to show Peni the template and generation techniques, she stood abruptly and said, "Let's go. Ask Ju Lo to accompany us. He is not yet settled to his new task. I need to show somebody what to do there."

Moments later, her remaining strength draining quickly, Kay transported to the exposition room. The sounds of war filtered through the large, oak doors. She had previously set the suspension pods Jack and Owain were in, to drain. She had presumed the reanimation process would be automatic, but it was not. "n'Gue, bring Gangling here, I am not good at Ogre."

n'Gue looked into her eyes and shrugged, his palms opening reflexively, as if in apology. Alarmed she asked, "He is dead?"

"No, I don't know. The battle rages within, and we cannot breach the Ogre shield. It needs to be overridden from here."

Kay's eyes flicked askance, both Jack and Owain appeared to be suffocating. She had to release them. "n'Gue, I need a dedicated messenger to work with us here. Ju Lo, pay attention, I will briefly explain the process as we go through, once I have understood it fully. I need a moment."

Chapter 31 ~ Homelands

Kay worked the strange Ogre consol, "Yes, there it is. I can reset this to Ancestor, but need the Ring of the Warrior, bring it to me."

As she worked, the Ring of the Warrior appeared to lose its venom, amplified the more she worked while wearing it.

Ju Lo implored, "Kay, hurry, they are dying in there!"

"Hush Ju Lo, one moment … there; the control is now back in Ancestor. We can understand it. Messenger, I need strong hands here now. Ju Lo, follow my keystrokes … and there, Jack's release mechanism activated … and Owain. Let's do Rambling next, we need the bulk. Watch carefully Ju Lo, you free the next one, OK?"

"How do you know what to do?"

"My mind was not locked down all the time, I watched what the Great Ogre was doing at this console, and committed it to memory. I was watching when he released my mother."

Teaching Ju Lo what to do, they were distracted when a cheer came from nearby. Focused, she finished the release of Rambling, before rushing to hug Jack. "Don't you dare leave me — Ever!"

She wanted to kiss his lips and hold him tight, but instead, gave his brow a smacker. "Nor you Owain, we need you both."

She kissed his forehead as well, before almost rising to her feet, and keeling over. "I need a moment. It's the effect of the mental containment device. Messenger, when you deposit Jack and Owain in our medical facility, see if Matron can find a remedy or tonic to keep me going."

Ju Lo said, "Bring me a chair. Kay, you need to watch me."

He worked methodically and was relieved when Ruaidhrí was released next. His confidence growing, he worked more quickly, and released his Empress, followed by the other leaders in turn. As he worked, Kay was given a serum by a medic, followed by a tonic made by Da Phai Nai. She felt a lot better, but was hungry and needed fuel. She asked for a takeaway and coffee to be delivered.

As they waited for pods to empty, Kay explained, "Shields are on this panel, and work much the same way as our own, same for the transporter, which is accessed by this rune."

n'Gue arrived bearing her request, burger and fries that she wolfed down. He said, "Jack is back with us, but weak, like you were. He needs time, but is in the War Room catching up and monitoring what is happening. The war is far from over this day. The others, including your mother, will be fine, but also need time to recover."

Kay nodded as she ate, and through a mouthful of food said, "We need a plan of attack. I hope the Ogre shield is still down?"

"Yes, but we are on borrowed time."

"How big is this place?"

"Indications are it is massive, an underground city."

"I need to speak to Jack."

At that moment, mighty blows came to the outside of the great oak doors. "I thought we were shielded and had troops outside."

n'Gue said, "We did. Their shield-draining technology is awesome. I must return."

"Send any troops you can, and presume the Ogres will break through at any moment. n'Gue, we must take their main control room, that's the only place we can end this."

"Jack just said the same thing. They are working on a captured Ogre shield, adapting it so only we can use it as they did to us."

"Good idea. Go, we need troops before they close us down. We must secure this bridgehead at all costs. Ju Lo, swap places, I have an idea."

As n'Gue departed, Ju Lo asked, "Kay, why are they still attacking? The Great Ogre is dead."

"No new orders will be issued, but the old ones will continue to be carried out. Regardless, I doubt any know of the fiend's demise, or would believe us even if we told them, unless…?"

Kay finished her food and felt much better. She worked quickly, locating the Ogre shield creation mechanism, and spending time reconfiguring a new transporter and shield. She placed it behind them. "Ju Lo, you followed all that? Good, I need several more, but do not set them just yet."

Her words were all but cut off as Ogres broke through the doors and ran towards them. She cast her eyes about, and noticed the Rings of Power still lying near the Great Ogre's ashes, and the Sword of Destiny. She ran for it, but paused before grabbing the hilt. "Apologies, Ræm, I need to borrow this for a moment."

Kay had no time to scoop up the rings or other artefacts. She rose swinging the sword at the nearest Ogre, decapitating him. She was fleet of foot, dodging, drawing the enemy away to follow her, and to protect the others in the room. Aroweena and a platoon of Ddwyrth materialised at her side, and immediately set to fight the horde. Support of others arrived moments later, Horovitz and Gung Loi with their special forces amongst the number.

The fighting was fierce, personal, the Ogre forces kept on coming, and allied support dried up. They defeated the first wave, each of them knowing others would soon replace them. "Horovitz, block the door, nothing comes in. Gung Loi, with me, we need a new plan, obviously the Ogres have reactivated their shields."

Returning to the console, she tied the scabbard to her waist and sheathed the Sword of Destiny, scooping up the rings of power and associated apparatus on the way. Gung Loi said, "The next reinforcements were bringing Ancestral weapons and our new shield draining devices. Without them we are done for."

Kay locked her eyes and retorted, "No we are not. It's time to play some games. Be ready to transport on my signal."

As Kay returned to the consol, Ju Lo said, "I have the shield made, an Ogre shield with our transport signature, but if we are locked down, the island also, we can't get out."

"Watch and learn." Kay set the new transporter before them in the room and said, "Gung Loi, this should work, you appreciate the alternatives. I am sending you to the Seventh, use their transporter as a link to reach our control room. Tell Jack, or whoever is in charge, that I'll place the next shield in the main Ogre control room. We will take the fight to the heart of the Ogre machine.

"Wait. This transporter is limited somehow and I don't have time to bypass it. It will not receive unless our own shields are dropped, which we cannot do. One moment, we need a work-around; I have a two-way interference to use, the old Ogre base at Lesotho. I'll use that as a transfer hub. Go."

Minutes passed, no word came back. Kay worked regardless of worry. There was only one way to win the war.

Ju Lo worked beside her, "The new shield for this room is weakening. They must be draining it."

"Ignore it. We must finish what we started. Focus. We've almost done it… Initiating deployment."

At that moment, the newly created shield failed and Ogres assaulted the doorway, dropping before Horovitz' Gatling gun. A fresh supply of Ogres appeared behind them. Kay rose in one fluid motion, drawing the Sword of Destiny. "Finish it Ju Lo. Place it."

Kay took out two Ogres with her first charge, but she was weak, and greatly outnumbered. Wary Ogres began to encircle her, as she worked her few options, and darted to one side, then feinted to the other, before striking a killing blow. More Ogres transported in. Some faced her but most ran past her to take the battle to those behind.

The air shimmered nearby and she half-turned to face the new threat, a killing blow already in motion. However, this was the transporter she had placed, and she wheeled aside, narrowly missing Owain. He was accompanied by a mixed troops of Ddwyrth, Trolls, and Twelfth.

"Well met, wee lassie," is all he said, before swinging his battleaxe, as he strode boldly into the ranks of the Ogres. Tenth and Allies continued to transport into the room. n'Gnung appeared, accompanied by Gung Loi and a platoon of men bearing plasma bomb launchers. The flow of battle shifted, but stayed nearly even, as Ancestral weapons, shields and shield drainers quickly came to the Allies. The Ogres likewise supported with reinforcements.

The Ancestors, still cocooned within their prisons, watched like the almost dead.

Kay said, "I need a controller who understand shields here now. Once we move forward, somebody has to back us up."

A messenger was sent, and moments later, Peni appeared. She exclaimed, clapping her hands together in delight, "Oh, isn't this exciting! It reminds me of downtown Detroit on Saturday night."

"Not now Peni. Pay attention."

The messenger said, "Lesotho is working. Jack wants you to compromise the main control centre immediately. We have support coming, but you need to drop the Ogre shields, all of them, everywhere in the world."

"That's why Peni is here, to assist. Protect us for one minute or less. I am seeding a shielded circle in the main Ogre control room now. I need the best team we have, here and ready to go.

"Peni, on my mark, press this rune to place the new transporter, and this rune to send us through. Then set about turning off Ogre shields. Ju Lo, you're with me, warriors come: three, two, action!"

Kay ran with the others, and drew the Sword of Destiny moments before they were engulfed in white light. Materialising moments later, Ogre controllers were killed before they realised they were under attack. Guards faced-off with Aroweena and n'Gnung, while more Allied troops came to support them.

Kay remained focused on the main task. "Work with me Ju Lo, watch and learn, I am decommissioning the main shield. OK. Main Ogre shield down, done. I am switching this back into Ancestor, are you following it? This is how to change the language ... and now to drop the rest of the Ogre shields in this city, and worldwide ... that's the first, now you do the next."

Several more shields dropped as Ju Lo took charge, before Kay said, "You've got it. Continue from the science station over there, it's the same as our old Guardian console. Wait, I'll need to activate it for you. Drop greatest threats first. The Eleventh, Twelfth, other Tribes — we are relying on you. Liaise with Peni."

Moments passed before Ju Lo said, "Peni has it almost done. What's next?"

"Maps. I need a detailed map of this entire place, significance first: control stations, troops, weapons and shields areas..."

"I have it. Working now."

Kay sat back to quickly review progress, before identifying what should be her next most important or helpful objectives. She knew the

Ogres worked on bravado, striving for physical and mental dominance of their opponents. She wanted to give some back.

It took her a while to find the recording she wanted, and minutes more to understand how to compromise the video feed that was set to repeat, to brainwash the Ogre subjects. She kept her narration simple, and in the Ogre language, hoping Gangling would appear soon.

Kay completed the recording and listened, "The Great Ogre is dead. A small girl killed him. Surrender at once. Drop your weapons or die."

She was putting the finishing touched to the recording, when she noticed a related application, 'Great Ogre Speaking'. Intrigued she opened it, and found a voice simulation package that would issue commands, as if spoken by the Great Ogre. She made a short sample statement, and it worked.

She was interrupted by a messenger. "High Lord of Destiny, Ogre shields are dropping to all the Tribes, but Ogres continue to transfer in, we do not have enough large shields to stop them. Can you assist?"

"Automatic transporters I presume. Yes, but I have a better idea. I'll order the Ogre troops to regroup somewhere that suits us best.

"Ju Lo, where are you with the map? I need a large area where troops would deploy from, a place they would assemble for battle."

"The general area will be southwest. I have what appear to be training, barracks, and drill areas identified. Sending to you now. I had thought troop deployment would cease now we have taken the control room."

"No. These must be orders already issued to troop commanders. We will need to kill them all to stop this." Kay looked at the area of the map, but it was still a work in progress. She had tried to avoid interfacing with the Core of the Ogre starship, but regards expedience and saving lives that was all that was left to her. She looked up as said, "n'Gnung, I'm glad you are still here. I must interface with this Core. Monitor me."

"Core, the Great Ogre is dead. I am now your controller, Captain Kay. Reveal soldier departure points and staging areas."

"Your Captain's ring is that of Taris, yet your wear the correct Warrior ring, as did your predecessor, computing … aggregated DNA match to Oma as close of that of granddaughter, you have the same black hair and white eyes, a feature only shared with the materfamilias Queen of the Eleventh, Oma's official daughter."

Kay was shocked, but the Core continued…"

"Reveal command accepted. This is a warrior command. For full access to ship's systems you must be officially inaugurated as Captain using Oma's Ring. Relaying results for deployment hubs to the Captain's console now."

Chapter 31

Kay punched her fist in the air. She had discovered the key to controlling the Core; any Core. She studied the detailed map and swiftly chose her preferred location. She worked quickly, composing a command, and setting the application to mimic the Great Ogre's voice. Satisfied she said aloud, "Great, that should do it."

She had forgotten she was still technically connected to the Core, which replied, "No it is not, Captain. The Great Ogre would not use those words."

Slightly shaken, but pleased with the response, she said, "What would the Great Ogre have said?"

The Core replied immediately, and Kay sent out the updated command, which translated as, "All combatants regroup at once for final battle deployment at staging area F. All Generals, join me in the War Room at once."

Kay smiled and said, "That should stop them dead in their tracks. I have suitable Ogre shields ready to be placed, in essence imprisoning the Ogre war machine. Once they attend, I will lock both locations out, and they will be trapped. Neat eh?"

n'Gnung smiled and placed a congratulatory hand on her shoulder, "Brilliant Kay, I will inform the Guardian as soon as it is done. You will need to confine the rest of the population as well, or we will have another uprising to deal with."

"Hmmm. No we won't, I have a plan for that also, what do you think about this..."

Some minutes later, Kay activated shields to isolate the Ogre army and generals. Nearly all were caught in the net. Once done, she activated her previous recording and set it to broadcast to the entire Ogre city.

The clip showed the Great Ogre's death, Kay's words a lance penetrating deep into the Ogre psyche. It ripped the heart out of them, confusion and inner conflict surfaced. They had no leader; they did not know what to do. There were no new orders to follow; some took up arms to defend themselves while others wailed bereft.

n'Gnung became the personal messenger between Kay and Jack, he being one of the few appraised of everything that was going on in both control rooms. Acting as Number One to both of them, he was able to ensure full communication and contemporaneous duality of purpose. He moved quickly between the pair, relaying their messages: "Kay, you did it! All Ogre shields are down, but fighting still heavy. I'm sorry, Elvenholme is a mess."

"n'Gnung, tell Jack I have isolated the Ogres into killing zones. Owain is systematically working through the upper reaches, despatching the few remaining outside containment. We need more troops to finish this."

"Kay, Jack states more Ogres are still appearing, where are they coming from?"

"What? Impossible. Core, 'Reveal' all Ogre troop placements."

Kay received a reply and looked annoyed. "Damn!"

"What is it Kay?"

"We missed it, obvious now we know. The Core only told me about this hub. There are many others. You remember the collapsed tunnel the Ddwyrth discovered, it led to a distribution point, yes? The corridors off it were not sealed by rock, but by rock plasma. We never checked to verify, it looked right. The tunnel collapse was not random, but deliberate. Each of the point corridors actually leads to another Ogre hub. Troop encampments of similar design to the one we overran. Ogres are still transporting out from each. There are eleven more in total.

"I'll lock out the transporters. Ju Lo, I need you and Peni to engage eleven shields, now. n'Gnung, tell Jack what I just discovered. I need to speak to him in person, to show him what we are up against."

A short time later Jack appeared and Kay rose with open arms. He hurried to her, engulfing her in a hug, like that of long lost lovers. He looked up into her eyes, as if exchanging inner commune. Breaking apart quickly, he said, "Apologies, I missed you. What's the critical situation?"

Kay smiled wistfully before replying, "O Captain, My Captain."

Jack's rugged, if cheeky smile appeared, "Captain Kay. Indeed, you have discovered a new world here, and the third spacecraft I presume. What do you need?"

"I want you. I need you ... to work with me, here. You see these eleven hubs I have marked on the map on screen, they are not yet under our control."

"Set a transporter in each and blitz them with plasma bombs. Job done. n'Gnung, delegate to action this immediately. Next?"

"You understand Ogre, which several systems are still using. They have no equivalent in Ancestor, and are of the Great Ogre's personal design. Ju Lo, Peni, and I are locking out the threats, but this is going to take days to finish."

"OK, but that can wait. Kay, all the other Tribes have been freed, but there was much loss of life. Troops are securing each enclave. Do they still need shields up?"

"Yes, we must assess each location carefully before any shield is dropped. Know there may be Ogres already in place, or transporting to other locations."

"What else do you need?"

"Troops and weapons, we have to erase the Ogres from all existence, there is no other way — at least, no other way to preserve the rest of humankind."

"Understood. Your mother wants to conference about the new world order, and I left them to it. She should be with her people. Have you seen what happened?"

"No, and I'd prefer not to."

"Like mother, like daughter. One of you needs to be there, come with me. Ju Lo, n'Gnung, Gung Loi, you know what to do here. Ready troops to transport in and Liaise with Langnor and Bufor."

"But…"

"Now Kay, your people need their leader. They need you."

Chapter 32 ~ New World Order

Jack

Kay and I returned briefly to the island, where we went to our homes at the hamlet; Kay having her own home adjoining mine. She donned the Sword of Deception, and handed the Sword of Destiny to me. I had a secondary purpose for going there, to finish something started years before by the Shaman. I needed to retrieve something special from my ready room, but before we could escape, a message came that we were required to attend Ælthrelntheine's meeting.

I had no time for the diversion, but Kay said, "No Jackie, they need their rings of power back. I'll leave them with Mother to disseminate; we will only be a moment."

We attended court on the Outlands, and were welcomed into the bosom of the Elf Queen's plans for the new world order. Kay produced the rings and accoutrements the Great Ogre had taken. She had placed them in a special purse, and opened it, showering them before handing it to her mother. Kay said, "Mother, please see to it that all leaders get their trinkets of office back. Meanwhile, we have work to do."

Kay turned and walked away. Ælthrelntheine commanded, "You will join us now."

"No. Somebody has to be with our own people. These leaders need to take back control of their own realms, Mother. The One Tree is no more. The people need the support of their ruler, but you are too busy with outside concerns, so it falls to me. Good day!"

I was aware of their exchange, but tending my wife, who was lying on a temporary bed nearby. "What's wrong, Jinnie?"

"Nothing of any consequence, I just feel so weak. Did we really win, defeat the Great Ogre?"

"Yes we did. You, I, and all of us standing together. We won."

I kissed her lips, but she shrugged me away after the initial acceptance. "Husband, what of Ræm? I hear she disappeared, again."

"She killed the Great Ogre. That's what happened. I witnessed it, so did you."

"No, I was aware of it, but my mind was … not there. I can't explain it. It was like seeing, sensing echoes, aberrant and with the wrong senses."

"Shhh, the Shaman took her to heal. She saved the world, us, and everyone alive today. That is our daughter's worth. She'll be a hard act to follow. Why are you lying down, the Great Ogre, he hurt you?"

"No, nothing like that. I am just weary in mind, and since my incarceration, in body. Something in the waters affected me."

"I am taking you to see Matron right now."

"Desist! I am not going. My life will remain under my control, and I will live it out according to my wishes and view of this world. Capisce?"

"You need me here, I must stay with you."

"No, go. If anything, we are now the strongest of the Tribes, excepting the Seventh perhaps. I need you to go and put things right. That is your calling. Now kiss me, and leave me in peace. Later I will need a word with you, but after all this kafuffle has died down."

"When you are strong enough, you must tell our own people. They are more important than this meeting, which can wait for several days."

"You are correct, I will go to Grimwaldi Rinns in a moment, but first I will tell everyone here where they should also be. Leave it with me, but join me for the announcement."

A short while later, Kay and I arrived in the control room of the Eleventh and were transported onwards to Angkrelguer. "Thank heavens you and mother are all right. Jack, great to see you, I can't imagine what you went through."

"It was rather strange, but we will speak of it another time. How can we help? What do you need?"

"There is still one band of Ogres we must finish off, otherwise the threat is neutralised. I have contacted the Community of Mages, and asked them to assist. I hope Ælthrelntheine will not be annoyed."

"She should have come straight here and made the decision herself. I agree with you, they were ostracised by our grandfather for no good reason and need to be brought back into the bosom of our Tribe. Where is Ælfreisia?"

"She is working with the injured and dying. I fear for our existence, so many have been killed."

"Were any sent to the Second for treatment?"

"No I ... we, er..."

"I'm going there now, Jack?"

We returned to the Elven control centre, where Kay used the scanners to quickly review what needed to be done. "They are not equipped to deal with these injuries, at least not so many of them."

"Kay, I'll return and send medics here to treat minor injuries. We'll treat major injuries and those that can be saved at the University hospital. A medic can identify any that could be resurrected."

That day became a blur. I worked with the Eleventh first, their Mages coming to assist in unusual but beneficial ways. Jinnie managed to adjourn Ælthrelntheine's meeting. I in turn accompanied her when she pronounced the Great Ogre dead, and victory for Allied forces. I could not stay, but watched concerned as she was carried on a litter back to her rooms in the palace.

The Second were returning to what remained of their full strength and order quickly. They, along with the Seventh, were the only two Tribes able to assist others to any great degree. The Ddwyrth were supporting with soldiers, labour for burials, and restoration works. A few Giants and Trolls also came to assist the greater good, but we knew they were sorely stretched themselves and a token of intent only.

Our control room and war room monitored and assisted. Bufor was dedicated to supplying troops to the Ogre city we had overrun. Seizing the opportunity, I said, "Langnor, great work. This is all tied down. I could use your expertise at the Ogre control room, it is like this Bridge used to be, and is now in Ancestor. I need your experience there to monitor the movements of any remaining free Ogres, and to lock down all containment areas."

I accompanied Langnor because I still had to review and disable the Great Ogres applications that were still running in the Ogre tongue. I killed a couple of processes, but others were too complex. I would need Volkar, Rambling, and Jason with me to be certain of what they were, and how to disable them. My time was also in short supply that day, so I sandboxed what I could, and took a brief review of handover. I wanted to relieve n'Gnung, and once Langnor had it under control, Gung Loi was released from duty there as well.

We began a tour of all the other Tribes. Kay joined us as we spoke to Rambling of their needs. "Mother has taken over at Elvenholme, as is her way. I got fed up with watching, so came to do something useful."

"Kay, you are always welcome in the lands of the Twelfth," said Rambling. "Come, join us, but I'm afraid the sight is not welcoming. We have lost most of our people."

We went with him and I asked after Gangling, but I was told he was mourning his granddaughter once removed. Constance Merryweather, Junior's wife, had passed on. We went to pay our respects, but I asked, "Constance, her colour is almost normal, and she is warm to touch. Explain."

"Ah, this is often the way Giants die. Their heart remains true, so they take a long time to cool."

I was not so sure, and summoned a medic right away. The automaton said, "This is most peculiar, I need to interface with our medical Core."

The Matron arrived moments later, running a scan immediately. She pronounced, "She is not dead, but lying dormant. She needs treatment at once. This is a fairly common condition of the Twelfth, when under severe trauma. It can be physical in cause, but is usually mental. They shut-down, comatose."

"Like they go into instant hibernation, you mean?"

"Yes, Guardian, that is an astute analogy. It is their race's self-preservation instinct. How many others?"

"You better check them all, I have a feeling Constance is not the only one."

And she wasn't. The Giants did not know this happened to them. Rambling put it into perspective, "We are so exceedingly grateful to you Jack, and all the other Tribes. We lost so much when Furlong Fourgay was assassinated, not only people, but knowledge. Remember, not only did we lose a King, we lost everybody, except the fledgling Prince and one serving girl."

"Temerity Shortfalls," I said, engendering empathy, "Rambling, I cannot but mourn your loss, repeated losses, but we will persevere. Look, your dead begin to rise."

We hugged man to man before Matron interrupted us. "Many of your dead are hibernating through trauma. I will ask Sylvia to send a field hospital here. No one is to be buried until they have been checked. Exhume any that have been interred. We may be able to reincarnate some of the terminally wounded."

"Jack, how can we ever repay you? You think you know yourself intimately, and then you discover death is merely hibernation. I'll need to think about that, but later. What of your own concerns this day?"

"I have one you can help me with. We have taken the Great Ogre's realm, as you are aware. Some of it remains in the language of the Ogres, and we desperately need a translator, if only to save lives."

"Gangling Shortfalls, consider him on his way as soon as he is able. He will need time to turn personal grief towards jubilation, and later, deeper understanding."

I departed as the saviour of their kind, well-wishers' tributes I could well do without. The scenes of massacre and decimation of humanity, played out as we visited every Tribe in turn of needfulness. We brought in the help they required, but it was beyond us to offer all they requested.

Finally, we were done, and transferred back to the Second. I felt drained, and knew others were functioning on adrenaline alone. I summarised, "We need to discuss priorities. The Eighth plead the loudest, yet I believe it is the Fifth who need our greater support first."

n'Gnung said, "Agreed, Guardian. However, every Tribe will survive for tonight, their injured are being treated, and they have enough food and drink. Shelter will suffice, if temporary, and many of their dead need burying. We should work on a plan for tomorrow, how about doing so at the shore? I have a mighty thirst to quench."

"I'll be with you in a minute. See if Owain is free to join us. We'll need his input regards future planning. But first, I need to check on my wife, she is not well and I am worried about her."

"Jackie, we better check on Langnor to ensure she's settled in OK."

"Good thinking, Kay, she's in charge of an alien stronghold and I want to offer her guards and backup crew. They need a dedicated canteen also. Kay, take n'Gnung with you and check on Langnor, while I check on Jien Noi, I doubt either will take long."

The Empress was asleep when I arrived, so I talked quietly with her Ladies in Waiting and the Healer, just before he left to prepare potions. The prognosis was good for one so relatively old. And that remained my ongoing problem. I sat by her bedside watching over her, wondering if I should overrule her wishes and have her rejuvenated at the ship's medical centre. I had just decided to do so, regardless of the repercussions, and reached for her hand as if to ask for her forgiveness.

She roused dreamily, "I knew you would come. Hug me, I feel cold."

We cuddled as she drew on my body heat, and warmed up considerably. I spoke softly to her, talking of greater things, and the inconsequential. Soon she was overly hot, a thing I had noticed about sleeping women. They tend to get hotter than the male. I made a mental note to ask Ami or Matron about the phenomena.

I thought she was asleep, and eased away to cool down. She clutched my hand and said quietly, "I know you well husband. I need you to promise me you will honour my wishes. I will not be rejuvenated. I will live my life as I wish. Take that away from me, then you are no better than the Great Ogre. Promise me, Jackie."

I made the vow, knowing I would keep it. I kissed her lightly and smoothed her brow, before easing aside and sitting on the side of the bed to escape her hyper-warmth. I remained to watch over her until the healer arrived with medicine and a sleeping draught. It was time for me to leave.

I ambled outside the Imperial rooms, lost within thought, my mind clouded with worry. My name was called, and I looked up to see n'Gnung and Kay waiting for me. "What's up?"

"The sky; I could ask the same of you, Jackie. Care to share?"

"Indeed, brother, what ails you?"

"Nothing ails me. But Jinnie is not well and refuses treatment at our medical facility. I just … Another time, why are you not at the shore?"

"Ræm dropped by and said you were needed at Elvenholme, and then she disappeared. How does she do that?"

"I have no idea, but I am going to ask her next time I see her. I presume she was fit and healthy."

"Fit as a fiddle, the epitome of good health. Guardian, I garnered the impression she needed you there fairly urgently."

"What of Langnor?"

"We just came from there, Jackie. Owain and Barph have everything under control, and Owain is looking forward to joining us later, but that may be tomorrow. It's too early to celebrate or drink good health. Langnor asked Gung Loi to stay, they are transporting Ogres into killing zones, and Gung Loi is brilliant at co-ordination. Stewart and his teams are searching every nook and alley of the city, Horovitz' platoons are acting as execution squad and backup. It's all under control, but will take time."

We took a brief review with Owain, attending to his needs, which were few apart from troops. Kay wanted to check on her mother. I also had a reason for going there, so we transferred at once, and found the Elven homelands to be recovering from the worst of the atrocities quickly. Ælthrelntheine had her finger on the pulse of the nation, controlling and delegating minutia. She was a little surprised when we arrived, but welcoming all the same. After brief review, we three looked at each other, wondering why we were there.

Kay whispered, "Come quickly, this way. We better get out of here before she finds us something to do."

We needed no urging, and slipped away unnoticed. The library was decimated, a burned out husk. Kay said, "My brother is clever. One of his first actions was to remove our knowledge to a safekeeping depository, and replace the tomes and scrolls with others of little worth, mainly blank paper. He did similar with our crops and larders, keeping the bulk safe. That is why we are recovering so fast."

"Perhaps, but the senate, the palace, the open-air forum are gone. You'll need the Ddwyrth to rebuild."

"Maybe, maybe not. Our Mages are powerful. Mother has pardoned them. "

"Their crime?"

"Disagreeing with my grandfather—they were correct in actuality, but wrong in body politick. They demanded powers above their station, but I think it was all a rouse to cover something else. What I do not know, so there's no point going into all that now."

"Sounds familiar, reminds me of my own world, and we know what became of them."

We had been walking away from the centre, circumnavigating, or climbing over the remnants of The One Tree. Kay skipped aside at times, gathering flowers for a posy. The skin near my groin started to itch, and I begged a moment aside to scratch. It was not a private place, but almost.

We continued walking, talking about how Elvenholme was similar, yet differed from the greater world at large. In time we came to the roots of the great tree, where Kay gave a blessing, and proffered the posy as simple honour. She added it to the hundreds already there, and bowing, said a few words in Elvenhua, and withdrew.

We wandered toward the gaping maw of a hole that used to be residence of The One Tree. I had to scratch my pelvis again; aware the condition was getting worse. I was feeling gratified by the relief of sharp nails on skin when my daughter appeared nearby.

"Father, what are you doing?"

I realised my hand was inside my jeans, my fingers gripped in a fist, scratching my groin vigorously. "It's not what you think…I can explain."

"No Father, you cannot. Please give your libido a rest and focus on the itch, what is it actually telling you?"

"Scratch me."

"No. Focus. Go; wander around until you figure it out. Only you know the answer."

I walked away in no mood for her games, and noticed the itch lessened. I ran further and it disappeared. Relieved, I turned and jogged back, the itch coming back again, as if it was trying to tell me something. I circled like a vulture, homing in on my target. Resisting the urge to scratch again, I took small steps until I divined the point where it was worst.

I marked the ground with the ancient dagger I always carried at my belt, and in so doing, moved my pouch aside. The itch changed place. I stopped on the brink of understanding, and opened the pouch. Inside lay the seed of The One Tree. I removed it and the itch stopped immediately.

"How do I plant this seed of The One Tree. Is there a ritual?"

Kay was surprised and said, "How? Why do you have it?"

"The Shaman gave it to me when we returned the old religion and her ring. She left me with a riddle as to when I should plant it. But the time is obviously now. A sowing ceremony?"

Kay said, "I think so. I'll bring my mother and the Magus Elder."

In consultation, Ælthrelntheine directed me how to plant the seed, a bed of moss lining the hole, before it was semi-filled with soft loam. I placed the seed in the centre, and filled in the divot, lightly tamping down, and stalled. The rhyme had been specific, "Fall waters aide you from a flask."

"Excuse me. Please don't do anything, and especially do not water. I will return in a moment," and I did.

I removed the stopper from the flask I had just filled with water from our fall, and looked up at Ræm. "Well remembered, Father. Aerated water is the best. Continue; we are almost done."

I watered and stood back. The Queen of the Eleventh said a blessing, and came over to thank me. When she turned her back,

Alberic, the Magus Elder came forward and offered incantations for the young tree. It seemed as if they were avoiding one another.

Distracted, I waved Ælthrelntheine's praise aside and explained the circumstances of how it came into my possession, adding, "I had almost forgotten about it, until I saw demise of The One Tree."

"Thank you. If the seed had remained here as normal, it would now be burned. The One Tree would be no more. She foresaw this — the Shaman was behind a lot of what occurred recently, or rather, our response to the situation. Ræm?"

"What you understand is correct, High Queen."

"Why were you not killed by the sword?"

"Oh that's easy. I would have been, but for the Ægus, the invisible cloak I was wearing. It protected me, just as the Shaman said it would."

"I always wondered why Rambling gave you that, and now I understand. The Shaman asked him to give it to you?"

"I believe so, but to know the truth, you better ask the King of the Twelfth. My work here is done. Please excuse me; I have other things I must do today."

"Ræm," I said, "Before you go, please explain how you come and go, as if by magic."

She giggled and said, "It is not magic Father, more like advanced technology, more sophisticated than that of the Ancestors — you will need to decide what you are going to do about them, and soon."

"Don't change the subject, how do you do it?"

"I cannot tell you. It is something you will have to discover for yourselves, as I did. I can tell you this though. You will find the key to unlocking the secret lies along the path of enlightenment. More I dare not say." And with that stated, she waved and disappeared.

"Guardian," n'Gnung enquired, "your daughter was correct, what do we do with the Ancestors?"

"Yes she was, but that can wait for another day. First, we need to consolidate our victory and right these wrongs. Then we need to carefully consider what we will do. Let's get out of here. I'm drained, let's forego the shore and recover at the Hamlet tonight. Tomorrow we will finish the all of this and celebrate."

Chapter 33 ~ Anathemata

By the following afternoon, the extinction of the Ogre Tribe was largely complete. To prevent unnecessary loss of our troops, we removed the warrior masses with plasma bombs sent into shielded areas. It was not war but obliteration of species. I had doubts and questioned my morality. Images of the Holocaust flitted through my mind. Was there any sign of remorse within their nation?

My closest and I walked shielded amongst the ordinary people. Ogre families, women and children, the aged, and were greeted at every turn with unprovoked, murderous attack. I gave up; there was no shred of humanity left within the entirety of their nation. So they came to pass into the annals of history. I was not proud of it, but prudence demanded justice must be meted out, if only for the security and continuation of all other life on Gaia.

Our investigation of the Ogre complex had been progressing on a relative threat basis, until all Ogres in the main city were eradicated. With the large, main area secure, we examined disbursed enclaves and tunnels. Several led to slave areas where Trolls were used for base labour. Some of the Trolls attacked us and were promptly dispatched, during which I noticed my sword, and Kay's flamed with a mixture of both blue and green. "Clones," she said. "Jackie, I hate this place."

"We must see it all, check everything out. One day this may form the basis of our first 'Starport'. It has everything going for it, including a launch bay."

"Yeah, just as well we got here before the Great Ogre figured out how to fly the thing."

"He worked out most of it apparently, later we must do the same."

"Yes, with our own spacecraft, but not this one. It cannot be controlled without Oma's Ring of Power, and that is still missing."

"We'll have to speak to her, cut a deal, her ring for either her life or death. Sounds fair to me; living in stasis, I, we..."

"Don't remind me, it was a nightmare! Dangerous. What of the other Tribes? They would all want a vote."

"Who all is here Kay? I and some of the Last, you are the only Eleventh, and without Owain and the Ddwyrth we would only have the remaining army of the Second. I would take Rambling's advice, and speak with Jinnie, but otherwise, we are it."

"At least until the new world order and Council of Tribes is convened. You're right; we should act now before anyone can stop us."

"Perhaps Kay, but we have already exterminated nearly all of the Ogre bloodline. Does that make us better or worse than them?"

"Better—we did it for the right reasons."

"Yes, the right reasons, from our point of view."

n'Gnung had been walking quietly to our side as the discussion progressed, he chose his moment perfectly. "Guardian, Kay, our new world needs an outright resolution, not government by committee, a plethora of provosts. Finish this before it begins. This new era needs to be in safe and capable hands, not those dithering for indulgence within a self-serving bureaucracy. Shared accountability is evasion of personal responsibility. I say do it. Do it now."

We had determined to do just that, when n'Gue appeared nearby, he did not look well. "Guardian, come. I have seen the devil's work today. It is macabre. I will take you to the doorway, but I am not going in ever again." He gulped and I thought he would vomit right there. "Excuse me, I'll show you the way, and then I'll go."

We were guided to what can only be described as a catacomb of genetic experimentation. Zombies with mutant bodies lunged for us. Beings with many arms and legs, plus several heads, attacked us unprovoked, and were despatched. Others scattered like spiders. The worst were the ones that appeared human, but weren't. The Sword of Destiny flared, Kay's sword likewise.

We three witnessed the wildest imaginings of Belial. I shook my head and said, "Enough, let's get out of here and retain our sanity."

"These are the Great Ogre's experiments gone wrong."

"But why did he keep them?"

"Maybe they were successful in some obscure way. Don't ask me. I'm never going there again."

I was still envisioning images of living things I wished were not, and without thinking said, "This. All of it has to go. Let's set a containment shield and nuke it."

"I'll use a plasma bomb Jackie, less fallout, you know."

We returned to the control room and set parameters for our imminent strike. Everything was set, but I had misgivings, it seemed we all did. "They need redemption, the chance at least. I don't know how to explain this. Otherwise this is murder."

"Forgive them, because they know not what they are?"

"Ask Aroweena and a small force to join us, we will do this one by one. Near the end of the warren there were some beings that did not affect our swords; we need to understand what they are."

"Correct, Kay. Guardian, wait one moment. I will ask Sun Kist to come here and advise us."

We returned to the catacombs and killed those that attacked us, or tried to. Our swords flared blue, or blue and green. Nearing the rear, we found more normal looking creatures that either produced a slight green flame, or nothing at all. Seeing the culling, they fled down an underground corridor, and we followed them to the outside.

There we found a troglodyte community, most living in burrows under the earth, some in caves set in the containing rock walls. We sheathed our weapons, but remained alert for attack, and maintained protection as we went amongst them. They fled from us at first, but in time became slightly curious, eyes peeping at us from behind shelter.

We had left two Ddwyrthen guards at the cave entrance, and they called out to let us know Sun Kist had arrived. We strode back to greet her and explained the situation.

"You were right to call for us, Guardian. Each horror needs to be addressed by an anathema, a blessing, forgiveness, or at least the spiritual chance of redemption if you prefer. These poor, underdeveloped souls need the release of either life or death. Currently they have neither one nor the other.

"Chein Tai will bless them so they find resurrection in a lifetime where they can grow as human beings. Your newfound wisdom becomes you, Guardian. I will send the whole team to you, so this place can be cleansed. Unfortunately, I cannot stay. The Shaman and Ræm are already facing a greater threat, but one perhaps not of your lifetime. I must join them, but will return before this is done."

High Priestess Chein Tai attended with her entourage, moments after Sun Kist departed. "We must sanctify the whole regardless, and better to start with the heart."

Chein Tai and her minions completed the blessings of the half-life we had already killed, and afterwards, we actioned the removal of the abomination of humanity. There were no smiles, no congratulations. We did what we had to do, and in so doing, perhaps delivered the blessing of death to those that had never been truly alive.

I asked the High Priestess if she would be able to cleanse and sanctify the entire city. "Yes of course, but it will take time, even with all our number. I will require a dedicated guide. Is Ju Lo available? He understands much of what we do already, having been the first, if temporary, High Priest."

"Yes of course, I will ask him to attend you. Where would you begin?"

"At the top, with the remains of the Great Ogre, and his palace."

"His ashes are still in the exhibition room, we intended to sweep them up later today."

"Leave it to us; we can perform a special ceremony of binding tomorrow. Sun Kist must be present."

"Good. We have located the palace, but not entered it yet. It is secure."

"I will attend when you do, we may need to clear a path for you, or your souls may become corrupt."

"Thank you, we must get about our business, there are still more unfortunates we shall have to kill."

"All must be offered redemption, Guardian, or you will be no better than the enemy. Priestess Siu Tao, please attend the Guardian and ensure justice for all. Remember, an individual's will, and that of their leaders is not necessarily the same thing."

She led us into the heart of the small community, and in time, some of the inhabitants prostrated themselves before her, and none offered us any threat. At no time did our swords show the slightest flare of blue or green. They were scared to death. "We need to speak to these creatures, but how? There is no common language. They have food and water, so let's lock this area down and move on, there is much more we must do, and these wretches can wait."

We returned to the Ogre control and Kay and I both heaved a heavy sigh. She muttered distractedly, "Now we must do something similar with the remains of the Ancestors."

n'Gue arrived and ripped the moment away from us. "You must come, Owain just discovered the slave quarters."

"Trolls?"

"Erm — perhaps? He's not sure what most of the creatures are."

We transferred to the area, which also lay on the outskirts of the city, and Owain briefed us. "Well met lads and lassies. These beings live in abject squalor, far worse than the city of the Trolls when we first visited them. I dunnae ken what to make of them."

The life forms appeared to be composed of bits and pieces from all manner of Tribes. They were humbled and scared. Some turned my sword green, but there was no hint of blue. We clung to our forbearance to witness the all of it, coming in time to the outside, where a long valley was home to them. We learned this encircled the city, like a moat filled with human damnation.

We walked on, the sameness of destitution appalling. "I didn't have the heart to kill them," said Owain as he sat down on a nearby rock in contemplation.

I offered my considered reply, "I could ask them if they want to live or die, but that feels like avoiding responsibility."

"I agree, Guardian. The easy way out is to find some cause or justification and murder them all. However, they remain victims, as far as I can see. They deserve a better fate, and that means offering them life instead."

"Ask a medic to attend; I need to know what sort of life they are capable of leading, and what they are. We will do likewise for the last community we found, and any others we come across."

"Hopefully there will be no others, Guardian."

The medic duly arrived and took representative samples. "They are mainly the results of genetic experiments on the Trolls and Last, although all Tribes are represented within the DNA samples. They are sentient beings, but of low intelligence. However, I must assert that they are all human."

"Thank you Medic. What do we do with them, offers anyone?"

Aroweena came forward and proffered her acquired hip flask brimmed with Raw Ogre Spirit, "This is the best I could come up with. Cheers!"

Her sense of humour was welcome, the liquor strong. Our thoughts were given voice as arbitrary mutterings, "They can't stay here."

"Neither can we set them free; they would never survive in the world outside."

"We can't just kill them for being different."

"Do they have any leaders?"

"No, they were controlled by the aged Ogres that we killed."

"What do they eat?"

"As far as we can determine, whatever they can scavenge or grow."

My ears picked up and I asked, "Where, show me."

We were taken to a secluded area where peasants were intent on some form of husbandry, harvesting root crops, whilst others prepared a form of broth, adding bits of rats and bugs for protein. They backed away whenever we came close to them, but there, within that valley floor of an offshoot ravine, we discovered their humanity, it being almost the same as our own.

"Jackie, we have to find them a new home, a place where they can live, yet be secure."

"Indeed, Kay. Guardian, I believe the perfect place would be the Ogre training ground we took recently."

"Brilliant, n'Gnung. It is certainly a large enough area, has barracks, a river, vibrant vegetation, and a great deal of land fit for cultivation. We should transfer those here as a beginning, and follow with the rest of them. Siu Tao, comments?"

"I am most pleased with the way you have dealt with this problem. Your solution is not perfect, but affords great hope for the future, not only for these poor souls, but also for your own. I must go first and sanctify the area. You stated it was once used as an Ogre training ground?"

"Yes it was. n'Gnung, Kay, we should also go there and check it is OK, and remove or obliterate all trace of the Ogre's occupation."

We attended to the task, physically clearing it of Ogre paraphernalia, as the Priestess did likewise in spiritual ways. It did not take long, there was little left, and we returned to the Bridge of Oma's spacecraft. Kay walked towards the Captain's console, and almost reaching it, stopped to stare at me. I said, "Captain Kay if you please, where would you like us to sit?"

Her immediate smile was almost lascivious, but tempered by fate and circumstance. "Hmmm. Captain Kay indeed, it has no *Ring* about it you know. The true Captain must wear Oma's ring of power, and be instigated by her as Captain. That is another reason we need her alive. Regardless, n'Gnung, Guardian's console if you will, Jackie, I need you as Gatekeeper. Cover all our backs."

By the time we had cleared the moat and associated areas, our sensors revealed that apart from one secured area, there were few life forms remaining within the city that were unaccounted for. The Great Ogre's palace was locked down and the spacecraft had been isolated as a separate area under its own shields. The adjoining labs and workshops were sealed by another shield, as was the Great Ogre's secondary control and exhibition room.

Owain said, "Let's clear the city, seal it off, and be done for today. I am in great need of a beer. Send them to us at this location, Guardian, and we will kill them."

We transported all in turn, a Priestess standing by to ask them to redeem their sins, and Gangling ready to interpret. We need not have bothered, but it mattered to us. As the Ogres saw our party, they wilfully attacked and tried to hack our people to pieces — there seemed little point in offering salvation to an enemy that was determined to kill us by any means, fair or foul.

n'Gnung put it in perspective, "They worship the Great Ogre and are his servants, even now. They will carry out his wishes, regardless of whether he is alive or dead. Seemingly, most religions of the Last are similar."

I grimaced and nodded, "Correct, my kind wasted many years at war with each other, and all over which of mankind's versions of The One God's Word, was the right one. Men, mainly exclusive of women, made it up to suit their own ideals of seeking and maintaining power to control others, especially their womenfolk.

"Where was the offer of redemption?"

"I am not aware they knew of that concept."

"Who, the Ogres, or the Last?"

We were interrupted when Owain's messenger asked for assistance. "Most you are sending to Llwydd from the latest secure compound are Trolls. He needs to know if they are green or blue, as in sword-fire."

n'Gnung said, "Go, Kay, Guardian. I'll send the rest in during the next few minutes."

Llwydd was standing beside his King, both in deep discussion. Llwydd spoke first, "They remind me of what we first found in Old Prussia. Are they green or blue?"

The familiar problem reasserted itself, how best to check the humanity of creatures with a drawn sword. They did not know of our intentions, and would either attack or flee. "I need the New Tenth here, now!"

Several minutes passed before Volkar joined us, and we all welcomed him as our brother, openly showing physical affection with manly hugs and bravado. He had been pre-warned of the situation, and was eager to add to their Tribe's number, replace those that had been lost during the recent conflict. During our embraces of unity, we formulated a ruse. Volkar would appear to be telling us what to do. Fortunately, Gangling was at hand to translate. This would be conducted in the language of the Trolls.

It was instantly obvious the captured Trolls were in awe, and hesitantly at first, did as their President instructed them. Volkar stood to the fore, Kay and I with swords drawn upright, as if in salute stood to either side. At Volkar's order, the Trolls came forward in pairs, and passed between us. Ddwyrthen warriors formed a corral behind us, where the Trolls regrouped. Siu Tao watched proceedings with an ambivalent air. They all passed the test, and Volkar welcomed them to their new nation.

The mood was congratulatory, when n'Gue appeared. "Guardian, my brother says there is one group left, maybe twenty Trolls. He has sent me to warn you, and said, 'I do not like the look of them, they seem different somehow.'"

"Different how?"

"He didn't know, but suggested you arm protection just in case."

We did as advised, and the last Trolls appeared. Immediately our swords set afire with blue and green. Volkar began to welcome them, but quickly retreated, commanding the Ddwyrth to protect his new citizens. The group attacked Owain and Llwydd unprovoked.

We ran to their aid, I glanced behind, and witnessed the Ddwyrth shoulder arms outwards against the new threat, their backs open to attack from those they protected. Volkar and Gangling joined them, but battle was upon me, and I swung the sword in a killing arc. Aroweena and others soon joined us, evening the numbers. The cull was over quickly, but Aroweena apologised, "Guardian, this one. I struck her down before I realised she was only green, no blue. I pulled the slay of my sword, but it was too late."

"Take her to medical now, save her. Aroweena, such things happen in the mêlée of battle. It is how we address the outcome of our inadvertent mistakes that gives us our humanity."

"Yes, immediately. But what if the healing machine, the Matron did not exist. This is a heavy blow to my heart, one I must right at once." She cradled the dead girl lovingly in her arms, and transported.

Gangling talked with Volkar, who in turn spoke with his new people. Several minutes later, we learned the whole story from Gangling. "The last group were not true Trolls, but clones sent as overseers, enforcers of the Great Ogre's desires. The girl you killed and took away, she was young and considered especially attractive, so the Ogres took her captive. Her family, her husband considered her dead. Perhaps she is better off now."

"We are trying to right this wrong, a moment please."

Aroweena appeared moments later and reported, "She will live, but it will take a few days. Please accept my apologies. I was not expecting to find such an innocent among the throng."

Her words were translated, and conveyed to the captive Trolls. Aroweena knelt and bowed her head, as if pleading for forgiveness. Several came forward and bowed in return to Aroweena. She did not know what to do.

I whispered to her ear as I gentled her to her feet. "Stand, bow back and smile. You did what you thought was right and discovering your mistake, instantly put right the wrong. I am proud of you, we all are. I will ensure they understand what happened. Come, we must speak with Volkar about assimilation of their new people."

We were interrupted when Siu Tao came to us, "Overall, I am very pleased. You have shown great fortitude and moderated your instincts regards being fair to all. However, do not place too much faith on hoping your charitable acts will turn out for the best. The application of wisdom applies to all seven virtues, not just the first four.

"That stated, I am pleased with the way you have conducted yourselves. These are the most trying of times, after all. We will return tomorrow to complete sanctification, including the palace area and exhibition hall. Please leave the latter unattended, but close down the secondary control centre."

"What do you mean, exactly?"

"Nothing, just an aberration the High Priestess mentioned in passing, but better to be safe than sorry. We must leave and attend Devotions, excuse me please."

The Priestess transferred back to the old capital, and I said, "That was odd. What did and didn't she actually say, Kay?"

Kay shrugged her shoulder in contemplation. n'Gnung replied, "Guardian, there is more afoot than we know of. I believe this has everything to do with the enmity between the Ogres and Ancestors. We will resolve this, tomorrow. Right now, we need to put ourselves first and recover. Let's lock this place down and head for the shore."

It felt like several hours later by the time we finally wrapped up for the day. We left Greenland in the early hours, arriving on the island at dusk. We all felt drained, and most departed for the shore, I going to attend my wife. She was asleep, but looking healthier. I learned from the Ladies in Waiting, she had improved much, but the Healer had already administered a sleeping draught. I lay with her for a while, she seeming to acknowledge my presence by flopping an arm around me.

The events of the day, and those that beckoned for the morrow came into my mind. I wanted to discuss them with Jinnie, but she was still recovering. I kissed her lips, and slid from her side. I glanced back, ignoring the automatic transporter we had fitted in the room, and walked outside. I looked up at the stars, and for a moment, became lost within the mysteries of time and space.

Later, the sounds of revelry from the Imperial Inn intruded into my thoughts, and I used my bracelet to return to the shore via the Bridge. I noticed Wong Kai was still working. "Why are you here so late?"

"What? Oh, Captain. Sorry, I am working on a task my mother set for me, and as far as I can see, the future is not set. How can that be?"

"You sound like your grandmother. She was a great Seer, but sometimes missed the obvious. Perhaps you should ask my daughter?"

"Yes, you are correct, the Gatekeeper knows much about the Third and Windy Way, more than she lets on. She was here today you know?"

"Mai Li?"

"No, Ræm. She spent hours in your ready room, and later in the medical unit. If you ask me, women appear to be a law unto themselves. Mom says I should not worry about such things, and focus. But on what?"

"Begin with the present, all of the present, the entirety — something Won Long occasionally overlooked."

"What do you mean, Guardian?"

"Don't let your personal feelings or view of this world, obscure the truth. We faced something similar today. Overcoming your prejudice or inherent beliefs is but the first step on the road to true wisdom. Come to me any time you have need, but I must leave you now, I need to relax. Never forget to unwind and release the stress."

I patted his back and was about to leave, when a thought occurred to me. "Wong Kai, you may be aware we are deliberating whether to reanimate the Ancestors, or kill them. There can be no other way. We will do one or the other tomorrow. Tell me, in your considered opinion, which is the prudent course of action?"

"Are you? I had no idea. I will ask my mother later, and see what I can find out."

"Don't ask her outright, be discrete, and try to gauge her preferred path. Thank you, and now I must relax."

I left him to his work. I had no idea what Ræm was up to and I was determined to find out, if I ever saw her again. She was like a butterfly, flitting hither and thither, following some unpredictable, perhaps predefined path of life. I was more than ready for a beer when I reached the shore. After a quick wash and change at our home, I had used the automated transfer circle, which took me to the back end of the community. I sometimes did this so I could soak up the atmosphere and normality of the place, as I walked down to the restaurant, my prelude to participating.

I was distracted, and closing on our table, when the swish of broom caned my behind. "Ahha! Here he is. The ringmaster has finally deigned to delight us with his company."

Thwack. "Your beer is going flat, your guests need entertaining, and you have been away too long."

We were almost at the table when I stopped running, swung around, and gathering her in my arms, kissing her briefly. It felt so good to be home. The table rose to drink our health, and I cajoled Da Phai Nai to join us. After all the horrors we had recently endured, it was not long before the strains of Old MacDonald cemented our camaraderie.

Chapter 34 ~ The Final Conflict

The next morning Jinnie was looking and feeling much better. I assisted her through to the Imperial restaurant and updated her as we ate. Once breakfast finished I broached the subject of the Ancestors.

She was quick to reply, "Jackie, do what must be done. Do it today before the Council of Tribes convenes. Either kill them or give them life, but only one lifetime."

"We came to the same conclusion. I thought to ask Rambling."

"No, he is far too preoccupied, and anyway, he would want Ælthrelntheine's opinion, which equates to the Tribal Council, as yet unformed. Finish this today."

"I will, if you will seek treatment at the medical centre?"

"You are impossible. No. Stop!"

"Jinnie, listen to me. I do not mean full rejuvenation, but please consider restoration of the functions of your joints. You would be freed from being virtually bedridden for days at a time, and able to walk and enjoy life without pain. We did that for Won Long, and I remember you remarked on the change in her, and Lo Si also. Look at Da Phai Nai. I'll say no more, but please, think about the quality of your life. You would want to play with your grandchildren, wouldn't you?"

"That's unfair, Jack Barleycorn, and you know it."

"I know, give me a kiss. I must leave in a moment. Hopefully today will be the end of it."

Minutes later, I joined our team on the Bridge, and took a moment to speak to Wong Kai. "I'm sure Mother suspected something, Guardian, but I bluffed my interest as best I could. She refused to comment directly, but her body language gave her away. I tried a different tack, and she said, 'To kill them now avoids a probable small trouble in the near future. To let them live will help with a larger trouble in the more distant future. More I cannot say'."

"Thank you, Seer Elect. That is a great help." Moments later, we transferred into the Greenland afternoon. Sun Kist was with us, and unwittingly, gave us the day's schedule. "I will stay until this is done. The Priestess' will continue to cleanse and sanctify, working with Ju Lo. Regards your plans for the day, I feel we must deal with the Great Ogre's palace first, and his trophy room last."

I felt something approaching unease regards her last comment, but moments later we actioned our plan. There remained three important areas: the spacecraft; the Great Ogre's palace; and his laboratories and cloning centre. The latter included the secondary control and exhibition centre — a part of the lab complex, but a separate entity.

As we made our way through to the transporter Kay said, "So, we will deal with the Ancestors last."

"Yes, but what we will do I still have no idea. We better focus on the palace, knowing the Great Ogre there may be traps and surprises."

We went in fully armed and prepared, Stewart and Gung Loi's platoons going first, securing bridgeheads, and scouting. Sun Kist accompanied us, insistent on going before us and cleansing, but what she did, did not make much sense. Owain led us through the complex; Horovitz our back up. Apart from the ground floor complex, it was a high tower. The few remaining staff were clones, and all were killed.

We worked progressively, securing one area before moving to the next. Reaching the top of the tower, we entered the private rooms of the Great Ogre with caution. There were several floors, the upper chambers being lined with spoils of war, some of which Kay and Owain recognised. "Guardian, me wee laddie, we must send all these items, plus the contents of the storeroom below us, to the High Queen for dissemination. It will keep her occupied and stop her interfering."

Kay patted his shoulder as she chuckled, "You know Mother well, Owain. But don't forget, her intentions are pure. She is High Lord Protector of all Twelve Tribes."

"I agree with you both, but don't send anything to her just yet. I want to thoroughly go through what we have discovered. I feel there may be more to be revealed, if we take our time."

"Indeed, Guardian, another time. Today we finish with the living, and those held in-between. What of the Ancestors? Are we determined to resolve this today, ourselves?"

Sun Kist had been working nearby, and completing a blessing, she said, "We will be there when you release them. They could turn out to be an ally for all time, or the deadliest foe. I see little in between. They created us. They could destroy us. The only way to discover the truth is to bring them back to life. If you do not, you will never know."

Kay and I nodded, turned away, and looked out from the balcony, talking and deliberating, presuming Owain would join us. Instead he said, "I hav'nae seen one of these for a long time. It's a King's Keepsafe."

We whirled in alarm as Owain continued, "Now let me see—Ah, yes, here it is." He tinkered with a panel, revealed a motif, and said, "This should only open with the Ring of the Warrior. You have it?"

Kay responded, "Yes, I had to take it off, it was affecting me in ways I did not like."

She put on the ring and accessed a hidden vault. A secret door slid aside, revealing a treasure trove. Owain eagerly strode through the door, as both Kay and I yelled, "This could be a trap."

"Owain, we must proceed with great caution, and leave this for another day."

Owain shrugged, his eyes fixated by gold and jewellery. We joined him to gawp at a large collection of priceless treasures.

Kay said, "This tiara was made by the Eleventh, look at the finely detailed craftsmanship."

"The missing crown of Boërwulf, an ancient Ddwyrthen king."

I looked at n'Gnung, who remained outside, and said, "This is a remarkable discovery, and there will be others. I need you all to focus on what we must do today. Come, tomorrow is time enough for this."

"Yes, you are right, Jackie. Time to get rid of whatever lives within the laboratories of the Ogre, and then we will face the final conflict."

"Agreed, young laddie, let's do it. However, I'll keep Boërwulf's crown if you don't mind. Kay, please bend so I may fit the tiara to your brow. Wonderful, it suits you perfectly. Guardian?"

"No, not now. Are you sure these items are not compromised by Ogre technology? Best have them checked just to be safe. Come, we have much work to do, and time flees."

After securing the tower and killing all the Ogres, we took a short break before attending to the next task. We entered the laboratory complex expecting to kill Ogres. We were greeted by a haphazard assortment of scientists and technicians. Gangling as translator, offered them redemption, which they all accepted and craved for. This response we had not conceived, never mind considered.

"We have a problem, what's the answer?"

I looked around hoping somebody would offer me a solution that gave us a meaningful way forward. I was rescued from the mental abyss by Sun Kist. "Meet thee well the game of three, but which path is the one to be? To live, to die, or other see, the key to life haunteth thee."

I gaped at her, and after absorption of her windy words replied, "Do you have a version of that we can understand?"

She giggled like the young girl I remembered, and answered, "We must honour our offer. Gangling will translate and I will perform the blessing to purge their souls. Guardian, they will either live or die. There can be no other outcome, be wary."

Proceedings appeared to be going well, the Ogres accepting the blessing and renouncing their sins. However, none would accept the healing process, adamant that it was a trick to enslave them once again. At my side n'Gnung whispered, "I do not like this one bit, Guardian. I feel we are in a trap yet to be sprung, but what?"

"I don't know, but I'm sure we'll soon find out. Let's spread out. n'Gnung stand aside ready to return and bring help. Something stinks about the all of this."

"The Ogre head count was exactly one dozen?"

"No, thirteen, a baker's dozen."

"There are only twelve Ogres here, Guardian."

"Go!" I cried out in alarm and reached for my sword. I was hit by an energy beam and frozen in place. The thirteenth Ogre had appeared clutching a gun-like device. Nearby, Kay activated her personal shield, moments before she was struck. She was not frozen, but her shield was locked in place. The remainder of our party met a similar fate.

Mere seconds later our fate was sealed, all except for Sun Kist were entombed in the freezing shield. I had expected Sun Kist to run, but she held her staff high and spoke clearly, "You asked for forgiveness, but lied. May your souls be damned forever and never ..."

A mighty Ogre hand clamped over her mouth cutting off her words. He raised her by her head to his eye level and leered at her. His other hand gripped her torso as if preparing to rip her head off. However, he seemed to falter, Sun Kist's eyes bored into his, and I picked up on a mental breeze, "Stop, it is wrong to kill me."

Those of us enabled took up the telepathic chant; n'Gnung's voice not one of them. He was our wild card, but would need to hurry. The Ogres armed themselves with lethal blades and spiked balls on chains. Sun Kist was thrown aside and landed badly, but she was alive. My attention was focused on the Ogres now coming for me.

They were haughty, bullying as they approached, intimating with their weapons how they were about to end my life. I knew they would need to drop the freeze shield, and the moment they did, I activated the protection of the Ring of the Ancestor, rolled forward and came to my feet swinging the Sword of Destiny at the leading Ogre.

He backed away in fright, presuming my target was either his head or heart. It was not. I severed his arm in one clean cut, and it, along with the freezing device, clattered to the floor. Falling backwards, prostrate he pleaded in English, "Please, I am truly sorry. I only did what the Great Ogre would have wanted me to do. I carried out his orders. I will repent. These were not my actions, but his."

Being conned once is culpable negligence, but twice, no. I stood over his dying form and plunged the sword into his heart. Words came unbidden to me, "I will heal you now."

The effect was not as cinematic as when Ræm, did it, but I saw runes flare to life and react with the Ogre blood, and knew at once my actions were vindicated. He had lied once too often. I swung away as a presence nearby drew my attention, already unleashing the Sword of Destiny towards its next victim. I pulled the sweep. n'Gnung had the Ogre's hand and was trying to prise free the freezing device.

I looked up, the room filling with our own, Horovitz and Stewart, Ddwyrth, and Elven Guarde. They had protection bracelets, Ancestral weapons, and shield draining devices. n'Gnung said, "Gung Loi monitored everything from the Bridge of this craft. We transferred Sun Kist to our medical unit; she seems fine, if slightly concussed."

"n'Gnung, find out how to use that thing, our people first."

"Sure, Guardian. Once I understand it I'll unfreeze the others."

His smile was that of a young boy with a new toy, and he quickly discovered how it worked. We soon freed our own and despatched the last of the so-called scientists, before exploring the complex in full. The sample room was distressing, the DNA extraction laboratory worse. There were sentient beings floating in containment pods, which looked like the rotting decomposition of an old grave.

I came to one that was human, except everything that should have been on the inside of the body, was on the outside; easy to take samples presumably. I shouted a warning, "Do not look at this. It is evil. I want you to go now. Any of us that remain will finish this."

Many came forward, but backed away when they saw what was in the stasis pod. There were few of us left resolute to face the worst horrors of Ogredom. Owain said, "Aroweena, is that hip flask of yours full? Time for a wee tipple before we eradicate this macabre."

The fiery liquor brought a tear to our eyes but warmed us to go on. We reached the end, and walked back along the adjoining and parallel hall that interlinked via dedicated laboratories. We witnessed deformed eyes, or genitalia being grown. The glass tubes we passed resembled a production line. Soon we came to the assembly area, just like that of a car plant, except they were putting parts of human beings together. Finally, we reached the exit; we had witnessed the all of it.

"That's it Jackie, I need to get out of here."

"Me too, Guardian."

"Leave it to the Ddwyrth, Guardian. We'll kill everything here."

I listened, but only one resolution gave me satisfaction, total obliteration of the whole damnation. "We will nuke this horror, and this time, Kay, I do mean we reduce the all of this to atomic particles. This is inhuman. It has no right to exist on this planet."

I turned away in disgust, but Kay caught my arm and we came face to face. "We don't actually have any nuclear weapons, Jackie. The Core is banned from deploying them. We could work around that, but it would take days. We need a resolution now, so I intend to send this entire area into the sun. That do for you?"

And that is exactly what we did. It was simple, and it was difficult. In essence, Kay shielded the area, dislocated it, and threw it up into orbit, where our spacecraft's carefully calibrated weaponry batted it towards the sun. Some minutes later, a flare confirmed the sun-strike.

The high of expectancy bequeathed a low. Our spirits had been uplifted by following the right path, and yet remained drained by the macabre machinations of a merciless and malignant mind.

We returned to Oma's Bridge in a frosty frame of mind. We had witnessed what no mortal should ever experience, and come out the other side. But it took a toll on our humanity. "Status report?"

"Everything is locked down, Guardian. There remain no Ogre life-signs, and all apart from one in the exhibition room are accounted for."

"What do you mean, 'all apart from one in the exhibition room'?"

"I have fourteen life-signs, Guardian, and I am aware there are only thirteen Ancestors. The other? Your guess is as good as mine."

"Is one of them pregnant?"

"No. It's not like that at all. It is one of the Last."

"Show me the room on screen."

"I cannot, there is no link, just like the palace tower, the Great Ogre liked his privacy. A penny for your thoughts?"

"A Peni indeed, Langnor, you are a genius. n'Gnung, assemble a small force, but I think I already know who is there."

As I expected, we found Peni operating the Great Ogre's control. I had ordered the place closed down and sealed-off. No one should have been there. I was in no mood for playing games, and strode towards her ready to bawl her out. My steps slowed as I passed the exhibition units; the Ancestors were being restored to full bodily function. I realised this was something we had overlooked. We could not release them until their bodies were whole once more.

My wrath had turned to intrigue by the time I reached Peni. "What are you doing?"

"Why, dearest Jackie, good of you to drop by. I have almost finished the rejuvenation process, they are coming along splendidly, don't you think?"

"Why are you doing this?"

"Because you told me to, don't you remember?"

"No I did not, Peni. Tell me exactly how you came to be here."

"Uh! Oh well suit yourself. After Sun Kist and Siu Tao cleansed the Great Ogre's ashes, the High Priestess gave me a message from you, 'The Guardian wants you to begin the reanimation process.' I tried to contact you, but you were off killing creatures of some sort.

"So I came here and a bit later you showed me what to do. It's actually quite simple, just like baking a cake."

"Peni, I was never here. I never told you, or Siu Tao."

"Yes you were, but you have changed clothes since this morning, these look much better on you."

"Was I wearing this sword when you saw me?"

"No, of course not."

"I have not taken this off since we began here. I think somebody has been playing mind-games, haven't you, Oma!"

I strode towards Oma and glared at her. My brief remonstration fell on deaf ears and blank eyes. I pulled the Sword of Destiny for effect, and she did not react, "Stop the mind-link Oma, now! We were considering letting you live, but I could just as easily kill you all now."

I thrust the sword towards her heart, stopping as it hit the glass door. I was getting mad again. "Let go of her mind, damn you, or I will end this, now."

The body of Oma continued to float serenely before me. There was no reaction whatsoever. n'Gnung came to my side, speaking in Ancestor, "Guardian, why bother, it's wasted time and effort."

I glanced at him, seeing a playful light dancing in his eyes.

He continued, "Come, we banquet to celebrate the death of the Great Ogre. Beers are flowing, food is waiting, and people are dancing. I say we leave now, lock the place down, and never come back."

"Correct; they can rot here for all eternity for all I care."

Before we turned away, I perceived a spark from deep inside Oma's eyes. It was fleeting, but it was there. In that moment, Peni's torso crashed onto the console, Kay was first to attend her. Peni was rousing as if from a swoon when I reached her, "What? Where am I?"

Her eyes seemed out of focus for a few moments, until she gathered her bearings. "Oh, why am I here, oh yes, Siu Tao said I should come. Why are you all staring at me?"

"When will the reanimation be completed?"

"In six hours. How do I know that? What reanimation?"

I went to her and lifted her up on her feet, "Come Peni, it is time for you to drink beer."

"Well I never did! The cheek of it; oh well, do you have any wine instead, a fine, dry Montrachet perhaps?"

As our team made its way to the door, I stopped before Oma and standing to attention, nodded my head in curt respect, "Thank you."

We locked the exhibition room down completely. It would require either Kay or I to remove the protective shield. We debriefed with Langnor, who had already assembled a crew to staff Oma's Bridge, twenty-four seven. We retired to the shore early that day, the perfect place to revive flagging spirits.

Peni came with us, and enjoyed the freedom of the strand, before the inevitable questions began, which we discussed openly. The only plausible explanation was that Oma had taken over the minds of her and Siu Tao.

Later, Kay said, "Jackie, I think I understand. Peni is marginally telepathic. Remember that time in Engineering, right after we remodelled the spacecraft. You and n'Gnung came to join us, and you whispered mentally to me. Peni picked up on some of that, her outburst about 'bees'. That was a warning, we should have been aware. How stupid are we?"

"Not much, I am sure of it. Kay, work with Peni and Siu Tao, enhance their mental protection."

Returning a little later, her duty done, Kay reported, "They should both be well protected next time. The Ancestors were subtle, and are masters of telepathy, but only within a short range, which is strange. In addition, due to the Ogre shield, they could only use telepathy inside that room, which is something I need to understand, we both do. Jackie, I need to protect all of us, mind-link with me."

When she was done, I understood what had happened to the women, and why. Kay fortified the others with us, those who would go in the next day. I left her to it, but spoke briefly to Peni, "Do you still know how to finish the release process, or stop it?"

"Why of course, dearest Jackie. It's terribly exciting, and I want to work on this. Imagine, reincarnation, ever-lasting life, and we know how to do it. I could spend a lifetime there trying to understand it all."

"We almost did, and you may well have done, had we not found you in time. They would probably have had you release them, and stuck you in one of those pods."

"Oh, how ghastly. But no, you are so sweet and caring Jackie, but it wasn't like that at all."

"How do you know?"

"Because I know. They were seeking release, nothing more. How would you feel if you had been locked up there forever? I bet you would have done exactly the same given half a chance."

"I almost was. Excuse me."

Disconcerted, I was surprised when we were joined by Sun Kist. We rose to greet her, but she bid us stay. "I am fine, and was not badly injured. I can't believe they lied to us, to me. Why?

"The Shaman once tasked me to study the Perception of Souls, and I found it quite complicated. Now I understand it relates to deception and enlightenment, judging a being's true worth against what they say, versus what they really think. People lie to gain advantage of one another. I can't understand that. Forgive me, I am still learning.

"We will deal with the Ancestors tomorrow. I need to recover. We all need to heal. Anyway, tomorrow is an auspicious day, the astronomical alignment of Theia's remnant core, Mars, and Gaia. That has to be the day we face the Ancestors."

"Walk with me a moment, I need to speak to you about Siu Tao and Peni. It seems that Oma..."

Chapter 35 ~ The Ancestors

I awoke when Jinnie nestled into me, her spirits light and airy. "Jackie, I have decided to take your advice, and will visit the medical centre after breakfast. I will not have the full program, you do understand, but a little help would change my life greatly."

I hugged her close. After recent events, I could not image better news, except for her having full rejuvenation. Be that as it may, it was something she needed and I determined to have a word with Matron, to make that something as large and broad-ranging as possible. However, I masked the thought with sincere jubilation, and felt in fine form to face the day.

After breakfast, I paid Weid Noi a brief visit. "We plan to release the Ancestors today, what are your considered thoughts?"

"I am not a fool. I know you spoke to my son; such are the ways of the apprentice. This day will revolve around truth versus trust, and the outcome remains as yet unclear. Today the omens are good. Guardian, Jack, trust your instincts. More I cannot say."

I left the enigmatic Seer and had a brief word with Matron regarding Jinnie. I then requested a medic to attend us. I wanted to be prepared in case we encountered any complications with the reanimation.

In due course our party formed in the control room of Oma's spaceship, where we initiated video feed to the Great Ogre's lair. I had entrusted n'Gnung with the Ogre's freezing device, and he was to use it, should he perceive anything untoward. Once all was prepared, we transported to the room.

According to our plan, Kay accompanied Peni to the console. I said, "Peni, show Kay what to do. I need both of you on this."

I waited while Sun Kist and her Priestess' prepared the room. Once everything was set, I toured the thirteen cubicles, noting all appeared to be back to full physical form. Kay confirmed moments later, "Jackie, physical restoration is complete."

I made directly for Oma. "I can offer you life, death, or never-ending stasis. Which do you prefer?"

I felt sure all thirteen paired eyes turned to me, a telepathic chorus of release ringing in my head. I cut it off at my will. The Ancestors would play by our rules, not theirs. I stood before Oma and repeated, "Life or death, which is it to be?"

I allowed Oma's thoughts to enter my mind. "I choose life, we all do. Oh to breathe again, to walk, to see. I never thought this day would come. We are all exceedingly grateful to you."

"Don't be, you've not heard our terms. If we grant you release, it is on condition that you live out the rest of your lives in peace and harmony with the Twelve Tribes. You may choose, within reason, where on this earth you would like to live. You are all expressly forbidden to enter the spacecraft, unless Ælkræleinnoire or I order an explicit exception. Do you understand?"

"Yes. This is understandable. We present a serious threat to you, despite the fact we gave you all life. You are known as The Guardian?"

"Yes. My duty is to protect the Second, and all of the Tribes."

"You mean they all still survive?"

"Yes, but several are few in number. The Ogres have been exterminated, but their cousins, the Trolls, are our allies. There is one final condition, you must hand over all your trinkets of power, and give your master ring of power to Ælkræleinnoire. You must do this immediately, and without trickery. You must officially renounce the captaincy of your spacecraft with the Core, and install Kay as the new captain. Fail and you will be killed. Is that understood?"

"You don't trust us, do you?"

"No. Why should I? Especially after what you did to Peni yesterday. Trust has to be earned, and it comes from acting and speaking truthfully, no matter the cost."

"Your price is far higher than I expected. Won't you reconsider; we could teach you so much."

"Thank you, you can still educate us. Nonetheless, we will be in complete control. I will give you a moment to consider."

"That is not necessary. I must escape this sarcophagus. I managed to hide the true ring of power from the Great Ogre. It should still be in the vault, but to access it I will need to attend the Bridge of the spacecraft. I will also need the decoy ring he took from me; it was a powerful controllers ring, but nothing more. He was wearing it when he was killed."

"Thank you Oma, if you are telling the truth I will trust you. If you lie, I will kill you. Do you understand?"

"Yes, Guardian, I am telling the truth, and I will not trick you. It is not our way. We live by our honour. Do you?"

"Yes, likewise. Good. I will return in a moment, and release you. Only you." I turned to the others and said, "Clear the room, everybody out of here."

Once the large oak doors closed, we transferred back to the Bridge. Gung Loi activated the shield for the room, and I sent Kay to get the ring back from her mother. Some minutes later they both returned, and Ælthrelntheine wasted no time in speaking her mind, "What on earth is going on here Guardian? I thought it was agreed the fate of the Ancestors would be decided at a full council of the Tribes. What have you to say for yourself?"

"No Ælthrelntheine, with respect, that is what you decided. It is we, here and now, who will decide the fate of the Ancestor..."

A difference of opinion ensued until finally, the Queen of the Eleventh backed down, "I am most unhappy with this turn of events, but you seem determined to do what you will, so be it. However, I hold you personally responsible for any repercussions, Guardian."

"Thank you Your Highness, we believe it is for the best."

"I should not admit this to you just now, but I am personally in favour of their release, provided suitable precautions are in place."

I beckoned towards n'Gnung and said, "Thank you, we are prepared for any eventuality. Let's get on with this. Kay, we need you affirmed as interim captain with the Core."

Kay made her way to the main transporter of Oma's craft for verification, and I wore the Ring of the Warrior to empower the Ancestor's commander's ring.

The process was quickly completed, and subsequently Kay ran several checks. "Oma told the truth, Jackie. This is an advanced commander's ring, and offers substantial, if ultimately limited powers. It is not as powerful as the Ring of the Warrior, but can access different systems, so the rings are quite well matched overall."

"OK, let's finish this now."

We returned to the trophy room with one extra member, Ælthrelntheine hesitant to enter. "This is a place of eternal damnation. I had hoped to never set foot here again."

We set about the task at once, Kay and Peni working the consol together, "Get ready for release."

We all watched the blue waters that had enclosed Oma receded, our mixed emotions covering a plethora of doubt, fear, and foreboding. These battled with excitement and expectancy, as we waited for the door to open.

Oma coughed when the tubes were withdrawn, and appeared startled when she took her first real breath in millennia. Although theoretically restored, it soon became apparent her muscles had atrophied, and she gradually collapsed as the waters bled away. I caught her as the door opened, n'Gnung standing back ready to freeze her. There was little weight to her, and I laid her gently on the floor, the robotic nurse attending quickly.

"Guardian, all her vital signs are extremely good, but she needs tonic and therapy. I recommend we look after her initial recovery. She has been entombed for an extremely long time, and there may be unforeseen complications."

"Take her, go."

Oma spoke, her voice a dry rasp, almost a whisper, "Wait. I must keep my promise first." Her physical words dried up, but she continued talking telepathically. "Take me to the Captain's day room; I will give you my ring. I can't believe I am truly alive again. It has been utter torment. Thank you, thank you all."

Her conversation stopped, she was close to losing consciousness. I picked her up and carried her, but said aside, "Nurse, I need Oma conscious for five minutes. Give her something to help. n'Gnung, come with us and remain alert. Kay?"

Oma was true to her word and retrieved her ring from a secret vault. I knew there was a DNA check controlling access to higher levels. She changed rings three times before bringing out the last. "This is my ring, and I will miss it dearly. Please look after it, Captain. I need to use it for a moment, to empower Ail Kray..."

"Kay"

"Kay. Ah, that's much better." They fixed each other in the eye. Oma's hands touched Kay's face, "Daughter? It cannot be."

Kay spoke, "Not so, grandmother. Your eyes are fascinating, disconcerting. Now I understand how others see me, see us. No other since our first Queen has had either white eyes or black hair. We are special."

"Indeed we are. I want to hug you, but first I need to sit down, to rest a moment before we finish this."

Once seated comfortably, Oma continued, "To know my genes still walk this Earth, but in the form of another, is an uncanny feeling. One moment please ... Yes, handing over my powers to my granddaughter feels correct, as if predestined, despite the æons in between. Come, Guardian, carry me. I must empower Kay as the new captain, before my remaining strength ebbs away. Now it is your turn to trust me. Do you trust me? Tell me the truth."

"No Oma, I do not completely trust you. But I trust you enough to take a chance you are telling the truth. Let's do this and get you treated. Remember, one false move and you are dead."

"Your trust takes a lot of earning, Guardian, but rightly so – that is your job. We should not have been so trusting with the original Great Ogre. Quickly now, despite my thrill and excitement at finally being released, I feel drained and am in dire need of revivification. Hurry, I weaken by the second."

We were wary, but Oma settled at the main control console and activated it with the most powerful ring. I was sure the whole room lightened when she did so, but I remained at her side, ever watchful. n'Gnung stood at her other side, weapon trained on her. Once finished, she removed the ring and handed it to Kay, "Go to the main transporter and..."

"Thank you Oma, I know what to do."

Seconds passed before Kay returned, and they interfaced with the Core from the Captain's day room. As soon as the handover of power was complete, Oma collapsed and was taken to our medical facility. I wanted full control of her, at least for the time being, so n'Gnung and I went with her to ensure there was no mistake.

"Matron, this is the resurrected body of Oma. Consider that she is under restraint, she is not allowed to go anywhere without my express permission. That stated she appears to be asleep."

Matron ran a quick check and said, "Her mind appears fine, but her body is in shock. Remember how you felt when you came out of that long coma after interfacing with the Core. This is similar, but far more traumatic. I will run deep scans in due course, but her sleeping is the body's way of self-protection, as was your own. I will let you know when her condition changes, but it won't be for several days."

"Thank you Matron. If this works out, know there will be twelve more coming to you in a similar condition."

"You mean the entire crew are still alive?"

"Yes, sort of, held in stasis is a better description."

"I must be there when you release the next, the procedure is rather complex, and I should be able to lessen the after-effects."

"The medic did not tell you?"

"No..."

I left Matron after agreeing to use the University hospital for recovery and therapy. Jien Noi was undergoing treatment, and I was not allowed to see her. Heartened she had gone through with it, I returned to the Bridge of Oma's craft, needing to speak to Kay.

"Jackie, this is amazing! Oma told the truth and I am now the official Captain of this spacecraft. I will tell all, but first, take this ring and I will empower you as my second in command."

I did as instructed, the situation seeming novel and just. Once the procedure completed, Kay led me through to the Captain's ready room and we interfaced with the Core, our positions reversed from normal. The level of information we had access to was far greater, and many things became clear. Kay also used the 'reveal' command to great effect, and we knew the next few days would be spent studying and understanding the all of it.

Having covered the primary bulk of revelations, Kay said, "There is one last thing to do Jackie, I need to officially instate you as captain of the other spacecraft."

"What, really?"

"Yes. Unless you want to be captain of this one, then we can swap over."

"No, I am fine as it is. Why do you ask?"

247

Kay chuckled and said, "Oma was the leader, not only of this craft, but also of the expedition. She and this craft have ultimate control, so does this ring. Now that is I. Sure you don't want to swap?"

It was my turn to laugh, "No, Kay, I am happy as things are. But empowering me as official Captain would solve a lot of my problems with the Core."

"I think it should solve all of them, let's go."

"Wait, I thought that could only be done by Space Corps."

"Ah, yes. What the Core did not tell you is that an official captain is automatically a member of Space Corps."

"But I was told Taris wasn't."

"Perhaps Taris wasn't the officially appointed captain. Let's find out."

I was eager to finally get full control of Taris' spacecraft, but stymied. "No Kay that can wait. We better finish-up here first."

That evening I attended Jinnie, who was still at the medical centre and under sedation. "We did as much as possible for her Guardian, but your wife was adamant on just how far we were allowed to proceed. Nevertheless, we went as far as was ethically correct. She has responded well to treatment, but we still have further work to do. She should be released within the week, and I will send word to you when she is able to receive visitors."

It was the morning of the third day after Oma's reanimation. In the meantime, we had finished all work at the Great Ogre's lair, with the exception of examining the Ogre treasure trove in detail, and freeing the rest of the Ancestors. Oma would determine the latter by what she did and did not do.

Kay had empowered me as Captain of Taris' spaceship, and I discovered he had been the First Officer. Kael had been the official Captain, but something had happened during entry into earth's orbit. I presumed this was why the spacecraft was forced into an emergency landing, and set about interrogating the Core.

"Commander Jack, the ship was damaged by remnants of the large meteor strike not long after take-off from Mars. The ship departed without full power and little shielding, the damage was substantial. Once in flight and space-critical parameters were in place, we began repairs. There was not enough time to fully restore the craft, and landing on Gaia was hazardous to life aboard.

"I recommended we orbit until repairs were complete, but that would have taken many weeks. We were much nearer the sun, and not prepared for the increased radiation, some of it life-threatening. The shields were still weak, and borderline regards protection. Worse was on the way due to sun-spot activity.

"Captain Kael decided to evacuate the ship, and set me the task of auto-landing once the craft was repaired. Taris was First Officer and he disagreed, stating he should remain on board, wearing a protective suit, and pilot the craft down. To do that, he required Kael's ring of power, and a struggle ensued.

"Taris managed to wrest the ring off Kael's finger, but was hit on the head in the process with a metal sculpture, part of which broke off and entered his skull. Kael tried to get his ring back, but Taris swallowed it. The other twelve jettisoned in the life-pods.

"Taris struggled through to medical, where he managed remove the ring via an unusual form of biopsy. He was clever, and knew ships systems intimately, something Captain Kael did not.

"Using the Controller's ring, he was able to pilot the craft. All was well to begin with, but we did not know about Gaia's foibles. Alarms sounded, our shield too weak to counter, and power critical. Taris tried, but the situation was impossible. We could do nothing to prevent a crash landing. In order to ensure integrity of critical systems, he initiated separation to the ship, moments before landing. The command module hit before his restraints were fully enabled, and he received more damage to his skull as a result. I actioned medics to attend him before all but emergency power died."

"Thank you Core, I think I know the rest. What of the twelve other crewmembers, did any survive?"

"No. The escape pods were incinerated upon entry into Gaia's atmosphere. The greater gravity and air density were beyond the pods' tolerance because pod shields had not been fully charged either as all power was needed for the main craft. This proved to be the same problem with our own landing, exacerbated by this planet's strong magnetic fields."

I had my answers, although I suspected I did not have everything. What I had dovetailed with the facts I knew, and corroborated what Matron had said. My thoughts were distracted when n'Gue arrived. "Guardian, Oma has asked to see you."

I visited Oma a short time later, n'Gnung as ever by my side. She seemed a lot brighter. However, she was struggling to control her body and to walk. "I know this isn't where I was held, Guardian. The days are almost equal in length and the air feels warm. Where am I?"

I had little reason to lie, "You are on the Island, the home of the Second."

"I need to see, to feel the sun. It has been so long. Help me."

I guided her outside, n'Gnung still covering her with the freezing device. Trust was being nurtured, but it would take time. She stopped just outside the main door, and raised her hands to welcome the sun on

Chapter 35

her face. "It's been so long. To be alive is such a wonderful thing. You don't realise it, until it's gone, the bit that matters anyway."

We soon returned inside as Oma weakened, but she was clearly thrilled with the treat of fresh air. Matron kept Oma on a strict diet and exercise regimen, but two days later, she was coming into herself. We had been sitting under the large oak near the automated transporter circles, but I still had misgivings about her presence, her intentions. She pre-empted the question I was trying to form, "What worries you, Guardian?"

My reply was impromptu. "Trust is a very big word. We are worried that once settled, you will turn on us and seek to regain the power you have given up."

Oma chuckled, "I do understand. We have placed you in an almost impossible position. That you are indulging us does you all proud. You fear what you do not understand.

"Guardian, I am not a megalomaniac, I am an astrophysicist. I was Captain of the escape ship because I thought about fleeing Mars by that means first, and initiated the project. It really is that simple. Vela is the only one with command experience of spacecraft.

"The others, as you will discover, are all highly skilled scientists, but in fields of botany, zoology, and human sciences. Our main work on Mars was related to soil, fertilisers, water to drink and for growing things, and maintaining biospheres where plants could grow. They were our main source of food. Our existence was precarious."

I absorbed Oma's words, and felt somewhat settled, but my misgivings did not entirely leave. I asked a considered question. "What would you do if Kay offered you your ring back?"

This time it was Oma who was left to contemplate, but she replied. "What is more important, the things you held high in a past life, or what treasures you will discover in the new, once you let go of the old? I have no desire for my ring back. It was only a fleeting position I once held. I would prefer to continue to do what I do best, study the properties of space, of time, the stars and their forms, and how they relate to our place within the greater whole."

"You should speak to Peni."

"I have, but Kay's knowledge is more aligned with what I do." She looked up as the sound of people heading for lunch drew her attention. "I can't believe all of these Tribes, so many different people are alive. We did something special you know. But we made one mistake. I'd like to meet them, if you will allow. But most of all, that Matron only allows me broth, tonics, and fruit juice. Is there any real food around here?"

Kay ran ahead to forewarn Helen, as I carried Oma to the door of the main University building, where I put her down, and she was introduced to John. I had given her a translation device so she could talk to others, and she was soon in animated conversation with the Chancellor as we made our way through to the refectory.

Although Oma ate little, she tried many dishes, her face often a picture of culinary bliss, sometimes not. I departed when I received a message from Matron, but others were already monitoring Oma around the clock, and she was on her best behaviour.

I arrived at Jinnie's bedside a short time later to find her looking fit and healthy. She had no difficulty with her joints and was in fine fettle. She was released the next day, and after taking a review of her realm, asked Oma to attend her.

The meeting went extremely well. Oma was surprised to discover we were married, and that our daughter was the one who killed the Great Ogre.

By the tenth day of her freedom, Oma had almost returned to full health and vitality. I spoke to Matron, who confirmed her recovery was virtually complete. We discussed reanimating the rest of the Ancestors the next day, Matron advising it would be better to bring them back in groups of three or four.

I spoke to John, "Oma is extraordinary. She knows so much, yet does not brag or belittle us. She spends most of her free time here and has helped us greatly, not telling us things, but encouraging us to look deeper, or in other directions. I would like to offer her a professorship, if you are willing? I have known many teachers in my time, and none holds a candle to her, she is terrific."

"Perhaps, but it is early days yet. Such an appointment would need the consent of the Empress, regardless."

"I understand, but I worry we will lose her to the NASA scientists, she is helping them also."

"Do not be overly concerned, we are considering releasing four more tomorrow, there are thirteen of them in total, so I am sure, if they prove to be as amenable as Oma, that you will have several new staff in due course."

The release of the next four Ancestors went smoothly, with both Oma and the Matron attending. They advised us on how to delicately adjust the process for each person, Vela being able to walk out of the pod herself, if only just.

The following week we released four more Ancestors, and one week later, the last of them. They all recovered at the University hospital, and naturally gravitated to the environment of the campus, and projects related to their areas of expertise. They seemed to be easing themselves back into being alive once more, but that was not without teething problems.

Matron assisted with their psychological adjustment, but Enok did not respond well. Oma suggested his mind be remapped by her spacecraft's facilities, and once actioned by Matron, he became a lot more settled. In time, this was done for all excepting Oma, Vela, and Iydm, who was the first to join us for an evening on the shore. He enjoyed the freedom and party atmosphere, always up for playing the fool. I remained wary, but was distracted, as Ræm had taken to spending a lot more time with us. She had taken special interest in the Ancestors, and was often in their company.

Although Oma and the Ancestors were formally banqueted and greeted by all leaders, it was not until the next Olympiad that they were presented to all of the Twelve Tribes officially. The Thirteen Tribes of Humankind stood together as one, fulfilling the Elven prophesy.

Chapter 36 ~ Webs of Subterfuge

2037

Some months later Oma and Vela came to see me. I had wandered down to the old Banyan tree whilst waiting for n'Gnung and Kay to join me for evening meal. "This is a lovely glade, how lucky you are. We haven't seen you around much recently, Guardian; you must be awfully busy with other matters."

"Yes I have been preoccupied, apologies Oma."

"I presume you are preparing to try to fly the spaceship — the one you have here, isn't that so."

I stared at her, unsure how to answer, before spluttering, "Perhaps, what do you know?"

"Only what many here have told us. In time, we learned enough to put Ju Lo on the spot, and he confirmed our suspicions. You also know of our history."

Vela cut in, "I would like to see the Corridor of Knowledge, if it pleases you."

"I will consider it. What don't you know?"

Oma chuckled, "If I knew that, I would tell you. This ship, it is Captain Kael's is it not?"

"Yes and no." I repeated what I had gleaned from the Core, revealing as much as was relevant, but not everything. I did tell them about the fight and subsequent crash-landing, adding, "Taris lived out his life here, but did bring the Second to this island for posterity. He died about twenty thousand years ago."

Oma reflected, "Taris, he was a good man, and should have been made Captain. I always suspected ill feeling between them. Taris was a much better Captain and pilot, but Kael pulled rank.

"Trust us Guardian, you will be well rewarded. We already have the knowledge you seek, let us share it with you. You do understand how the infinity thrusters work, don't you?"

"You mean the Boson Drive, yes we do."

"No Guardian, the infinity thrusters are required for sub-light, intra-solar navigation to the nth degree. They are essential for things like take-off, landing, and geo-synchronous orbital positioning. Shields also have to be calibrated for take-off and landing in Gaia's atmosphere."

"Yes, we understand how to do that."

"Magnetism shielding from the earth's core?"

"No. We have much to learn I admit, but we are learning in a structured and progressive way."

"That could take years, decades even. We offer to teach you now. You could be flying the craft next week. How about it?"

I did not reply, and before I had reasoned everything through, the two rose to leave. At last I found my tongue, "Why are you doing this? What's in it for you?"

"As distrusting as ever, Guardian, or is it Captain Jack? The rest of my crew are scientists and University life suits them, although you should consider giving them purpose-built laboratories. They excel in advanced biosphere environments, and can grow what you cannot. But no matter, that is for you and them to decide. I don't have an opinion on that matter."

Vela said, "We alone are experts in time and space, and I am bored. I am not a teacher of infants, no disrespect intended. I am a scientist, a Starship Captain, and I need to function as one."

"Enough Vela, hold your tongue," Oma commanded. There was silence, and they appeared to be having a telepathic conversation. Oma nodded in agreement, "It is true, Vela is more forthright than the rest of us. She was the best pilot we had, that's why I chose her as my Second. Had it not been for her skills, our craft would likely have crashed also.

"I am so glad to be alive once more, but I crave to do something more useful, something I as a person am good at. I can make a big difference, but only if I, if we, are given the chance. Come Vela, our words fall on deaf ears. Good day Guardian, we are sorry to have troubled you."

Later I spoke to my closest, and the next day we learned about infinity thrusters, magnetism affecting spacecraft within earth's gravity well, and one hundred other factors that could precipitate in-flight disaster. I saw my ambition as akin to a child close manoeuvring a cruise ship in a stormy harbour. Days passed as we continued our efforts to learn how to fly the spacecraft, but by the fourth day, we had had enough, and I called a council of the learned.

It was agreed we would show the Ancestors the Corridor of Knowledge, which occurred a couple of days later. We invited other races to attend, Ælthrelntheine and Gangling being first on our list. The Magus Elder of the Eleventh also joined the party, his role being one of learning, and also protection of us all — which I did not understand, but apparently, knowledge comes with risks, and that I understood.

Ælthrelntheine had been in good spirits and buzzing with energy until she saw Alberic. She immediately hurried over and spoke to Kay, who was standing beside me. I overheard her mention a pressing matter and moments after she was gone.

Kay looked confused so I asked, "What, did something happen?"

"Apparently, but I'm not sure what. Leave it alone, Jackie, later."

Instead of answers, we studied the record Taris had created and many were amazed. Time passed by quickly, the Ancestors passing on their wisdom and higher interpretations of what was recorded. Ræm become a glutton for deeper insight and understanding. The result was more like a series of co-joined forums that stretched along the corridor. Ju Lo and his grown children effected an unintentional cohesion, but later spent great time with the Magus Elder.

That evening I took a walk with Kay and asked, "Tell me something, although I don't wish to pry. Why do your mother and Alberic avoid each other?"

"I don't know what you mean, Jackie. Maybe it's because the mages were banished. Why do you ask?"

"Because of the way he looks at her, at you, I think there's more to it. They were banished just before you were born weren't they?"

"Yes, some months before because of a disagreement. But nobody knows the real reason, as those given don't make sense."

"I bet Ælthrelntheine and Alberic know, you should ask them. Your father must have been a very special man."

"I never met him, nor know who he was. I think he passed on, but this is old news, Jackie, best leave it be. Now, about the spaceship…"

So I let the matter pass, but my suspicions remained to be aired.

We continued to study the corridor the following day, Kay's and my focus remained dedicated to learning about the prehistory of the Ancestors, and flying the spacecraft. Alberic was often nearby but it seemed coincidental. However, I saw him glance at Kay a few times. He had a curious smile on his face that made me wonder.

That evening on the shore, Oma confirmed, "We are Centaureans, we came from a planet of Alpha Proxima, which may or may not have been the birthplace of our species. Our line fled when the star began to change, just before it became a red dwarf. We came to this solar system. Others made homes on other planets of the known cosmos, or fled to distant stars. That is our ancient history, but what of the future? Will you allow us to help you fly the spacecraft, to explore new worlds?"

Vela added, "Guardian, we had almost reconstructed a spacecraft carrier on Mars, and I would presume the shield will still be intact. What do you say? I will never mention this again, but know my question remains open until answered."

"Consider this under imminent resolution, but first, I have a question for you. I need to know all about the craft of Obsidian, and what he was doing with all those transfer circles. Enlighten us please."

"Obsidian? How do you know about him? He went down with the third spacecraft, it burnt up on entry."

"No it did not. We are currently repairing the ship, but it will take decades. He left behind a cobweb of interlinked transporters that either he, or somebody else, instigated to seed the more recent development of the Last. What do you know about this?"

"Nothing. How recent?"

"During the last twelve thousand years, from a time we know of as The Great Flood, arguably the result of a comet striking the Earth. Much of life on Earth was extinguished, but many were saved by ancestral-like powers. It gave rise to a new religion, that of The One God with three faces."

"That is strange; it does not make any sense. We were entombed ninety thousand years ago, and that is a long, long time to be undead. Obsidian, he is still alive?"

"No, I discovered his corpse' ashes at the captain's consol, he was wearing this ring, an intermediate ring of power—he had hidden his version of the Ring of the Power. We also hold the Rings of the Last, of Taris, Obsidian, and you, Oma. Explain."

"When did he—Obsidian die?"

"It was probably two and a half millennia ago, but that does not fit with all the facts. Half a million years would be closer to what we know. That would be about the time you all came here?"

"Yes. But one and a half million years ago, more or less, you are well informed."

"You cannot be serious. You are still alive after all that time!"

"Yes, and no. I would explain, except it does not make sense, even to me. Everlasting life is not what it is cracked up to be. I've been cryogenically frozen and cloned millions of times, and sometimes, I feel something is missing, well, from whom I was. Does that make sense?"

"No. Maybe yes. Misinformation abounds. By extending your lives unnaturally, you denied your human nature. That is wrong. Real life doesn't wait for you to be ready, it happens to you. You either live or die by the consequences of your deeds. I live and die by my word of honour, by my will to survive, and by my sword.

"Even so, I understand. I'll share something with you. We have crystal memory devices that are encrypted, ones we cannot unlock."

"Ah, well…"

"Even with the correct Core and Ring of Power."

"Impossible!"

"Trust, blind faith in this instance is a big concept, Oma. Care to share, reveal the past to us, so our knowledge of the present and future grows?"

"Guardian, Jackie. It is overdue time we shared more openly with you all. Shall we begin now?"

"Thank you, but no, I'd prefer to start in the morning. First, we need to show you what we have discovered so far—it is utterly amazing, and convoluted by turns. Our research shows Obsidian died shortly after crash-landing, from meson irradiation.

"My problem is, the transporter web we discovered, bears the signatures of Taris, Obsidian, and yourself. How?"

"Two of them were dead, and I held in stasis. We knew nothing of either Taris or Obsidian. The Great Ogre, his forebearers I mean, only they would have the power, the perspicacity to do this, but why? Tomorrow we should dedicate ourselves to solving this riddle. First tell me all you know."

"Tomorrow Oma, we reveal all, not tonight. Enough. I need to call on others, Finity for one, Pomfrey another, perhaps."

"One last thing. Taris, he was there in this 'cobweb'?"

"No, impossible, he was either here, or dead. I managed to open vaults using his rings of power, that is all. I never felt his presence, does that sound strange."

"No Guardian, the ring and the wearer become one. You would know if Taris had been there, the ring would have told you."

We agreed on a plan for the morrow, as the first strains of chorus rang out, being led by Owain. Oma enquired, "Guardian, this looks like fun. What are the rules of this Old MacDonald?"

The next day Finity acted as tour guide of our cobweb, showing us the highlights, and explaining relationships of the Last as we moved back in time. We did not visit every destination, but eight of the most interesting, before entering the remains of Obsidian's craft.

I allowed Oma to interface with the Core using Obsidian's ring of power. "Guardian you have done well. Allow me to adjust some of the remodelling parameters, it will speed restoration work and aid human safety. Let's do this together from his ready room, so you learn what to do, and why."

Oma explained what she was doing, with Vela assisting, then taking over; she was the expert. Kay, n'Gnung, Gung Loi, and Peni also paid great attention. Once finished, the prognosis was five years for craft integrity, and six before we could fly the thing. It was a great result, and our esteem for Oma, Vela and their knowledge grew.

Afterwards, I showed them the crystal memory plumbs, but they got no further than we had done. "This is strange. These are definitely Centaurean recording devices, but the encryption is unknown."

"We have tried them here, and on the Invincible. They reveal only low-level data. They were hidden extremely well, so must contain vital information. The answers we seek, I presume."

"Indulge us, Guardian. Show us where these memory devices were found."

We did, and Oma and Vela examined the motifs. "These are not Centaurean motifs, Oma. They are very good copies."

"What are you saying, Vela?"

"That they were not created by us. Only a Core can manufacture them, so that means they were deliberately altered, but why?"

"To leave us a clue. Could that explain why some motifs would not lock with my ring of power, even though the fit was correct?"

"Yes. Somebody sabotaged the motifs, to prevent others opening them, no doubt. You did that well, Guardian."

"Unknowingly it seems. It was trial and error."

n'Gnung spoke for the first time, "Indeed, Guardian. If we presume Obsidian was the saboteur, it follows the Great Ogre of the day was who he deceived. I think we should pay a visit to Greenland."

Oma was wary to enter the exhibition chamber, but Vela marched in and kicked her pod as hard as she could. During her subsequent rant we learned a few new swear words. We made several attempts before letting Peni have a try. The key came not from the main control centre, but from the Great Ogre's personal command station.

"Some files are still in Ogre. They are application files, which means they do something specific. Can anyone read Ogre?"

Oma nodded, "As project overseer, I understood it pretty well, but Carro, the tenth member of my crew knew it best, he invented it. Want me to send for him?"

"Perhaps, but take a look first, Oma."

I had to return for the Ring of the Warrior before we could unlock the files. At Peni's request, I also fetched her sister and Jason, our two best at Ancestral computer code.

It took a while before we found the encryption key, as we tried to access what appeared to be the least important of the memory crystals. It contained precise details of Ogre cloning technology, including mind- moulding and mapping. The next crystal gave details of other Ogre systems, and was apparently a failsafe backup of vital information. The third was more a history of the pre-Christian era, containing great information about Egypt, and also noted an Ogre as King of Knossos for a short period, named Minotaur. He was executed by the Great Ogre of the time.

The last crystal was astonishing. It laid out the successive Great Ogre plans for domination and subjugation of the world, right up to the Roman Empire. The cobweb of transporters was revealed. It was a means of access for Ogre generals to control their new creations.

"Jack," Finity stated aghast, "The Ogres created the Hittite, Sumerian, Babylonian, and Assyrian royal houses, and set them to war against each other, and Egypt. This is incredible. You are copying these files I hope. I need to study them."

"Wait until you get to the Romans, Finity. From what I just read, the Great Ogre considered one of his best inventions was Caligula. His birth was the first time they altered a foetus' brain before it was born."

"Oh my God! You cannot be serious."

"That's what is written here. I think you are going to be occupied for quite a while. My problem is that that particular Great Ogre disappeared in the prime of life, and he was replaced with the present one. Little information appears to have been passed between them, as if the line stopped dead. Was he murdered?"

Several spoke up, but there was nothing said that rang true. n'Gnung had kept his own counsel, listening and thinking, before speaking. "Guardian, I get the connection with Oma, and by extension, the Ring of the Last. But how does this relate to Captain Obsidian?"

Oma reacted, twitching her head to gawk at him. "Guardian, what was in Obsidian's personal log?"

"What? I've no idea. I did not know the Captain had a personal log. Show me."

"We better return to Obsidian's spaceship and find out. I warn you, I may need to use my ring again, but only for a moment."

"I should be able to do that, I am installed as Captain of that ship."

"No, Guardian, you are not. Your position is that of acting Captain. Obsidian did not hand over power to you. I may be able to override the Core. And anyway, you cannot fly two ships at the same time."

The upshot was, only Oma could unlock Obsidian's personal log, as mission controller, because her DNA matched the Ring of Power. The Core rejected all other authority. The revelations came only after Oma had been reinstated as Captain of her craft. It was a risk, but one we felt obliged to take.

The personal file was copied before we studied it properly, to get a picture of what had occurred. Oma revealed, "Obsidian was resurrected many times over æons. The previous Great Ogre made special use of him, treating him for all intents and purposes as his slave. Nothing new there then.

"It appears Obsidian was complicit, but working secretly on a greater plan, in time earning the Great Ogre's trust. They worked on the cobweb together, Obsidian having greater and greater input. His ideas were exceedingly good, and usually implemented without question. I can imagine Obsidian's inner rage, an obedient Centaurean is a nice pet to have.

"That changed here in the record. The Great Ogre needed to hibernate, which is what they term reanimation. Obsidian used the time wisely, first recording events on the crystal memory, and acquiring rings of power when he could.

"He created an emergency, which resulted in the Great Ogre being brought out of regeneration. Ogres are susceptible at such times, and Obsidian brought him to this spaceship. He took the Great Ogre into the armoury to supply weapons, but returned to the control room and subsequently shielded the forward module only, and dropped the shields for the boson drive. Meson radiation resulted, which killed the Great Ogre instantly, and himself some time later.

"Before the command module shield faltered, Obsidian had time to hide the greater rings of power. There was no opportunity to pass the Ogre's heritage on to the next generation. You discovered what was left of him. I am proud of Obsidian. This calls for a celebration."

We had our answers, bizarre though they were. Oma insisted Kay be reinstated as Captain of her spacecraft, even before our work was finished. After she completed the handover she said, "You should consider Vela for Captain of Obsidian's craft, she was a spacecraft carrier Captain and fighter pilot. I'll say no more, but think about it."

In due course, our scans revealed a large pile of ashes in the weapons locker, the previous Great Ogre presumably. In ebullient frame of mind, we all gathered on the shore some short time later, and drank in celebration.

During that evening, the Ancestors showed their true humanity, which was unsurprisingly similar to our own. They gave their knowledge to us freely, and we by return gave them fun and laughter, full enjoyment of being alive. Owain was with us and, Oma and Vela got completely trashed drinking lethal spirit. Iydm did also. Although I was sure Ræm was fairly sober, she encouraged him within the moment. I, too, helped them to their demise.

Later Kay said, "Jackie, guess what? They let their mental shields drop, and I poked around inside. I should not have done so, but we needed to know — Jackie, they are genuine in their desire to help us."

"That may be so, Kay, but I'm sure they would double-cross us given half a chance."

She shook her head, "No. What I saw within them wasn't like that at all. Granted, if they had a ring on their finger they could commandeer the craft, but would they? Where would they go? What would be the point? Oma had that option today, yet handed control of her craft back to me at the first opportunity, and without prompting."

Hmmm. Yes, I felt exactly that way when I first arrived here. I wanted to escape, but there was nowhere for me to go. Apologies, we need to consider this more carefully and with open minds."

Chapter 37 ~ Taking Flight

The following afternoon I spent time with Finity, suggesting ways she could restructure, since she was short of staff. I began to regret limiting numbers of newcomers, but I did what I thought was best at the time. She gave me a list of names, detailing pre-eminent scientists and historians that would be valuable additions to the team. John added others, the 'I told you so' left unspoken.

I found a number of them, and most chose to come to us, relieving some of the pressure Finity and her teams were under. We also recruited the brightest minds of our own, and found volunteers from other Tribes who were willing to assist the greater good.

Professor Urquhart, or Doc U as he preferred to be called, was a cuneiform specialist. He had arrived with those from the British Museum, and had concluded the initial deciphering of The Twelve Commandments. He and Finity presented their results to me, which were interesting. I needed independent consideration of the bigger picture.

That evening I cornered one who would know at dinner. "What were the original Twelve Commandments, Oma?"

"They were the basic rules of our culture, adapted for life on Gaia, let me show you how to write them in our language." That meant attending my ready room, which we did moments later.

The creation was simple, a mental exercise, which I completed quickly, once I became accustomed to the interface. I created a tablet of stone, in Centaurean, and showed Kay the results. She was impressed, and did likewise. Nonetheless, we were both amazed moments later, when Oma created the original Commandments, handing the tablet over for us to study.

Primary Principle: To create new life in your own image, to become better, to progress as a species, and seek enlightenment.

Love and honour your mother, your creator.

Love and honour your father, your sustainer.

Do not lie; tell the truth.

Do not steal; give excess to those that have too little.

Do not cheat; respect grows from another's faith in you.

Treat others as you would treat yourself, your standards will give others hope of emulation.

Honour the official union of one woman and her husband, and do not come between them for personal gain or gratification.

Do not kill another, except when an enemy would kill you, or take from you what is not theirs.

Be fair in judgement of others; understand why they do what they do. [Justice.]

Indulge freely in the pleasures life has to offer, but do not become a slave to addiction. [Temperance.]

Stand up for what is right for all; the greater good. Speak up for the rights of the worthy and the less fortunate. Challenge wrongdoers, and bring them to account, even if you agree with them. [Courage.]

Practice the wisdom of knowing, of choosing right from wrong, even to your own shortcoming. Often the immediate disadvantage is for the longer-term greater good of all, especially yourself. [Prudence.]

The next day we had a more serious discussion about the Ancestors, with the larger team and Jinnie. The result being we would show Oma and Vela, only, our ship. Some considered it was a grave risk, but if they proved genuine, it would be a mammoth step forward for us.

When they entered the Bridge for the first time, Oma stopped to stare. Vela's eyes were full of wonder, her body walking as if of its own accord, imbibing the ambience of the control room, feeling, touching everything. Her eyes appeared to be filled with starlight as she ran to Oma and hugged her close, their kiss on the lips lasting a fraction longer than I expected. Nonetheless, their paired jubilation was infectious, and they hugged me first, Kay, and others in turn. However, when they reached the Empress, they both stalled to bow. "Thank you. We are extremely happy."

Once they calmed, the questions came thick and fast. The ship was now a battle cruiser, designation hunter-killer, and it appeared they did not know how to do that. After a full tour of the craft, and lunch, training began in earnest. All of our crews learned what to do, and each covered most, if not every station. I had actioned n'Gue's general log entry to the fullest implementation.

Jinnie continued to use my ready room. She was ostensibly there to continue her autobiographies, but became increasingly interested in learning how to fly the craft. The heady rush of enthusiasm and discovery affected us all, including the Ancestors.

On the eighth morning, we attended our stations, Oma preparing to give us the day's tasks. Vela walked forward, and standing in front of the main screen said, "I'm sure we've all had enough of the classroom. Time to fly this thing, don't you think. First, we need to get this craft outside of the rock coffin it is trapped within. What is the best way to do that?"

Oma stood and stared at Vela, who was already distracted, taking possible and probable solutions from our junior controllers. She made a game of it, and her enthusiasm was infectious. However, we knew the real answer was much more complicated. Kay and Peni, had been working on the same problem for some time.

When Peni was asked, she proposed our most promising hypothesis, a dedicated, external transfer circle with only one objective, get the craft above ground. That was when our real learning began.

The spacecraft was in essence, the core of the island, supporting shielding and numerous other systems. We could not remove it without affecting everything, unless there was a dedicated control centre outside of the craft, related only to island shields and concerns. Thus we created a new campus of the University, that would in time incorporate NASA. It took several days to create, what with the construction, recruitment and training operational staff, setting parameters, and switching over shielding and internal island transporters from the spacecraft's direct control, to the new entity. I proposed a name with a laconic air of irony that few understood. I was surprised when it was accepted: Houston.

The following morning Houston gave the command, and the spacecraft was transferred to the open air. Oma monitored us from the new island central control, which was aligned with her skills. Vela kept check on me at the Captain's console, but our team knew what to do.

"Flight shields set."

"Engines online. Powering. Ready."

"Shields one hundred percent."

"Proximity clear."

"All checks complete. Ready for take-off, Captain."

I rose from my seat, and eased Jien Noi into the chair, whispering into her ear. She stared at me, before focusing, and pressing the helm activation. "Take us up Geldar."

"Destination?"

She pointed forwards, upwards, "There, the sky's your limit."

The main screen showed us where we were going, smaller inserts at the corners showing side, the ground below, and rear views. It was breathtaking. At first, the upper atmosphere was our limit, because we were still running checks and honing systems. Incredulously we took in Gaia's size as we skimmed and surfed the air, sometimes hovering as if to land, and at other times rounding the globe in minutes. Vela tested all our basic skills, and was impressed. She hardly said a word, but it felt good to know there was instant back up, should we need it. In the event, we did not.

The next phase was more complicated, and could have been handled automatically by the Core. Vela insisted we learn how to do it ourselves, and I agreed with her. I told her of captaining a ship, of steering by the stars, the sextant, charts and plotters, and physical means of determining wind speed and sea current, tides.

"Jackie, that is a great analogy. Exactly! In battle, the ship can be damaged, areas cannot send the Core information, or receive. It is then that humans need to take over. They are no good if they don't know what to do instinctively. Now, take helm control and show me how to hover."

The following day we set course for the Moon, and dropped into orbit several times to hone our skills. But, Gaia's beauty was alluring, and she seemed a long way away. We set a return course, and came close to the Space Station. I spoke to Ah-Nei on comm., "Patch me through to Captain Williams in the space station."

"Howdy Jack, what can we do for you?"

"Look out of the window, earth-side. We got the old bird flying again. You want a ride next time?"

"Holy Cow! Are you serious? Count me in."

"Tomorrow OK? We plan to practice docking with you, manually. You better prepare to be amazed."

Geldar managed to flip our wings in respect and we headed home. It had been an enthralling buzz and we celebrated in big style that night. During the days and weeks that followed, we learned how to fly the ship properly. The Ancestors never put one foot wrong. I let Vela pilot on occasions and she really put the craft through its paces. She knew so much more than us, I was seriously considering Oma's suggestion to install her as Captain of Obsidian's ship. But would I?

The next phase was flying Oma's craft. I had to ask Oma to help sort out one persistent glitch, and she worked with Captain Kay to find a resolution. We all suspected an Ogre trick, but Vela eventually found a partial component failure.

I was there with n'Gnung to monitor, and take appropriate action if required. It never came to that. We were gelling as a team, acceptance of our creators seemed assured. A moment of clarity came to me, and I realised the real reason why homo sapiens sapiens could never be called the First. That title already existed in the form of the Thirteenth. They truly were the first of our kind.

Oma spoke openly to me later that evening. "Jackie, I have had enough of this. Yes, of course, I will assist you to attain your destiny, and fly the pathways between the stars, that is what Vela lives for. But I am growing old, mentally tired.

"I have already lived, abjured, too many lifetimes. I just want to live out the rest of my days in happiness, and die. Would you deny me that? What is it like have children? We rarely can, hence the cloning and reincarnation technology."

Ju Lo was close by, and answered as I gathered my thoughts. "Oma, life is all about being born, living, changing, creating, and dying. What you have done, by unnaturally extending your lives, is to deny your spirit the chance of development in a future life. This is why the Ogres found themselves in a spiritual cul-de-sac.

"For your spirit to grow, attain enlightenment, you need to die, yet be reborn through your seed, as in the next generation; the next natural reincarnation of the life-spark of your own being. You need to bear a child, physically. I'm sure the medical facility can rectify the problem; Matron is exceptionally gifted. Care to try? Consider it at least."

Jinnie lived comfortably during that period. She had entered into early old-age, as with her kind, but often acted with the fervour of youth. Ræm had effectively become second in command of Taris' spaceship for the season, on merit. She flew the thing as well as Kay or I did, although Vela remained several steps ahead of us. But she had learned much from the Ancestors, always spending time with Oma, Vela, and Iydm.

We were all busy preparing for the next Olympiad, one month away, when I was asked to attend Grimwaldi Rinns for the evening meal, in my official capacity as Emperor. I was aware several young men needed Empirical blessing regards forthcoming marriage proposals, and I was looking forward to the fiesta.

Ræm had taken her official seat as Empress Elect, ostensibly to learn what to do during the ceremonial formalities. She adjudicated on some, with her mother's final word. It was not in fact a big thing, because everything had already been sorted out via the Provost and court staff. That was until Iydm stepped forward, and my instincts flared, but it was too late for prior knowledge. I would have to deal with this head-on. I looked at Ræm, who gave me her 'please Daddy' look, one I had never managed to master.

By the time the Centaurean stood before us, I already had a shrewd idea what was about to occur, and I was not disappointed. Iydm spoke officially to me. "Emperor, Empress, in harmony with your traditions and culture, I humbly beg your indulgence in a delicate matter. Since my release from captivity, I have once more been captivated, this time by a woman. I would ask you to permit me to marry your eldest daughter, Ræm. I would not wish to become Emperor of the Second, during or after your day, nor ever lay claim to that title. I wish to spend my remaining days as husband and truest supporter of her, as my wife."

There was not a sound, but it felt as if I heard the howl of ancient winds buffet my soul. The Empress' voice broke the spell, "The decision lies with my husband, but as a point of law, if you duly honour our culture, the Empress welcomes this union. Jackie?"

I turned to look at her, "So finally, your wish will be granted, to recreate the Thirteenth Tribe in our own image. Ræm?"

Chapter 37

I looked over to our eldest child, who seemed to be on tenterhooks, her radiant smile about to explode. She nodded her head enthusiastically. What was I to do?

One last question remained. "Iydm, I am aware the Ancestors seldom procreate naturally, but this marriage demands offspring. This is of the utmost importance. Neither will my grandchildren be grown in some test tube, answer me, truthfully."

"Be assured, Ræm will conceive our progeny, Emperor."

I was against the union, when Ræm spoke up. "Father, I'm not stupid. We resolved the issue. I will be impregnated with Iydm's seed. I spent a lot of time researching this, and his spermatozoa will be introduced to my eggs, it will be quite natural."

"So-be-it. Iydm, you must complete the Trails of Passage, and build a house fit for my daughter—I expect the extraordinary."

The marriage was scheduled to be held on Spring Day, the beginning of our year, and the day before the Olympiad. Members of all Thirteen Tribes would be present and made welcome.

§

Ten months later, Jinnie was first to be offered Ræm's baby to hold, fittingly a girl, the product of an immaculate conception. "What will you call her?"

"Eve Ning. We thought it fitting because she was born at the end of the day."

I marvelled the wonder of creation, and said, "Good Evening, Good World, that has such people in it."

The End of Star Gazer Book Three

Star Gazer

The chronicles of Jack Barleycorn continue with
the Second Star Gazer Trilogy,

Book Four

The Centaureans

The Aleutian-Hallion Alliance drone passed into the remote Alpha Centauri system, in a distant and unpopular part of the Galaxy. It was there to monitor the aftermath of the inhabitant's destruction. This was a standard verification of little significance, as 'AC' was in the outward spiral of the most undeveloped region of the Galaxy.

The unmanned space drone picked up a faint signal pulse as it passed by, but one that was so distant, slight, and old that it was not even flagged, but set aside for review at a later date.

Fortunately, for Gaia and her progeny, that proved to be at a much later date...

§

The first Star Gazer Trilogy was mainly adventure science fantasy set in the contemporary world, and questioned the origin of species homo sapiens, and the existence of God.

The second Trilogy continues the adventure, but is set in the near future, and is more science fiction in orientation. We explore our Solar System and venture to others nearby. However, the twin cores of the reason we exist, and what of God, remain to be answered.

Book Four, The Centaureans, is already written, but moves away from our solar system much too quickly, so I have already begun review. That in turn means that Book Five is already half written.

Book Four begins with the arrival in Earth orbit of Poh, captain of a Centaurean spaceship, so let's get on with the story...

Ræm's backstory is appended below.

Part one may be read at any time.

Part two is best read near the end of this book when all appears lost. It presages what Ræm and the Shaman were preparing for regards eradication of the Great Ogre.

§

http://www.star-gazer.co.uk
The official Star Gazer website, offers a vast array of additional information, full character descriptions with personal history, intriguing details, and images.

The website also includes large-scale maps, character backstories, and other interesting details. Sections explain the Ancestral science, while others provide full references, timeline, and much more.

This free online resourse gives a tremendous amount of further information, such as resolving the issue of Kay's parentage. I have given easy clues in this book, but Book Four will explore that revelation in depth and attend to other things deliberately left to hang in this trilogy.

Ræm's Backstory ~ Part One

Ræm enjoyed a happy childhood, despite the community's irregular wars with the Great Ogre and the unleashing of the Wrath of Gaia. She had never seen the Sun, Moon, or Stars, and her days were filled with dark heavy clouds and incessant rain. But for the great shield her father devised, her life would have been intolerable.

This instilled a deep yearning in her to one day see these wonders for herself. As a result, she was drawn to stories of how life used to be, and grew to appreciate everything around her. Learning from infancy to cherish the smallest gifts that life bestowed, she took great pleasure in the beauty of nature and its great diversity. Her dreams of brighter days and of new beginnings became her overriding desire. These shaped the young girl to reach for the stars.

Unlike many, she did not blame Mother Earth, but understood it was her way to cleanse terra firma and begin afresh.

Ræm loved to spend time with her mother and father, growing to admire the strange assortment of permanent companions that always seemed to accompany them wherever they went.

Her mother groomed her from an early age to be the next Empress, and the next Gatekeeper. Life in the Imperial Palace was quite formal and extremely boring, while times spent at their home and especially on the shore became her escape. She loved the ocean and the sense of freedom that it released within her heart. She spent many long days with To Mo and To Ma who taught her how to swim, fish, and hunt.

Meanwhile Ræm's quest for knowledge was unquenchable. Of her own volition, she attended school just after her fourth birthday. Six was the usual starting age, but it provided her with an escape from the confines of the Palace and brought with it a liberating sense of freedom. Ju Lo and his language assistant Suzy Wong, accepted her and encouraged her in many disciplines, including languages, science, and deeper knowledge of their combined hereditary.

When she grew older, she became an irregular crewmember for the outgoing Australians, Gary and Shirl. At first, they took her along for the ride and occasional sea fishing. However, her inquisitive nature and determination to help led them to train her informally as a sailor. By the time she was eleven, she could sail the boat herself and had learnt how to read the navigation charts. With the passing of another year, she had not only become competent, but also a talented mariner.

One day her Father came to her early in the morning and said they were going on a trip. They left quickly with n'Gnung and Aroweena and arrived on the shore, immediately making their way down to the small harbour at the end of the beach. Gary greeted them and handed her a piece of paper. It had a location on it.

Ræm stared at it for a moment, determining immediately there was a secret to be unlocked, and went below to check the charts. She took her time to fix a point near the small island across from them, but on the other side where there was a natural harbour. She bounded back up to the deck and told them. Gary looked at her father who nodded his head, a curious smirk and twinkling eyes only adding to her confusion.

"Your crewmember today is Aroweena, and she has never sailed before [true]. When you get to the location I gave you, go to lobster pot number eight, and bring back whatever is inside. We are not here."

Gary started laughing as he finished speaking, and Ræm's mouth dropped wide open in astonishment. She screwed up her face thinking this was a joke, before stuttering, "You cannot be serious!" but it was not a joke and she soon realised they were deadly serious.

She had done the trip many times, but had never before done the whole thing herself. However, she had done each of the parts, so she sat down and reasoned through what she had to do. Speaking to no one in particular, she said aloud, "First I need to know the direction and speed of both the wind and the current, plus the state of the tide. Then I can work out which sail to use to get us into the lagoon." Gary looked at Jack, and both turned to watch the gifted youngster.

Satisfied with her reasoning she went below and checked the tidal data first, the current, and finally the wind. It was a fairly calm day compared to others recently and conditions were ideal. She stood in the cockpit and said, "You all set this up didn't you. Well I'll show you.

"Aroweena, hoist the jib, that's the sail at the front of the boat." The Ddwyrth did as instructed and when the wind caught lightly, Ræm released the front mooring rope, thus allowing the boat to turn against the rear mooring and drift around slowly towards the open sea.

Ræm was practiced with this manoeuvre having done it countless times before. She had never done it as Captain before. She watched as the nose came round slowly and waited until the jib stalled before telling Aroweena to set the sail to the other side of the boat. Gary was ensuring Aroweena carried out the commands correctly and quickly.

Meanwhile Ræm started to let out the looped rear mooring rope so the boat continued to spin in the water past the 90-degree mark and came under power again from the front sail. Watching intently as she positioned and locked the rudder, she gauged the moment perfectly and released the captive eye of the mooring rope, pulling back the now long single rope quickly into the craft and stowing it aboard.

She had Aroweena hoist the mainsail, before attending to tune both sails to get maximum drive from the wind. Set fair, the boat began to glide through the water, as a large cheer went up from the four people who were theoretically not there. She took a moment to plot the course around the outlying island, and returned on deck to relax.

Ræm felt a burst of pride, her eyes watered slightly as her Adam's apple caught a lump in her throat. The moment passed and she knew she could not have done this alone, so took a dedicated moment to thank Aroweena for her skill and assistance.

The outward leg was easy being downwind, but the girls had to work much harder on the second leg into the wind. Their respect for one another grew during the day, as they melded into a team, understanding what was required of them. They collected the lobster pot and found it contained several large lobsters, a belligerent crab, also discovered it contained two strange tokens.

The third leg was again a continuation into the wind, but soon they rounded the tip of the islet and set the final course for the simple run home with the wind to their backs. Ræm stood commandingly at the wheel and felt a great sense of achievement. She knew docking could sometimes be tricky, but conditions were perfect and did not worry unduly about the final task. With everything going exactly to plan, she relaxed and enjoyed the entwined feelings of power and confidence.

Her contentment was shattered moments later when Gary screamed aloud, "Man overboard."

She whirled and saw n'Gnung wearing a buoyancy aid, jump into the water. Her mind went momentarily blank, but the reality of the situation made her to respond. She remembered the drill and had performed it on several occasions; in fact she had done this same thing only a few days ago. Was that a coincidence? She realised they had all connived to set this all up. 'I'll show you' she thought to herself. Her only ally was Aroweena, so she gave her a look of encouragement and a thumbs-up, before returning to her thoughts.

She remembered the drill, go on for three boat lengths, turn into the wind, and complete the first loop of a figure of eight. There would be a chance to get n'Gnung back if she was lucky, otherwise she would complete the figure of eight and come back, in theory at least, to exactly where the lost sailor was.

Her watchful eyes judged distance before commands flowed from her as both sails reset after 140 feet, and the boat heeled to come about on its new heading. She watched intently judging the positions of the man in the water and the boats relative position, before making her last call to complete the first loop.

Ræm had purposefully sailed slightly farther windward than necessary in order to ensure they were on the correct side of the wind and current in relation to n'Gnung. She slackened both sails little by little and later slowed by turning them into the wind, so they were hardly driving the boat at all.

Gary and Jack, both held Yachtmaster Ocean (Sail) qualifications, whilst Shirl was as good without ever being tested. They watched intently as Ræm brought the boat in perfectly on the first pass, a risky manoeuvre for all but the most experienced of sailors. She dropped both sails at precisely the right moment and let the current push the boat the last few yards towards n'Gnung.

Aroweena stood ready with a lifeboat ring, but Ræm's positioning was so accurate that n'Gnung came into the lee of the boat and bumped against the hull. He was handed down a rope with which he was able to crab sideways to the stern and climb back aboard via the rear ladder.

Standing inside the boat, n'Gnung high-five'd Ræm as the others joined to cheer her. She took Aroweena's hand and raised it with her own arm, so they shared the honours equally. n'Gnung was handed a beer, as other bottles were broached for the remaining passengers.

Ræm let them have a piece of her mind, which only brought forth more cheers and howls of laughter. She almost managed to keep her stern face, before succumbing and joining the delight. Everyone aboard knew she had done good, real good.

Ræm completed the trip by bringing the boat in perfectly and moored with Aroweena's help. They held a small and impromptu party, with Aroweena ready for her first beer, and as a special treat, Ræm being allowed a small can of Australian original.

They laughed and shared until Gary asked, "Why did you attempted the more risky first loop and not the easier figure of eight."

Ræm spoke with the emphatic belief of the young, "Because I know there are many sharks in these waters, and I also knew that if I stayed windward I could secure the rescue more quickly. The longer you are in the water the greater the chance of being eaten you know."

Both Jack and Gary began to reply and compliment her wisdom, when the stage was stolen by n'Gnung, "What! There are sharks in these waters? You didn't tell me that before I jumped into the sea."

n'Gnung played the fool to perfection, elaborating on his initial comments as everyone broke into uncontrollable fits of laughter. He stomped around, making vague swimming motions, whilst imitating a giant and hungry shark in between the spaces of his performance.

They all knew that he was very aware of the danger the sharks posed, and had taken a sword with him as protection, but there was no need to let that ruin the comedy. Aroweena came to his aid as the straight person, and together they made a remarkable improvised performance that remains one of the funniest things they had ever had the pleasure of witnessing.

Finally, all gathered to drink their beer. Shirl gathered everyone around Ræm and before the girl knew what was happening, they had grabbed her arms and legs, and gave her three bumps of 'hip, hip, hurrah'. Securely held, she was thrown upwards on each hip, but on the final throw, she was tossed into the sea nearby.

Ræm had been expecting the ploy and had already planned her reply before she hit the water. She spluttered to the surface, indignation flailing rapidly from her rabid tongue. They howled with laughter, except for one who stifled her mirth out of newborn admiration.

Instead, Aroweena leapt into the water and came immediately to Ræm's side. Both knew it was out of a new and growing respect for each other. Then the others bombed into the sea nearby to join them and a water fight ensued. It was fun while it lasted, but as soon as Ræm tired of it, Jack went to her, and despite the torrents of water aimed at him, picked her up and carried her out of the water secure in his arms.

He spoke to her gently, "Know I would never ask you to do something if I thought for one moment you could not conquer it. How do you feel now?"

"I very wet, but I have a great sense of triumph," she giggled.

He enquired, "Now you know you can sail a boat all by yourself. Why do you know that?"

"Because I have already done it," Ræm stated as a matter of fact.

"Exactly. That was the lesson I wanted to teach you today. Knowing how to do something is one thing; actually doing it is something quite different. Doing something yourself is an accomplishment. Never forget this.

"It also brings with it greater confidence and the respect of others. Just now Aroweena went instantly to your aid, and know she is not easily impressed by anyone, I can assure you."

Ræm knew her Father spoke the truth, because she did feel more confident and self assured. She said to her Father, "Thanks, I love you."

Her new confidence transmitted into her everyday life. Every new challenge she faced and conquered would only add to her feeling of worth in the years to come.

That evening, Jack organised a small celebratory party. Ræm wanted to know what the two mysterious tokens they collected were for, but he refused to say anything other than she would find out after dinner. She was not impressed, but knew not to push him once his mind was set.

Dinner was an informal affair and consisted of the usual suspects and a few others such as Billy, Mavis, and Gilly. Dinner took its natural course, Jack hoping his daughter would mix and discover new attitudes and make new friends. He was of course, misguided. In time, it fell to her mother to rein in Ræm's socialising excesses.

To complete festivities, Jack stood and spoke to the diners, "Friends, we are gathered here this evening to welcome into our midst a new Able Seaman. Aroweena if you please."

The Ddwyrth was taken by surprise and stood to the applause and whistles of the onlookers. Knowing she was not one for formalities and medals, Jack kept the proceeding brief. At his nod, Gary came forward and presented her with a bracelet that bore the sign of an anchor. It had one band, which Jack had commissioned personally to be made of the finest gold, by Owain and the Ddwyrth. Aroweena's eyes glazed for an instant as she stood to more applause, before reaching for her drink, mumbling a reply and downing the draught in one.

She returned to her seat directly, but many were aware she kept touching and glancing at her new jewellery occasionally, her inward pride almost hidden. Sometimes in the future, people would come to ask her why she wore it and what it signified. She dismissed the issue out of hand, saying, "It was something I was given because I helped out on a boat. It is of no worth and I must remember to take it off," although she never did.

In time, Jack called upon his daughter, "Ræm, today you passed the most serious challenge of your young life with flying colours. Know you have earned this right through your own efforts, and now join Gary and myself as being the only three properly trained and qualified sailors. Please may I have a big hand for the new and third Captain of our fleet."

Again cheers erupted and Gary had to call for order. He presented her with a bracelet of similar design, also made of pure gold by Owain and his smiths. However, this one has four bands signifying rank. With the official presentation complete, Ræm held her arm high and showed the seal to everyone. She followed with an impromptu short speech, and publicly thanked Aroweena for her assistance; making it known, she could not have completed the day's trial without her backing.

After that evening, Ræm came to love evenings spent on the shore, especially the cheery, boisterous humour of Owain, and later as she aged, the clever and intricate stories of Rambling. However, one unforeseen result was that a month later she went to live with Billy and his people for a few days. She revelled in the simple yet satisfying experience of connecting deeply with nature and Mother Earth.

Another and more unexpected result was that she became a regular, if erratic visitor to Gilly and his tribe of Hells Angels. By the turn of another year, they had formed a rock band and she saw both words and music as languages in their own right.

Jack had serious qualms about someone so young being exposed to that kind of culture, although at heart he loved it himself. Jinnie knew of his misgivings, and they talked about it sometimes. It wasn't until one evening some months later that the talk again came to centre upon Rebel Ræm, when who should put it into perspective but n'Gnung. He began, "Tell me of your daughter and her destiny?"

Jack raised an eyebrow to the cheery enquiry and immediately knew he was up to something. However, he replied, "As far as every indication I have confirms, she is destined to become some sort of saviour, and rescue mankind from ultimate destruction. She commands the Sword of Destiny, and has many rare gifts. What of it?"

Jack had hoped to throw the question back at n'Gnung, not expose himself to subtle probing of his own motives, "So you have freed her mind to learn, and know she absorbs everything. She is a wonder in that respect. Yet all her tuition is either: practical, academic, theoretical, or comes from our establishments, is this not so?

"And yet, if what we fear is true, then one day she will stand alone against an impossible foe of unimaginable power. She already has the confidence and self-belief, but there is more to this. She needs to become her own person. Now, I will ask you all here, what is the one thing that all people who overthrow a regime have in common?"

They were surprised at n'Gnung's depth, but Jack became determined to work through his logic, as those around all offered answers and observations. Suggestions such as leaders, freethinkers, and similar were evaluated, and n'Gnung sat there patiently, his smile growing conspiratorial and his eyes increasingly sparkled. In time, they admitted they did not understand his point.

"Then let me state the obvious. They are all rebels and have a revolutionary heart, a drive that spurs them to achieve the impossible; the unthinkable even. If you wanted to create a rebel, where on this island would you go?"

Jack could not fault his logic; "The first place I would go is to the Cavern, and join Gilly and his friends. If I were not her father, my heart would be entirely at ease."

However, Jack learned to let Ræm have her head, leave to join the rebels at her will, knowing she would return and grow from exposure to the rogue elements of their society, and even their music. That was not to say he felt entirely at ease, and spoke to her about matters that were more adult on occasions, with mixed results.

Ræm's Aunt, Weid Noi, also spent much time with her and introduced her to the unusual work of the Seer. Weid Noi took time to nurture her inquisitive mind and teach her concepts of an entirely different nature. On one of these occasions just before the next Great War with the Ogres, they were joined by the Shaman, who when finished with her Aunt, took Ræm for a walk in the forest, and told her a very great secret. She learnt the truth about the Sword of Destiny, and that in a year or so, she would become the Shaman's apprentice.

Growing up with so many diverse influences in her life, led Ræm to become very self-assured, to the point of being precocious; like when she pleaded to be allowed to learn the language of the Ancestors. Within months, she had become a match for her teacher, and one year later was better than everyone except Gangling, Kay, and her father.

As her age moved into teenage figures, so she also moved to spend more and more time at the University. John was always kind and paid her special attention, making her feel very special. Faye Wong admitted her curiosity to a depth she did not often offer others, and she became a regular fixture on campus.

Perhaps because of her dedication to purpose, she homogenised with like-minded students. By contrast, her daily schedules became ever more complicated and fulfilling, as her band also played at the University regularly. Jack admitted later, "I must admit, the first night I was filled with trepidation, and later wonder, because they were damned good. Perhaps more importantly, she was not fazed by the crowd and led the band from the front, bewitching the throng as the group played their magic on stage, backing her vocals and guitar."

Later they threw open the stage and she encouraged floor artists to come up and have a go. Jack ended up playing lead and singing, before someone shouted out another song request he vaguely remembered. Their Stairway to Heaven would never better Led Zeppelin's, but then again, the crowd loved it and called for an encore. They passed the buck to Ræm, and she stole the night, singing modern songs some had never even heard of before, but the student population loved.

John joined them as the evening wound up and asked bluntly, "How old did you say she was?"

Jack turned to greet him, and offering a toast stated, "Almost thirteen going on infinity. Why did you ask?"

John looked back at Jack and dolefully said, "I thought so," before raising his glass to chink; and from that very moment, they both knew they were already a generation older.

As they sat to talk and share, John mentioned, "I need to think about my replacement, at some point in the not too distant future. I am good for many years yet, but the next generation, as we see here tonight, are already finding their feet."

Jack heard him, and after assessing replied, "Why not take several deputies and make them responsible for various departments? Your job would become overseeing them. Finding an actual replacement for the perfect person is never easy."

The next day brought changes to the University hierarchy, and a few months later, similar changes came to Jack and Jinnie's home. The day after Ræm's thirteenth birthday, when the Shaman came to visit, leaving with her new apprentice.

Ræm's Backstory ~ Part Two

Ræm's apprenticeship with the Shaman was unusual, but Sun Kist helped her greatly to adjust to the strange ways and even stranger speaking of the sage. After two weeks, she became very homesick, and after two months asked if she could finish and go home, because the teachings appeared to be of little value.

The Shaman listened to her, and explained about the seed and how it grows. Sometimes it grows quickly from planting requiring but a little water to initiate development. At other times, as in her case, the seed lies dormant until precisely the right conditions are met. Abruptly it bursts forth into a magnificent creation, a wonder of great worth. Ræm agreed to stay for a while, and before she knew it half a year and more had passed, so complete was her absorption.

Completed also was the first phase of her training, so one morning she was given leave to return and spend the day with her parents. Her only task was to return at dawn under her own means. She leapt up and hugged the Shaman, who was quite shocked by her reaction, and also very pleased. The reunion at her home became a feast of thanksgiving for her safe return. It reinforced that she was simply working away and walking a different path in life of a while. Their family bonds grew stronger, and the loneliness and melancholy was replaced by renewed faith and love.

The short day taught her a great deal, which the Shaman used to great effect over the coming months and years. She took great pains to nurture and equip this special child for the dire battle that was destined to shape her future, or herald her untimely death.

Although yet still a girl in many ways, Ræm always knew she had a destiny to fulfil, one within which the balance of life on the planet may depend, and also may turn upon her own salvation. She had already devoted many years of her small life in the quest for knowledge. She had gained from exposure to the lessons of nature and the physical world, the structures of science, of many languages, and of the hearts and desires of people.

Ræm never consciously recognised that she quickly became far more advanced than Sun Kist over those passing years, but kept her shamanic peer close and guided her at times of distress towards the enlightenment that would surely follow. They were not natural sisters, but they were all each other had, and bonded to become more than themselves alone.

Whilst Ræm was far more educated and exposed to life, Sun Kist had a very deep affinity with nature and knew things instinctively that Ræm took longer to comprehend. This in turn brought them closer unto a true understanding, and so much so that true sharing came between them to form its bonds.

Later they truly became good friends as they travelled the land and learned together about the wonders of nature. Meanwhile the Shaman kept a watchful eye on them. She understood that without Sun Kist, Ræm would never understand the truer nature of Gaia, nor heed her lessons. Eventually she saw the spark of understanding flare within Ræm's heart, and waiting just long enough to kindle it, swiftly moved on, for the times were soon to change once more.

And so it came to pass that during that last year with the Shaman, Ræm studied the Tablet of Enlightenment and other heady scripts, yet felt she had achieved nothing, except gaining confusion. Some of what was written within the tablet conflicted with her understanding of the metaphysical and physical worlds, plus the endless riddles of the Shaman had done little to unravel the mysteries hidden long within the depths of perception.

In time, Ræm sought once more the guidance of the Shaman, stating, "Great Mother, what of my destiny, for the Tablet only offers confusion and distraction. It offers a path to enlightenment, but the road is long and may not be for me in this lifetime. You have taught me the subtleties of how right and wrong may deceive as to their true nature and intent if we are not vigilant.

"You have taught me the power of love, acceptance, and of understanding different peoples, as opposed to cursorily judging them because they are different. The tablet always speaks in extremes, and yet real life is not like that. There is no pure black or white, merely many shades of grey, and colours so many as to be uncountable. I believe that everything is composed of the white, and the darkness contains nothing.

"Yet the light is a beacon along the road to self-improvement, and the darkness is but the way to sin and a signpost to great evil and death. Therefore, white and black together represent the whole, and surely would contain half each. But then the darkness grows and walks amongst us, while the light recedes as if in fear. It also seems one cannot exist without the other. How can this be?"

The Shaman heard her words and smiled, because at last she was beginning to ask the correct questions. She considered her reply before answering, "Speakest plainly to thee this day I will, for this one time alone. You cannot judge Good and Bad alone and without context. This is why I began by instilling within you the strongest understanding of telling what is Right, from that which is Wrong.

"What if I told you a story of a great King who made his empire and dominated the world by wiping out a whole race of beings. He thought he lived by his honour, but his sword alone killed thousands, and so did those of his companions. Would this man be Good or Bad?"

Ræm immediately started to reply, "Bad…" Then she stopped to think deeper, before making her considered reply, "You did not give me the situation, by which I mean was the killing in the name of Right or Wrong. Therefore, I withhold my answer until I know more.

"Ahha! Great spirit, you are speaking about my Father and contrasting him with the Great Ogre; then know he is not perfect and sins as all people do; with and without their greater knowledge or comprehension. If this man is my Father, then know he is Right and Good – A Soldier of the Light.

"But if this man were the Great Ogre, then know also that he is evil and does Wrong intently and on purpose so as to hurt others and make their lives a misery. His heart is empty where my Father's is full of compassion."

The Shaman chuckled at her bright student and pushed her further with an observation, "How can this be foretold, for do they not both want to rule the world?"

Ræm smiled and replied, "That is an unfair assumption, which I will eschew. The difference, as we have already witnessed, is that the Great Ogre would enslave the world and all its beings to be tokens of his untouchable will. My Father would fight to give all people their freedom, and the choice to make their own futures as they see fit, even if this prejudices his own beliefs and desires. He respects the differences between all living things and delights in them. He does not try to bend them all to his own will, or kill all those that refuse."

The Shaman was greatly pleased with her response and depth of understanding, yet probed her student one more time, for this one needed to break free, and not be broken, "Tell me of the Sword?"

Ræm knew the answer, because it was simple, but also knew this was not what the Enlightened One was asking her. In a few moments she replied, "The Sword of Destiny was created by the Eleventh and Seventh, and is reported to have magical powers. I now consider these powers to be runic in nature, which means you, or another like you had something to do with the casting. I also have known for a long time that it is a weapon of healing, not death. It is also my birthright, or so I have been told."

The Shaman immediately replied, "Kind to you I have been this day child, for still the future resolved be not. Determine as the days turn soon and sours, the souls survival or extinction of the fayre or foul. Destiny of Sword was cast in womb of female earth, and graces thee her love and compassion undue. The Ddwyrth and Eleventh laboured hard and long at forge for casting. Then added was thy blood to blade with runal blessing in whitest, bluest hue of fire.

"Leave me now oh daughter fayre, for thee must learn the blade. Come to me once more and bare, when you can call it to your whim or wishes made. Learn no more the Tablet of Enlightenment, for sagacious ye are without its guide."

Ræm thanked her gratefully; at last free of the cursed Tablet of Enlightenment, which to her had become a millstone around her neck.

She was about to leave when the Shaman added, "Fayre child, know you should also spend more time with the ones you love these days, for soon comes your sixteenth year, and Trials of Passage must ye take. Build your home and of it make, a place no other could forsake."

Ræm did as the Shaman instructed, becoming a regular visitor to her parents and others. She instructed Dan Nai to build her home beside her parents in the Valley of Knowledge, and made it similar in some ways to the home of the Shaman. It had a large patio outside the front door, with steps leading up to it and the central door. There was another balcony set back above where her bedroom would be, which also faced the Sun. It was the first ever fully, two-storey building on the island, and built around a variation of the gazebo principle. It was heavily influenced by her Father's knowledge of constructions of the Last, and had an arched roof covered with grass bundles akin to thatch. Like the Shaman, she had a fireplace built to ground and upper floors, the downstairs one being grand and open for the enjoyment of friends on chilly nights.

Ræm's thoughts turned to the future and she prepared like all the other adolescents for the trials. She decided to take both the male and female versions, but not a husband. "I have no time for me," she thought. "What need have I of a husband to waste my precious time? One day perhaps, when all is settled and the Great Ogre dealt with, but not before. He would need to be very special and measure up. No matter the now, I must prepare for my life and live this day as I will."

She was tempted to try to break her Father's record, but knew this was not her calling, so instead took one trial each day, the female for the first week, and the male for the second. This allowed her ample time to work with the sword, trying to call it whenever she had free and dedicated time.

One day shortly after her coming of age birthday party, she heard her name being called telepathically. It was not the sword, the Shaman, but the Seer who was trying to attract her attention. Curious she attended her dear friend in order to offer her assistance.

Weid Noi also knew the world was turning once more, but could never see the Third Way. They discussed the matter for some time until Ræm said, "The third and windy way is left to chance, where the powers of nature hold sway. The Shaman taught me to divine and augur. I could show you my way, but you should speak to Sun Kist."

"Augury is an art we lost a long time ago. I will speak with her. Thank you Ræm, I feel my feet now tread the right path."

Throughout this period, Ræm's studies progressed rapaciously, but yet for all her newfound skills and knowledge, she always failed to call the Sword to her. She could feel the blade sometimes, but it was a fleeting whimsy.

She desperately wanted to attend the Olympics in 2036, but the Shaman forbade it. When she pressed the point, she was told that all would soon be revealed, and she must be kept safe from harm. Mollified, but not happy, she continued with her studies, and tried to call the impossible blade to her hand.

This changed the morning Sun Kist rushed in all of a fluster, mumbling that everyone was lost. Through her garbled uttering's, Ræm deduced that her Mother, Father, and all the Kings' and Queens' had become captives of the Great Ogre. Ogres, who killed indiscriminately, had invaded the Olympics and destroyed what should have been a festival of sharing. Her rage flared as she determined the Sword of Destiny to answer her bidding. Nothing happened and it felt more remote than ever.

Sun Kist departed, but periodically retuned with reports of atrocities committed by the invaders. Overburdened, Ræm's heart wept for the innocent killed that day, and for the loss of so many world leaders. Her heart erupted in grief and brotherly love. For just one instant, she wished the sword was in her hand to right this grievous wrong … and there it was!

Stunned, she stared down at it, and drew her fingers lovingly along the blade, learning of its secrets along the length as if by divination. Trancelike she knew within the moment that she and the blade were one. Their destinies were irrevocably linked, and that if she had faith in the impossible, then all would come to pass, and even the sun would finally put on his hat.

Her reverie is broken by the Shaman,
"Done well thee hast, and better still.
Blade commanded by your will.
Return to safety, scabbard fill,
Till cometh time for the blade to kill."

The Shaman turned away as if to depart, but added,
"The call of sword ye must attend
World turns once more with Ogre's end.
Send back the sword of love and light,
And tarry not for Ogre's plight."

The Shaman repeated for surety, and waited, as she watched her young and gifted charge.

The Sword disappeared from Ræm's hand; the difference being, that now Ræm knew what it felt like in her hand, and was confident she could summon it at will, if only because she had already done it.

The Shaman spoke her last,
"Attend me now to take review,
As die be cast and nearness due.
Your calling be to make, to slew,
Great Ogre crimes of darkest hue.
When sword taken be your cue,
Steps boldly make the world anew.
Believe the Good, the Right, the true,
Trust to your heart, your love to sue.
To save or send this be your lieu,
And heal unto his death imbue.
For Ogre Great his last curfew,
His life to lose, to mourn, to rue."

www.ingramcontent.com/pod-product-compliance
Lightning Source LLC
Chambersburg PA
CBHW031256170626
46807CB00001B/168